PENGUIN BOOKS

The One That Got Away

Melissa Pimentel grew up in a small town in Massachusetts in a house without cable and much of her childhood was spent watching 1970s British comedy on public television. When she was twenty-two she made the move to London and has lived there happily for ten years, although she has sadly never come across the Ministry of Funny Walks. Before meeting her husband she spent much of her time trawling the London dating scene for clean, non-sociopathic sexual partners and blogging about it, which became the inspiration for her first novel. These days, she spends much of her time reading in the various pubs of Stoke Newington and engaging in a long-standing emotional feud with her disgruntled cat, Welles. She works in publishing.

The One That Got Away

MELISSA PIMENTEL

PENGUIN BOOKS

PENGUIN BOOKS

UK | USA | Canada | Ireland | Australia

India | New Zealand | South Africa

Penguin Books is part of the Penguin Random House group of companies
whose addresses can be found at global.penguinrandomhouse.com

First published 2016

001

Text copyright © Melissa Pimentel, 2016

The moral right of the author has been asserted

Set in 12.5/14.75pt Garamond MT Std

Typeset in India by Thomson Digital Pvt Ltd, Noida, Delhi

Printed in Great Britain by Clays Ltd, St Ives plc

A CIP catalogue record for this book is available from the British Library

B FORMAT ISBN: 978–1–405–92373–6

www.greenpenguin.co.uk

To the Pimentel-Robertsons

Now

It was a Monday night. The remains of a chicken Caesar salad were congealing gently on the side of my desk, and the mug of coffee next to my elbow – my fifth of the day – was now cold. I looked at the tiny clock at the edge of my screen: 9:23 p.m. There was no way I was getting out of here before midnight.

'Do you need anything?' I looked up to see Jennifer, the assistant I shared with the other account directors, standing in front of me. She'd arrived with the apple-cheeked, milk-fed look of a woman who had wandered in straight from the farm (even if, in her case, that farm was Yale). Now, after only a few weeks with us, her skin had already taken on the vitamin-D deficient pallor of someone unfamiliar with daylight. I felt a twinge of guilt: she was like a sweet little lamb being slowly, methodically sheared by the city.

'No, I'm all set, thanks.' I looked at her more closely. She was wearing lipstick. Red lipstick. 'Are you going out tonight?' I asked.

'No!' she said, nervously fiddling with the gold chain around her neck. 'I mean, sort of. I had plans or whatever, but I can stay here as long as you need me.'

She was wearing a dress, too, a floral tea dress that suited her tiny waist. It was definitely a date. 'Don't worry about me,' I said. 'I don't need you to stick around, honest. What time are your plans?'

She shifted her weight to her other foot and tried to look casual. 'Um, twenty minutes ago?'

'Then what are you still doing here? Go!' I said, shooing her away.

Her eyes widened, her mouth breaking into a wide grin. 'Are you sure?'

'Absolutely.'

'Oh my God, thank you!' she said, scrambling around her desk and gathering her bag. 'I really, really appreciate it. I'll be in super early tomorrow morning, I promise.'

'Relax, you're fine. I'm off for the rest of the week, but I'll be on email all the time, so just drop me a line if there are any major fires. Hopefully I'll wrap most things up tonight.'

Jennifer hesitated. 'You're sure you don't need me? I don't mind staying, really.' Half of her body was already out the door.

'I know, but I'm fine. Really.'

'Okay, well . . . have a good trip! Let me know if you need anything!'

'I will. And Jen?'

'Yes?'

'You look great.'

She beamed at me and slipped out the door. I heard her heels clacking down the stairwell and the sound of the fire-exit door swing open and clang decisively shut.

I sighed and turned back to one of my many color-coded spreadsheets. I was working on a major new digital campaign for Spike, a low-cost airline that had been plagued with a myriad of health and safety scandals recently: salmonella in a batch of their in-flight meals, child harnesses that snapped when tested, and one particular incident where a marauding band of mice chewed through a nest of wiring during a flight to San Jose. We were rebranding them as the 'Airline of Adventure', complete with GoPro footage of various lunatics jumping off buildings and abseiling down crevasses. Because surely, at this point, it was only those lunatics who would willingly board one of their rickety planes.

Regardless of my thoughts on the ethics of fudging airline safety, the Spike business was a huge slice of the BlueFly budget, and it was essential that the campaign went off without a hitch. As a result, I'd been pulling sixteen-hour days for the past three weeks, taking phone calls from the nervous CEO late into the night and early in the morning. One of my eyes had developed a twitch a week ago, and now that twitch had a twitch. And, of course, with the worst possible timing, I had to take a week's vacation to travel to the north of England because my sister had insisted on getting married in a castle (which, if you'd met Piper, wouldn't come as much of a surprise). And to add insult to injury, my ex-boyfriend would be there, too. Trust Piper to marry the best friend of the one man I never wanted to see again. And at this rate, I wouldn't even have time to wax my legs before I left.

My phone flashed up with a message.

Are you bailing on me tomorrow?

It was my best friend Jess, who had defected to the wilds of New Jersey two years ago with her husband and baby son, and who I had since managed to visit a grand

3

total of three times. I know, I know, I'm a terrible friend. Something Jess hasn't held back on telling me. Another text flashed up.

Let me rephrase that. DO NOT BAIL ON ME TOMORROW. You do not want to piss off a pregnant lady because I will crush you.

I'd promised her I'd swing by her place on the way to the airport the following morning, but had, in all honesty, already been planning to make my excuses and spend the morning in the office. But seeing her text messages, I knew I was toast.

Of course I'm still coming! Can't wait. Xxx

I placed the phone back on the desk and turned back to my spreadsheets. I saw the phone flash up again from the corner of my eye.

You're a liar but I love you. Let me know what train you're on and Noah and I will meet you. X

I took a sip of cold coffee and grimaced. Midnight, I thought to myself. I won't stay any later than midnight.

I woke up to the mechanized chirrup of crickets.

My eyes stuttered open and I fumbled in the dark until my fingers curled around my phone: 6:33 a.m. I let out a plaintive moan. I thought about closing my eyes again, letting sleep pull me gently back under, but the little blue envelope on my iPhone had an angry red number hovering

4

above it: fifty-seven new unread emails. The Shanghai office had been busy overnight. I tapped with a reluctant index finger and scanned through a series of minor and major disasters that would need rectifying, and felt my chest tighten with each swipe.

6:37. Time to get up. I swung my legs over the side of the bed and suddenly regretted my decision to take an Ambien last night. I shielded my eyes from the sun, now streaming through the window, and sat for a moment while I made a mental calculation of what I had to do today: gym, train, Jessica, plane. England. The ex. I let out another groan and glanced down at my pillow longingly.

I forced myself onto my feet. I had a 7 a.m. training session this morning, and Jeff would make me do extra burpees if I was late. Tuesday at 7 a.m. had been spent with Jeff for three and a half years now, ever since I had tried to squeeze myself into a dress I used to wear back in college and couldn't get it past my knees. All the days and nights spent at the desk had caught up with me, and the only solution was to subject myself to twice-weekly punishment sessions with Jeff, and frequent pre-dawn runs along the river. It was brutal. It was endless. It was, it appeared, the routine I would be following for the rest of my life. Why couldn't exercise be like money, or Starbucks points, where you could amass a stockpile and then spend it gradually over time for the rest of your life? Instead, I found that if I took even a week off, my lungs reverted to their previous flaccid state, and my ass started inching towards the backs of my knees. And so, onward I fought.

I padded into the bathroom and flicked on the light, wincing slightly before switching it back off again. Brushing my teeth in the dark felt safer and more humane. Face washed and hair tied up in a fresh ponytaïl, I pulled on the gym clothes I'd left carefully folded for myself the night before, and scooped some coffee grains into the French press. I glanced up at the clock hanging above the range. 6:48: two minutes to spare. I straightened the covers and double-checked that I had everything I needed for the trip, including the lurid green monstrosity that Piper had decided was the maid of honor dress. I was going straight to the station after the gym and couldn't afford to come all the way back to the apartment for an errant shoe.

Dress, shoes, make-up, Ambien all accounted for, I had a quick last look around the apartment before heading out the door. It was a tiny studio, but it was all my own – the first place I'd been able to afford by myself in the city. There comes a time in a person's life when, if single, one should live on one's own, mainly because the only possible room-mates available to one are the deranged and mentally diseased. The commute from Bay Ridge – where I'd lived for the past seven years, ever since I moved out of the place I'd shared with Jess in Sunset Park – had been brutal, but not as brutal as the feeling of being the oldest, and lamest, person in the neighborhood. When Len, the grizzled old bartender at McDougall's, was replaced by a smirking twenty-three-year-old wearing a Hypercolor tank top, I went home, prepared a financial spreadsheet, and called a real estate broker: I would move to Manhattan, where I would be poor but would at least feel young. (I felt more poor than young, but it was still worth it.)

The new place, nestled in an old tenement building in the East Village, was tiny and extortionately priced, but I could afford it (barely) thanks to my recent promotion to account director. It was beautiful – all exposed bricks and high ceilings – and I'd been slowly replacing my old Ikea furniture with purposely distressed vintage pieces that had originally been bought at a garage sale in Michigan and resold at a tremendous mark-up to city rubes like me. I was fine with this.

I tore down the stairs and burst onto the street. It was a beautiful morning: the sky was a faultless blue, the day's inevitable mugginess had yet to descend, and the street sweepers had already come through, so the road wasn't littered with the previous night's detritus of beer bottles and vomit. I sipped my coffee on the way, and listened to the quiet rhythms of the city waking up: the metal shutters sliding open, the pails of water being tossed onto the sidewalk, the quiet tick of town car engines cooling as they waited for their breakfasting businessmen. I walked into the gym, the familiar smell of sweat, chorine and overpriced air freshener welcoming me. 6:59 on the nose.

A large, muscular man with a head shaped like a triangle and a sadistic grin stood up when I walked through the door: Jeff.

'Morning, Ruby,' he said. 'Ready for the pain?'

'Not really,' I said, but it didn't matter – it was going to happen anyway.

I sweated my way through the usual series of increasingly grueling and bizarre exercises, Jeff standing over me and occasionally bellowing what he thought was encouragement, but would more accurately be classified as harassment. 'Lower! Deeper! Faster! Harder!' he said, over and over. Taken out of context, it would sound as if he were directing fringe porn. I squeezed my eyes shut and thought about the coffee and bagel that awaited me at the end of this, and considered, not for the first time, the irony of working out this hard in order to maintain some semblance of the body I'd had at nineteen, when my diet had consisted entirely of Cheetos, Diet Coke, slices of processed cheese and cheap vodka. I pushed the thought out of my head and did another rep. This is about being strong and healthy, I told myself, not about being thin. (Okay, it was a little bit about being thin.)

In addition to allowing me to eat a guilt-free bagel, exercise helped temporarily to dislodge the tight knot of anxiety that had nestled itself in my breastbone – like a tiny, fluttering baby bird with an extremely sharp beak – ever since the promotion. With every squat thrust, it flew higher and lighter until, by the end of the hour, I couldn't feel it at all. Today it was particularly useful, considering the amount of pre-travel/wedding/family/ex-boyfriend anxiousness pressing firmly on my shoulders.

'One more circuit and we're done,' Jeff said, idly flexing a bicep in the mirror as I began yet another set of weighted lunges. I suppressed the urge to thwack him over the head with a kettlebell.

Workout done, shower taken and personage assembled, I made my way to the subway, wheeled suitcase dragging noisily behind. The city had stretched its limbs and was fully awake now, and I had to shoulder through a crowd lined up outside Birdbath Bakery, all desperate to get their hands on a freshly baked cronut despite the fact that no one in the city ate gluten anymore (except me). I dodged a woman struggling to free her stiletto from a subway grate, a vagrant pushing a shopping cart full of dismembered mannequins and a squall of hungover-looking college students before descending into Second Avenue station.

The subway was, as ever, a minefield of smells and sounds and strangers' limbs. I normally avoided the sub-way – the BlueFly office was within walking distance – but there was no way I could walk the thirty-plus blocks across town to Penn Station, and a cab would take twice as long to snake its way through the morning traffic snarls. I pushed my way onto a busy F train, enraging everyone in the vicinity by having a suitcase with me during rush hour, and let my face arrange itself into its Don't Fuck With Me expression (a mix of boredom, stand-offishness and vague menace). I found a (hopefully) non-living place to hold on, and spent the next twenty minutes scrolling through my iPhone – thirteen new emails had come in during my gym session – and trying to ignore the truly appalling stench coming from the man next to me. I stole a glance at him: he looked normal, handsome even – fortyish, with an appealing shock of salt and pepper hair and wearing a good suit – but he smelled like he'd rolled around in a mix of garlic and wet dog hair.

I looked at him again, more closely this time. There was something familiar about him . . . maybe I'd worked with him before? Did he go to my gym? And then I remem-bered: I'd swapped a few messages with him on Ok Cupid the month before. We'd even arranged a date, but I'd had to cancel at the last minute because of a work emergency.

I felt his eyes on me and stared hard at my phone. Please don't recognize me, I prayed silently. Please, garbage man, leave me in peace.

'THIRTY-FOURTH STREET, HERALD SQUARE!' The conductor's voice crackled across the loudspeaker and I pushed my way through the door and onto the platform, leaving a wake of disgruntled *tsk*s as I pulled my suitcase off behind me. The doors started to close and garbage man locked eyes with me, a look of recognition written across his face. I looked away and the doors clanged shut behind me, whizzing him up to 42nd Street. I smiled to myself as I lugged the suitcase up the stairs: another tiny victory won.

I emerged from the station and began my cross-town journey on foot. The heat of the summer had started to press down on New York like a thumb, and by the time I walked into Penn Station, sweat had begun to trickle down my back.

'Can I interest you in free highlights? Our brand-new salon has just opened . . .' 'Free sample of I Can't Believe It's Not Chocolate! The first chocolate substitute made entirely of beetroot!' 'Half-price tickets to the Knicks!' I hustled my way past the tourists and ticket touts and promoters pressing leaflets into any passing hand. There was a time when I would have taken the handsome man up on his offer of a free haircut, but experience had taught me the hard way that by 'new salon' he meant a back-alley joint in Chinatown where they would bleach my hair orange and charge me $110 to fix it. That is the thing about New York: its beautiful, maddening essence. No one gets anything for free here. You have to work for it.

I hurried down the long, curved white corridor, flying past Nathan's and the souvenir stands and the bookshop stacked high with the latest pulpy bestseller. The floors were now scattered with the detritus of the morning commute: splashes of coffee splattered on the polished concrete, along with flimsy paper bags that had held now-eaten croissants and egg sandwiches, an abandoned sports section lying limply on a nearby bench. The rush had ended, and an echoey calm had fallen on the station. I saw my train listed on the board – the 6929 to Millburn – and headed towards the platform. I was early, so I stopped at a bagel cart on the way and ordered a wholewheat bagel (cream cheese on the side) and a coffee (black).

I was furiously blowing on the scalding coffee when something caught my eye: staring out at me from the magazine rack was none other than my ex-boyfriend, his face smiling smugly out from the cover of *TechCrunch* magazine. 'Can Ethan Bailey Save the World?' the headline asked, as if specifically designed to annoy me. 'I'm guessing not,' I muttered as I pulled a copy from the rack and slapped it down on the counter.

'Four dollars,' said the unsmiling man, hand outstretched. I peeled off the bills and shoved the magazine deep into my bag, where I could feel it throbbing, and then headed off to catch my train.

The Morris and Essex line is a miniature socio-economic tour of the Greater New York area. I stared out of the window as we chuntered through Chelsea, speeding past the boutique shops and expensive cocktail bars, out past the High Line and over the Hudson River into New Jersey. Through Hoboken and into a sea of squat industrial parks dotted with billboards advertising strip clubs and loan sharks and auto-body shops until the first ad for West Elm appeared and you knew you were out in the suburbs.

I finished off the last bit of bagel and pulled the magazine out of my bag, holding it gingerly between thumb and forefinger as though it might be radioactive. Which it sort of was, at least to me. The coffee I'd gulped down made an unwelcome reappearance in my oesophagus. I leaned in and inspected the photograph. He hadn't changed at all. If anything, he was now better looking. He had the confident sheen of wealth shining out of every pore, and had obviously used some of his apparently now-vast fortune to have his teeth straightened and whitened. His dark hair was slightly shorter, but still curled around his temples, and his eyes were the same greenish-gold I remembered. Yes, it was definitely him: a beacon of success, heralded the world over as the designer of a generation, and presumably described as one of the city's most eligible bachelors somewhere in the article. At least he was still a bachelor the last time I'd allowed myself to Google him (once every two months, no more) following his split from some leggy fashion editor.

I skimmed the article, which contained the word 'genius' so many times I seriously considered sending a thesaurus to the sub-editor, and allowed myself to stare at the accompanying photographs for exactly four minutes. There he was with the late Steve Jobs, arm tossed jovially around his shoulder as they grinned out at the camera in matching turtlenecks. Now he was at the Met gala, aforementioned leggy fashion editor wrapped around him like a baby monkey on a tree branch. And finally, there was a picture of him with his business partner, arms slung around each other's shoulders and smiling at each other as if they both couldn't believe their luck.

I couldn't believe it, either. If you had told me ten years ago that Ethan would end up designing one of the most used and best loved apps of all time, I would have laughed in your face. Actually, first I would have asked what an app was, and then I would have laughed in your face.

I closed the magazine and shoved it back in my bag. You know that feeling when you put coin after coin into a slot machine without winning a single penny, only to walk away and watch the next person who drops a quarter in win the jackpot? That was the feeling that I had been living with for the past seven years, ever since Ethan's face appeared in *Wired* in an article entitled 'Rising Stars'. I drank half a bottle of vodka with Jess that night, eventually setting fire to the magazine and placing it in a garbage can in what Jess had promised would be a 'cleansing ritual', but which ended up just melting the (plastic) garbage can to the living-room carpet and resulted in a serious deduction from our security deposit.

The trees whizzed by as the train sped deeper into New Jersey. I closed my eyes and leaned against the window, head knocking rhythmically against the pane as the train clicked over the tracks. Tomorrow, I would see him again – the first time in nearly ten years. What could I possibly say to him? Would he even talk to me? What if he still had feelings for me? Or, worse, what if he didn't? I swatted the thought from my mind like an errant fly. The man opposite caught my eye and gave me a friendly smile. He was dressed in a suit, but the edges of his cuffs were frayed and his collar slightly yellowed, and he had the harried look of a man teetering on the brink. I looked back at the whizzing trees, which were thinning slowly and being replaced by identikit clapboard houses and the occasional strip mall. What if I still loved him after all this time? What the hell was I supposed to do then?

'NEXT STOP, MILLBURN!'

I bumped my suitcase down the steps and onto the platform, waving away the frayed man's offers to help. It was deserted at this time of day, and I felt strangely criminal being outside the confines of the city and out in the open on a weekday morning. I blinked into the bright sunshine before pulling my phone out of my bag and scrolling through my emails: no major disasters, thankfully. I breathed a small sigh of relief and headed out of the station.

'Ruby! Over here!' I heard Jess's voice before I saw her, standing by an enormous silver SUV and waving her arms maniacally despite the fact that she was the only person in the parking lot. A smile burst onto my face and I broke into a run.

Jess wrapped me in a hug. 'Thank God you made it – I was worried you'd get lost or something!' She was pregnant – heavily pregnant – but she was still all long limbs and blonde hair, though the peroxide had been replaced by more honeyed tones, and her limbs were swathed in a pair of leggings and an expensive-looking maternity tunic. She looked like a glowing, glorious little egg. It was strange to imagine a tiny person swimming around inside her, all tiny fingernails and nose and presumably tiny internal organs squashed inside. It made me feel a little nauseous to think about it. Babies are miracles, sure, but sometimes the specifics veer a little too close to science fiction for comfort.

'Jess, I'm thirty-two years old and I was at your house three months ago – how could I have got lost?' I peered through the back window and waved at Jess's two-and-a-half-year-old son, Noah. He gave me a long, wary look from his car seat in return. Children are like bears: they can smell fear.

I hauled my suitcase into the trunk and climbed into the passenger seat. The soundtrack to *Frozen* was playing on the stereo and Jess shot me an apologetic smile as she pulled out of the parking lot. 'He's obsessed,' she said, nodding towards Noah. 'It's all he'll let us listen to. I keep trying to introduce other things to him, but he's not buying it. The other day I put on Pharrell because another mom told me she'd used it to break her daughter's *Frozen* addiction, but he just screamed the whole way through. Didn't you, buddy?' Noah let out a triumphant shout from the back seat, and she rolled her eyes. 'So for now, we're stuck with Elsa and that snowman guy until we can stage an effective intervention. Sorry.'

'I'm actually kind of into it,' I said. This was a slightly gray shade of the truth: I'd taken myself to see *Frozen* on a particularly dark day back in January and had found myself sobbing uncontrollably during 'Let It Go', much to the horror of the multitude of dads who had been shooed out of their homes for the afternoon to take their children to see it for the tenth time. The experience had been mildly cathartic, but not one I was particularly keen on replicating. I'd been struck by waves of retrospective humiliation for weeks, usually while in client meetings.

We cruised into downtown Millburn, which felt more like a 1950s simulacrum of a town than an actual place. 'I feel like I'm in a tank,' I said as we drove past a succession of coffee shops, children's clothing boutiques and ye olde candy stores. The SUV was a few feet off the ground and made everything – the other cars, the neat rows of shops, the moms pushing their kids along the street in strollers – look puny and vulnerable, like the plastic figurines lining the toy store window.

'I know,' Jess said, 'it's a little ridiculous, but Noah generates so much stuff. The kid is like a pack mule. Plus it's great for when the in-laws are in town.'

We pulled into the driveway, stopping just short of a Radio Flyer tricycle that had been abandoned in front of the garage. The house, a three-bed that Jess and her husband had bought two years ago, was a dove-gray Cape with daffodil trim. There was a wraparound porch with a trellis on which ivy climbed, and flowerboxes along the railings and on the windowsills. It looked exactly like a dollhouse I'd had as a kid, and I was always surprised when I walked inside and discovered that the furniture was real sized, not miniature. The yard was dotted with Noah's various toys, including a wooden Peter Pan house and a tiny cherry-red car, and I took a moment to marvel at the idea of leaving stuff out in the open and not worrying about it being stolen.

'Your house continues to be sickeningly perfect,' I said, shutting the car door and gazing up at the whitewashed shutters and neat slate roof.

'It's a little small, but it does the job. We just had the lawn reseeded, and Ben is obsessed with watering it. As soon as he gets home from work, he's out there with a hose and a magnifying glass, checking on his sproutage. We'll need more space soon, though,' she said, idly stroking her swollen stomach. 'This is just a starter home, really.'

I murmured something noncommittal and smiled. Noah was only three feet tall, and the baby would be the size of a volleyball when it was born: did they really need more than three bedrooms? It seemed that as soon as someone turned thirty, they suddenly needed at least three times the amount of space previously required, regardless of how many children they had or how many things they owned. Square footage, front- and backyards, his and hers sinks – everyone seemed to be in the grip of their own personal Manifest Destiny. I thought about my cozy studio, everything tucked neatly into its rightful place: surely, at a push, Noah and the baby could fit in there? Maybe they could each sleep in a drawer, like an illustration from a children's book. Not that I wanted to test out the theory. First of all, it would be kidnapping. Second, they would definitely get drool over my sweaters, which would be gross.

Jess unhooked Noah from his seat and he flopped forwards onto her shoulder. I saw her stagger slightly against his weight and rushed to help. 'Do you want me to carry him?' I asked.

Jess waved me away. 'I'm like an ox these days. You should see my biceps – I could win strongman competitions. Ben keeps saying that he's going to sell me to the circus. Now, are you hungry? I've got some stuff in the fridge I could throw together for a salad, and I baked some cookies this morning. Oooh, and Ben brought back these amazing salted caramel truffles the other night – you have to try one. Let me just get this little guy settled and I'll make some coffee.'

Noah ran ahead into the kitchen, shouting something indecipherable and punctuating each statement with a loud whimpering noise. I looked at Jess for a translation.

'He's hungry,' she said, hurrying after him. 'We're late for his lunch.'

I stayed back in the hallway for a moment, breathing in expensive cedar-scented candles and freshly baked cookies, undercut by the faintly sour smell of often-spilled milk. There were pairs of shoes lined up neatly by the door; I slipped mine off and placed them next to Ben's neon-green running sneakers. The air settled around me, the dust motes sparkling in the late-morning sun streaming through the window. The inside of the house was as beautiful as the outside, all polished hardwood floors and walls painted in tastefully muted colors. There was a framed wedding photo sitting on the mantelpiece over the little brick fireplace, next to a photo of Jess looking exhausted but deliriously beautiful, holding a newborn Noah to her chest. There was an old wine crate full of toys tucked into the corner of the room, and the coffee table was stacked with Early Reader books. I felt like an alien that had been unexpectedly beamed onto the surface of an unfamiliar planet.

In the kitchen, Jess was assembling a peanut butter and jelly sandwich with military precision. She cut off the crusts, sliced it into long, thin fingers, and placed it on a plastic plate featuring the cartoon face of a lion. I watched from the doorway for a minute and was struck, as I always was by these little domestic tableaux in which Jess now starred, by both a violent, primordial jealousy and a desire to run screaming out of the house in order to take deep lungfuls of clean, free air. The flight instinct was usually the more dominant.

'Lunchtime, buddy!' Jess placed the plate on the tray of his highchair and gave his hair a light tousle.

Noah took one look at lunch and started to whimper. 'Jiffy! Jiffy!' he cried.

'Okay, sweetie, I'll get it.' Jess took another plastic plate from the cupboard, this time featuring a cartoon giraffe, and slid the sandwich onto it. She spotted me in the doorway and smiled. 'His favorite plate,' she said, rolling her eyes but still displaying a level of saintly patience that had materialized as soon as Noah had been suctioned out of her after a long and difficult labor. Before motherhood, Jessica would have been described with a long line of colorful adjectives, but patient would not have featured on the list.

Noah now happily munching away, Jess turned to me, her hand resting calmly on her bump. 'You want coffee, right? Ben does this cold press thing that he's obsessed with. And please, eat a cookie! Ben can't eat them because of his stupid Paleo diet, and I'll just end up throwing them out when you leave to stop me and Noah from eating them all.' Noah let out a little moan of despair and started licking the jelly from the sides of his sandwich fingers to comfort himself.

I plucked an oatmeal and raisin cookie off of a sunny yellow ceramic plate, Noah eying me with undisguised rage as I took a bite. 'These are delicious,' I said, sending a gentle spray of crumbs onto the oak table.

'All done!' Noah called. His plate was empty – the kid must have a hoover inside him. Jess lifted him out of his highchair and handed him a cookie, which he accepted with a look of happiness usually reserved for Oscar winners, before scooting off into the living room.

'You're like Queen Etsy or something out here,' I said, gesturing around the room.

Jess shook her head. 'Seriously, this is nothing. You should see some of the houses Noah's friends live in – not a single surface that hasn't been slapped in chalk paint and decorated with vintage seltzer bottles. We went to a birthday party for a two-year-old last week and the mom had made carob and quinoa cookies and balanced them on top of these tiny little milk bottles. It was nauseating. I was, of course, insanely jealous.'

'How are you getting along with the other moms? Are you guys all playing nicely?'

'A few of them are pains in the ass, but most of them are cool. Lots of former Brooklynites who've come here to breed and die – they should probably just set up a shuttle service between here and Park Slope. It's like the hipster version of Florida or something.' She got up and started fussing around with an expensive-looking coffee maker.

'I'll do that!' I said, lunging towards the counter.

She shooed me away. 'I'm pregnant, not crippled. Besides, this machine is like the Enigma code – I'd never ask you to try and crack it. Now, where did Ben put that Jamaican blend? It's to die for – you've got to try it. I can only smell it at the minute, obviously, but seriously – it's heaven.'

I watched her with a sense of quiet disbelief, still not quite able to reconcile the domestic goddess in front of me with the woman I'd shared a room with in college. It was as if a little switch had gone off. One day, she was smoking like a trooper and telling expletive-riddled stories about interviewing New York's latest playboy in a strip club in Queens, the next she was worrying about the provenance of her artichokes and the competitiveness of Monkey Music class. This was the woman who had once hijacked an idling limousine and demanded that it take us to a pop-up cabaret in Williamsburg, and who had slept with not one but three of the New York Yankees. I wondered briefly whether Jess's lifetime season ticket to Yankee home games was still valid.

But it wasn't just Jess who had undergone a transformation. A few years ago, it was as though a high-pitched whistle had sounded and all of the women who I'd spent my twenties carousing with pricked up their ears. One by one, they disappeared, swept away to a suburban enclave or less 'intense' city, never to be seen in a dive bar or nightclub again, all citing the same reasons: it was too expensive, there was nowhere for their existing or hoped-for children to play, the competition for schools was crazy, there was no space. On the rare days I got out of work early enough to have a drink with someone, there was now no one to call. I felt like one of those Japanese soldiers hidden in the jungle years after the Second World War had ended, vowing never to surrender.

Noah wandered in, a pile of board books stacked precariously in his hands. 'Story, Mommy?'

'In a second, sweetie,' Jess said. 'Why don't you do a puzzle?' He toddled off looking mildly disgruntled. Jess placed a mug in front of me – in the same sunny yellow as the cookie plate – and sat down with a sigh. 'Okay,' she said, 'tell me everything. Bring me all of your dispatches from civilization.'

I shrugged. 'There isn't much to tell, really. Work's good. Crazy busy, but good. A new restaurant opened up on Jane Street that you'd love – they do amazing Thai food . . .'

She waved away the pad thai talk. 'Ruby, we don't have much time. That kid in there is a ticking time bomb, so let's get to the good stuff. Have you had any decent sex lately?'

'Nothing noteworthy,' I said, flicking an errant crumb off my lap. I didn't have the heart to tell her I hadn't been on a date in months, let alone had sex.

'What about Mark? Is he still buzzing around?'

'No, he buzzed off a long time ago, thank God. He kept telling me about what he ate and how much exercise he did every day, in minute detail. It's like he thought I was his Fitbit or something. Anyway, I have more important news.'

'Go on . . .'

I reached into my bag and pulled out the now dog-eared copy of *TechCrunch*. 'So this is happening,' I said, waving the magazine in front of me slightly maniacally.

Jess stared at the cover in silence for a minute before snatching it out my hand. 'You have GOT to be kidding me. How the hell do they expect him to save the world through a food delivery app? What, General Tso's chicken for all?'

'Something about redistributing restaurant food waste to the poor,' I said. 'Anyway, that's not the important thing. The important thing is that I am going to see him in' – I glanced up at the kitchen clock – 'thirteen hours, and I have no idea what I'm supposed to say to him. I mean, what do I say to this?' I jabbed a finger at Ethan's grinning face.

'I think I'd start with hello,' Jess said. 'And maybe ease up on the finger pointing.' She looked down at the cover. 'He is super hot. He wasn't this hot when you were together, was he? I know I only met him once, but I feel like I would remember it more clearly if he had been this good-looking.'

'I thought you couldn't remember anything about 2005,' I said.

'True. But still, I think this would have made an impression. So, what's your game plan?'

I threw myself back in the chair. 'Avoid him as much as I can, I guess.'

'Why would you want to avoid this?' Jess asked, gazing at Ethan's face. I snatched the magazine back and shoved it in my bag.

'Um, because he's my ex-boyfriend? Because we haven't spoken since we broke up a decade ago? Honestly, it's embarrassing that I'm even worrying about it – Justin Timberlake still had curly hair when we were together, for God's sake.'

'You never forget your first love,' she said wistfully.

'You're telling me that you remember that bartender from the Last Drop?'

'I do, actually. Sometimes, in a low moment, I think about his forearms.'

'Okay, well, I do not think about Ethan's forearms, or any part of him for that matter. It's ancient history.'

'Stop being such a Grinch. I think it's romantic! The two of you getting thrown back together – at a wedding, of all places! A wedding that's happening in a castle! It's like a fairy tale or something!' Jess reached over and took a bite out of a cookie, chewing contemplatively. 'You should at least try to have sex with him.'

'This isn't a fairy tale, this is my life, and no one is having sex with anyone.'

Jess raised an eyebrow.

'You know what I mean.'

'Unfortunately, I do,' she said. 'That's exactly my point.'

Noah's voice broke the silence. 'Mommy! I spilled!'

'It's just water, right, honey?'

'I spilled the blue!' he called back, voice quavering slightly.

'The blue? Oh Jesus, the finger paints,' she said, taking off with impressive speed. 'Coming!'

We rushed into the living room to find a puddle of thick blue paint spread across a patch of hardwood floor. Noah was sitting in the middle of it, blue-tinted tears streaming down his face. 'My blue!' he wailed.

'My floor!' Jess wailed.

'I'll get the paper towels,' I said, turning on my heel and heading towards the kitchen.

'Wait, I'll get them,' she said. 'You hang onto this one and make sure he doesn't rub anymore of it into the floor or his eyes or whatever.' She thrust Noah into my arms and hurried out of the room.

'Hello!' I said brightly. My voice sounded oddly strangled.

He eyed me suspiciously, his legs and arms dangling limply as he considered the situation. 'I want to get down,' he said. He started to wriggle. 'Down now.'

'Just one sec, buddy,' I said, tightening my grip to keep him from slipping to the floor. 'Mommy will be back in just one second.'

'Down!' he shouted, kicking out. 'Down! Down! Down! Down!' The sound was not unlike the police siren I'd heard while on a work trip to Copenhagen last year.

'Noah! Don't kick your aunt!' Jess lifted him out of my arms and replaced him with a wad of damp paper towels. 'I'll take care of him – do you mind clearing up the spill?'

'Of course!' I crouched down and started scrubbing the stained floorboards while she carried Noah upstairs. I couldn't remember the last time I'd been more grateful to be on my hands and knees.

Twenty-five minutes later, the paint puddle had been wiped away (thankfully it was water-based) and Noah had been cleaned up. Jess had found two fingers of peanut butter and jelly sandwich stuffed down his pants, which explained the speed at which he'd earned his cookie, and he was now playing with a fire truck in a slightly desolate manner.

'Where were we?' Jess said, settling back into the sofa cushions and keeping a wary eye on Noah. 'Oh yeah, you were planning on ignoring your handsome, rich ex-boyfriend. Don't do that.' She reached over and took my hand, and I knew exactly what was coming.

'Please don't,' I said. 'Not the speech.'

'Ruby, you are smart and sexy and funny and generally wonderful. You deserve to be happy.'

'Enough already.'

'And I watch you going through this life of yours, so focused on your career, so determined to shut out any distractions, and I worry about you.'

'There's no need to worry about me.'

'Just do me a favor and keep an open mind, okay? That's all I ask: just be open to the idea that you might still have feelings for the guy.'

'I really don't think that's going to be a problem.'

'In that case, you shouldn't have a problem with promising me you'll keep an open mind.' She sat back, triumphant.

'Fine,' I groaned. 'You win. Now can I have another cookie before we go?'

'Of course you can,' she said, patting me on the head. 'Good girl.'

Jess drove me to the airport, Noah burbling excitedly as the planes came into view. She hugged me hard when we got to the curb. 'I know this is stressful, but it's going to be fine,' she said. 'Text me when you land. And when you see him. And when you get to the castle. Seriously, just text me all the time.'

'Will do.'

'Noah, say goodbye to Aunt Ruby!'

I leaned into the back and planted an awkward kiss on Noah's hand, which he promptly wiped off. I gave Jess a hug and opened the door. 'No giving birth until I get back, okay?'

'Trust me, I'm not in any rush. Have a safe flight and keep me posted! Don't do anything I wouldn't do!'

'That leaves me a fair amount of liberty.'

She glanced at Noah in the rear-view mirror and quickly flipped me off. 'Love you!'

I watched her car speed off and felt a pang of anxiety. Jess meant well, but with all the will in the world, there was no way I could just relax about seeing Ethan again. I had to be prepared.

I spent the flight sandwiched between a gangly man wearing a safari jacket and a teenaged boy who had doused himself in Drakkar Noir before take-off. I wasn't sure whose benefit this was for, but it certainly wasn't mine. I swallowed my usual in-flight cocktail of zinc, vitamin C and Ambien, and woke up as they were urging us to return to the upright position. One of the gangly man's legs had migrated into my leg space over the course of the flight and I gave his foot a nudge and shot him what I hoped was a polite but firm smile. He pretended to be too engrossed in the latest Cameron Crowe movie, as if that were even possible.

The plane landed at Heathrow. I shuffled silently through passport control and baggage claim, eyes bleary and legs stiff. When I finally emerged at the arrivals gate, it was nearly eight o'clock in the morning. Piper and Charlie's flight from Boston wasn't due for another hour, so I found an empty bench, switched on my iPhone, and bedded in for a long wait. Turns out I didn't have to wait very long.

I looked up to see *TechCrunch*'s pin-up striding across the concourse towards me. He had the same walk, loose-limbed and slightly swaggering, though his shoulders were broader and his clothes fell differently now, more easily. His hair was the same shock of black curls, but I could see a few threads of silver scattered through them, and it was more closely cropped than before. His eyes, though. His eyes were exactly the same. I was shocked – appalled, actually – to find my bloodstream suddenly coursing with dopamine. It's him, I thought to myself. Of course, it's always been him.

'Ruby,' he said, more of a statement than a greeting. He leaned in and kissed my cheek perfunctorily, leaving a good inch of air between his lips and my face.

In that moment, two things were immediately and immutably certain: I was still in love with him, almost giddy-ishly so, and he was not in love with me. In fact, he seemed very much the opposite.

'Ethan!' I did a sort of half-salute that I instantly regretted.

'Good to see you,' he lied.

'You too!' I said, too brightly. 'What are you doing here?'

'I live here now,' he said. 'Not at the airport. I mean, in London.' I was pleased to see him a little flustered. 'I came to pick up Charlie and Piper.'

'Oh,' I said. 'That's nice of you.'

'Yes, well . . . Did you just get in?'

'A few minutes ago.'

'Good flight?'

'Fine, thanks.'

We settled into an awkward silence, both of us staring intently at the arrivals gate, willing Piper and Charlie to appear. A few minutes passed. I caved first.

'I'm just going to run to the bathroom. Would you mind watching my bag? I promise there are no explosives in it!' I caught the look of confusion on his face as I walked away and hurried towards the bathroom. Inside, I splashed my face with cold water and inspected myself beneath the harsh fluorescent lights. My face, as feared, had puffed and swelled during the flight, and I could see the insistent black stub of an errant hair springing from my chin. My hair, which I'd had blown out two days before, hadn't fared much better, and was now an odd combination of flat and flyaway. In what cruel universe did a first encounter with an ex-boyfriend occur immediately after a long-haul flight? Why the hell had I just mentioned the threat of explosives to him? And how was it that I could see him again after ten years and still feel that same flip in my stomach, like driving over a speed-bump too fast and being momentarily weightless?

Get a grip, Atlas. I slicked on some red lipstick, but it only succeeded in making me look more sallow. I sighed and trudged back out to the arrivals area.

Thankfully, a distraction had arrived in my absence: Ethan was now clapping Charlie on the back and pulling my sister in for a hug. I took a deep breath and strode towards them.

'Ruby!' Charlie gathered me up in a bear hug and shook me back and forth, my feet dangling in the air. 'You made it!' He put me back on the ground and put both hands on my shoulders. 'I am so glad you're here. Piper, aren't we glad she's here? Man, that flight was amazing. They had all of the Rocky films on board – even *Rocky 5*! Can you believe it?'

'I can believe it,' I said.

'And they gave us these little miniature ice-cream bars halfway through. Did you get ice cream on your flight?'

'I slept most of the way.'

'Well, that's a shame. We'll have to get you an ice cream today to make up for it. Ethan, do you know any good ice-cream places?'

'Uh, sure, there's probably one at the train station . . .'

'I'm fine, thanks.' I extracted myself from Charlie and walked over to my sister, who was frowning at her phone. 'Are you going to say hello to your big sister already?' I asked, pulling her in for a hug. She was tiny – even smaller than usual – and her fine blonde hair was piled on top of her head, displaying her long, thin neck and delicate ears. She'd always been the ballerina of the two of us – graceful and fine-boned. I was built a little more hardily.

'Sorry,' she said, accepting the hug reluctantly. 'It's nice to see you and everything, it's just – I mean, do they even have 4G here? I'm not getting any reception and I need to call the caterer.'

'It's nice to see you, too,' I said, releasing her. I was used to Piper's somewhat reserved approach to familial affection: when we were kids, she'd scream bloody murder if anyone tried so much as to hold her hand, let alone kiss her. The Ice Princess, we called her. I still did, when she wasn't around to hear it.

'Here, you can use mine,' Ethan said, handing her a shiny new smartphone.

'Is this the new model?' she asked, eyes wide. 'It's not even out yet!'

'Perk of the job,' he shrugged, running a hand through his hair. My guts twisted a little tighter.

'Did you see the photos of the Beefeaters? Aren't they just darling?' We turned to see a middle-aged couple struggling with a trolley loaded high with luggage come steaming out of the arrivals gate. 'Sorry we're late,' the man called. 'Barbara wanted to freshen up before she saw you, Ethan.'

'Oh hush,' Barbara said, landing a lipsticked kiss on Ethan's waiting cheek. 'Don't listen to a word he says. It's so good to see you, though! Isn't he looking handsome! My other son, that's what I tell people when I see you on the television. "Look!" I say, "That's my son Ethan!" And they say, "Barbara, I didn't know you had another son!" And I say, "Well, he might not be blood, but he's as close as you can get."'

'It's good to see you, too,' Ethan said. 'And you, Bob.'

'Hello, son.' The two men shook hands, the older man pulling Ethan in for the manliest of hugs.

'Enough already!' Charlie laughed. 'A guy could get a complex listening to you two. Ruby, you remember my parents, right?'

Barbara squinted at me for a minute before a smile broke out across her face. 'Ruby Atlas! I haven't seen you in years and years! You haven't changed a bit!'

I watched Ethan's eyebrows rise almost imperceptibly. 'It's so nice to see you,' I said. 'And you too, Mr Armstrong.'

'Please, call me Bob. Where's that father of yours? Is he off selling sand to a beach somewhere?'

I ignored the dig and the jocular laugh that came with it. 'He and Candace are going to meet us at the hotel in Bamburgh,' I said. 'They decided to make a little road trip out of their visit.'

Barbara's eyes widened. 'Is he still with Candace? Well, isn't that nice.' I could tell that she didn't think it was nice at all, and felt a flash of pity for my stepmother. 'Your mother was a doll,' she said, placing a hand on mine. 'It's too bad she can't be here to see this wedding. She would have loved it. Such a class act, your mom.'

'We all miss her,' I said, pulling my hand from under hers. At this moment, on top of everything else, I couldn't allow myself to think about my mother, or her absence.

'We should get going,' Ethan said. I could see that he'd overheard the whole thing from the embarrassed look on his face. 'There's a car waiting outside.'

We gathered our bags and headed out towards the parking lot. He strode ahead and I hurried to catch up with him. 'Thanks for the out,' I said, quietly. 'I couldn't really handle that conversation right now.'

He nodded and then walked faster, nearly breaking into a run. It was obvious to anyone that he was trying to get away from me, so I dropped back and let myself be left. There was no point chasing someone who had no interest in being chased, at least not by me at that particular moment in time. I followed slowly behind the group, wheeled suitcase clacking on the pavement slabs.

Then

Ruby woke up in the night to the deafening sound of crickets and felt a sudden, deep pang of alarm. She was in a room so dark that there was no discernible difference between opening and closing her eyes, and her neck was bent at an awkward angle, thanks to her head being held aloft by an enormous pile of scratchy pillows. Disorientated, she sat up in bed and blinked a few times, willing her eyes to adjust to the dark. After a few seconds she could make out the faint outline of the Letters to Cleo poster, and a photograph of Jared Leto.

Finally, the penny dropped: she was back home, in her old bedroom, in the middle of fucking nowhere.

How could a bunch of tiny bugs make such a racket, she wondered. The constant thrum of traffic and drunken people that used to float up to her apartment window in Boston had been soothing white noise compared to this cacophony of crickets chirping away at each other. The darkness was scary, too – who knew what was lurking out there in her father's mammoth backyard? A few years ago, a perfectly normal-seeming, chino-wearing, Saturday morning soccer practice-type man had cut off his wife's head and impaled it on a stick in their garden because she'd burned the spaghetti. These sorts of things didn't happen in the city. You might get stabbed, but you'd get stabbed by the guy who was waving a knife around and cackling maniacally – not by the accountant standing quietly next to him. Ruby found that level of transparency comforting.

She glanced at the digital alarm clock that had been perched by her bedside since time immemorial: 4:12 a.m. She sighed and clicked on the light, squinting into the brightness as she felt around for the copy of *Glamor* she'd picked up at CVS on the way home. She stared at Jessica Simpson's smiling face for a minute and flicked through a photo shoot featuring models in what appeared to be Romany-gypsy costume. She made a mental note to buy a peasant skirt and moved onto an article debating the various merits of self-tanner.

The next thing Ruby knew, she was being startled awake by the sound of an almighty crash. She peeled away the magazine that had glued itself to her face and blinked into the sun now streaming through the lace curtains. She looked at the clock: 6:33 a.m. There was another crash, followed by a stream of expletives. Her father was evidently awake.

She pulled on a sweatshirt and a pair of shorts and padded into the bathroom. The smell of freshly brewed coffee had wafted up from the kitchen downstairs and she paused on the landing to take in a deep breath of it. Being home did have a few perks.

She peered at herself in the mirror, realizing with slight despair that a pimple that had been threatening to emerge had finally unveiled itself during the night. She prodded it with the edge of her nail and sighed: she'd have to dig out her high-school stash of Clearasil. Twenty-one and still getting acne: how was this fair?

Ruby pulled her hair into a slightly neater version of a ponytail and trudged downstairs into the hall. She could hear her father's voice echoing hollowly across the kitchen and reverberating through the house, but couldn't see him. The kitchen was basically in another wing.

The scale of the house – bought by her father five years ago shortly after he had married her stepmother, Candace – never ceased to amaze her. She'd grown up in a three-bedroom bungalow across town with a cozy living room and a sweet little front porch, complete with swing, but as her father's real estate business – and, concurrently, his bank balance – grew, it was deemed insufficient for a man of his stature. So he and Candace had bought a mini-mansion in one of his swanky new developments, and had decamped there. Ruby had only spent a year there before shipping off to college, so it had never fully felt like home. The development was called 'Songs of the South', and their house – the largest and perched at the top of the hill – was modeled after Tara from *Gone with the Wind*, the inappropriateness of which Ruby could never fully convey to Candace or her father. Candace had had a pair of forest-green velvet curtains custom-made for the living room, and it was one of her more well-worn party tricks to stand at the top of the curving staircase and say 'Well, fiddle-dee-dee!' before descending to greet her awaiting guests.

Ruby wandered through the living room, marveling at the enormous crystal chandelier that had appeared since the last time she'd been home, and into the kitchen. Her father was in workout gear – a high-tech-looking T-shirt that zipped at the throat and a pair of Lycra shorts. He was on his cell phone, talking to someone in plaintive tones about landscaping costs. He gave her a quick smile and gestured towards the coffee pot before walking into the laundry room to continue his phone call.

She poured herself a cup of coffee and sat at the breakfast bar, flicking through yesterday's copy of the *Beechfield Gazette*. Local charity auction, small fire burns down shed, cats that look like their owners, summer practice for high-school football begins: standard. On the front page, there was a photograph of a small girl in pigtails with an enormous ice-cream cone. *'Maisy Parker, four and a half, enjoys a raspberry ripple on a scorching afternoon.'* No doubt about it: she was back in the suburbs. She folded the paper and set it aside.

Her father, conversation finished and landscaper on the other end presumably duly admonished, walked in and started stretching his calves on the countertop. 'About to go for a twenty-miler with Kevin,' he said.

'You're going to run twenty miles?' she asked in slight disbelief. She'd known he'd gone on a fitness kick recently – she'd noticed the bottles of spirulina lined up in the fridge and the large-scale jars of protein powder in the pantry – but hadn't realized he'd turned into an ultra-runner.

'On the bike,' he said, looking slightly defensive. 'We're going to cycle around the lake. Great workout. Big cardio burst. My stomach is tighter than it has been for years. Feel that,' he said, offering up his abdomen. She gave it a tentative poke and made vague approving noises. He beamed. 'Candace says I look younger every day. Started calling me her wildcat.' He did a funny little growl and pawed at the air.

'Dad, please. I don't want to hear about what Candace calls you.'

He laughed and slapped her on the back. 'Well, kiddo, just thought you'd want to know there's life in the old man yet!'

'I definitely don't!' she said, shooing him away. 'Gross.'

'So, what are you doing today?' he asked, tossing an apple in the air before taking a bite. He looked at her with an appraising eye. 'You should try to get some sun,' he said. 'You've been locked away in a library for too long – you're too pale. If you turn up at the club looking like that, they'll think they've got a ghost. They'll call in Bill Murray and the gang!' He smiled and jabbed a finger towards her. 'Who you gonna call?'

'Ghostbusters,' she muttered dutifully. 'Anyway, they love pasty white people at the club. In fact, it's you that needs to be careful,' she said, assessing his deep mahogany tan. 'If you get any darker, they'll ban you.'

'Now hey there, you know that rule was overturned a long time ago. That club is a prestigious part of this community, not to mention your sister's employer, so I'd watch it before I went around saying that sort of stuff. People will get the wrong idea about this family.'

'Don't worry, I'm not about to lead a march on the golf course or anything.'

He frowned. 'There are some things that we don't joke about in this house, Ruby. You'll be meeting a lot of members when you start in the office, and I don't want to catch you giving them any of that attitude.' Ruby groaned inwardly at the mention of her upcoming job as receptionist at her dad's real estate agency. She'd applied for

37

internships, waitressing gigs, even for a job in which she would have had to dress up as a hot dog outside a car wash, but they had all turned her down. In the end, it was Atlas Realty or nothing.

'Hey, you two early birds! Catch any worms yet?' Candace sauntered into the kitchen wearing a black sports bra and matching leggings, a strip of toned, tanned abs on display in the middle. Ruby had to hand it to her, as much as Candace drove her nuts, she did look amazing for someone who was pushing forty.

Ruby's father necked a shot of wheatgrass and pulled on his cycling shoes. 'Morning, sweetheart! Just off to meet Kevin on the bike. Gotta keep myself in shape for my lady,' he said, giving her ass a little slap.

She giggled and kissed him on the cheek. 'You better,' she said, slapping his ass back. Ruby wondered if he could feel it through his padded cycling shorts – his face remained suspiciously unmoved. 'Is Piper up yet?'

'Of course not,' Ruby said. 'She never surfaces before ten. Besides, she was complaining about allergies last night, so presumably it'll be more like noon.'

Her father's brow wrinkled. 'I hope her nose doesn't get red. She's got her first day at the club tomorrow.' Ruby took some consolation in the fact that her sister – whose idea of work up until that point was peeling the shellac off her fingernails – would soon be a hostess at the local country club, with a uniform and everything. The idea of Piper in polyester filled her with inestimable joy.

A horn honked outside and her father grabbed his backpack. 'That's Kevin. I'll see you two ladies after work!' He trotted out of the house, shoes clicking neatly on the tiles, and Candace poured Ruby another cup of coffee and herself a cup of green tea.

'What's up for today?' she asked with a smile. 'I'm heading to the mall later on if you want to come?'

'No thanks,' Ruby said. Even though she suspected that a shopping trip would result in free things, she couldn't face trying on clothes with turbo-stepmom and her pneumatic breasts. It was her last day of official post-graduation freedom: tomorrow, she would start work and commence her summer of atrophying underneath the steady hum of an office air conditioner. She needed to make the most of today.

'Okay, you just stay right here and work on your tan. I'm going to run to the grocery store on my way home – is there anything in particular you think your sister would want?'

'I think she's on Gwyneth's macrobiotic diet,' Ruby said, 'so I guess just stock up on loads of beans and vegetables.'

Candace wrinkled her nose. 'Poor thing. She's going to be all kinds of gassy eating beans all day.' She swept up her Chloe Paddington and the Longchamp tote she used as a gym bag and gave Ruby a quick wave. 'Okay, I'm off to spin! Have a nice day by the pool and try to get some color on those little legs of yours, missy!' She floated out of the door in a cloud of Clinique Happy.

Ruby slathered herself up with Hawaiian Tropic oil (SPF 4, safety ever the watchword) and spent the rest of the day dozing in and out of sleep and lazily flipping the pages of her novel. Piper appeared next to her at around noon and grunted at her before stealing her oil and drinking the last Diet Coke. The two of them bickered gently until Candace came back home and paraded her purchases in front of them, including a microscopic white denim miniskirt that the sisters were united in hating.

By the time Ruby's father arrived home from work, all three women were irritable and suffering from mild cases of prickly heat. Oblivious, he rattled off his day's triumphs to them: his new personal best on the cycle this morning, the three condos sold over lunch, the cut-down price he's secured on lawn fertilizer, and a joke he'd told that had caused Buddy Cartwright to spit up his Mountain Dew. Candace and Ruby listened and took turns making appreciative murmurs over a dinner of grilled chicken salad (hold the dressing) while Piper munched sullenly on a plate of lentils. She made one last gallant attempt at getting out of work the next day (citing the beginnings of a trapped nerve in her finger) but her father shut it down quickly.

At nine o'clock, Ruby slid her plate into the dishwasher and gathered her bag. 'I've got to go,' she said, hoping to make a quick exit. 'I'm meeting some people from high school down at Billy Jack's.'

Her father's eyebrows shot skyward. 'Billy Jack's! Why the hell do you want to go to a dump like that?'

'Ruby thinks slumming it makes her seem sophisticated,' Piper said, unhelpfully.

'I do not.' She did, a little bit.

'Do too.'

'Shut up!'

'Girls,' Candace said, smiling brightly, 'try to get along, for your dad's sake. You know what the doctor said about his blood pressure.'

Ruby swiveled to face him, suddenly panicked. 'No,' she said, 'I don't know what the doctor said. What did the doctor say?'

'It's nothing,' her father said, stretching his arms out above his head. 'Just a little high, that's all.'

'He's put your father on beta blockers. All the stress from work.' Candace speared a piece of chicken and gave him a meaningful look.

'Why didn't you tell me?' Ruby said accusingly. 'How could I not know about this?'

'Uh, because you're never home?' Piper again, still unhelpful.

'Sweetheart, it's nothing. Honest. Now you go out and enjoy yourself. Do you need any money?'

'I'm fine, Dad. Thanks.'

'Probably for the best. You don't want to be carrying much cash in a place like that. Now if anyone asks you to go outside with them, or into the bathroom, or anything like that, you just tell them no, okay?'

'Okay, Dad.' Ruby fought the urge to point out that, for the past four years, she'd lived in a corner of Boston best known for its colorful collection of prostitutes and meth-heads.

'Why don't you take your sister with you?' Candace suggested. 'It might be fun!'

'Over my dead body,' Piper said, reaching into the fridge and pulling out a miniature wine cooler. 'Like I'd be seen in that place. Anyway, I'm going out with Kimberly tonight.'

'Piper, I'm sure you're used to drinking at college, but you're under my roof now, and you know how I feel about underage drinking.'

Piper rolled her eyes. 'Oh please – it's a wine cooler, not Bacardi 151. It's, like, juice.'

'Piper . . .'

'Please, Daddy?' She flicked her eyelashes at him a few times and he assented with a shrug. She skipped out of the kitchen, but not before grabbing another little bottle from the fridge.

Ruby climbed into her car, cranked up Sheryl Crow, and sped off to Billy Jack's, feeling like she was a senior in high school all over again. Only with a real ID this time.

When she got to Billy Jack's, she pulled open the saloon-style doors, the opening strains of 'Sweet Child of Mine' welcoming her in. She saw a group of old classmates tucked away in a corner, all of them sipping nervously on their Buds and eyeing the townies warily. The bar was packed and muggy with people's beery breath, and Ruby felt her shirt begin to stick to her shoulder blades. She ducked past two women in denim cut-offs and backless shirts dancing enthusiastically, and grabbed the edge of the bar to steady herself.

'What can I get you?' the bartender asked, bending his lean frame across the bar towards her.

She looked up, and there, cleaning up a swill of beer with a dirty rag, was the most handsome man she'd ever seen.

He had a swirl of black hair curling across a wide, smooth forehead. His eyebrows were thick and perfectly straight, and under them lay two enormous eyes fringed with long, dark lashes. A thin, almost girlish nose led to a full, wide mouth.

'Um . . .' She looked at him blankly for several beats.

'A woman of few words,' he said, 'I like it. I'm Ethan.' He stuck out a (perfect) hand and flashed a (perfectly) crooked grin.

She stared in stunned silence. Ethan, she thought, rolling the name around in her head like a smooth stone.

He gave her shoulder a little nudge. 'You okay?'

She was startled back into the moment. 'Ruby,' she said, offering her hand in return. 'I'm Ruby.'

'Cool,' he said. 'Like the song.'

Ruby had no idea what he was talking about, but it didn't matter. All that mattered were his green-gold eyes, and her reflection in them.

Now

'What do you mean, he hates you?'

'I mean he hates me. Do you need me to draw you a diagram or something?'

I was hissing down the phone at Jess from behind a potted plant in King's Cross station. The vaulted glass ceiling soared above, and the concourse rang out with the hurried voices of passengers rushing to catch their trains. Ours wasn't scheduled to leave for another hour, so Ethan had taken the rest of the group to St Pancras for lunch at the champagne bar. I'd made up some excuse about buying emergency tights – a pretty bad excuse considering it was July and London was in the grip of a heatwave, but one he accepted unquestioningly – and had darted off to call Jess.

'I don't understand. He doesn't know what happened, right?'

'No!' I shouted. A woman pushing a sleeping toddler in a stroller shot me a dirty look and I rolled my eyes at her. 'No,' I repeated, more quietly, 'and he's not going to, but it doesn't matter – he still hates me. Actually, it's more like he's totally indifferent to me, which is worse if you think about it.'

'How can he be indifferent to you? You're adorable!'

'He looked at me like I was a can of wallpaper paste.'

'Okay. Well, how do you feel about him?'

'That's the problem,' I said, swallowing hard. 'I think I still love him.'

'Holy shit!'

'It's ridiculous, right? I don't even know him anymore, how can I love him? It's probably just hormones, or exhaustion from the flight or something. Maybe they pump something in the air over here. Anyway, just forget it. Ignore me. I'll snap out of it. In fact, I feel like I'm already snapping out of it. Yep! It's totally fine, false alarm.'

'Ruby, get a grip.'

'Just forget I ever said anything. Temporary insanity.'

'Ruby, if you have feelings for him still — and it totally makes sense that you would, considering how you guys left it — you have a duty to yourself to see where they might lead.'

'Did you not hear the part where I said he thinks I'm wallpaper paste?'

'He's probably faking it! I bet he's secretly roiled up just as much as you are.'

I picked at a stray cuticle. 'He does not look like a man who gets roiled up.'

'Why, because he's rich now? Rich people get roiled!'

'Stop saying roiled!' I said, tearing the cuticle off with my teeth and wincing as a tiny bead of blood appeared. 'And no, not because he's rich now, because he's . . . I don't know. Different. I'm telling you, he doesn't give a shit about me anymore. There's nothing there.'

'Give it time,' she said. 'Don't just shut it down because he hasn't immediately come running into your arms.'

I sighed and leaned against the cool stone wall of the concourse. The station was a hive of activity, filled with packs of confused tourists whacking into one another with their maps and selfie sticks. I watched a woman push through the barrier gate and sprint towards a man who was waiting for her with outstretched arms. 'It's so embarrassing,' I said. 'I feel like some idiot teenager.'

'Love is embarrassing. That's just the way it is. Let yourself be embarrassed for once.'

I sighed. 'I should go. I've got to go buy tights from somewhere.'

'What do you need tights for? Is the weather really that bad there?'

'Long story.'

'Okay, well, remember what I said. Don't freak out. Just go with the flow.'

'You know as well as I do that the last time I went with the flow, I had J. Lo highlights and you were dating a Yankee.'

'And I stand by both of those choices. I love you.'

'Love you too. Keep your phone on – I have a feeling I'm going to need you.'

I hung up and headed over to join the others in St Pancras, stopping first to buy tights in Boots and ending up with an armful of exotic-sounding beauty products in the process. I showed Piper my haul when I reached the table.

'I'm stealing this,' she said as she inspected the ingredients list on a tub of sugar scrub. 'And this,' she added, nudging an overnight serum towards her.

I stuffed them back in the plastic bag. 'The store is literally two minutes away. I can just take you there and you can buy your own stuff.'

She snatched the bag away. 'Why would I want to do that? There's champagne to drink. Here, have some.' She poured half a glassful and handed it to me. 'Now,' she said in a fake whisper, 'how are you doing about . . . *you know*.' She nodded meaningfully towards Ethan, who was seated at the other end of the table and was busy trying to explain to Bob and Barbara why he hadn't yet met the queen, despite having lived in London for three years and being, as Barbara didn't tire of pointing out, a Very Important Person.

'Fine,' I said. I worried she'd be able to see my heart frantically beating from underneath my thin cotton T-shirt. I loved my sister dearly, but there was no way I was going to tell her the truth about Ethan. The girl couldn't keep her mouth shut to save her life, and anything I said would go directly back to Charlie . . . which meant it would go straight to Ethan. 'It was a long time ago. No big deal,' I added, with what I hoped looked like a nonchalant shrug.

'Okay, phew! That's exactly what Ethan said, but I just wanted to make sure you were okay, too. I know it must be awkward, being at a wedding with your ex-boyfriend when you're still single. Especially your little sister's wedding.'

'Thanks for that, Piper.' I tried not to show my mortification, both over her having spoken to Ethan about me and him confirming my suspicions about how he felt. It was official: I was wallpaper paste.

'I'm just saying, I would totally understand if you were feeling a little insecure about the whole thing. Especially now that Ethan's so insanely successful. Did you know that he was voted one of *Time* magazine's 100 Most Influential People?'

'I did not know that.' Of course I knew that.

'And he's in the process of setting up a charity providing tech training for underprivileged kids.'

'Wow.'

'I'm just saying, he's kind of amazing, so I think it's really impressive that you're being so cool about it.'

'Well, like I said, it's all water under the bridge now.'

'It's super brave of you.'

'Ancient history.'

'I mean, if it was me, and my ex-boyfriend had turned into this, like, *demi-god* –'

'Piper, I'm fine, okay? I appreciate the concern and I'm very happy that you think I'm being brave or whatever, but honestly, I'm totally fine about the whole thing. Completely and totally unaffected.'

'Okay! Okay! Sheesh, I'm just trying to be a good sister.'

'I know you are,' I said, and believe it or not, it was true. Piper was self-obsessed, often infuriating and at times showed a lack of awareness that was truly astonishing, but her heart was in the right place. Most of the time, at least.

'It's probably time we made a move,' Ethan said, leaning away from the table and signaling a passing waiter for the bill. There was a small smile playing at the edges of his mouth and I could tell that he'd overheard our entire conversation. The irrational teenage lust that had gripped my insides since I'd laid eyes on him a few hours ago suddenly flipped to irrational teenage anger.

'I'll get this,' I said, reaching for my bag. 'Since you got the car here, and the train tickets. You don't have to pay our way for everything, you know.'

He waved me away. 'Honestly, it's fine.' He slid a credit card into the leather billfold and handed it back to the waiter.

'Let's at least split it,' I said, pulling a card out of my wallet and holding it out to the waiter. I was determined to prove that he wasn't the only one who had the ability to pay for things. I'm a success, too! I wanted to scream. I'm also considered a Very Important Person in some circles! Or at least an Important Person. Even just a Person. 'Take it,' I said to the waiter, waving the card in his direction. 'Please.'

'No,' Ethan said, more insistently this time. 'I've got this.'

'I don't see why you should pay for everything,' I said, narrowing my eyes at him.

'Because it's a nice thing to do?'

'Then why can't I do a nice thing, too?' I spat back. I turned back to the waiter. 'Ignore this man,' I said, nodding towards Ethan. 'Put it all on my card.'

'Shall I come back?' the waiter asked nervously.

'No!' We shouted in unison.

'This is ridiculous,' Ethan said. 'We have a train to catch. If it means that much to you, go ahead and pay the damn bill. Knock yourself out.'

'Thank you,' I said loftily, and tried not to blanch visibly when I saw the amount on the card reader the waiter handed me. Do not think about the exchange rate, I chanted in my head as I typed in my PIN.

'Right,' Charlie said as he gathered up the bags. 'Let's get this show on the road!'

Then

Ethan was in the middle of an argument when he first saw her. Mick Dewey was giving him shit about the change he'd given him – again – and he was explaining simple math to him – again – when he looked up and saw her leaning on the bar. A few tendrils of hair had plastered themselves to her forehead and she had the faintest sheen of sweat above her upper lip. She was looking around the place as if it were a museum of curiosities rather than a shitty dive bar, and there was a faint look of bemusement on her face that he'd soon learn was pretty much permanent. Two truths were immediately apparent: she was absolutely gorgeous and she definitely didn't belong there.

He leaped along the bar to get to her.

'Hey, what about my change?' Mick called. Ethan gave him the finger, which was maybe not the best customer service, but was pretty standard when bartending at a place like Billy Jack's, perpetually full of loudmouth drunks (all of whom he loved dearly, of course). Anyway, he'd gone to high school with Mick, who used to beat the shit out of him when they were playing basketball, so it was nice to exercise a little power over him now. A little retribution.

'Hey,' he said to the beautiful girl, leaning across the bar in what he hoped was a casual-yet-rakish way. 'What can I get you?'

She looked up, startled, and stared at him for a couple of blank seconds. 'Um . . .' she said. He realized it wasn't going well.

'A woman of few words,' he said, 'I like it,' and then kicked himself for sounding like a dick. 'I'm Ethan.' He stuck his hand out, feeling like a door-to-door salesman who had just agreed a nice deal on a deluxe vacuum cleaner. She continued to stare at him as if he'd just pulled a rabbit out of somewhere unmentionable. He worried briefly that she thought the foul smell that constantly permeated the bar was coming from him. It's the dishwasher! he wanted to shout. It stinks! Well, that and Mick Dewey, who was staring intently at his palm and counting out the change for the fifteenth time, lips moving soundlessly as he did it. The staring continued for a few more beats. It was brutal, his hand just dangling there in space. Dewey was going to look up any minute and see him get shot down by this beautiful girl, and he'd never hear the end of it. He couldn't let that happen. He reached across and gave her a little nudge on the shoulder. 'You okay?' he asked.

She snapped out of it, her eyes refocusing on him. 'Ruby,' she said, placing a soft hand in his. 'I'm Ruby.'

'Cool,' he said. 'Like the song.'

'Oh, sure,' she said, and he could tell by her uncertain smile that she didn't have a clue what he was talking about. Normally he had a rule against dating women who didn't have an innate knowledge of late 1960s rock (other deal-breakers included not loving *The Big Lebowski* and not hating Jeff Koons) but she was so cute standing there in front of him that he decided he could overlook it. Just the once.

'You from around here?' he asked.

'Born and bred,' she said, and her tone suggested she wasn't too proud of the fact.

'Oh yeah? How come I've never seen you in here before?' To his knowledge, every citizen of Beechfield had filed through Billy Jack's double doors at least once in their lives. The poor kids came in because the beer was cheap and the jukebox was good, and the rich kids came to marvel at the poor kids and feel superior to them. The poor kids didn't mind so much because sometimes the rich kids would challenge them to a game of pool and the poor kids would clean up. And if they didn't win, there was always the fun sport of beating up a rich kid.

Ethan was one of the poor kids.

Ruby gave a little shrug. 'I'm only back for the summer,' she said. 'I just graduated from Boston College and I'm moving to New York in the fall so . . . just passing through, I guess.'

'But you grew up here? In Beechfield, I mean. Not in Billy Jack's.' He was rambling. He leaned over and poured himself a finger of whisky – normally he didn't drink on the job, but talking to her had him a little off balance. 'I'm just surprised I never ran into you at school or whatever.'

'I went to County Day Prep,' she said, a little embarrassed.

'Oh, a private-school kid. That explains it. I was Beech-field High all the way. Go Greyhounds.' What was he even doing, he wondered? It was as if he were hovering outside of his body, watching himself make a total asshole out of himself, but powerless to stop it.

'Yeah, well, my dad's Alec Atlas,' she said, as if that answered everything. Which, in fairness, it did.

'Oh yeah? I've heard of Alec Atlas.' Everyone had heard of Alec Atlas. A poster of the man hovering above a genie's bottle was plastered on every bench, corkboard and window in town. ALEC ATLAS: YOUR WISH IS MY COMMAND. The town was littered with 'Atlas Specials', as they were known, developments stacked with mini-mansions and called things like 'Whispering Pines' or 'Venetian Dreams'. Over the previous ten years, Atlas Specials had replaced nearly every single field, apple orchard and wooded area in the town, much to the displeasure of some of the older residents, Ethan's father very much included.

'Yeah, everybody's heard of my dad,' she said. She didn't look pleased about it.

Ethan felt for her: he knew what it was like to live under a parent's shadow in a small town. 'What do you want to drink?' he asked. 'On the house.'

'Oh, you don't have to do that.' She flushed slightly, which he found adorable.

'It's the only perk of the job.'

'Okay, then . . . I'll have a whisky. Bourbon, actually.'

'A girl who drinks bourbon, huh? I like it.' He poured her a generous measure and handed it to her. She took a sip and he saw her wince – not much of a bourbon drinker after all. 'Do you want some Coke in that?' he asked.

'Just a little,' she said, relieved.

'Hey, Ethan! Who do I have to screw to get a drink in this place?' He looked up to see Charlie Armstrong leaning over the bar and waving at him.

'Why don't you start with yourself?' he shouted back. He tried to send a meaningful look Charlie's way – a look that said 'I think I'm talking to the woman of my dreams so get fucked' – but, as ever, Charlie didn't clock it. Charlie was his oldest friend, and Ethan loved him like a brother, as in half the time he drove him crazy.

'C'mon, buddy! I'm dying of thirst over here!' Charlie wrapped his hands around his throat and pretended to pass out, knocking into a disgruntled-looking Mick Dewey in the process. Ethan had been counting the number of scotches Dewey had been drinking that night and knew that he was close to fighting level: he'd have to intervene or Charlie would end up dying of something other than thirst.

He turned back to Ruby with an apologetic smile. 'Sorry, be right back. Don't go anywhere, okay?'

'I won't,' she said, smiling over the rim of her glass, and at that moment he thought he might be in with a shot. At least he hoped he was.

Now

We boarded the train, each of us clutching a plastic bag full of snacks and bottles of water we'd bought from M&S, and took our seats. Charlie, Piper and the Armstrongs filled up a table of four, which left Ethan and me sitting in a cramped two-seater. We shuffled awkwardly next to each other, careful not to touch accidentally across the armrest, and after a brief 'All set?' he proceeded to stare out of the window and ignore me. The London suburbs whizzed by, rows of gray- and red-brick houses backing onto tiny squares of garden, and then out into the countryside, where patchwork green fields spread neatly outwards, occasionally dotted with a few scattered sheep. From the occasional glimpses I had around the back of Ethan's head, I could tell the views were beautiful, but I forced myself to concentrate on the paperback thriller I'd bought at the airport. Eventually, I dozed off, lulled by the dull whir of the engine.

I woke up to find Ethan nudging me – not all that gently – off of his shoulder. 'We're almost there,' he said, not all that nicely. 'Time to wake up.'

'Sorry,' I mumbled. I figured I'd probably been asleep for a couple of hours, and judging by Ethan's reserved air and the – oh God, mortifying – slightly damp patch on his shirt, I suspected that I'd spent most of that time unconsciously cozying up to him. I jumped up and started gathering up the detritus that had coalesced under the seat during the trip. 'Almost there, guys!' I said, leaning over the neighboring table, where all four present-and-future Armstrongs were asleep, open-mouthed.

Barbara startled awake. 'What have I missed?' she asked, staring frantically out of the window at yet another sheep-scattered field.

'Nothing,' Charlie said, raising his arms in a stretch. 'Just a load of grass. What time is it?'

'Nearly six o'clock,' Ethan said. 'We're the next stop, so we should get the bags together.'

The train pulled into the station with a groan, and the six of us tumbled out through the door and onto the platform. It was still a bright, blue-skied day, but the air in the north had a crisp edge to it. At the end of the platform stood a man with a round, florid face, wearing a slightly-too-small suit. He was smiling and holding a piece of white paper with the name 'Bailey' scrawled on it.

'Oh, Ethan, what have you done now?' Barbara said, her face flushed with pleasure.

'I thought it would be easier to book a driver for the week rather than having to rent a car,' Ethan said.

'Just look at his cap! Isn't it darling?'

'You must be Ethan,' the man said, holding out a large, calloused hand. 'The name's Victor, but please just call me Vic. Can I give anyone a hand with their luggage?' He took Barbara's over-stuffed Vera Bradley bag out of her hands and swung it over his shoulder without waiting for an answer. 'Follow me,' he said, striding down the steps and out into the parking lot.

'All right, Vic,' called a man smoking a cigarette by the front entrance.

'All right, Carl,' he called back. 'You still owe me a tenner for those Tom Jones tickets I bought!'

'Aye, you've been after that tenner for months, and I keep buying you pints and saying we're even!'

'A pint is not a tenner, it's a gesture of hospitality, you cheap bastard!' The two men erupted in laughter and Vic led us on to an enormous black SUV, Barbara shooting nervous glances back at Carl.

'He wasn't very nice to call Carl a bastard!' she whispered to Ethan.

'I think he was just kidding, Mrs A,' he said. 'Here, let me take your suitcase for you – you must be exhausted.' He dragged the case to the car and loaded it into the trunk with the rest of the luggage before wordlessly reaching for mine.

'I've got it,' I said. I distinctly felt something snap behind my kneecap when I swung the suitcase in, but refused to let myself wince.

Barbara climbed into the van and settled herself on a seat. 'Ooh,' she said. 'This is just like what Charles and Camilla travel in!'

'Oh yes, I remember from that documentary we watched,' Bob said, buckling himself in to the seat next to her. 'They seemed like a nice couple.'

'Well, no one will ever replace Diana, and I'll never forgive him for –'

'How long until we get to the hotel?' Piper cut her off from the back seat – I suspected she'd already heard

Barbara's thoughts on Princess Diana more than a few times in the run-up to the wedding. 'I'm so hungry I could die, and my skin is literally shriveling up back here. I need to hydrate, like, yesterday.'

'It's not a long drive – about three-quarters of an hour or so – but I thought I'd take you the scenic route,' Vic said. 'Beautiful countryside around here, and I'll take you past a few castles on the way.'

'Did you say a few castles?' Bob said, leaning forward. 'You mean to say you've got more than one castle around here?'

'We've got shedloads!' he said with a booming laugh. 'Can't get bloody shifted for castles around here! Border country, you see. Someone always trying to invade us. Good luck to them, I say.'

'The scenic route sounds great,' Ethan said smoothly. 'Piper, I've got some water in my bag if you want it?'

'It's fine,' she said, but I could tell by the tone of her voice that it definitely wasn't, and that we'd all pay for it later.

Vic was true to his word. 'Castle!' he called out every five minutes, pointing to a block of tumbling rock perched precariously by the side of the road, or the faint outline of a turret a few miles away. 'There's another one!'

'It's like castle bingo,' I muttered after we sped past the fourth, and was pleased in spite of myself when I saw Ethan crack a smile.

Finally, the car pulled into a circular sweep in front of an imposing sandstone mansion, the front portico flanked with graceful fluted columns. Tall windows stared sightlessly out, some of them hooded with damask blinds. The well-manicured lawn stretched out in front, punctuated with thick tufts of pink roses and purple crane's bill.

I climbed out of the car and shook out my stiff legs. My eyes were gritty and stinging from travel, but they still widened with awe when I saw the size of the place. 'Is this another castle?'

'What, this place?' Vic lifted my suitcase out of the trunk and placed it next to me. 'No, love, this is just Bugle Hall! It's only been around since the eighteenth century – practically a new-build around these parts.'

I took a moment to process the idea that something from the eighteenth century could be considered 'practically new', while the rest of them tumbled out of the car, each of them stretching and blinking and gaping at the enormous house in front of them. Even Ethan, whose own home was presumably the size of an oil tanker, seemed impressed. Vic pulled the cases into the lobby of the hall, where a blue-haired woman wearing a tartan skirt and a blouse buttoned up to the neck was there to greet us.

Vic turned to us with a smile. 'Right, well, you're all settled then, so I'll be off, unless there's anything else you need me for?'

'Thanks very much, but I think we're fine for the rest of the evening. I have your number if we need anything.' He reached over and shook Vic's hand, sliding a wide purple note into it as he did so.

'Lovely, thanks very much! Tarrah, everyone! See you in a tic!'

The blue-haired woman – whose name was Mrs Willocks, and who assured us several times that she ran a very tight ship – showed each of us to our rooms and told us that we had time to 'freshen up' before 'tea is served in the drawing room'. Every phrase she uttered sent Bob and Barbara into further paroxysms of delight, and soon they had cornered her into walking them through the line of oil paintings hung in the hallway, inspecting each of them for a possible Armstrong family resemblance. (Barbara had done some light family tree research before the trip and they were now convinced that they were directly related to William of Orange.)

I used the distraction to slink off to my room – the smallest, of course, wedged at the top of the house in the old servant's quarters – and prepare myself. This being the modern age, and me being a thoroughly modern woman, I knew just how to go about it. I pulled out my phone, waved it around until I found a signal, and typed the name Ethan Bailey into the search bar. Sure, I'd looked him up before, but now I needed to go deep. I needed to go full Mach-ten Google-stalk.

I was hit with a wave of entries – reams and reams of them, all extolling Ethan's many creative and capitalistic virtues. I scrolled past the *New York Magazine* piece and the subsequent *AP Wire* mentions, had a quick look at his company profile – 'Ethan Bailey, widely regarded as one of the leading technological designers of the age, founded Albion in 2006 and currently serves as Head of Creative Development' – before moving on to his social media. His Facebook feed was protected – smart guy – but his Twitter was public. There was a thumbnail image of him smiling confidently into the camera and wearing another very expensive suit. Most of his tweets were links to design articles and retweets of Albion company news, but there was the occasional direct tweet – a 'nice to meet you' or a 'sorry I missed your call' or, once, a 'great connecting with you the other night. Dinner soon?' – that led me down Twitter-link rabbit holes, staring beadily at the tiny photographs of women who may or may not have slept with Ethan. I hated all of them on sight.

I was halfway through an article likening him to Steve Jobs when I was interrupted by someone pounding at the door. 'Ruby!' Piper's voiced called, 'What are you doing in there? Dad and Candace are here and we're all waiting for you!'

'Coming!' I croaked. I stumbled over to the basin – there was one in the bedroom rather than in the adjoining bathroom – and splashed cold water onto my face. I looked in the mirror and winced: the puffiness from the plane had lessened a little, but my eyes were bloodshot and there were dark hollows underneath them. I slapped my cheeks a few times to see if it would perk them up a little, but I still looked like death warmed up. There was no way I could compete with the Twitter ladies, at least not in this state. I sighed and trudged downstairs.

Bob and Barbara had obviously taken the suggestion to 'freshen up' seriously, because Bob was now wearing a beige linen suit, and Barbara was trussed into her Country Casuals separates. Both of them balanced a cup and saucer awkwardly on their knees. Piper, wearing a pair of Lululemon yoga pants and a cashmere sweater, Coach bag nestled neatly by her side, was scrolling idly through her iPhone. 'She *told* me there was Wi-Fi,' she *tsk*ed. 'How am I supposed to get our wedding hashtag going if I can't even tweet?'

And there, perched on a heavily fringed velvet divan, luggage stacked around them like fortress walls, were my dad and stepmother.

'Hey there, champ!' Dad called as I walked in. He pulled himself heavily to his feet and enveloped me in a hug. 'How's my girl?' he asked. 'You look fantastic!'

'You're a liar,' I said, 'but I'll take it.'

It took me a minute to adjust my eyes to the sight of him. He was very, very orange, as he had been ever since they'd made the move down to Florida to, as he always said, 'live the dream'. The reality was more of a nightmare. In the boom years of the mid-noughties, and riding high on his success with the Beechfield developments, he had drunk the Floridian Kool-Aid and bought up as much of Orlando as he could get his hands on, miles and miles of tract housing built on the promise of an endless supply of young professional couples, eager retirees and cheap money. After the property crash, he and Candace had decamped to one of their few remaining unforeclosed properties, a bungalow in Clearwater set in an Italianate village that they insisted on calling Botticelli's Grotto. I'd never been able to imagine Botticelli living in a a pale-pink stucco ranch, but I knew when to keep my mouth shut. Sometimes.

'Well, you're always beautiful to me. You and your sister are both the apples of my eye. And Candace, of course. She's my Candy Apple, aren't you, sweetheart?'

Candace shot him a tight smile. Candace, also orange, had embraced the Miami side of the Floridian aesthetic and was wearing a pair of slightly shimmery purple leggings, a low-cut blouse covered in a palm-frond print and a pair of wedges so high they were almost vertical. She'd been a knockout when she got together with my dad, all legs and breasts and long, tousled waves that I'd spent hours in the mirror trying to replicate. She was still beautiful, but she was softer now – her face had lost its sharp angles and her waist had thickened a little. But you could tell that, in my dad's eyes, she was still up there with the best of them.

Dad hitched up the waist of his plaid shorts and shrugged. 'She's a little pissed because we got lost on the way here.'

'Alec, you drove us halfway to Glasgow!'

'A little road trip!' he said with a smile. 'We had fun, didn't we, Candy?'

Candace sighed and pulled me in for a hug. 'Your father is going to be the death of me yet. How are you doing, sweets? You look a little washed out. Have they been working you too hard at that agency again?'

Dad leaned forward and punched me lightly on the shoulder, nearly clipping Candace in the process. 'Nothing wrong with a little hard work, right, kid?'

I smiled weakly. 'I'm fine, really,' I said, extracting myself gently from her Poison-infused embrace. I had never adjusted to Candace's Californian touchy-feeliness, even after nearly twenty years as my stepmother. 'I'm just a little jet-lagged. How are you doing? How was your trip?'

'Oh God,' she said, throwing up her hands. 'It was an absolute nightmare. We had three connections – three! At one point, we were in Dubai, though God knows why. And your father forgot his heart medication –'

'Dad!'

He held up his hands. 'I'm fine! I'm fine! I've been meaning to get off that stuff for a while. Makes me feel a little loopy.'

'You're not supposed to go off it cold turkey!' Candace said.

'Hey, I'm a tough guy,' he said, thumping himself on the chest. 'This old ticker of mine isn't going to give me any trouble, I can promise you that. I'm fitter than I was when we met!'

I looked at the small paunch hanging over his belt buckle. 'I feel like you should try to get your medicine over here,' I said. 'Maybe we could get your doctor to call a local pharmacy or something?'

'Ruby, I'm fine.' His tone had turned stern, and I raised an eyebrow at him. He thwacked me in the shoulder again, harder this time, and cracked one of his patented Alec Atlas Winning Smiles. 'Hey, how's work? You killing them out there?'

'I'm trying,' I said.

'Good for you, good for you.'

Piper, who'd been silent until this point, looked up from her phone with a frown. 'What's the emoji for "living my best life"?'

'How's the golf game, Bob?' Dad asked, pushing past me and settling himself in an armchair next to a startled-looking Mr Armstrong. 'You still bogeying all over the course?' He let out a guffaw and slapped Bob on the back. I was starting to worry that all this joviality would end up with an assault charge by the end of the trip.

'My handicap has actually gone down a couple of points recently,' Bob said, stiffening.

'Is that right? Are they letting you use the kiddie course or something! Ha ha!'

'Bob and I won the Spring Fling Couples Tournament,' Barbara said, placing a protective hand on Bob's thigh. 'We were given matching blazers.'

'How sweet!' Candace said, hoping to smooth things over. From the look on Barbara's face, it hadn't worked.

'It's something, all right,' Dad said. 'How is the old club, anyway? Surviving without me?' One of the great injustices of my father's life was being kicked out of the Beechfield Country Club for non-payment of dues after the crash. On his last night, he made a rousing speech on the front lawn and burned his membership card, but I knew how hurt he'd been by the whole thing. It was like watching a teenage girl get kicked off the cheerleading squad: swift, brutal and socially annihilating.

'The club's doing just fine. We just got a new sauna, in fact.' Bob was a board member at the club, and a staunch defender of its principles and traditions – even if those principles and traditions meant kicking his son's future father-in-law out of the club. My father hadn't forgotten, and, from the look of it, hadn't forgiven, either.

'I hear those saunas are breeding grounds for bacteria. Better watch it, Bob – you might sit in something you'll regret.'

'Now, hang on a minute –'

'Why don't you guys drop off your bags and get a little sleep?' I hoisted my dad out of his chair and steered him and Candace towards the door. 'You must be exhausted after all the traveling.'

'You're so right,' Candace said, looking at me gratefully. 'Did I tell you we almost went to Glasgow?'

'Let me help you with that,' I said, taking my dad's suitcase from him and shoving him firmly up the stairs. I noticed that the stitching on the LVs didn't match up. A few years ago, Candace wouldn't have been caught dead carrying anything other than the real thing. Times were apparently still tough in Florida.

'It's definitely prayer hands,' I heard Piper say as I lugged the heavy case up the stairs. 'Kimberly is going to *freak* when she reads this Facebook post.'

Then

Ruby parted the curtains and peered out of the window. The day had been hot, another in a long string of humid days where the pavement turned sticky and the smell of exhaust seemed to permeate the air, but a thunderstorm had cut through it an hour ago and the driveway was now slicked black with rain. The air smelled of freshly cut grass. At the end of the drive, a lamp shone yellow, but otherwise it was dark.

She'd dressed up for the occasion and was wearing her favorite sundress, a little vintage number she'd bought at a thrift store in Boston a couple of years ago. It was sunshine yellow and had a nipped-in waist and a full skirt: much more girly than she usually went for, but it seemed to fit the occasion. She'd been waiting at the window for twenty minutes, even though Ethan wasn't due to turn up until eight. She couldn't help herself. She couldn't wait.

Finally, she heard the sound of a car engine getting closer and then saw the flash of his headlights as he pulled into the driveway. Her father appeared next to her and glanced out of the window to see what she was looking at. 'Is that Bill Bailey's son?' he asked as Ethan climbed out of the car. They both watched him lope up the driveway towards the front door.

'I don't know who his father is,' she said, 'but his name is Ethan.'

'Hmm,' he said, watching Ethan accidentally step on one of his geraniums. 'Looks like Bill's son to me.'

Ruby opened the door, and there he was, in a white T-shirt and a pair of worn-in jeans, smiling his crooked smile. 'Hey,' he said, and Ruby's heart flipped and soared.

'You must be Ethan!' Ruby's father pushed past her and stuck out his hand. 'I'm Alec Atlas, Ruby's father.'

'Nice to meet you, sir,' Ethan said, shaking his hand. 'I've heard a lot about you.'

'All good, I hope!' he said, forcing a laugh. 'Now, I know you two are grown-ups and all, but Ruby is my little girl –

'Dad, I'm twenty-one, not twelve,' Ruby said. She heard the peevishness in her voice and hated herself for it.

'I know, I know, just being your typical overprotective dad.' Ruby wondered where that overprotectiveness had been when he had locked her and Piper, as kids, in the house with a pizza and a VHS so he could go on dates with a seemingly endless parade of leggy blondes, but decided to bite her tongue.

'Sir, you don't have anything to worry about with me,' Ethan said. 'I'll take good care of her, I promise.' He flicked Ruby a wink when her father wasn't looking and she gave him a sly smile.

'Glad to hear it, glad to hear it. You're Bill Bailey's son, right?'

'That's right,' Ethan said evenly.

'Nice guy, Bill. You tell him when he finally decides to sell that old place of his to give me a call. I know a couple of developers who would pay a pretty penny for that plot of land.'

'That land has been in our family for five generations, so I don't think he's planning on selling anytime soon,' Ethan said, voice still even.

'Well, you never know what the future might hold, so you just pass my message on to him and give him my regards.'

'Will do, sir,' Ethan said.

'Well, I won't keep you two any longer. Have fun and be safe!'

'Bye, Dad,' Ruby said, before grabbing Ethan's hand and making a break for the car.

'Don't forget to tell your father!' her father called after them. Ethan waved a hand in acknowledgement but didn't turn back.

'Man,' he said, when they were safely out of the driveway, 'is he always like that?'

'Trying to wheedle business out of everyone? Yeah.' She remembered the high blood pressure and felt a twist of guilt. 'He means well, though.'

'I'm sure,' he said, 'but he's barking up the wrong tree with my dad. He always said he'll be carried out of Beechfield in a pinewood box, and I don't see that opinion changing anytime soon.'

'Honestly, I can't see a pinewood box stopping my father.'

Ethan drove them out to a little Italian restaurant by the river. 'It's not much to look at,' he said with a shrug, 'but the food's good.'

There was a chorus of 'Ethan!' when they walked through the door. A stout, blousy woman with tinted red hair charged towards him and wrapped him in her arms. 'I haven't seen you in ages! Where have you been keeping yourself? Look at you, you're too thin! Is that father of yours not feeding you? I'll have a word with him next time I see him down at the Elks.'

'I feed myself these days, June,' he said with a fond smile.

'I know, I know, you're all grown up now, but I don't care – you'll always be the little boy who peed on my rose bushes. Do you remember that? Lord, I could have killed you! But then you looked up at me with those big eyes of yours and told me you were "helping the flowers", and oh! My heart just melted. You were such a cute kid.' Her eyes swiveled over to Ruby. 'And who's this? Is this your girl-friend? Ethan Bailey, I didn't know you had a girlfriend! And a pretty one, too! Now don't you go breaking this boy's heart,' she said, wagging a finger at a shell-shocked Ruby. 'I don't want to have to kill you.'

'Auntie June . . .!'

'I'm kidding! Of course I'm kidding! Now come in and have some supper! You both look like a couple of starving little birds!' She took Ruby's elbow and led her over to a table. 'I wasn't kidding,' she said in a low voice as she pulled out Ruby's chair. Ruby looked up and nodded, eyes wide.

'Sorry about that,' Ethan said when June had bustled off to the kitchen. 'She's a little . . . overprotective of me.'

'That's okay,' Ruby said. 'It's kind of sweet, actually. So she's your aunt?'

'I mean, we're not related or anything, but yeah, she's basically my aunt.'

'Oh, right.'

'I've got lots of fake aunts in this town,' he said. 'I'm like a walking example of the whole "It takes a village thing". My mom . . . well, she wasn't really around.' There was a pause as this settled in the air above them. 'Anyway, sorry. Enough with the heavy stuff.'

'I'm sorry,' she said quietly.

'Who's ready for some antipasti?' Auntie June hovered above them, holding aloft an enormous platter laden with cold meats, cheeses and olives. She set it down in the middle of the table with a flourish, alongside a basket of bread. 'I hope you're hungry!' she said. 'I'll just go get the pepper.'

'How the hell are we going to eat all this?' Ruby whispered. Her dress was already a little tight – who were these women from the past with their tiny wasp-waists? – and she worried the seams wouldn't survive that much Parma ham.

'This is just the appetizer,' Ethan said, folding a chunk of parmesan into a slice of prosciutto and popping it into his mouth. 'There are four more courses after this.'

'Here you go!' Auntie June reappeared with a pepper mill the size of a baseball bat. She ground a generous helping of pepper across the platter before leaning over and pinching Ethan's cheek. 'Look at you – adorable!' she said, giving them both a wink before rushing back towards the kitchen. 'Let me know if you need more bread!' she called over her shoulder. 'I'm just doing your fish now!'

Ruby tore off a piece of bread and balanced a piece of cheese on it. 'So how long have you been a bartender?'

He shrugged. 'About three years.'

'And you . . . like it?' She wasn't sure if there was a way of asking without sounding patronizing. From the slightly guarded look on his face, there wasn't.

'Yeah,' he said. 'I like it a lot. I get to hang out with my friends and get paid for it, and it gives me the days free to do whatever I want. What's not to like?'

'What did you want to do before this?'

'You make it sound like I've had some kind of accident that resulted in me only being able to bartend,' he said with a laugh.

She blushed. 'Sorry, it's not that, it's just . . . there must be something you want to do aside from bartending, right?'

'Not right now.' He tore into a piece of bread with his teeth and chewed it defensively. 'I know it's not what you or your friends – or your father, I'm guessing – would classify as a career or whatever, but I'm happy.'

'I think you're making a lot of shitty assumptions,' she said, taking a swill of wine and sucking it down through her teeth. Being Alec Atlas's daughter hadn't exactly been a walk in the park – all those ads with him grinning out at potential customers, seasonally appropriate hat perched on his head. Witch hat, pilgrim hat, Santa hat, Abe Lincoln hat, tri-cornered hat: as a kid, she'd been able to predict the impending holiday by whatever novelty hat her father was wearing in the local newspaper. Sure, he was successful now, and that success had afforded her an expensive private education and a car on her sixteenth birthday. But Ruby knew exactly how hard her father had had to work to get where he was, and she was also all too aware – more than her father, for sure – of how his success was perceived in their small town. She knew they called him Greenback Atlas at the country club because they could smell the new money on him, the same club where he paid twice the annual dues as everyone else (something she learned from her lab partner in high school, a Beechfield blue-blood whose ancestors had once worn the actual pilgrim hats that her father wore in those cheesy advertisements).

'What, you're going to tell me your father is thrilled that you're on a date with a bartender?' he asked. 'I saw the way he looked at me tonight. Like I was the delivery boy or something.'

'I should go,' she said, draining her glass. Her chair scraped the floor as she pushed back from the table. This had been a mistake, she saw that now. What was she even doing here, on a date with this random – albeit good-looking – townie? She was moving to New York in two months! New York, a city that was bound to be full of handsome, erudite men who used words like . . . like erudite! Who had careers! And swanky apartments! And shoes made of real leather! She stood up and gathered up her bag. 'Well,' she said. 'Goodnight.'

She was in the parking lot by the time he caught up with her. 'How are you going to get home?' he asked, a question she'd already started asking herself.

'I'll just walk,' she said, gesturing towards the two-lane highway without sidewalks that was the only route home.

'Seems a little dangerous,' he said. 'At least let me give you a lift.'

'I'm fine, thanks. I'm perfectly capable of getting home on my own. I used to live in Boston, so I think I can handle Beechfield.'

'Ooh, Boston, eh? Bright lights, big city! I hear they've got a museum there and everything!'

She rolled her eyes. 'Look, this obviously isn't working, so let's just agree to disagree, say our goodbyes and hope we never see each other again. Okay?'

'Fine by me,' he said. 'Just as soon as I get you home in one piece. Come on,' he said, taking her by the elbow and leading her to his car. 'I promise we won't even have to talk. I just can't have it on my conscience if you get flattened by a pickup on the walk home. Even if you are a big-city girl, and perfectly capable of taking care of yourself.'

'Fine,' she said. She was secretly relieved – she'd always found the suburbs a lot more frightening than the city at night, mainly because in the city all of the lunatics were in plain sight. In the suburbs, they could be hidden any-where – in the woods, or a Volvo.

They began the ride home in silence, Ruby thinking how much she regretted not having taken the rest of the bottle of wine with her when she left, Ethan wondering if Charlie was still at Billy Jack's. They were just pulling onto Hosmer Street when a doe leaped out in front of the car.

Ethan braked, hard, and the car screeched to a halt. The doe stood in the headlights, black eyes blinking blankly at them, and then stalked off the road and into the woods. They could hear each other's breaths coming in quick, sharp gasps as they watched her disappear.

'Fuck,' Ethan said. 'Are you okay?'

'I'm okay. Are you okay?'

'I think so. Fuck.'

She glanced over at him and saw that he was pale with shock. 'Are you okay to drive?'

He nodded. 'Fine,' he said. 'Just give me a minute.'

'Just pull in there,' she said, gesturing towards a clearing on the side of the road.

He pulled in and switched off the car. They listened to the engine tick cool, and to each other's breaths as they began to slow.

'My dad killed a dog once,' she said. 'I was in the car when it happened. I'll never forget the look on his face.' She could still picture it, as clear as day. Shock and guilt and grief all rolled into one. 'He loves dogs,' she said, as if that made the fact he'd killed one both better and worse.

'Me too,' he said. 'I mean about loving dogs, not about having killed one. I hate cats, though.'

'Really? How come?' She loved cats.

'They always look like they're plotting against me.'

'Maybe they are. Maybe they know you hate them, so they're plotting their revenge.' She unbuckled her belt and turned towards him. 'Thanks for not killing the deer.'

'I didn't not kill it for you,' he said, 'but you're welcome. I'm happy that nothing – and nobody – got killed just then.'

They sat in the darkness for a minute.

'I didn't mean to get all defensive back there,' he said. 'I just get a little prickly around the whole "where are you going with your life" thing. I hear it from my dad all the time, so . . .'

'I get it,' she said. 'My dad asked me at least once a week when I was in college if I'd made any good connections yet. I'm pretty sure he cried when I told him I was majoring in English.'

'You majored in English?'

'With a minor in business. My small concession.'

'So what's your favorite book?' He pushed his seat back from the wheel.

'That's such a hard question,' she said. 'I don't know . . . maybe *Tender Is the Night*? I love anything Fitzgerald. Or maybe *Vanity Fair*? I was obsessed with *The Bell Jar* for a while, too. And anything by Jane Austen.'

He nodded. 'I love Austen, too,' he said.

'Wait, you've read Jane Austen?' She tried to picture him thumbing his way through *Emma*.

He shrugged, embarrassed. 'I know I'm not supposed to admit that because I'm a guy and everything . . .'

'No, it's not that, it's just . . . I didn't think you'd be into literature.'

'What, you didn't think bartenders could read?'

She felt herself blush and was thankful that it was too dark for him to see her. 'No, of course not. I think you're the first guy I've ever met who admitted that he liked Jane Austen.'

He shrugged. 'I try to read a little bit of everything,' he said. 'Right now I'm in a big Chandler phase –'

'I love Chandler! *The Big Sleep* is incredible. Have you seen the film?'

He let out a little scoff. 'Of course I've seen the film. Watching the entire collected work of Humphrey Bogart was pretty much mandatory growing up under my father's roof. The book is better, though, I think.'

'I don't know,' she said, putting her feet up on the dashboard. 'You can't really beat the Bogart–Bacall combo . . .'

He looked across at her and smiled. 'This is fun,' he said. 'I'm sorry I was a jerk earlier.'

'I'm sorry, too. I shouldn't have walked out,' she said. 'It was a dick move, even if you were being kind of a jerk.'

'Tell you what,' he said, pulling his seat forward and turning the key in the ignition. The engine coughed and spurted to life. 'Why don't we start over again? Auntie June is probably still making the pasta for the main course, anyway. We'll sit down, have a bottle of wine – well, you will, I've got to drive – and talk about books and movies and anything other than the socio-economic disparities of growing up in Beechfield. I promise not to be a jerk if you promise not to walk out on me again.'

She slipped her seat belt back on and grinned at him. 'It's a deal.'

He pulled out onto the road and put his foot on the gas. He wanted to hurry in case she changed her mind, but of course she wouldn't. Her mind was already made up.

Now

'Are you guys ready to go?' Ethan's voice boomed up the stairs from the downstairs hall.

'In a minute!' I called down. I bundled my hair into a topknot and pulled on another sweater, my third. I hadn't thought to pack a jacket, considering it was the middle of summer, but any of the day's remaining heat hadn't made it past the cold stone walls of Bugle Hall. Earlier, I noticed that the tips of my fingers had turned pale blue. I glanced in the mirror – still pale, still puffy, and now bulked up like a weightlifter underneath several layers of knitwear. There was no way to salvage things at this point – I just had to go with it.

I poked my head over the banister. 'Is Piper down there yet?'

Ethan was standing at the bottom of the stairs, Bob and Barbara close behind him, all of them looking irritable and impatient. 'We're starving down here,' he called up to me. 'Can you tell your sister to hurry up?'

'I heard that, Ethan!' Piper called from inside her room. 'Stop trying to rush me! Ruby! I can't find my blue heels!'

'Give me a sec!' I walked into Charlie and Piper's room to find scraps of silky fabric strewn across the four-poster bed. Charlie was sitting on a velvet pouffe, staring mournfully at his iPad – 'The Sox are six down in the bottom of the eighth,' he muttered, shaking his head – while Piper stood in the middle of the room, brandishing a J.Crew wedge like a weapon. 'Just put those on,' I said, nodding towards the wedge. 'They're cute.'

'I can't wear these!' she sulked. 'They're the wrong shade of pink!'

'Piper, we're walking to the pub. I think you need to go for something a little more sensible anyway. Did you bring a pair of sneakers?'

Piper looked at me aghast. 'Ruby, you *know* I only wear sneakers for SoulCycle. I only packed them in case I found a class over here, though that's obviously not going to happen –'

'I feel like tonight you're going to have to make the exception,' I said, shoving her sneakers into her arms. 'Come on, we need to get Bob and Dad a drink before they start talking about golf again.'

We set off for the pub, filing down the gravel driveway like little ducklings. It was still light out, but the clouds had thickened and there was a cool breeze. I hugged my arms to my chest. The air smelled of freshly cut grass, bell heather and foxglove, and underneath it all was the sharp salty tang of the ocean. We were close to the coast, and if I listened closely, I could hear the waves breaking against the cliffs.

'Vic said the pub was just across here,' Ethan said, pointing towards a field in which a smattering of slow-eyed cows were chewing their cud. There was a wooden fence encircling it, onto which had been hung a large wooden sign painted with menacing red lettering: PRIVATE PROPERTY.

'We should probably just stick to the road,' I said, pointing towards the sign.

'It's not like in America,' Ethan said, charging ahead towards the gate. 'Some redneck isn't going to appear with a shotgun or anything. They're used to people walking across their land.'

'I didn't realize that you were now a member of the Northumbrian Agricultural Council, in addition to everything else.'

I watched his jaw tighten and felt a little frisson of happiness: it was kind of fun getting under his skin. 'Vic said that this was the best way to go, so that's the way we should go,' he said.

'Fine,' I said, 'but if anyone shows up with a shotgun, I can promise you this: I'm pointing the finger straight at you and ducking for cover.'

Ethan slid through the gate wordlessly and held it open as the rest of us filed through. He rolled his eyes at me as I went past and I shot him a winning grin.

'Eww, Ethan! There's cow shit everywhere!' Piper looked at the cowpats in dismay and held her delicate nose shut. 'This is gross.'

'Nah, we're just getting back to nature!' my dad said, slapping Ethan on the back. 'Nothing beats a little fresh air. Besides, the walk will give us some time for me to tell you about a business venture I've been cooking up.' He took Ethan's elbow and steered him ahead, head bent conspiratorially low as he described his plans for a floating casino in the Everglades. 'We'll call it Gambling with the Gators . . .' I heard him say.

'Wait, is that a pheasant?' Charlie bounded off to explore the edge of the field, leaving me to support a crabby, unsteady Piper on one arm, and a tipsy – she'd discovered the complimentary vodka miniatures before we'd left – Candace on the other. Bob and Barbara brought up the rear, resplendent in matching tweed. The cows gazed at us impassively, blinking their heavily lashed eyes and occasionally swishing a fly away with a tail.

'Ethan!' I called ahead. 'How much longer?'

'Almost there! It's just through that bush, I think!'

'Through a bush?' I called back, but he didn't respond. Instead, Ethan and my father plunged straight into a thicket of brambles before crashing back out, cursing and rubbing their forearms.

'Jesus H. Christ!' my dad yelled as he came stumbling towards us. 'Turn back! It's not safe! Something bit me in there!'

Candace rushed forward, weaving dangerously close to a cowpat as she went. 'Shit! Are you okay?'

'I think it's some kind of poison ivy or something,' Ethan said, inspecting his hands, which were now blotched with red and covered in small white bumps. 'Only it's really painful. Like a sting.'

'I think it's nettles,' I said, leaning down to inspect the offending bush.

'Is it poisonous?' Candace asked, brows knitted together with worry. 'Has he been infected with something?'

'Yeah, it's definitely nettles,' I said, after taking a closer look. 'Don't worry, they're harmless.'

'Speak for yourself,' Dad said as he rubbed at the splotches on his arm. 'This hurts like a sonofabitch.'

'You'll be fine. We just need to get you to the pub so you can rinse it off.' I turned to Ethan, eyebrow raised in triumph. 'Any bright ideas on how we get there from here, Magellan, or shall I give it a shot now?'

Ethan scowled at me and rubbed his sore arms again. 'Be my guest,' he muttered.

Ten minutes later, having followed the little blinking blue dot on the Google Map straight onto the road running adjacent to the field, we were sitting inside a cool, low-beamed pub, nursing our drinks and – for some – wounds. Piper had discovered a tube of aloe vera cream at the bottom of her bag, and my dad and Ethan were now slathered in it, their pints slipping out of their hands each time they tried to lift them.

'Can't get any Bud over here, I guess,' Dad said, staring disbelievingly at his pint of Stella. 'No American beer at all, according to the guy at the bar. Said this was the closest thing to it, but I don't think so.' He took a sip and screwed up his face. 'Too bitter for my taste.'

'How does the old joke go?' Ethan said. 'What do American beer and having sex in a canoe have in common?'

'Fucking too close to water,' I said. We looked at each other and smiled, and for a minute all the weirdness fell away.

'Well, hey now, I don't approve of that kind of talk!' My dad was indignant. 'You're talking about the greatest country on earth here, and that includes its beer. Our country was built on the honest hard work of Bud-drinking men.'

'I think you're reading a little too much into this, Dad.'

'I've got to say, I like this stuff,' Bob said, taking a sip from his pint of Old Peculier.

Across the bar, a group of men in their early twenties erupted into jeers. 'YOU SOFT SOUTHERN SHITE!' One of them, a beefy redhead, leaped to his feet and pointed a finger at a nervous-looking guy in a Newcastle United top. 'What do you mean, you bought a fucking JUICER?'

Piper's ears pricked up. 'Wait, you can get a juicer over here? Thank God – I thought I was going to starve. Have you seen this menu?' She picked up a laminated piece of paper and waved it at the table. 'The only vegetables they have here are potatoes! And there's something called a "steak and kidney pie" – they're kidding, right? How is everyone not, like, a thousand pounds?'

'Bud tastes like piss.' Charlie had been staring at the television mounted above the bar up until then, trying to work out the rules to cricket, and had suddenly tuned himself into the conversation, if a little late.

'Charlie!' Barbara said.

'You fucking PRICK!' bellowed the red-headed man across the bar. 'You're going to be telling me you eat salads next!'

'What's this game they've got going on?' Dad asked, pointing towards the television. 'It looks like baseball, but they're doing it all wrong.' The batsman on the television hit a particularly elegant cover drive and began to take three runs. 'Why's he running back and forth like that? What are you doing, you idiot!' he shouted. 'You're at home base! You can just stop there! Ah, this game is screwy,' he said, shaking his head. 'They don't know what they're doing out there.'

'Charlie, come with me while I ask that guy where he got his juicer from,' Piper said, taking a sip from her glass of Chardonnay and gathering up her bag. Charlie stood up reluctantly, eyes not leaving the television, and followed her across the room to the group of young men.

'Is that a cigarette machine?' Candace, who had previously sunk into a post-vodka gloom, suddenly brightened. She poured the contents of her change purse onto the table and started counting out the coins.

'I don't think the machine will take quarters,' I pointed out gently.

'Here you go,' Ethan said, handing over a handful of shiny pound coins. 'They're on me.' Candace took them gleefully.

'Candy, you haven't smoked in years!' Dad said. 'What's got into you?' But I could tell he was secretly delighted: he was always up for a little bit of mischief, especially from his women.

'Oh, screw it, we're on vacation. Besides, I don't have many opportunities to have fun left these days. Got to get it where I can. Are you coming or what?' Candace flashed Dad a smile – the first genuine smile I'd seen her give him since they'd arrived – and he looked up like a dog who'd finally been let back inside the house after a night in the rain. The two of them headed for the cigarette machine, giggling conspiratorially as they went.

'Nice to see them so happy,' Ethan said, watching Candace slap my father on the ass as they slipped outside to smoke their forbidden cigarettes.

'I'm not so sure how happy they are,' I said. 'The past few years have been a little rough on them.'

'I heard,' Ethan said, his face softening. 'Sorry about that.'

'It's not your fault,' I said. 'I mean, I know you're a master of the universe and everything now, but I don't hold you personally responsible for my dad's financial solvency.'

Barbara had been scanning the room, her eyes suddenly lighting up when they landed on an elderly man wearing a flat cap and a pair of worsted wool trousers hitched up to his armpits. He was sitting at the bar nursing a half-pint of dark ale, rheumy eyes cast down towards the paper spread out in front of him. 'Bob, doesn't that man look exactly like my great-uncle George?'

'It's uncanny.'

'Do you think he could be a distant relation?'

'Well, let's buy the man a drink and ask!'

Bob and Barbara took their pints of bitter – a half for her – and charged over to the elderly man, who swayed slightly at the sight of them before greeting them with a mouth full of broken teeth.

'He's going to turn out to be the town drunk, isn't he?' I said.

'Oh, absolutely,' Ethan said.

It was just the two of us at the table now, and we stared into our drinks in nervous silence. 'Your dad will pull through,' he said finally. 'He's a smart guy.'

'Well, he's persistent, I'll give him that. I'm assuming he's already told you about his latest business venture, whatever it is now.'

He laughed. 'Floating casino,' he said, 'in the Everglades. I tried to point out that it might not be the most accessible place for gambling, but he seems pretty convinced.'

'It'll be something different by the end of the week. Just whatever you do, don't let him get you to sign anything.'

'I learned that a while ago, but thanks.' He took a long sip from his pint. 'So what are you up to these days? Still in New York?'

'Yep, still there. Can't get rid of me. I made the move to the mainland last year, so it's official: I'm never leaving.'

'Fair enough.'

'Still can't stand the place?' I asked. Ethan had never shied away from telling me how much he hated my adopted city, and I couldn't imagine it had changed. Once a Yankees hater, always a Yankees hater, he used to say. I believed it.

He shot me that crooked smile of his and my heart lurched. 'You know it.'

'Fair enough.'

We looked at each other for a minute, the acknowledgement of our shared past sinking into our bones like a hard frost. He looked the same as he did ten years ago, but his success had given him another layer, a glossy, confident sheen. The air of nervous energy he'd carried with him had cleared, like the air after a thunderstorm, and it had been replaced by something more solid and intractable. There wasn't much trace of the mechanic's son in him now: he was all smooth edges and quiet confidence.

'Married?' I asked, knowing full well he wasn't.

86

'Nope. You?'

'Nope.'

Another pause, longer this time.

'So you're still advertising?'

'I'm an account director at BlueFly. Have you heard of them?' I tried to sound casual, but I was desperate for him to recognize it, acknowledge the fact that I'd become a success. A marginal one on his terms, maybe, but a success.

'Sorry,' he shrugged. 'I leave the advertising side of things to someone else. I don't have the patience for it – no offense.'

'None taken,' I said, stung. I felt a sudden urge to punish him. 'I'd ask you what you've been up to, but that would just make me look like an idiot who's never read a newspaper,' I said. I could hear a bitter edge entering my voice. 'Can I just ask, how the hell did it all happen? I mean, when I knew you, you were a bartender!' I let out an unkind snort of derision here, and instantly hated myself for it. 'Sorry,' I said, softening my tone, 'it's just . . . I mean, how?'

He sighed and leaned back in his chair. 'I met this guy at school . . .'

'Wait, you went back to school?'

'I enrolled in this tech design course a few months after we split up,' he said. Hearing him acknowledge the break-up was like a sucker punch to the gut. 'He had this idea for a computer chess game, but one you could play on your cell phone.'

'So an app,' I said, wanting to sound informed.

'Right, only they weren't really a thing back then. Anyway, the guy wanted me to help design it – super basic graphics, pretty rudimentary stuff. We spent a couple of weekends kicking around ideas above the garage, and we basically realized that the game would only be interesting if you could play against other people. So we looked into the tech on it, and ended up building our own platform for it, and . . . I don't know, it just sort of exploded from there.'

'The entire Albion empire sprang from a computerized chess game you built over your dad's garage?'

'Pretty much.'

'So you're basically living the dream.' I thought back to my inbox, currently filling with client emails about production schedules and budget concerns and last-minute changes to the art director's precious copy, and felt a tiny flinch of despair. My success felt more marginal than ever.

'Not exactly. It was great at first, but ever since we went public . . . Most of my time is spent trying to appease a bunch of old white guys in suits.'

'I know the feeling,' I said. 'Old white guys in suits are the single most appeased group on the planet. Though I guess you'll get to be one someday, so there's a silver lining in your dark cloud.'

'I'm not so sure about that.' He shifted uncomfortably in his seat. 'There's been an offer for the company. A big one.'

'That's great!' I said. I saw the look on his face. 'Isn't it?'

He shrugged. 'My partner thinks we should take it, and the board members do, too.'

'What about you?' I asked gently.

'I don't have a fucking clue. It's for a lot of money, so it's not like I can complain or anything . . . it's just, what the hell am I supposed to do with myself if I don't have the company?'

'But what about the charity you were setting up?'

His eyebrows shot into the air. I shrugged. 'I'd heard something about it somewhere.'

He shook his head. 'The tech for it is part of the buyout. So that really would leave me with a lot of free time.'

'I get it,' I said. 'My job basically rules my entire life, and the idea of not having it anymore is just . . . weird. But you could literally do whatever you wanted! You could travel, or train for a triathlon, or start a new company. You could gamble away a small fortune at illegal poker games in various Chinatown basements. You could buy a remote tropical island and found your own dictatorship. Seriously, anything.'

He laughed, and I was happy to see his face brighten a little. 'An island dictatorship does sound appealing. Do you want another drink?'

'I'll get this one,' I said, waving him away. 'I've got pounds burning a hole in my pocket.' I squeezed between two tall wooden stools and placed my elbows on the long wooden bar. My head was spinning from the unreality of it all. Here I was, jet-lagged as all hell, standing in a sixteenth-century pub in the middle of nowhere and giving my ex-boyfriend advice on how to spend his magnificent fortune . . . it was all a bit much. I glanced over at him sitting gazing down at his hands stretched out on the table. A dark curl had fallen over one eye and there was something inside me that itched to run my hands through his hair and push the curl back behind his ear.

'Hello! Are you in there somewhere?' I looked up to see a gruff-looking man mopping up a puddle of bitter with an old cloth and looking at me impatiently.

'Sorry,' I said. 'I wasn't paying attention.'

'I'd clocked that.' He placed his hands on his hips and let out a long, weary sigh. 'Now, what can I get you?'

'Two pints of Kronenburg, please.'

'Are you sure you don't want a half? Little lass like you.'

I felt myself bristle. 'I think I can handle a whole beer, thanks.'

'Fair enough, it's your own funeral. Two pints coming right up.' He lumbered off to pour the drinks, muttering quietly to himself as he went.

'Enjoying the local hospitality I see?'

I looked up to see a tall, grizzled-looking man in an Irish-knit sweater holding a tattered paperback in one hand and a pint of dark amber ale in the other. 'I'm not doing so well with him, am I?' I said, jabbing a thumb towards the barman.

'Don't pay him any mind,' he said. 'He's an old crab apple, him. Never recovered from Bobby Charlton going to play for United – been in a foul mood ever since.'

'I don't know who Bobby Charlton is, but I wish he hadn't done whatever he did.'

'You and half of the North East, pet,' he said. 'You with the American bunch?'

'What gave me away?'

'I've always been renowned for my powers of deduction around these parts. Up here for a wedding, I presume?'

'How did you know? Other than your renowned powers of deduction, obviously.'

'There are two reasons Americans end up in the north: either they've made a wrong turn in Edinburgh or they're going to a wedding. Who's marrying the Geordie, then? Not you, I hope. You look far too sensible for that.'

'No one's marrying any Geordies,' I said. I wasn't entirely sure of what a Geordie was, but I didn't think Charlie was one of them. 'My sister wanted to get married in a castle – she has a thing about Kate and William.'

'This is the place to come for castles,' he said. 'Can't take a piss around these parts without some of it splashing on one.'

'Yeah, I gathered that from the ride over.'

There was a roar from the table in the corner. Piper was sitting primly next to the group of loud young men, scrolling through her phone, presumably ordering the nearest juicer. Charlie was in the middle of the scrum, wiping his lips on the back of his hand and triumphantly holding an empty pint glass in the air. 'Get fucked!' the red-headed man bellowed at him, splattering his own unfinished pint down his top.

'That's her with her fiancé over there,' I said, nodding towards them.

'Looks like he's making friends, though you might want to drag him away from our Liam before he gets too pissed, otherwise Liam'll make him play brag and he'll end up walking out of here without his shirt.'

I squinted at him. 'I don't understand anything you just said.'

'Wouldn't be the first time I've heard that,' he said with a grin.

The barman placed two pints in front of me. 'That'll be seven pound ten.' I handed him a crisp fifty-pound note, which he looked at as if it were a slab of rotting fish. 'That all you've got?'

'Sorry, that's what they gave me at the currency exchange at the airport.'

He heaved a long, pained sigh and made an elaborate show of inspecting the note in case it was counterfeit. Eventually, and under obvious duress, he rung it through the till and thrust a handful of crumpled notes and loose change into my hands. 'Come back with proper notes next time,' he said with a scowl. 'Bloody Americans.'

The grizzled man beside me laughed. 'Don't think you've done yourself any favors there,' he said. 'Thanks for that – he'll be in a mood for the next week!'

'I thought he was already in a mood about Bobby Charlton?'

'Ah, but that's just his base mood. That man there has more moods than Joseph has colors on his Technicolor dream coat.'

I picked up the pints, lager splashing onto my fingers and running in rivulets down my arms. 'Anyway,' I said, raising the pints in half salute, 'goodbye. Thanks for . . . well, no. Just goodbye.'

I heard him laughing as I walked back to the table, and Ethan raised an eyebrow as I set the pints down.

'Making friends?' he asked.

'Failing spectacularly,' I said. We settled into another silence, but this one felt more amicable. 'So,' I said finally, 'how's your dad? Is he still in Beechfield?'

'No, he had to sell up a few years ago. Had a stroke when he was working on a car, and the doctor said it was too much for him. He lives with me now.'

'What, in London?' I could not picture Ethan's father living in a city, never mind a *foreign* city.

Ethan must have clocked the surprised look on my face. 'I know, right? I guess we missed the announcement about pigs flying.'

'Is he doing okay now?'

'Apart from driving me nuts? Yeah, he's okay. He's on some low-fat healthy diet that he never stops complaining about. That and the British weather. This is a man who was not meant to take it easy. Though he has learned to use a computer, God help me. Spends all day sending me emails about things he's "improved" in the house – that generally means he's taken some expensive and highly calibrated piece of technology and destroyed it – and complaining about the cat.'

'He has a cat?' Jesus, Bill Bailey must have changed. First London, then a cat?

'No, I'm the one with the cat.'

'Wait, *you* have a cat? You hate cats!' A few strays used to congregate outside Billy Jack's – Ethan would always refer to them as 'fancy rats'.

'No,' he corrected me, 'I *used* to hate cats. Now I love cats.'

'You do not.' I couldn't imagine him having a fancy rat living in his house.

'I can show you a picture and everything if you don't believe me.' He took out his phone and flicked to a photo of a large, lazy-looking ginger cat with an overly fluffy tail and a surly look on his face. 'See?'

I looked at him sceptically. 'Cat pictures are ninety per cent of the Internet, so that doesn't prove anything. Anyone can show me a picture of a cat. What's the cat's name?'

'Willy Nelson,' he said, without hesitation. 'He doesn't have any teeth.'

'Why doesn't he have any teeth?' I asked, horrified.

He shrugged. 'He had some weird thing where all his teeth were getting sucked back into his gums. I had to take him to a specialist cat dentist and get them all taken out. It cost a fortune.'

'Jesus.' I tried to picture Ethan wrangling a large orange cat into a cat carrier and schlepping it to a pet dentist. I rested my chin on my hand and looked at him across the table. 'Okay, so tell me how a guy who hated cats so much that he'd cross the road to avoid one ends up with a toothless cat called Willy Nelson.'

He looked pained for a split second before his features rearranged themselves back to neutrality. 'An old girlfriend found him one day in a bin outside a sandwich place. I got home to find the two of them curled up on the couch together. The look on her face, on both of their faces . . . well, I couldn't say no.'

My stomach soured at the thought of this little domestic tableau: a silky-haired, milky-skinned goddess swathed in cashmere and silk, cat purring contentedly on her lap, the two of them staring up adoringly as Ethan walked through the door of his inevitably expensive and (thanks to the girlfriend's impeccable taste) beautifully decorated townhouse. 'That's nice,' I said.

'Yeah, well, it wasn't so nice when she walked out on me three months later and left me with a moulting cat who kept throwing up on the carpet.'

'Poor Willy Nelson,' I said, but I couldn't keep the grin off my face.

'Thanks for the sympathy. Anyway, he's better off without her, mainly because I always forget to buy cat food so he ends up eating whatever I happen to be cooking for dinner. That cat eats better than most people.'

'And you?'

'Yeah, I eat pretty well. I mean, I could probably lay off the booze a little, but . . .'

'No, I mean . . . are you better off without her?' I tried to keep my voice neutral, but I could feel the tightness in my throat as I asked. I realized it meant a lot to me how he still felt about this ex-girlfriend, as if it could be some sort of barometer about how he felt about all ex-girlfriends of his, ever. This was a losing game I was playing, of course: if he said he was still in love with her, it would hurt, and if he said he couldn't give a shit about her, it would hurt. At least I knew what I was setting myself up for.

'Ancient history,' he said with a swat of his hand. I felt like a tiny gnat about to feel the full force of his palm. 'I mean, it sucked for a while, but it was a couple of years ago now. I can barely remember her name.'

'Oh. Cool.' I ran a test for internal bleeding: severe, but not life-threatening.

'You know,' he said, taking a swig from his pint, 'it's cool we can talk like this. I've got to admit, I was a little nervous about seeing you again.'

'You were?'

'I was worried it would be awkward. You know, after all these years or whatever.' He rubbed the stubble on his chin and grinned at me. 'You probably think that's stupid.'

'Not at all!' I said, too quickly and too loudly. 'I mean, I was sort of nervous, too.'

'But just hanging out and talking like this . . . it's cool, right?'

I looked at him across the table, so handsome, so like the person I'd loved so long ago, and felt something inside of me click. This was it. It was me and him again, us together. 'Really cool,' I said, and the little swallow of hope inside me soared. We held each other's gaze, and in that moment I knew – I absolutely *knew*, as sure as I knew my own name – that he still felt something for me. After a few seconds, he would break off the gaze and start flicking through his phone for more photos of Willy Nelson to show me, but there had been a moment between the two of us, however brief. I was sure of it.

Then

Ruby tapped her teeth with her fingernail. 'I'm not sure,' she said. 'Maybe a whale?'

'A whale? Why the hell would you want to be a whale?'

'Because they get to swim around all day and eat stuff and no one ever messes with them.'

'Sharks,' Ethan pointed out. 'Sharks might mess with you.'

'Not if I was a really huge whale. I wouldn't even feel it if they tried.'

Ethan turned and looked over at her. Her face was in profile, and he could see the curl of her eyelashes in the moonlight. She tapped her teeth again with her fingernail. 'Or maybe a seagull,' she said. 'It would be nice to be able to fly, and they get to hang out at the beach all day.'

'Do you always do that when you're thinking?' he asked.

She looked at him. 'Do what?'

'Tap your teeth with your fingernail.'

'I don't do that!' She looked mortified.

'You do it all the time!' he said, laughing. 'You're like a little woodpecker over there. Maybe that's your real spirit animal.'

'God, how embarrassing,' she muttered.

'Nah, I think it's cute.' The truth was, he thought everything she did was cute. She could probably turn around and spit on him right now and he'd think it was adorable.

He reached out and took her hand in his. 'So do you always go parking in your dad's developments, or is this a new thing?' They were lying on the hood of his car looking up at the blanket of stars above. She'd sat in the passenger seat on the ride over, telling him to take a left and then then second right, and now they were high up at the top of a half-built development that, according to the sign outside the gate, promised to be Beechfield's first ever English-style hamlet. There was a show home at the bottom of the hill – complete with faux-thatched roof – but the rest of the land was peppered with cranes and diggers, sitting like hulking, sleeping dinosaurs. He'd left the radio on when he'd parked the car – fuck the battery, he could always get a jump – and Van Morrison was now singing softly about a ballerina in the background, the crickets chirping noisily along from the tall grass nearby.

'What can I say? I've got a thing for MDF and shoddy workmanship,' she said with a laugh.

'Kinky!'

'Actually, I've always just come here on my own before. In high school, I liked driving around at night. I'd just go around and around in circles, listening to music and being all angsty or whatever, and I'd usually end up parked in one of my dad's developments scribbling shitty poetry in my journal.' She shot him a sideways glance. 'I was pretty cool back then, in case you couldn't tell. Pretty popular.'

'I think it sounds cool,' he said. 'I love that you write poetry.'

'Used to write,' she pointed out. 'I haven't done it in years. Too mortifying.'

'Well, you should start again. I bet you're really good.'

98

'I promise you, I'm not. It's completely embarrassing to read the stuff I used to write. I was so melodramatic.'

'We're all our own worst critics,' he said, propping himself up on his elbows and looking at her. 'That doesn't mean we should stop trying to create things.'

She wriggled up onto her elbows now, too, and their faces were so close they were almost touching. 'What kind of stuff do you want to create?'

'I don't know. I like fucking around with computers and stuff, and I've always loved art.' He glanced away for a minute and then looked back at her. 'There's not one specific thing I want to create, I guess. I just want to be creating.' He tucked his shoulder up to his ear in a sort of half shrug and he looked so vulnerable and earnest in that moment, like a little boy not quite able to tack down the edges of a dream he'd had. She leaned across and kissed him.

'You're adorable,' she said. 'You know that, right?'

'I was going for handsome and manly, but I'll take it.'

'What were you like in high school? I'm guessing you weren't sitting at home alone reading *The Bell Jar* like me.'

He wrinkled his nose. 'I don't know,' he said. 'I played sports, dicked around with Charlie and everybody down at the pit, smoked a fair amount of weed. The usual stuff, I guess.'

'So you were, like, popular.' She said this as a statement rather than a question, and a slightly irritated one at that.

He laughed and gave her a playful shove on the shoulder. 'What, is this *The Breakfast Club* now or something?'

'Well, if it was, you'd totally be Emilio Estevez. The handsome jock with a heart of gold.'

'Nah. If I was anyone, it was Judd Nelson. Cutting class and smoking under the bleachers before practice.'

'Oh, of course!' she said, smiling now. 'You were so cool you didn't even have to try to be cool.'

'Whatever. So I guess you were Molly Ringwald, right? I can totally see you being a preppy little goody two-shoes. I bet the teachers loved you.'

She leaned back on her elbows and looked up at the sky. 'Not really. I was more of an Ally Sheedy type, all black clothes and attitude. Let's put it this way: I spent a lot of time listening to Tori Amos. Like, a lot.' She looked over at him. 'I had a lot of anger as a kid,' she said with a little smile.

'About anything in particular?'

'The usual.' Her voice had a clipped edge to it and she turned her body away from him. It was obvious that there was no room for follow-up. 'So now you know the dirty truth. I was a weird nerd in high school.'

'I always liked girls like you when I was in school, actually,' he said.

She let out a derisory little snort.

'I'm serious! I had a massive crush on a girl who sounds a lot like how you were.'

'Oh yeah? What was she called?'

'Lily,' he said. 'She used to stomp around the halls in these massive Doc Martens with her headphones on. I remember she always used to carry this book around with her – the *Collected Poetry of Anne Sexton*.'

'I love Anne Sexton,' she said.

'Why am I not surprised? Anyway, I got the book out of the library once, and my plan was that I'd casually leave it out on my desk so she could see it, and then when she did, I'd strike up a conversation with her and she'd fall madly in love with me once she saw what a cultured, sensitive bastard I was.'

'And did it work?'

He shook his head. 'She took one look at it and snarled at me. Actually snarled!'

'She probably thought you were making fun of her. That's what I would have thought. She probably thought that the only reason a guy like you, a popular guy' – she wiggled her eyebrows – 'would leave her favorite book on his desk would be to make fun of her.'

'That's a pretty dim worldview,' he said.

'That's high school.'

'Well, she basically scarred me for life. I mean, she literally drove me into the arms of Courtney Albertini.'

'Wait, the Courtney Albertini who's now one of the New England Patriots cheerleaders? I saw her poster in the mall the other day. She has her own calendar!'

He nodded gravely. 'It was a very difficult time.'

She rolled over and started punching him in the chest. 'You are such a jerk!' she tried to say, but she was laughing too hard to get the words out.

'I don't believe this!' he said. 'I tell you about my darkest moment of adolescent pain, and you abuse me! Abuse!' he shouted. 'Abuse!'

'Shut up!' she yelled.

He grabbed her wrists and pulled her down onto him. 'Just imagine, a Judd like me getting together with an Ally like you. We're like the Montagues and the Capulets.'

'Or J. Lo and Ben Affleck.'

'Julia Roberts and that country singer – what was his name again?'

'Lyle Lovett!' she said. 'Please tell me I'm not Lyle in this.'

'You could never be Lyle,' he said. 'I've heard you sing.' He pulled the blanket over their heads. It was pitch black, the moon and the stars locked outside, and their breath soon turned the air fuggy and hot. The hood was still warm from the engine. In the background, the late-night DJ was playing Fleetwood Mac, and the crickets had finally fallen silent. 'I like you,' he whispered to her.

'I like you, too,' she whispered back. 'Kind of a lot.'

'Looks like we're both in trouble.'

Now

I woke up at 6 a.m., my mouth stale and lightly furred from the remnants of last night's dynamic cocktail of beer, vodka miniatures from the ransacked mini-bar and, eventually, half an Ambien.

'What the . . .' I opened my eyes and felt a rush of dis-orientated panic. The walls, which I could barely see in the dim early-morning light, were papered with sprigs of lilac, a deep purple border running through the centre of it. Every perceivable surface was covered with tiny ceramic animals – goats, squirrels, fluffy little dogs, all of them staring out at me from the shelves. I sat bolt upright, my heart jumping into my throat and nestling in with the left-over vodka fug. I blinked once. Twice. Three times. I finally remembered. I was in England, in a giant old – but apparently not that old – house with my family and the Armstrongs and – oh, God – Ethan. I rolled over and smiled into the pillow, remembering the way we'd locked eyes last night. It had been brief, but it had meant some-thing. I just knew it.

'Baby, I need water! I'm literally dying of thirst, and my skin is going to freak out if I'm dehydrated. Please?' Piper's voice rang out as clear as a bell through the paper-thin wall. I listened to my future brother-in-law walk across the room and turn on the tap in the bathroom. He let out a long, gentle fart, followed by a long, gentle sigh before the pipes groaned and I heard water thunder into a glass. 'Thank you!' Piper sang. 'Now get your cute butt back in bed.' It became rapidly apparent that I needed to get out of earshot of the two of them, and fast.

I struggled to my feet. The room looked vaguely menacing, all those flat painted animal eyes staring at me from various shelves and nooks, and I wanted out of it as soon as possible. I pulled on a pair of sweatpants and an old T-shirt I'd packed as pajamas – even though I had never once in my life worn pajamas – and crept downstairs. I could hear Mrs Willocks getting ready for the breakfast rush in the kitchen, and slipped past. I opened the front door and headed out onto the lawn, where a dew had settled overnight. I rubbed my arms for warmth and checked the time on my phone: 7 a.m., which meant it was 2 a.m. back in New Jersey. To hell with it, I decided, desperate times called for desperate measures. I hid next to the gardening shed and pressed dial.

Jess picked up on the third ring. 'Hello?' she said. There was an angry edge behind the grogginess in her voice, and I felt a stab of guilt for waking up a pregnant lady is the middle of the night.

'Jess, it's Ruby.'

'Thank God you woke me up. I was having a nightmare that I had to give birth without painkillers. What's up?'

'I'm in England,' I said, somewhat redundantly.

'Yes, I am aware,' she said. 'Hang on, I'm just going to get up.' I heard her grunt as she lifted herself out of bed, and then the sound of her footsteps padding down the hall. 'Okay,' she said, 'I'm in the clear. Now give me the full update: have you and Ethan had sex yet?'

'No, but . . .' I chewed at a stray cuticle and stared out across the grass. 'I think we had a moment.'

'No shit. Tell me everything.'

'There's nothing to tell, really. We just – I don't know. We were at the pub and we ended up alone at the table and he was like, "it's really cool seeing you again" and I was like, "me too".'

'And then you lunged across the table and licked his face?'

'Not exactly. Dad and Candace came back from having a cigarette –'

'They were smoking? Is it 1997 over there?'

'– and the moment was sort of lost. But it was definitely a moment.'

'Did you invite him back to your room?'

I pushed down a flash of irritation – I felt like she wasn't taking me seriously. That said, I'm sure Jess would have preferred it if I'd just pulled him into a bathroom stall at Heathrow and asked questions later. She was always a lunatic, but since settling down in the sticks she was taking this whole 'living the single life vicariously' thing to a new level. I was secretly thankful she'd never got into *Fifty Shades* – I'm sure she would have bought me a ball cock for my birthday.

'Of course I didn't! We're in the same hotel as my dad and my sister – gross. Plus, I didn't really get the chance to talk to him again. We got back and he basically went immediately to his room.'

'Well, obviously I would have liked you to have made more progress, but I'll take what I can get.'

'Come on, it was a good moment!'

'Okay! Okay! You had a moment.' I could practically hear her grinning down the phone at me. 'So you're happy?'

'It's so weird – all of this time has gone by, and then it's like – BAM! – here we are again.' I *was* happy. It felt good to be letting go a little, opening myself up to new possibilities. I sighed – I knew what was coming.

'I don't want to have to say it but, I told you so!'

'You're a liar – you so wanted to say it.'

'You're right, I loved it. But still, it's so romantic!'

'I guess it is.' I had wandered off into a tiny daydream about Ethan's hand on the small of my back when I heard the sound of liquid splashing onto porcelain. 'Wait, are you peeing while you're on the phone with me?'

'It's called multitasking, and yes, I am. What's the big deal? You've seen me pee a million times!'

I thought back to the dingy frat room bathrooms, disabled stalls in throbbing New York bars, and the occasional Brooklyn alleyway where Jess had pulled down her underwear without warning and said, 'Cover me.'

'All unwillingly,' I pointed out.

There was the flush of a toilet. 'There, finished. Now, where were we? Ah yes – romance!'

'I feel like the atmosphere has been slightly punctured by the bathroom break, to be honest,' I said.

'Then you wouldn't last a day in married life.' Her voice dropped, suddenly serious. 'If things do work out with you and Ethan, are you going to tell him?'

Her words felt like the equivalent of popping a child's balloon at his own birthday party. 'No,' I said quietly. 'I don't think there's any need. It's all in the past, remember? Better just to move forward.'

'I think you're right,' she said, though I don't think either of us was fully convinced. 'No point in airing out dirty laundry now, right?'

'Exactly. Now go back to sleep. I'm sorry I woke you up – I hope you won't be too exhausted tomorrow.'

'Please, between the bowling ball sitting on top of my bladder and Noah's night terrors, I'm used to operating on about an hour and a half of sleep a night. I had my quota before you called.'

'I love you,' I said. 'Thanks for picking up the phone.'

'Always. Love you too. Let me know as soon as you have another moment, only for Chrissakes, kiss him next time.'

I hung up the phone and crept back to my room, wincing every time I stepped on a creaky floorboard. A soothing voice coming from the radio in the kitchen was discussing the results of a recent census of the local otter population, while Mrs Willocks tutted rhythmically to herself. All of the doors were still shut tightly, everyone desperate to sleep off their jet lag or put off facing each other around the breakfast table. The light was now streaming in through the window in my room, and I threw open the sash and thrust my head out, sucking in great lungfuls of fresh air and feeling it carry the musty, close smell of the house out with it.

I lay on the bed and flicked through my emails, several of which had been marked urgent. I battled my way through as many as I could before finally trundling downstairs, my stomach tied in a neat bow of anxiety. So much for a vacation.

I seemed to be the first to arrive for breakfast, and settled into one of the tall oak dining chairs. The table was spread with a starched white cloth littered liberally with crocheted doilies, and in the centre was an ornate urn over spilling with lilacs. It was beautifully laid out, but the overall effect was more funereal than I was used to for breakfast. I slid a heavy beaded napkin ring off and spread the linen napkin on my lap. I felt my posture improve immediately.

'Morning!' I looked up to see Mrs Willocks sail into the room, holding what looked like a knitted rooster in one hand and a heaped, steaming plate of food in the other. She was wearing a stiff white apron over a floral-sprigged dress, and her legs were encased in shiny taupe tights, the kind that Piper had worn at tap-dancing recitals as a kid. 'Tea?' she asked, gesturing towards the rooster.

'Sure,' I said. I actually wanted coffee, but I was too fascinated by the rooster contraption to stop her. Mrs Willocks lowered the rooster to my cup and poured a long stream of weak-looking tea from it.

She must have clocked the look of incredulity on my face because she nodded towards the rooster and said, 'Tea cozy. Sweet, isn't it? I'll get you your milk in a second.'

'Very,' I said, looking down at the plate of fried eggs and sausage and trying not to appear disappointed. 'You don't have any yogurt, do you? Or some cereal?'

'Do you not like a hot breakfast?' Mrs Willocks asked, eyes narrowing. 'It's the best way to start the day, you know.' She gestured towards the sausages. 'Lovely, those. Fresh from the butchers yesterday!'

They did look amazing – plump and golden, the meat escaping its skin at the ends. I felt my stomach growl. Tomorrow I'll go for a run, I promised myself. I speared a sausage and took a bite. It was delicious. And I'll do some sit-ups, I added.

'And where are the rest of your party?' Mrs Willocks asked, clucking impatiently. 'The Armstrongs were down here at seven a.m. sharp, but I haven't seen hide nor hair of the rest of them, and it's nearly half-eight!'

'Jet lag.' Or they're all nursing their incapacitating hangovers, I added silently. When I'd finally climbed up the stairs to my room the night before, Candace was leading my dad and the Armstrongs in a rousing chorus of 'If You Like Piña Coladas'.

'Well,' Mrs Willocks said, hands on hips, 'I hope they show their faces soon – it'll get cold sitting out here much longer!'

'More for me!' I said merrily. And maybe some squats, I thought. I reached over and buttered a thick piece of white toast. I sank my teeth into it, letting the butter dissolve on my tongue. I hadn't had white toast since Bush was in office – I'd forgotten how completely, utterly perfect it is. Definitely squats tomorrow.

Just then, Candace and Dad rounded the corner, both looking bloated and exhausted.

Dad summoned up his best showman's smile. 'Good morning, sunshine!! How's everybody doing this morning? What a feast! I have to say, Mrs Willocks, this looks absolutely fantastic! Candace and I overindulged a little last night, so this will clear out the old cobwebs. Won't it, sweetheart?' He squeezed Candace around the waist. She swallowed, hard, and then lowered herself carefully into a seat and started nibbling at the corner of a piece of dry toast.

'Poor Candy is a little under the weather,' he said, nodding towards her. He reached over and helped himself to a couple of eggs and a few tomatoes, all of which he piled onto three pieces of heavily buttered toast. 'Now's not the time to worry about my cholesterol, am I right, kiddo?'

'How's your head?'

'Oh, fine, fine. You know me – constitution like an ox! How about you? Did you sleep off your jet lag? You seemed pretty spaced out when we got back.'

I had a vague memory of staring at a strip of flocked wallpaper in the drawing room and replaying the look that Ethan and I had exchanged while my dad and Bob shouted over each other about Tiger Woods. I blushed. 'I slept like a log,' I said.

'Good, good. I tell you, Mrs Willocks, that mattress of yours – like sleeping on a cloud!'

I thought back to my own bed, which was lumpen, hard, and topped with a pair of flaccid pillows, and raised an eyebrow at him. He winked back.

'Oh, I'm so glad to hear it, Mr Atlas. I do like to make sure my guests are comfortable.'

'Like a pig in shit,' Dad said, and the look on Mrs Willocks's face suggested he'd gone too far. 'Pardon my French,' he added before turning his full attention towards demolishing several rashers of bacon.

Ethan walked in, followed by Charlie and Piper. Ethan was wearing jeans and a slightly-too-small T-shirt that rode up to reveal a slash of his torso when he reached across the table for the ketchup. His hair was rumpled from sleep and his eyes slightly bleary. The morning had taken the edge off him, and the wealthy, confident sheen of yesterday was replaced by something like the boyishness I used to know. I wanted to reach out and touch him, feel the warmth of his skin and the solidity of his bones. But instead I sat up even straighter in my chair and tried to catch his eye. When I finally did, across a plate of slowly congealing eggs, he gave me a quick smile before turning his attentions to his toast.

Well, I thought, a guy's got to eat, right? We can't always be having a moment, particularly when there were sausages to be eaten. I speared another and took a bite, but it was cold now and the fat stuck to the back of my teeth.

'Let me get you a fresh plate of eggs,' Mrs Willocks said, bustling in and sweeping the platter off the table. 'And some fresh tea and toast, too.' She addressed all of this to Ethan, and from the pinkish glow in her cheeks I could tell she'd developed a crush. 'Or do you want something else, pet?' she asked. 'I could knock you up some porridge as quick as you like! Or some of those pancakes you Americans love so much?'

'This is wonderful, thank you,' he said smoothly, and I saw his polished surface begin to re-emerge. 'Don't go to any extra trouble on my account.'

'I'd love some porridge,' Piper said. She looked like she could faint with relief as she pushed away the plate of eggs she'd been idly forking. 'I'm not really meant to eat eggs or meat or stuff with gluten,' she said with an apologetic shrug.

'Of course, love!' Mrs Willocks said, and disappeared into the kitchen with a flourish of her apron.

'I didn't know eggs were on your hit list now,' I said. 'What the hell is left? Chickpeas and kombucha?'

'I can't help if I have a sensitive stomach,' she said, chin held defiantly high. 'And chickpeas make me bloated.'

'If your stomach got any more sensitive, it would be writing you love poems and leaving them in your locker,' I said. I saw Ethan crack a smile and felt disproportionately proud.

Bob and Barbara walked in, both pink-cheeked and windswept and bedecked in matching fluorescent technical jackets. 'Who's up for a bit of adventure?' Barbara cried, waving her umbrella in the air. In the twenty-four hours she'd been in the country, she'd managed to pick up a faint English accent. 'We'd better get a move on if we're going to make it to Alnwick before the tourists!'

There was a collective suppressed groan around the breakfast table. I took another bite of cold sausage and washed it down with a swallow of tea: I was beginning to suspect I'd need all the energy I could get today.

'Come on, chaps!' Bob called. 'Chop chop!'

Then

Ethan rolled out of bed and stepped into a pair of shorts before stumbling into the bathroom. He stared at his face in the mirror as he brushed his teeth, but his eyes didn't see anything. His mind was elsewhere, still in the night before, in the park on a blanket with Ruby, a canopy of stars spread out above. He swallowed the ghost of a smile before spitting out his toothpaste. He knew if his father saw him grinning like an idiot, he'd never stop giving him shit.

He trundled downstairs, grabbing a banana from the kitchen before heading into the shop. He glanced at the clock: 11:13. His father was on his fifth car of the day already, and he was only just surfacing. 'Morning,' he called as he walked into the garage.

'Morning, kid,' his father called from underneath a 1996 Pontiac Bonneville that was in the process of getting new shock absorbers. 'Can you hand me the PB Blaster?'

He rolled out from under the lift and Ethan handed the can to him. He was already covered in grease, though it was hard to determine the fresh grease from the old, caked-on grease. For as long as Ethan could remember, his father had black half-moons of embedded grit under his fingernails. He used to soak them for hours and go at them with a nail brush, but it never made any difference. When Ethan's mother left, he stopped trying. 'Take me as

I am,' he'd say with a shrug, and surprisingly enough, a few women actually took him up on that, though Ethan was never sure if it was because they actually liked him or just felt bad that his wife had left him with a kid. That was the hard thing to determine when you were a small-town single father, or a motherless boy: the line between affection and pity was thin and often blurred. Ethan thought of Ruby's face in the moonlight, the smile that lit up her face whenever he took her hand, and smiled. The line was clear with her, thank God.

His father caught Ethan's smile. He sat up on the mechanic creeper – which was just a couple of boards of plywood he'd glued to an old set of rollerskate wheels, ever-resourceful – and gave him a long, hard look. 'What are you looking so happy about?' he asked, before sliding back beneath the Pontiac.

'Nothing.' Ethan busied himself with organizing the tire valve caps, sorting them first by make, then by size, then by color.

'Cut the shit,' his father called out from under the car. 'I can tell when you're happy, so there's no point in trying to hide it from me. What are you all goofy-eyed about? Let me guess: it has something to do with that girl you've been seeing.'

The grin made an involuntary reappearance on Ethan's face. 'Maybe.'

'Don't play coy with me – I know a man in love when I see one. Hand me the rag on top of the table, will you?' Ethan passed the dirt-smeared cloth down. 'So that's – what? – three nights in a week? Must be pretty serious ...'

'She's cool.' He tried to keep his voice casual, but the catch of excitement in it gave him away.

'It's love all right. So what's this girl's name?'

This was the moment Ethan had been dreading. 'Ruby Atlas.'

'Alec Atlas's daughter?' The incredulity in his voice was clear even from underneath a Pontiac.

'Yeah.'

'Well, look at you,' he said, shimmying out from under the car and tossing the rag back at him, 'wining and dining Mr Country Club's girl. Now I know why you bought that fancy rotten cheese yesterday. Next thing I know, you'll be eating Grey Poupon.'

'It's called blue cheese, and you know the mustard thing is just an ad, right?'

'I never thought I'd see the day when my son was eating blue cheese and dating Alec Atlas's daughter. He sold you a shitty house yet? Called something like Gypsy Bungalow or Pocahontas's Lighthouse?'

'No, but he did tell me to tell you that he'd be happy to sell this place for you.'

'Over my dead body. Alec Atlas has been selling the whole town out from under our noses for the best part of a decade. If he thinks I'd sell him my family's heritage so he could build another bullshit Disney World crap house on it, he's got another thing coming.'

'That's basically what I told him.'

'Good. The goddamn vulture.' There was a pause while they both waited for his blood pressure to return to normal. 'But this daughter of his – Ruby? You like her?'

'Looks like it,' Ethan said. And then, more seriously, 'Yeah, I do. A lot.'

'Well, Alec's a nice enough guy, I guess. Kind of a jackass sometimes, but who isn't? Sad what happened to his wife.'

'Ruby hasn't really talked about it much.'

'Cancer,' he said, wiping his hands on the front of his trousers. 'She went pretty quick, thank God, but she was heartbroken to leave those two little girls behind. Nice lady.'

'Jesus,' Ethan said quietly, 'poor Ruby.'

'Yeah, it was pretty hard on all of them. Man, my son and Ruby Atlas. This really is the land of opportunity. So, you think it's serious? Because you sound serious.'

'It is serious. I'm heading over to hers for dinner, actually. With the, uh . . . whole family.' He swallowed nervously.

'No shit,' his father said with a grin. 'I hope you can remember how to use a knife and fork. I don't think you're going to be getting a burger over there. There'll probably be a goddamn cheese course, knowing Atlas.'

Ethan shrugged. 'Ruby said it would be casual.' Not that it mattered. His stomach had been twisted up with nerves all morning – he doubted he'd be up to eating much of anything.

'Son, I'm guessing Ruby has a different idea of casual than you do. Make sure you bring flowers,' he said, chuckling to himself. 'And wear a shirt with a collar for once!'

Shirt buttoned (well, not all the way up) and flowers in hand, Ethan pulled into the Atlas driveway that evening and killed the engine. He'd been there a few times now to pick up Ruby, but he still hadn't adjusted to the size of the place. It loomed over the top of the hill like a giant wedding cake. The rest of the houses in the development looked tiny in comparison, even though even the smallest house was twice the size of his father's. The lights were on in the windows and Ethan could see into the dining room, where Candace and Ruby were laying the table. Oh Christ, he thought before stepping out of the car, a tablecloth and everything.

He raised his hand to knock, but Ruby pulled the door open before he made contact. 'You made it!' she said, throwing herself in his arms, as though he'd traveled from across the country rather than down Main Street.

'Here,' he said, pushing the bunch of flowers towards her.

'Save them for Candace,' she whispered. 'She'll love you for ever if you give her flowers. That's basically the only reason she's still married to my father – he has the florist on speed dial for every time he screws up. Which is pretty much all the time.' That last remark tossed over her shoulder as she led him into the kitchen. He'd never made it this far into the Atlas compound before, and was astonished – truly – at the amount of marble everywhere. The floors, the countertops – even the refrigerator appeared to be somehow made of marble.

He let out a low whistle. 'Hell of a place,' he said, and felt immediately like his father.

'I know, it's a little much,' she said, rolling her eyes. 'They kind of got carried away during the design process. I didn't grow up here,' she added hastily. 'The house

I grew up in was' – she looked around despairingly – 'normal.'

'Are you kidding me? This place is incredible!' He looked around at the shiny gadgets lining the counters. 'I don't even know what half these things are,' he said, gesturing towards something that looked like it could either be an espresso machine or a remote control helicopter.

'Neither do I.'

'Ruby!' A woman's voice called from another room. 'Do I hear the sound of a handsome man?'

'In the kitchen!' she called back. She turned to him and took both his hands in hers. 'Are you ready?'

'Always,' he said, though standing in the middle of this marble palace, he felt more nervous than ever.

'They're going to love you,' she whispered as Candace walked into the room.

It took a minute for his eyes to adjust. Her dress was gold – bright, glittering gold – and she was wearing a pair of stilettos with heels so thin and so high it looked like she was levitating. She came towards him and wrapped him in a hug, crushing the flowers between them in the process. 'Ethan!' she cried. 'It is so lovely to meet you, sweetheart!'

'These are for you,' he said lamely, holding the slightly mangled bouquet out to her.

'Aren't you just the sweetest thing?' She plucked them from his hands and immediately began arranging them in one of the enormous vases lining the ornate French dresser in the corner. She finished and stepped back to admire her handiwork. 'They are absolutely beautiful,' she said, 'the prettiest I've ever had. Thank you so much!'

'You're welcome, Mrs Atlas.'

'Please, call me Candace. Mrs Atlas makes me sound ancient. Now, I'll just call Alec down and then we can sit down to supper. I hope you're hungry!' She bustled out of the room, the back of her dress winking as she went.

'So that's your stepmother, huh?' He suddenly felt a newfound respect for Ruby's father.

'Yeah, that's her,' she said, rolling her eyes. 'I never thought I'd have a stepmother who was hotter than me, but there you go.'

'She's not hotter than you,' he said.

'You're a terrible liar,' she said, reaching up to kiss him. 'Okay, ready for round two?'

They walked into the dining room (solid walnut table draped in a lace tablecloth, full silver table setting including tureen – though no one, including Candace, knew what that was for – and windows draped inexplicably in heavy red velvet), where Candace and Ruby's father were arguing quietly over the drinks trolley. 'Alec, I really don't think that's a – Ethan!' Candace beamed at him. 'Meet my husband, Alec!'

'We've already met,' Ruby's father said. He fastened Ethan's hand in a vice-like handshake and pumped with abandon. He was wearing a pair of jeans with creases ironed into them and alligator-skin shoes, and had the look of someone who was in a constant battle against being too well fed. His face was as pinked and plump as a ripened peach. 'Good to see you again. How's that father of yours?'

'Still kicking,' Ethan said, wincing as the pain in his hand traveled up his arm.

'I'll bet, I'll bet. Would you like a drink? I was just about to make myself another Manhattan. I did thirty miles on the stationary bike this morning so I think I deserve a little reward, though my wife here disagrees.' He winked at him here, a real, honest-to-God, non-ironic wink. Ethan nodded mutely: he felt powerless to protest in the face of such persuasive winking. 'Excellent! You all just have a seat and I'll play bartender. Though I guess I should be letting you do the honors, since you're the professional!' He let out a roar of laughter, but stopped himself when he saw the looks on Ruby and Candace's faces. 'Only kidding,' he added, but Ethan wasn't entirely sure what he was kidding about – the fact that Ethan was a professional bartender (which was true and, to his eyes, not a joke) or the fact that he should be letting Ethan mix the Manhattans (also true, though Ethan knew enough not to point this out). Instead he just smiled benignly, sat down at the table, and watched him mix (badly, as suspected) a shaker of Manhattans.

'So Ethan,' Candace said as she placed a platter of artfully arranged king prawns on the table, 'Ruby tells us you're a computer genius!'

'Not really,' he said, scratching the back of his neck. 'I like to play around with them and stuff, but I definitely wouldn't call myself a genius. I didn't go to school for it or anything.'

Ruby's father handed him a drink and sat down across from him. Ethan took a sip: it was blisteringly strong. 'What did you go to school for?' he asked. 'Cheers, by the way.'

'Cheers,' he murmured. He took another sip and felt a layer of skin slough away from the back of his throat. 'I didn't go to school for anything,' he said. 'I mean, I didn't go at all.'

'Oh? Why's that?' Ethan saw him shoot Ruby a sideways look.

'I had to get back to the shop to help out my dad,' he said, which was partly true. He didn't want to tell the whole truth, which was that, after graduating high school by the skin of his teeth, the last thing he'd wanted to do was to set foot in a classroom again. Not that many classrooms would have had him.

Ruby's father raised his glass to him, and Ethan wondered, irrationally, if he was about to throw his drink in his face. 'That's very noble,' he said. 'I took a few years off before going to college myself.'

Ruby stopped dunking a prawn in a dish of cocktail sauce and looked up in surprise. 'You did?'

'Sure. There was no way my father was paying for my college tuition. Even if he could have afforded it – which he couldn't – he made it pretty clear that he expected me to be out of the house and paying my own way just as soon as I tossed my graduation cap in the air.'

'I can't believe Grandpa Joe would be such a jerk,' Ruby muttered.

'Those were just the times,' he said with a shrug. 'Real men went out to work, they didn't sit around reading books all day.'

Ethan felt a little fizz of pride at being classified as a real man. 'So what did you do?' he asked.

'I worked on building sites for a few years,' he said. 'Learned everything there was to know about the trade. I can tell a dovetail joint from a tongue and groove at fifty paces. I can tell you when a foundation's been poured crooked just from eyeballing it. And, most important in my business, I can tell when a builder is trying to Mickey Mouse me out of some money.'

Ruby looked astonished. 'Dad, I have never seen you pick up a hammer in your life.'

'That doesn't mean I can't. It just means I don't want to and can afford to pay someone else to do it for me. And that, son, is the definition of success.' He leaned back in his chair and took a triumphant sip from his Manhattan.

Ethan wasn't sure if that was his own definition of success – he actually enjoyed working with his hands, and more importantly, he couldn't imagine getting to a point in his life when he was able to pay anyone to do anything for him, ever, but he admired the sentiment nonetheless.

'Yep,' Ruby's father said, swiping a prawn off the platter and tossing it into his mouth, 'I've always thought it was a good idea to get out in the real world, get a sense of what work is like before you commit to an education.'

'You never said that to me!' Ruby said. A prawn was dangling from her hand in mid-air and was now dripping cocktail sauce onto the tablecloth.

'Why would I? Your heart was set on going to college from the time you stopped wearing diapers. I used to call her Little Einstein,' he said to Ethan, shooting him another one of those winks. 'Besides, your mother would have killed me if I hadn't encouraged you to go to a good university. That's the one thing she made me promise her before she died.'

A silence fell on the table. Ethan wondered what the correct response was. Should he offer his condolences? Was it too late, considering how long she'd been gone? Would Candace be upset by it? In the end, he took another sip of his drink – still like battery acid on the stomach, but tasting a little better now – and stared down at his lap.

'Well,' Candace said brightly after a few beats had passed. 'I'll go get dinner plated up.' She pushed back from the table and tottered into the kitchen.

'I can't believe I didn't know that about you,' Ruby said. The prawn had finally made it into her mouth and she was chewing it contemplatively.

'I've still got a few tricks up my sleeve,' her father said. 'Anyway, Ethan, my point is that we're not all like my beautiful daughter here. Some of us were put on this earth to do something other than stick our noses in books all day.'

'Dad! I did more than just read books all day at college! I wrote papers! I got a business degree! I have a job lined up with one of the best advertising firms in New York!'

'I know, sweetheart, and I'm very proud of you. I know you worked your butt off, too – I'm not taking that away from you. I'm just saying there are many paths in this world, and I'm sure Ethan will find his one day.'

'Thank you, sir.' Ethan didn't want to point out that he was already on his long-destined path, one that would see him working at the bar until his dad was ready to retire, at which point he'd take over running the garage. He'd stay in Beechfield, probably in the same house that he grew up in, and get drunk with the same people at the same bars. Even as he sat there in that glittering dining room with its fancy curtains and crystal platter full of shellfish, he could felt their world receding from him. Ruby would go to New York and start her real life, one that would be bigger and more important than his could ever hope to be. And soon she would recede from him, too, like a star fading in the early-morning light.

'Another Manhattan?' Ethan looked up to see her father standing over him, holding out a hand for his empty glass.

'I'd love one,' he said, and reached over and plucked the last prawn from its bed of chipped ice.

Now

To: Bill Bailey
Sent: 15 July 2015 10:53
From: Ethan Bailey
Subject: re: Doctor's appointment

I know you didn't go because Jasmine told me (and before you ask, yes, I am spying on you, and no, I don't think it's an infringement of your civil liberties). There was a two-month waiting list to see that guy. I'll see if I can get you in again, but you have to promise to go this time.

Everyone's getting along okay so far. Bob and Barbara are convinced that they're descendants of Henry the Eighth (you will not be surprised to hear). It's like the time he ran for president of the club, but worse.

The shareholders are on my back about a decision. I'm kind of glad to be off the grid for the next week so I can get some space to think.

Tell Jasmine not to feed you too much mac and cheese. Maybe some green stuff every once in a while, just to keep your colon on its toes.

E

Now

Vic appeared at the end of the driveway at the wheel of a small bus. 'Your secretary told me you'd need something for eight,' he said to Ethan with a shrug, 'and this was the best I could do.'

'This is great, thanks,' Ethan said. Vic beamed: even he'd been won over by Ethan's charm.

I thought about this as Vic barreled through the hairpin country lane curves. I looked at Ethan's profile as he chatted with Vic in the front seat and wondered what it must be like for him now, living this enchanted life. He'd seemed completely unfazed that someone had commissioned a bus on his behalf, like it was something that happened every day. Like it would be weird if it *didn't* happen. The world seemed to bend to his will, the very air around him shaping itself to accommodate him. And yet there he was in the centre of it, dark hair curling haphazardly over his eyes, the same boyish grin playing on his lips most of the time. I wondered whether he could let me into the centre, too, if there was still room for me there.

We pulled into the grounds of Alnwick Castle and parked in the gravel parking lot. It was before noon, but already the place was filled with groups of Chinese tourists wearing matching red-and-yellow striped vests, documenting their every move through the beady eye of their phones, and harried mothers toting bags stuffed full of wet wipes and packed lunches, tugging their children towards the gate. Vic decided to wait outside – 'I've seen enough castles to last a lifetime, cheers' – and waved us off before putting his feet up on the dashboard and cracking open the *Mirror*.

Ethan strode up to the ticket window and said a few words to the woman behind the counter, and suddenly we were being whisked off on a private tour. 'I pulled a couple of strings,' he said with a shrug.

Bob and Barbara looked as if they were about to combust as we walked through the gates and into the castle. 'You know, the Armstrongs were once very close to the Percys,' Barbara said as they were led into the Lower Guard Chamber.

We followed the guide up the Grand Staircase, treading gingerly on the red oriental carpet and admiring the gilded cornicing on the vaulted ceiling. It shone despite the dim light, and occasionally a beam of sunlight would track through the window and set it alight. For a moment, I was too overwhelmed to breathe.

Dad let out a low whistle. 'This must have set them back a few bucks.'

'The castle has been in the family for over seven hundred years,' Bob said, taking a discreet snap of the carved banister with the Canon hanging around his neck. 'The building itself is nearly a thousand years old.'

'Jeez.' Another whistle, longer this time. 'How the hell did they build something like this a thousand years ago?'

'A feudal system reliant on peasant labor,' Ethan said with a wry smile. 'Makes building things a cinch, apparently.'

'Well, I can't say I don't miss the old ways of doing things,' Barbara said. 'I'm sure it was much easier in those days. More civilized.'

'I think it would be pretty hard to find much civilization in these parts a thousand years ago, Mrs Armstrong,' Ethan pointed out. 'They spent a lot of time killing each other with spears.' I looked over at him and smiled, and he shot me a wink that nearly made me double over.

'Well,' Barbara said, bowed but unbroken, 'they made some beautiful things.'

'We need to talk.' I looked over to see Piper hovering over my shoulder. She grabbed my elbow and led me into what looked like the library. Both the carpets and walls were red, and there was a massive, imposing chandelier hanging in the centre. Bookshelves towered above us, each filled with leather-bound books and the occasional heavy-looking bookend. I was desperate to see if one of them led to a secret passageway.

'What do you want?' I asked as my eyes scanned the room for hidden buttons or levers.

'It's Candace,' she said. 'She's totally embarrassing me.'

'What, because she got a little drunk last night? Who cares? Everybody was hammered.'

'It's not just that,' she said, hands on hips. 'That outfit she's wearing today' – too-tight white jeans and a bright pink halter top, point somewhat taken – 'and the fact that she keeps telling me how excited she is to be the mother of the bride . . .'

'Most people would classify that as nice,' I said.

'Ruby, don't you get it? She's not our mother!'

'She means well,' I said. 'She's been our stepmother for a long time now, so I think she's just trying to –'

Piper's face crumpled and her bottom lip began to tremble. 'I want Mom,' she wailed. 'Our real mom.'

I sighed and pulled her in for a hug. 'I know, kiddo,' I said. 'I know. Me too.' I was surprised to see her so emotional about it – Piper and I almost never talked about Mom. She never brought it up and I was always too scared to, in case she didn't remember. She'd been so young when she died, just a blonde little baby toddling around in pigtails at the funeral. I wasn't sure if she had any real memories of her, beyond the photos Dad and I had shown her over the years and the stories we'd told.

'It's not fair that she's not here,' she whispered into my shoulder.

'You're right,' I said. 'It's not. It's really, really fucking unfair. But you've got me and Dad and Candace, and now you've got Charlie and his family, too. We're all here for you. It doesn't make up for Mom not being here – but it's not nothing, either.'

She straightened up and nodded, wiping the mascara from underneath her eyes. 'I know Candace means well, and I like her, I really do,' she said with a sniffle. 'I just wish she wouldn't wear so much Lurex.'

I linked my arm through Piper's and led her out of the room. 'There are some battles you can't win,' I said. 'Now, let's go see if Dad's broken anything yet.'

Luckily, he hadn't, though he had made the mistake of flicking through the pages of what turned out to be an original copy of the Domesday Book, eliciting a sharp intake of breath from the private guide, who told him, in her most polite tone, that he was never, ever to do that again. Meanwhile, Candace was busy inspecting an Italian silk tapestry and wondering aloud if it wouldn't make a great material for a cocktail dress. Charlie had wandered off to inspect the jousting equipment on display – 'I bet it wasn't *that* hard. Do you think they'd let me try it?' – and Bob and Barbara had begun curtsying to everyone who walked through the Upper Guard Room in the hope that one of them might be the duchess. Ethan was standing off by himself, quietly admiring an oil painting of a woman with long, blonde hair wearing a deep-scarlet dress. I felt a twinge of jealousy even though I knew she was probably long dead.

Eventually, the guide couldn't stand to see another set of fingerprints appear on another highly polished surface and suggested that we take the tour of the gardens.

'I don't know why I'd come all the way here just to see a couple of flowers,' Dad grumbled as we made our way outside. 'Got plenty of them in Florida.'

'I don't think it's really the same thing, Dad,' I said, nodding towards the expansive manicured grounds stretched out before us. Through the arches, I could see an enormous water fountain spilling down a set of stone steps, flanked on either side with perfectly trimmed hedges. School children tossed coins into the fountain, each shutting their eyes tight as they silently mouthed their wish. I patted my bag instinctively, thinking of all the coins lingering at the bottom, and wished for a minute that I wasn't too old for wishes.

We walked through the rose garden, Barbara exclaiming over every bloom, her fingers clearly itching to take a cutting for her own backyard. Piper joined her, both of them wondering aloud about possible last-minute changes to the already-extortionate wedding flower arrangements, while Bob quizzed the long-suffering guide on the Latin names of each specific variety of rose. Poor Candace quickly added hay fever to her lingering hangover, and Dad had to lead her out of the garden, eyes streaming, and away towards the relative safety of the café. Charlie and Ethan strode ahead, heads bowed towards each other in conversation.

I watched them all walk ahead without me and sat down on a bench. The stone was cool against the backs of my legs, and I closed my eyes and breathed in the scented air. I thought about what would be happening back at the office – it would just be opening now, people stumbling in smelling of soap and shampoo, clutching their bagels or smoothies or thermoses full of coffee. New York felt like a far-off dream from here, all of the steel and glass and crowds and hectic energy seeming like something out of another dimension. I gazed up past the vined trellises overhead at the blue sky above and the high walls of the castle just beyond. I felt as if I was receding back in time somehow, and wondered if I was going to end up in a loincloth by the end of the trip, bashing a ferret over the head with a rudimentary club and marveling over the wheel.

I heard Charlie and Ethan's voices behind me from the other side of the trellis and froze.

'Hey, you don't have to tell me. I read that Steve Jobs book,' Charlie was saying. 'So what's going on with you and Ruby? You two looked pretty cozy last night.'

There was a rustling noise, like someone kicking at leaves. 'Nah, it's not like that,' Ethan said.

'Come on, don't give me that. I remember when you guys were together. You were totally obsessed with her! Remember I used to call her Beer-flavored Nipples?'

I felt a curious flash of pride mixed with indignation: I had never wanted Charlie to refer to my nipples, but I guessed this was the best possible scenario.

I heard Ethan let out a low laugh. 'I remember.'

'So?'

'That was a long time ago, man. Things change.'

At this point, my blood began to run cold.

'Yeah, but you've got to admit, she's still hot.'

'I guess. I think it just took me so long to get her out of my system that . . .' A pause, more rustling. 'There's no way I'd go back. Besides, there's nothing there now.'

'You sure about that?'

'Positive. Whatever we had, it's long gone.'

And there it was. He didn't love me anymore, and he never would again. The world rushed away from me and I felt lightheaded. For a moment, I genuinely thought I might be sick, and if it wasn't for the fact that Ethan might have heard me retching in the roses behind him, I probably would have been. I listened to their footsteps recede and tried to suck air into my lungs. My heart ached in my chest. I was hurt, of course, and bitterly sad, but the thing I felt most was shame. Deep, unrootable shame. Because I knew exactly why he would never love me again, and the worst thing was, he didn't know the half of it.

I had been a fool to think there could ever be anything between us again. The one thing I hated more than anything else was being embarrassed, and yet here I was, sitting on a cold stone bench and getting scratched by rose thorns, humiliated. At least he didn't know, I thought to myself. At least I hadn't said anything and made an even bigger fool of myself.

I stood up and dusted the dirt from my legs. I could still save face in all this. I didn't have to be the loser who turns up to her sister's wedding and makes a fool of herself by throwing herself at her ex-boyfriend. Ethan could never, ever find out how I really felt about him. I vowed to myself then that he never, ever would.

Then

Ethan was out back, tapping a new keg of Miller Light. He could hear Ruby and Charlie making stilted conversation at the bar, and he hurried so he could save them from each other. Charlie made Ruby deeply nervous with all of his bluster and wilful bro-fulness, and Ruby flummoxed Charlie with her mix of slight primness and sharp-tongued wit. Ethan was the buffer between the two of them, smoothing each other's edges and making sure that the conversation didn't veer too far in either direction.

He sealed the tap, wiped his hands on his jeans, and headed back behind the bar. It was a Wednesday night and there wasn't a game on, so it was fairly quiet. The regulars were perched in their usual spots, and in the corner, a group of teachers from the nearby high school had come in after their summer-school classes and were still there, empty bottles littering the tables, the occasional collective laugh or shriek rising and falling. They would be sorry tomorrow when their alarm clocks went off and their hangovers kicked in, but in the meantime Ethan was happy to keep supplying them with wine and plates of nachos he microwaved in the back kitchen.

'Ethan, did you know that your girlfriend has never seen *The Big Lebowski*?'

Ethan shrugged noncommittally. When the three of them were together, a lot of the conversations were led by one of them asking him if he knew something apparently abhorrent or ignorant about the other, and over the past month he'd become an expert at polite distance. To them, he was Switzerland, though his allegiance did swing slightly towards Ruby, as she was better looking and let him sleep with her. 'She was probably too young.'

'Dude, it came out like six years ago! It's not like she was a baby back then.' Charlie swung towards Ruby, eyes intense. 'Seriously, it's the best movie ever made. How have you not seen it? I mean, you don't even know about the Dude!' He swung back towards Ethan. 'Your girl-friend doesn't know about the Dude!'

'It's a good movie,' Ethan said to her. 'We should watch it sometime.'

'A good movie! How can you stand in my presence and say that *The Big Lebowski* is just "a good movie"? You only drank White Russians for, like, three years after you watched that movie! We watched it so many times the tape got demagnetized! How can you not remember this?' Charlie had worked himself up into a fury now, and was taking his frustrations out on a beer coaster that he was methodically shredding.

'I'm not saying it's not a good film!' Ethan said, holding his hands up. 'You need to relax, man.'

'Okay, okay, I'll watch your stupid film,' Ruby said, roll-ing her eyes at Charlie and pulling the frayed coaster away from him. 'But if I watch *The Big Lebowski*, you have to read Jane Austen.'

Charlie was horrified. 'Why the hell would I want to read some old chick talk about love and shit?'

'She's not just some old chick,' Ruby said. She began to shred the already-shredded beer coaster between her fingers and Ethan gently took it out of her hands and replaced it with a new, unshredded one. 'She's one of the greatest English novelists. And it's not just about love, it's about . . . she writes about the human condition!'

'Yeah right. I know boring chick stuff when I hear it.'

Ruby looked at Ethan beseechingly. 'Ethan, please tell your friend that Jane Austen is not just "boring chick stuff". If she could hear this right now, she'd probably be rolling in her grave.'

'If she could hear it, she wouldn't be dead,' Charlie pointed out, smug.

'Oh for God's sake – you know what I mean! Ethan, tell him that Jane Austen is amazing!'

Ethan sighed. He did a lot of sighing around the two of them, but secretly he loved it. The two people he loved most in the world – apart from his dad, of course – sitting together and keeping him company while he worked. It made him almost giddily happy, even though they argued all the time. Or maybe *because* they argued all the time. 'Jane Austen's cool, man,' he said with a practiced shrug. '*Pride and Prejudice* is actually pretty funny.'

'Dude, when did you become such a pussy?' Charlie said, visibly sickened. 'Do me a favor and get me another beer. Or do you need to change your tampon or something?'

'Don't be such an asshole!' Ruby said, reaching over and swiping him on the arm.

'What?' Charlie asked, rubbing his arm. He looked genuinely confused.

'How are you ever going to get a girlfriend if you say things like that?' Ruby asked.

'Don't worry about me,' he said, tilting dangerously on the bar stool. 'I do just fine.'

'Liar,' Ethan said, stifling a laugh.

'Hey, fuck you, man. Just last week I had a girl from Wentworth practically begging me to take her number.'

'Really?' Ruby asked, eyes narrowed mischievously. 'I used to be on a swim team in Wentworth. I know lots of girls there. What was her name?'

Charlie looked temporarily flummoxed. 'I . . . uh . . . I can't remember.'

Ethan burst out laughing. 'Dude, come on! At least make one up!'

'I can't remember, okay? I was wasted! But she was super hot, I know that.'

'I'll bet,' Ruby said.

'Speaking of super hot, how's your sister doing?' Charlie asked. 'Now she is someone I would like to get to know better, if you know what I mean.'

'Gross! Don't talk about my sister being hot!'

'Why not? It's basically a compliment for you!'

'How do you figure that you telling me you want to have sex with my sister is a compliment to me?'

'Because of genetics, or whatever! And you're the one who mentioned sex, not me, you pervert. Though now that you mention it . . .'

Ruby reached over and smacked Charlie again, harder this time, and his stool wobbled precariously beneath him. 'Stop talking about having sex with my sister!'

'All right! All right! I'm just saying, if you ever feel like spending some quality time with her when I'm around, especially with you going off to New York soon . . . I mean, I'm a guy who appreciates the importance of family, that's all.'

'Very kind of you to be concerned about my familial bonds,' she said, rolling her eyes.

'We could even double date, if you felt that would bring you guys closer . . .'

'Enough already!'

'Guys, guys, take it easy,' Ethan said, tossing the rag he'd been using to clean up a grenadine spill over his shoulder. The group of teachers looked up from their wine fug in confusion. They'd forgotten there was anyone else in the bar a bottle or two back, and Ruby and Charlie's argument had rattled them unpleasantly back to reality. They glanced at their watches and began muttering to themselves, their minds whirring into gear as they calculated how late it was and how few available hours for sleeping it off they had left before they had to be back at summer school. They gathered their belongings and said their goodbyes, hugging each other too long and too tightly and slowly, steadily clapping each other on the back. 'Hope you guys all have rides home!' Ethan called to them, and one mousey man, who had spent the evening tucked invisibly in the corner of the table nursing a watery glass of Coke, held up his keys and said, 'I have a van.'

The door opened and they filed out into the night, ushering a blast of warm, muggy air into the bar. Ethan glanced up at the clock: an hour until closing. 'Do you want to stick around tonight?' he asked Ruby. 'I know you have to work tomorrow and everything.'

'Of course I want to,' she said, placing a hand over his. 'Who needs sleep anyway?'

'I'm staying too,' Charlie muttered, 'not that anyone asked.'

'That's because everyone knows you've never left a bar before closing in your life,' Ruby said, tossing a peanut at him.

'Damn straight,' Charlie said, catching it and throwing it back at her. 'And I'm serious about your sister. I'll be a gentleman and everything.'

'I didn't realize the word gentleman was even in your vocabulary.'

'Ha ha. You're hilarious. Look, just put in a good word for me, okay?'

'Give me the rest of the peanuts and we'll talk.'

'Deal.'

Ethan watched the two of them bicker with each other and realized that he had never been happier than he was, at that moment, past midnight in a dingy bar in his tiny hometown. It was happier than he'd ever been before.

Now

To: Mathius Sondergaard
Sent: 16 July 2015 14:21
From: Ethan Bailey
Subject: re: Buyout

Mat –

I don't feel comfortable making a decision just yet. Sorry, I know you're going crazy down there but can you give me a little more time? It's a big decision, and I'm not sure I'm ready to put myself out to pasture just yet.

Call if there's anything urgent – otherwise more soon.

E

To: Bill Bailey
Sent: 16 July 2015 21:16
From: Ethan Bailey
Subject: re: House alarm

It wasn't broken, you just put in the wrong code. I'll get
someone to come over and fix it. Next time that happens, just
leave it alone – I don't want to worry about you climbing
through windows or shimmying down drainpipes. Just try to
take it easy, okay?
Heard the Sox hammered the Giants the other night. I can't
believe I missed it.

E

Now

I sat in the back of the bus on the ride home from Alnwick and tried to hold my shit together. I felt stunned, and numb.

Candace craned her neck to look at me. 'You okay, baby girl?' she asked. She'd recovered from her hay fever attack, but her eyes were still puffy and slightly bloodshot. I felt for her: so far, England wasn't agreeing with her.

'Yep, fine!' I trilled back. I pretended to look through my bag as tears stung my eyes. Get your shit together, I thought to myself. Don't go soft on me now.

'You don't look so hot,' Candace said. 'Can I get you anything? Maybe a cold drink? I'm sure we could stop off at the shop if you wanted.'

'I'm fine, really,' I said. I heard the edge in my voice and saw the look of hurt on her face and instantly regretted it. Great. Not only was I unloved, I was also a bitch. This day just kept on giving.

The bus finally pulled into Bugle Hall's long sweeping drive. Ethan's phone rang and he grimaced before answering. He gave all of us a quick wave and then shot into the house, his voice low and his face dark.

Dad appeared by my side and nudged me in the ribs. 'What do you think that was about?' he asked, nodding after him.

'I have no idea.' And at this point, I really didn't care.

'Bet it's important. Guys like him only have important conversations.'

'Dad, that's an insane thing to say.' It was probably true, though. He was probably finding a solution to world hunger or setting up a charity to help blind Sudanese kids, the asshole.

My dad was undeterred. 'I've been reading up on the guy,' he said. 'Do you know what his estimated net worth is?'

'No, and I don't want to.' Besides, I already knew. I'd Googled it yesterday. It wasn't information that I would currently classify as 'helpful'.

'Let me tell you, it's a lot. He could own his own baseball team if he wanted.' I knew that this was the ultimate mark of wealth for my father.

'Good for him.' I pushed past him and walked into the house. I needed a break from all the Ethan-worshipping. Either that or a stiff drink. Ideally both.

Instead, I found two glossy brunettes perched on the sofa in the living room, Bob and Barbara buzzing around them like a pair of bumblebees around a particularly fragrant flower patch. 'Ruby, Alec, you remember the Duffy girls?' Bob said excitedly. They were the type of women I would normally remember because of the mix of contempt and self-loathing they inspired. They were long-legged and coltish, the sort of women who swung enormous, expensive handbags from their tiny wrists, handbags that tended to thwack into me when I passed them on the street back in New York. They looked familiar to me, but not just for those reasons. They looked familiar because I used to babysit for both of them when I was a teenager.

'Taylor? Madison?'

'Omigod, Ruby! Hi!' Taylor leaped to her feet and entangled me in a long-limbed hug. 'I can't believe it! I haven't seen you since I was seven!' I tried and failed not to do the mental math. If I'd been fifteen when I looked after them, then they were now . . . Oh God. Twenty-three. Fully-fledged handbag-carrying adults. I felt my ovaries shrivel just thinking about it.

Madison reached up and grabbed my hand. 'It is so good to see you,' she said. 'You haven't changed at all!' I thought back to my fifteen-year-old self – replete with Jennifer Aniston haircut and muffin top protruding above my low-rider jeans – and felt mildly offended. 'You . . . definitely have changed,' I said, gesturing towards them both. They were twins, but not identical. Madison was slightly taller and more fine-boned, and her eyes were deep sapphire blue to Taylor's sky. Both were almost painfully gorgeous. 'What are you guys doing here?' I asked.

Taylor tossed a wave of caramel highlighted hair over her shoulder and looked at me with surprise. 'We're bridesmaids! Didn't your sister tell you?'

'No, but that's nothing new,' I said. 'I didn't even realize you guys knew each other.'

'Oh, we've been friends for a few years now,' Madison said. 'We held a conference at the club a couple of years ago and Piper ran the event for us.'

'You held a conference?' They barely looked old enough to hold a bottle of beer.

'It was this young digital entrepreneur thing,' she said, waving it away with her hand. 'It was kind of stupid. I mean, who holds a physical conference for digital entre-preneurs? And in Beechfield of all places? So embarrassing.'

'Totally,' Taylor said. 'But we were just babies then.'

'So you guys do digital stuff?' Even though part of my job was to know what was cutting edge in the digital world, the idea of a 'digital entrepreneur' was still some-thing of a mystery to me, like the meaning of 'Netflix and Chill', or who Grimes was.

'Taylor is basically the queen of Instagram,' Madison said proudly. 'She has almost half a million followers.'

'Jesus,' I said. 'What do you do?'

Taylor shrugged. 'I'm a yogi, so I take a lot of photos of yoga poses I'm working on.' I pictured her doing the pigeon and those half a million followers started to make sense. 'Plus stuff on health and nutrition. I just launched my own juice company, actually, which delivers fresh juices to offices around New York. It's cool.'

'She's being modest,' Madison said. 'The girl is a goddess.' I felt touched watching how proud she was of her sister – I doubted that Piper and I had ever expressed even a fraction of that much genuine sincerity towards each other.

'How about you?' I asked Madison. 'Are you a digital entrepreneur, too?'

'Please, Madison is a way bigger deal than me,' Taylor said. 'She basically owns an empire.'

'Really?' I tried to arrange my face in a way that at least partially hid my jealousy. How did all these people have empires? Where the hell was my empire? Suddenly my studio was looking pretty cramped.

'I have this fashion thing,' Madison said. 'It's no big deal.'

'Maddie, don't do the whole false modesty thing. Don't listen to her,' Taylor said to me. 'She runs one of the most influential sites in fashion. The shop aggregator she designed is a work of total genius.'

'So you're a coder, too?' I couldn't believe it. Who were these people?

Madison shrugged. 'I took a few courses in college. Anyway, enough about us. What have you been up to?'

'I work in advertising.' It was normally a sentence that filled me with a smug sense of *Mad Men*-esque pride, but faced with twin mogul millennials, I suddenly felt like a dinosaur. I might as well have said that I make abacuses for a living.

'Cool!' they cooed.

Dad walked in eating a cookie and whistling to himself.

'Mr Atlas!' Madison cried. 'How are you?'

From the look on my dad's face, it was obvious he had no idea who either of them were. 'Hey, you two!' he said. 'How the heck have you been?'

'Oh, you know,' Taylor said. 'Same as ever! My dad told me to tell you that he hadn't forgotten about the bet you two had!'

The look on my father's face turned from confusion to panic. 'He did, did he?'

Barbara tossed him a few breadcrumbs to peck up. 'Taylor and Madison were just saying that their parents decided to go to St Andrews before the wedding,' she said. 'You know how much Larry loves the links, and I'm guessing Joanne went with him to make sure he actually came back!'

'Joanne and Larry!' he near-shouted. 'How are they doing, those son of a guns? I haven't seen them in donkey's years!' I guessed from the look on his face that the long absence hadn't pained him particularly.

'Good!' Madison said. 'They'll be here tomorrow, so get ready for lots of boring golf stories.'

'Can't wait!' my father said, smile stretched tightly across his face. 'Your dad didn't happen to mention what that bet was about, did he? I can't seem to remember off the top of my head. I can't imagine it was for much money . . .'

'Dad said you'd say that!' Taylor said.

'There's no pulling the wool over your old man's eyes,' Dad muttered.

'Are those my girls I can hear?' Piper charged into the room emitting a high-pitched squeal and lunged towards the couch. She was quickly consumed in a tangle of toned arms and Kérastased hair.

Taylor emerged briefly and yelled 'You're getting *married*!' before getting dragged back into the scrum. I watched impassively from the other side of the room, polite smile plastered to my face. I suspected this was the point where I was meant to pull out my pompoms and start doing wedding cartwheels, but I didn't have it in me, not after today.

Piper finally extracted herself and perched on the arm of the sofa, holding each of the girls' hands (which was going a little too far – she wasn't Oprah) and gazing at them adoringly. 'Taylor,' she said to caramel highlights, 'I absolutely *love* your hair. It's kind of Jennifer Lawrence, but not *American Hustle* Jennifer Lawrence, when she looked kind of trashy. Like a fancy Jennifer Lawrence.'

'Oh my God, don't,' Taylor said, running a hand through her caramel waves. 'I look like I fell out of a garbage can today.'

'You do not,' Piper said. 'You're gorgeous!'

'Can I just say how amazing you look?' Taylor said. 'Have you been juicing?'

'Yes!' Piper said, delighted. 'I followed your advice and got a NutriBullet. It's amazing.'

'I can totally tell. I said to Madison on the flight over, I bet Piper has been juicing and she is going to be glowing. And you totally are!'

'Taylor is going to help digitally style the wedding,' Piper said, addressing the room. 'We really want to get the wedding to go viral, so everyone has to start tweeting and Instagramming now. It's hashtag PipsGetsHitched.'

'Are you sure you want to have anything to do with a virus?' Dad asked. 'It sounds dangerous.'

'Madison is going to direct the photo shoot,' Piper said, ignoring him. 'And she said that she might feature it on her website! Isn't that amazing? I would just die. No pressure,' she added to Madison, who looked like she understood exactly how much pressure there was.

'You guys are going to be like Kate and Wills, only, like, a blonde Kate and a William with more hair,' Madison said, beaming. 'It's going to be amazing.'

'Great!' I envisioned myself being photographed jumping into the air clutching my bridesmaid's bouquet, or perched awkwardly on a hay bale at Piper's feet. 'Look like you're having fun!' the photographer would say, and I wouldn't be able to list all the reasons why it was impossible for me to do so convincingly.

'You girls are going to look gorgeous,' Dad said.

'Absolutely,' Barbara said, nodding approvingly. 'Amazing.'

'Amazing,' I echoed, and thought longingly about the row of tiny vodka bottles awaiting me upstairs.

Ethan walked in, phone still in hand. He looked at the Duffy girls like a little kid finding a shiny red tricycle under the Christmas tree. Two shiny red tricycles. 'Sorry,' he said, 'I didn't realize we had new guests.'

I caught the look on his face and immediately decided that I needed to get as far away from the living room as possible. 'I'm going for a walk,' I announced, and the rest of them glanced up at me quizzically, as though they were surprised I was still there.

I pulled on a jumper and set out down the drive. I pulled my phone out of my pocket and pressed dial, worrying briefly about the size of my phone bill. Jess picked up on the third ring. I could hear the sound of Noah screaming in the background.

'Is this you calling me to tell me you have just left Ethan in a state of post-coital bliss? Because while I'm very happy for you, I'm also literally up to my ankles in toddler puke right now, so I don't know if I can work up the requisite amount of excitement.'

'It's over,' I said, maybe a little melodramatically. 'He never wants to get back together.'

'What? Wait, hang on.' She placed her hand over the phone. 'Noah, go play with your fire truck and Mommy will be there in two minutes, okay? Okay,' she said, coming back on the line. 'Tell me what happened. I'm sure whatever it is, you're overreacting.'

'He literally said that there was nothing between us. I don't see how I can be overreacting.'

'How – I mean, why would he have said that? Did you ask him or something?'

'I overheard him talking to Charlie. He was pretty decided on the whole thing.'

'Oh, please. He has no idea what he wants! He was probably just doing that to save face. What you need to do is –'

'Jess, I'm not doing anything. I told you, it's over. Done. I don't know what came over me, anyway. I mean, what was I even thinking? It's like I had some kind of sickness, a kind of temporary brain disease.'

'Such a healthy way to describe love . . .'

'It wasn't love,' I said. 'It was temporary insanity.' I walked through a kissing gate and into the nearby field, careful to keep to the well-trodden path. The sky was bright blue and marbled with wisps of cloud, and there was a cool edge to the breeze. There was a cow standing in the field a few feet away, and it blinked impassively as I passed.

'I honestly don't think that having feelings for someone you used to love can be classified as temporary insanity.'

'Well in my case, it was. At any rate, it's over now, and I can just put the whole humiliating episode behind me and move on.'

'How was it humiliating? There's nothing humiliating about admitting you have feelings for someone!'

'Um, it is when that person has absolutely zero interest in reciprocating those feelings. It's completely embarrassing!'

'Ruby, there's absolutely nothing for you to be embarrassed about. You like the guy! There's nothing wrong with that! Besides, I'm sure he'll change his mind. Maybe you should flirt with him a little more, remind him of what he's missing.'

'Are you kidding me? Have you completely lost your mind? I told you, he doesn't want to have anything to do with me. Why would I go throwing myself at him after hearing that?' The field sloped upwards and I struggled to catch my breath as I climbed the hill. I looked behind me: the cow was still watching.

'Because you have feelings for him? Because it's good to take risks in life?'

'There's a difference between a risk and a kamikaze mission. No, my whole plan for the rest of this trip is just to save face and make sure that he doesn't get even a whiff of what I was thinking earlier. I'm going to be cool as a cucumber. I'm going to channel that "cool girl" thing from *Gone Girl*.'

'You know that character was a sociopath, right?'

'Whatever. You know what I mean.'

I heard Jess sigh. 'I wish you weren't so hard on yourself.'

'I'm not hard on myself,' I said. 'I'm just being realistic. This whole thing has been traumatic enough – I don't need to make a complete fool of myself on top of it. From now on, I'm going to be a fortress of self-control.'

'Sounds like fun. I don't mean to lecture you or anything, but I feel like you're so closed off to –'

'Sorry, you're cutting out,' I lied. 'The reception up here is terrible! I'll call you later – love you byeeeee!' I switched off my phone and slung it in the bottom of my bag.

I reached the top of the hill and looked down on a patchwork quilt of grass and wildflowers in which sheep grazed and lounged in the sun. The sheep were bigger than I'd expected, and, from the smell, dirtier, not quite the little cotton balls on legs I'd imagined. I stopped and watched them for a minute, feeling jealous of the freedom and ease of their lives – except the slaughter part, I guess. Though these sheep looked like they were too old for the chop, and would probably be safe. No one wanted mutton – too tough. They only wanted tender little lambs.

I pressed on, encouraged by the brightness of the skies above. I could get used to this whole country-living thing, I thought as I straddled a fence and hopped into a field filled with tiny yellow flowers. I imagined myself in the pub afterwards, talking to the locals – lovely weather for a walk, they'd say, very rare – wearing an Aran sweater and those giant rubber boots everyone seemed to have in the countryside, nursing an enormous pint of ale. Yes, I could definitely see the appeal. The green was unrelenting, hill after undulating hill of it. My eyes were so used to living in New York, where you couldn't see further than ten feet without your eyes hitting a building, that this much free space felt almost . . . luxurious. The silence, too, was a novelty: there was nothing except for the occasional low buzz of a tractor, or a cow lowing in a nearby field.

I saw a little stone bench up ahead, perched neatly on top of a bluff, and decided to stop there for a minute. The view was gorgeous, the hills rolling down and out and, beyond them, a thin slate-gray sliver of sea. I closed my eyes and let the weak sun warm my face. Ethan's words were still rolling around in my head, and I let myself feel one final wrench before I pushed them out of my mind. I'd been chasing some stupid silly dream, a dream that had died a decade ago in a basement bar in SoHo. I remembered what I'd said to Jess about being a fortress. I sat up straight and clenched my fists tightly. You're a fortress, I thought to myself. You are tougher than this.

'Cheer up, pet. It might never happen!'

I opened my eyes and saw an elderly man wearing a flat cap, a newspaper tucked neatly under his arm. I blinked a few times, unsure of whether he was real or a mirage sent from the tourist board for local color. He smiled at me, revealing a row of teeth that had eaten too much cinder toffee. He was definitely real. 'Pretty girl like you shouldn't be scowling on her own like that,' he said.

'I'm not scowling,' I said, forcing an icy smile. I knew that the old guy meant well, but men telling me to smile got my back up at the best of times, and this, as previously established, was not the best of times. 'I was just lost in thought for a minute.'

'From the looks of it, you weren't thinking very pleasant things,' the man pressed on.

Jesus, let it go already. 'I'm fine,' I said tightly. 'Really.'

He looked at me through narrowed eyes, as though he was trying to place me. 'You're up at Bugle Hall, aren't you?'

'How did you know that?' This, it seems, was one of the main drawbacks of living in the countryside: everyone knew your damn business all the time, and you had to make small talk with people, even when it was literally the last thing you wanted to do.

'A little village like ours, you know everyone's comings and goings,' he said with a proud nod.

'So I've noticed.'

'Are you the one getting married then? Are you up here on your own trying to recover from your cold feet?'

'No,' I said. 'My sister's the bride, I'm just a bridesmaid. She's getting married at Bamburgh Castle on Saturday.'

'Ah, it's lovely there. Some say that it's not a real castle, but don't pay them any mind. It's as real as my right eye,' he said. 'The left one's glass,' he explained, pointing towards it.

Now that he mentioned it, it was all I could look at. I'd never met anyone with a fake eye before, so I wasn't sure how to respond. 'I'm sorry?' I ventured.

He waved me away. 'Don't be silly, pet. Happened ages ago. Willy Crannock got me in the eye with a poker. Anyways, what have you seen of this land of ours so far? I expect you'll have been to Alnwick.'

'We went this morning. It was beautiful, especially the garden.'

'All tarted up, thanks to that bloody duchess,' he said with a scowl. 'Do you know she diverted water from the local villages to water those silly plants of hers?'

'I – n-no,' I stuttered. 'I didn't.'

'Well, she did. Bloody aristocracy. They should be lined up against a wall and shot, the lot of them.'

'Hmm,' I mumbled, trying to seem as noncommittal as possible. He seemed to be getting very worked up over an admittedly somewhat over-preened garden and, while he looked harmless, you never knew what people were capable of. I knew that better than most.

'You're sitting on my wife, you know,' he said abruptly.

I started up from the bench and looked down. As suspected, there weren't any old ladies hidden underneath me. Maybe he'd lost his mind as well as his left eye.

He moved forward and brushed the dust from the plaque mounted onto the back. I leaned down to read the inscription: Lily Cramer 1934–2008: Always On My Mind. 'Lily was your wife?'

'She's still my wife. Just because she's passed on doesn't make her any less my wife.'

'I'm sorry,' I said gently. He'd been driving me a little crazy with all of his questions, but now I felt a twist of sadness to think of him on his own. He probably lived a solitary life, biding his time in thin scrapings of margarine across dry toast. I felt a lump form in my throat and had to swallow it down, hard.

'We had fifty-odd good years,' he said fondly, 'and I was lucky to have them, even though she was always giving me gyp about betting on the horses. Gave me four beautiful children and nine little grandchildren, though, so I cannae complain.'

'You have grandkids?' I asked. I perked up at the thought of him doting on a brood of tow-headed little cherubs. 'So you're not alone?'

'Alone? I barely get any peace! If it's not one of the grandchildren pulling at me leg, it's the bingo night at the club or a trip to St James. Plus I've got all the old grannies in the village running after me, cooking me casseroles and asking if I need anything darned.' He smiled at me kindly. 'No, pet, don't you worry about me. I'm not alone.'

I felt absurdly relieved. If this slightly odd one-eyed man could live a full and happy life on his own, maybe there was hope for me yet. 'And the bench?'

'Aye, she loved coming up here, so when she passed I commissioned a fellow in the village to make her this plaque, so everyone would know it was her place.'

'It is gorgeous up here,' I said, gazing out across the hills to the sea.

'God's own country,' he said with an approving nod. 'Well, I'd best be off. I told Willy I'd come round and watch the races with him, and he'll give me bother if I keep him.'

'I should get going too,' I said, but I found myself sitting back down on the bench and staring out at the view.

'Hard to leave, isn't it, pet?' he said, following my gaze.

'It is,' I said. 'Besides, I'm not in any rush to get back.'

'Weddings can be right pains in the arse,' he said with a smile. 'Stay as long as you like. I'm sure Lily will be happy for the company.' And then, with a wink and a doff of his flat cap, he was off.

I closed my eyes and tilted my face towards the sun.

Then

Ethan and Ruby lay on their backs and tried to catch their breath. It was deep into August, and the walls of his tiny room had started to sweat in the humidity. The tang of sex hung in the air and clung to the bedding – it was beyond the power of Tide now; he would probably have to throw out the sheets. The window overlooking the garage's lot was opaque with steam, which was probably a good thing under the circumstances.

'Four times in one day,' he said. 'How is it even possible?'

Ruby rolled over and propped herself up on her elbow so that she could look at him. His arms were stretched above his head and he'd kicked off the sheets, exposing the long, lean line of his torso and his slim hips. Ruby swung her leg over and straddled him, dipping down to kiss his collarbone. 'I can't get enough of you,' she whispered. That was the feeling: one of ravenous hunger. She imagined herself as a python, jaw unhinged and swallowing him whole, but didn't tell him this in case it scared him. Which it probably would, considering how much it scared her.

'Let a guy catch his breath,' he said, rolling out from underneath her. 'Do you want the last slice of pepperoni?' he asked, reaching down into the open pizza box on the floor. He didn't wait for the answer: he folded the slice in half and took a bite.

Ruby leaned over and licked a smudge of tomato sauce from the corner of his mouth.

This was how their nights were spent: hiding in his room, eating take-out pizza, and having more sex than they'd previously thought physically possible. It was like nothing Ruby had ever imagined. Of course, she'd had sex before. There was her sweet high-school boyfriend, Dan, who she lost her virginity to in his parents' conservatory, Dave Matthews Band on the stereo. Dan was followed by a handful of guys in college, each encounter hazy and generally unsatisfying thanks to varying degrees of inebriation. But this – this was something else. Sex with Ethan was like a drug, like one long, continuous roll. They were both out of their minds.

Ethan pushed the last nub of crust into his mouth and scrambled out of bed, suddenly possessed by a frenetic burst of energy. 'Check out what I found today,' he said, digging around in his closet. He pulled out an old Polaroid camera and held it up for her to see.

'Cool,' she said. 'Where did you find it?'

'In the junk shop down by Delaney's. It still works.' He framed her in a shot and pressed a button, the camera's mechanics whirring into life and spitting out a stiff piece of card. He plucked it out and started waving it around in the air.

'What are you doing?' she laughed.

He shot her a disbelieving look. 'It speeds up the development time! Everyone knows that. See?' He held the bit of card up, and she saw a faint outline begin to appear. He resumed his flapping, more wildly this time, and after a few minutes the image had sharpened. There she was, wrapped in his bedsheet, smiling shyly up at him, the light hazy and smudged around her face. He looked at it admiringly. 'Look at you.'

'I think you're just a good photographer.'

'No way,' he said, jumping on the bed and kneeling beside her. 'It's all you.' He gazed down at the photograph. 'Man, I love Polaroids. They make everything look like a Beach Boys album cover.'

'Totally,' she said, even though she'd never seen one. Ethan's cultural knowledge was of oceanic depths; hers felt like a kiddie pool in comparison. She tried to bluff as much as she could, but he usually saw through her.

'You don't know what I'm talking about, do you?' he asked, bouncing lightly on the bed.

Images of sun-kissed boys in various Californian settings flashed before her eyes. 'Sure I do,' she said. 'You know . . . the one with the surfboard on the cover?' she guessed weakly.

'Wait, have you ever listened to *Pet Sounds*?' he asked, eyes wide and intense.

She shook her head.

'Oh my God, amazing. It is going to blow your mind.' He hurried over to the old record player set up in the corner of the room and started thumbing through a stack of frayed record sleeves. 'Got it!' He dropped the record on the turntable and lifted the arm of the needle, sending the record spinning. 'Close your eyes,' he said.

The opening strains of 'Wouldn't It Be Nice' *plinkety-plink*ed through the room. She remembered the song from long car rides with her parents as a child, the two of them singing along together. Her father had a terrible voice – couldn't carry a tune if it had handles – but her mother had had a clear, high voice and would always somehow manage to harmonize with him. The thought of it made her smile. 'My mom loved this song.'

She felt the mattress shift as Ethan lay down beside her. He moved towards her and put his arm around her, pulling her towards him. He started singing softly, his chin resting on the top of her head. She leaned back and pressed herself into him. He stroked her hair as he sang the rest of the song, kissing her when it ended. 'What was she like?' he asked softly.

She tried to think of words to describe her, but could only think in sounds and smells: the sound of her laugh when her father had told a joke, the sound of her voice when she'd wish her goodnight, the smell of her shampoo when she was freshly showered. 'She was great,' she said.

'You never talk about her. Tell me about her.'

Ruby tried to fight her way through the thicket of memories and grab hold of something tangible. 'She used to make Piper and me pancakes every Saturday after soccer practice,' she said, surprising herself as she said it. 'She would let us pour our own syrup over them, even though we'd always drown them.'

'Nice,' he said, stroking her hair. 'What else?'

'When she'd cut up a banana for snack, she'd always cut it lengthwise a little at the top first. It made this little banana mouth. She'd make it talk to us – I think it was called Billy Banana or something like that – and we'd have a little conversation with Billy Banana before he got cut up into little pieces.' She paused. 'It was kind of sick if you think about it, talking to our food before we ate it, but we loved it.'

'I don't think Billy Banana would have minded much. What else?'

She leaned back and sighed. 'I don't know. It's been a long time since I really thought about it, you know? Really thought about her and tried to remember things about her. Dad never talks about her these days – I think he's worried that it would upset Candace, or maybe it's too hard for him, too. And Piper . . . well, I don't know what Piper thinks. I feel like she might have been too young when Mom died, and now she doesn't remember her.'

'Have you asked her about it?'

She shook her head. 'I'm too scared to find out the answer. What if she really has forgotten Mom – what am I supposed to say to her?'

'You could tell her what you just told me,' he said. 'You could remember for her.'

'Piper doesn't really work that way,' she said. 'She's . . . I don't know. All three of us sort of shut down one way or another when Mom died. But with Piper, I feel like she shut herself off for good or something. It's like she made some decision along the way to be a complete and total bitch and to not care what anyone thought of her.'

'And what about you? What did you do when she died?'

'I decided that I had to take care of my dad,' she said quietly. 'That was the most important thing. And Piper, too, but she didn't need me as much, even though she was so young. Dad needed me the most. I was so scared that I'd somehow lose him, too. I basically didn't let him out of my sight for the next four years. I was like a dog in the window whenever he went out, just counting the minutes until he came back home. Poor guy must have felt like he had a tiny little stalker.'

'Nah, I bet he loved you looking after him like that.'

She shrugged. 'I think it cramped his style, but I couldn't really do anything else.' She thought about the morning that Candace had appeared at breakfast, and how betrayed she'd felt, but also a tiny bit relieved that he was someone else's responsibility now. She shook the memory out of her head and turned to Ethan. 'Okay, you've got enough out of me for one night,' she said. 'Your turn now. What was your mother like?'

He let out a low, nasty laugh – one that didn't sound right coming out of his body. 'She's not my mother, not anymore.' He sat up and pulled on a T-shirt that was lying next to the bed. 'You want to go get a beer or something?'

But Ruby wouldn't let him off that easy, not after all the soul-baring she'd just done. An eye for an eye, a tragic mother story for a tragic mother story. 'Come on, she couldn't have been all that bad,' she said. 'Tell me something about her.' She moved to pull him down towards her, but he shrugged her off.

'There's nothing to tell, Ruby.' He was trying to keep his voice light but there was an edge to it. 'She was a drunk, a mean one at that. Best thing she ever did for me or my dad was leave. Look,' he said, pulling away further, 'I don't want to talk about it, okay? She's not worth our combined breath.'

'Okay.' Ruby stroked his arm as if he were a spooked racehorse. She'd heard the stories by now. Everyone had. Lucille Bailey: seventies wild child turned nineties drunk, left her husband and her only son without so much as a goodbye note. She thought of Ethan as a little boy, small and alone as his mother raged above him, and then him as a thirteen-year-old kid, coming home one day to a still, empty house. She felt a sudden, heart-twisting urge to protect him, to wrap all the versions of Ethan up into one big blanket and hold it tightly and tell him he was safe. 'Come here,' she said gently. She pulled him back towards her and this time he let himself be pulled. She kissed him lightly on the cheek. 'What a pair we make, huh?'

They were still for a moment, listening to each other's quiet breaths, before Ethan leaped out of bed and started rummaging through his desk drawer.

'What are you doing?'

'I want to show you something.' He ran over to his computer and started pecking out numbers. The screen went blank and then an image of a woman's face – her face – appeared.

'Wait,' she said, 'how did you do that? Did you put my picture in it or something?'

He laughed. 'It's not a scanner, it's a computer. I drew it.'

'You drew it using a computer? How did you do that?'

He shrugged. 'I read up on 3D modeling. They use it a lot in video games so I thought I'd try it with a portrait. What do you think? I know the eyes are a little weird.'

'It's seriously incredible,' she said. 'I look way better as a computer graphic.'

'Impossible,' he said.

She stared at it for another minute. Every strand of hair had been sketched out, every eyelash. 'I knew you messed around with computer stuff, but I had no idea you were so talented.'

'Honestly, it's no big deal. Lots of people can do this sort of stuff.'

'I don't think that's true, especially since you haven't gone to school for it or anything. Imagine how good you'd be if you trained for it!'

'It's just a stupid hobby.'

'No, it's more than that. Don't undersell yourself: you have a real gift. You have to do something with it,' she said. 'Have you thought about going back to school?'

'Ruby, we've talked about this. Your father even agreed with me.'

'My dad hasn't seen what you're capable of. This is your path! You could come to New York with me! There are loads of amazing graphic design schools there. Or you could just do straight up programming! I mean, it's probably too late for the fall semester, but I bet we could get you in for the spring semester.'

'I don't want to go to school with a bunch of techy assholes. Besides, what about my dad? I can't leave him in the lurch just to go chasing after some stupid fairy tale. He needs me here to help at the shop.'

'You can't just stay with your dad for ever. And it's not a fairy tale, it's your life! You're really talented! Don't you want to do something with that? Don't you want to get out of this place?'

He shook his head. 'I didn't show you those sketches so you could give me some kind of life-coach pep talk,' he said. 'Just forget it, okay?'

'Fine,' she said. 'We can stop talking about it. But I'm not forgetting about it.'

Now

I arrived home just in time to see Ethan wrapping his arms around Madison. She was holding a croquet mallet and he had his hands over hers, guiding her swing. She was wearing a pair of denim shorts cut so tight I worried for her bacterial levels. I thought about going to get some cranberry juice just to be on the safe side.

'See?' he was saying, 'It's easy. It's just a little back and forth motion.'

'Is that what you say to all the girls?' I called out as I walked up the drive. You are a fortress, I thought to myself. You are cool as a cucumber.

Ethan dropped his arms and stepped away. A small smile pushed at the corner of his mouth, as if in spite of itself.

'Ethan was just showing me how to play,' Madison said. Her hair had fallen in the sort of long, tousled waves that fashion magazines describe as 'beach hair', even though everyone knows that beach hair consists of a topknot slicked in sun cream.

'I didn't know you were a croquet expert,' I said.

He took a swing and hit the ball with a sharp clack. It sailed through the wire hoop. 'Simon le Bon taught me the last time we were at Babington House.'

'Of course he did,' I muttered.

'I love Babington House!' Madison cooed. 'We did a whole shoot there last year. *Such* a cool place. But who's Simon le Bon?'

I stifled a laugh at the look of horror that flickered across Ethan's face. 'I'll see you guys inside,' I said, moving swiftly past. 'Careful of your back, old man.' Score.

Taylor appeared in the doorway. 'Guys! Dinner's ready! Ethan, you're sitting next to me since Madison has been hogging you all day. I have, like, a billion questions to ask you about outreach conversion.'

We found the rest of the group huddled around the heavy oak dining table, listening nervously to pots and pans clattering in the kitchen. Mrs Willocks was in the final throes of preparing dinner and, from the sound of it, it wasn't going down without a fight.

I slid into the empty chair next to my father. 'Kiddo!' he beamed. 'You're back! Where'd you go? Did you see anything good?'

'I just wandered around for a while. I found this amazing spot at the top of the hill – the view is just incredible. There was this bench up there . . .' I realized that my father had stopped listening and looked up to see Mrs Willocks carrying a tray of pies, the steam still rising from them. 'I hope everyone's hungry!' she trilled, setting the platter down with a proud flourish. 'I've brought a nice variety for you all to try,' she said. 'There's steak and ale, chicken and leek, and plain old pork.' She sliced into each of them, the shortcrust flaking before yielding under the knife.

She slid slices of each pie onto our plates, all of us eyeing them greedily. 'Thank you, Mrs Willocks!' we chorused. I took a bite of the chicken and leek: it was incredible.

I'd never been much for savory pies before, but this woman was some kind of pie sorceress: I already knew I'd be going back for seconds (and adding push-ups to tomorrow's workout).

'And I've done something special just for you,' Mrs Willocks said, turning to Piper. She returned from the kitchen holding aloft a plateful of very brown food. 'Liver and bacon,' she explained, 'as I know you can't eat pastry because of your . . . disposition.'

'Liver? As in the organ?' Piper asked, eyeing the plate Mrs Willocks placed before her queasily.

'That's right, love. Full of iron for you, and it's completely gluten free – I dialed it up on the Internet and checked!'

'Great,' Piper said weakly. I had to feel for her – as delicious as the pies were, nothing – not even Mrs Willocks's wizardry – could make a plate full of liver and bacon appetizing. 'Do you have any vegetables?' Piper asked, a panicked note in her voice. She was regarding the congealing slab of liver, which was modestly draped in a slice of bacon, with unvarnished horror. 'I definitely need to eat vegetables, or my alkaline levels will be, like, dangerously low.'

'Of course, pet! Coming right up!' Mrs Willocks dashed into the kitchen and returned with a bowl piled high with roast potatoes. 'Can't have liver and bacon without the veg!'

Piper made a small mewling sound, like a cat in distress. 'What am I going to do?' Piper hissed when Mrs Willocks had returned to the kitchen for more gravy. 'There is no way I can eat this!'

'Piper, chill out. I think it looks pretty good,' Charlie said. 'I'll eat it if you don't want it.' And that, ladies and gentlemen, is love.

True to his promise, Charlie polished off the liver and bacon after quickly dispatching his own plate of pie. Mrs Willocks looked like she wanted to kiss him when he asked for seconds, not knowing that Charlie had spent the afternoon getting quietly stoned with the gardener in the shed at the top of the garden. Taylor and Madison glee-fully spooned roast potatoes onto their plates and asked Mrs Willocks for more gravy, taking full advantage of their twenty-three-year-old metabolisms (which no amount of juicing could replicate). Ethan whispered something to them and they burst into fits of laughter, revealing rows of even, pearly-white teeth. I pushed my plate away: I'd finally lost my appetite.

Dad polished off the last of his pie and pushed his chair back from the table, placing a protective arm over his gen-erous stomach. 'That was just wonderful, Judy!' he called to the kitchen. Leave it to my father to be on first-name basis with Mrs Willocks after a day and a half. 'Now, who's up for a little whisky and a game of charades? What do you say, kids – just like when you guys were little!'

'*Dad, no!*' Piper and I groaned in unison. We didn't agree on much, but we were of the same mind when it came to charades. We had spent our formative years watching Dad contort himself into ever more unlikely shapes, gesticulating madly before eventually – inevitably – blurting out the answer when we failed to guess correctly. The thing was, he was terrible at acting, and we were ter-rible at guessing, and yet somehow it was the game he always wanted to play. It always ended in someone stomping off in a rage, so adding whisky to the equation felt doubly risky. Besides, I never drank whisky.

'C'mon, it'll be fun!' he insisted.

'I love charades!' Taylor announced, jumping up from the table and skittering towards the drawing room on her baby colt's legs.

'Me too!' Madison chimed, following close behind. 'This is so old school, guys! I love it!'

'Well, I don't see the harm in it,' Bob agreed. 'I'll bring down a bottle of the good stuff, Alec.'

'I'm in if you are,' Ethan said, turning to me with a smile. 'What do you say?' It was an act of breathtaking cruelty – he knew just how much I hated charades. But there was no way that I was going to let him show me up like that.

'What the hell,' I sighed, and followed the rest of them into the drawing room. I'd already suffered a lifetime of humiliation that day – what harm would another few hours be?

Now

To: Bill Bailey
Sent: 16 July 2015 23:48
From: Ethan Bailey
Subject: re: Sox

I know, I heard they really screwed it in the sixth inning. Porcello can't throw for shit. 82 million for a guy who couldn't get a ball to the plate if he had a waiter helping him serve it! It's the 2012 season all over again.

Hey, do you remember the Duffy girls? Taylor and Madison? They're here now, too. Arrived this morning. Seem nice.

E

Then

'I can't believe I agreed to do this.' They were sitting in the parking lot of Beechfield's fanciest French restaurant, Le Boeuf, waiting for Charlie to arrive. It was late August, and the nights were getting dark earlier. It was just before eight, and the street lights were already on. The heat of the day still clung to the inside of the car, though, and Ruby's thighs were stuck to the leather upholstery. She unpeeled them and put her feet up on the dashboard.

'Neither can I,' Ethan said. He rolled down his window. 'I can't believe that you agreed to it in the first place. I want it on record that I was coerced.'

'You're his best friend!' She reached over and swatted him on the shoulder.

'Yeah, that doesn't mean I want to double date with the guy.'

'At least he's paying,' she said.

'He'd better be. The only reason I'm here is for the free frogs' legs.'

'If you go anywhere near those frogs' legs, don't even think about kissing me tonight. They probably dredged them out of the Assabet River.'

'I'm ninety per cent sure I saw a body floating in that river when I was a kid.'

'I wouldn't be surprised. Hang on – I think that's them.'

They both watched as Charlie's cherry-red Corvette – a twenty-first-birthday present from his parents, to replace the sixteenth-birthday Audi he'd crashed into a tree the year before – pulled in and parked next to them. Charlie got out first. He was wearing – and neither of them could quite believe this – a white collared shirt and a navy blazer, and his hair was neatly combed. 'Holy shit,' Ethan said. 'He's actually serious about this.'

Charlie walked around the car and opened the passenger door. One long, tanned leg appeared followed by the other. Ruby immediately recognized the shoes – strappy blue sandals – and cursed under her breath. 'She's wearing my shoes!' And with that, Piper unfolded herself from the car and gave them both a little wave.

'I can't believe she agreed to this,' Ethan muttered.

'Honestly, she was excited about it. She said she thought he was cute. The fact that he's basically the richest guy in town probably isn't hurting, either.'

'It never does. Come on,' he said, opening the car door. 'It's show time.'

The four of them were shown to a table in the middle of the restaurant and were painstakingly seated by the maître d', who insisted on arranging napkins on each of their laps. He handed Charlie the wine list and disappeared with a flourish and a bow. Charlie closed the wine list without so much as a glance. 'Everyone happy with champagne?'

Piper hadn't looked so delighted since J.Crew had forgotten to charge her for a pair of yoga pants.

'This place is so fancy!' Ruby whispered. Ethan's eyes widened in agreement as they looked around the room. They were the youngest people in there by at least twenty years, unless you counted the miserable-looking Russian woman reluctantly spoon-feeding chocolate mousse into the mouth of an elderly man.

'I feel like everyone is watching me to see if I'm going to steal something,' he whispered back.

All around the table, white-shirted waiters swooped and sailed around like gulls circling a fish-teeming sea. Champagne was produced, poured and placed in an ice bucket next to Ruby's elbow. They clinked glasses and toasted each other and attempted to make what they considered adult conversation until Charlie made a joke about the shape of one of the bread rolls. Things deteriorated quickly from there until finally, fifth bottle of champagne drunk and bill paid with much fanfare by Charlie, the four of them stumbled out into the night, the door almost – but not quite – hitting them on the way out.

The parking lot was all but abandoned now, only Charlie's shiny red Corvette and Ethan's rusty Ford sat lonely underneath the lights. A couple of kitchen porters were squatting by the back entrance passing a joint between them. They barely looked up when the four of them passed.

'What are we going to do now?' Piper asked. She was swaying gently in her heels and her hair had come loose from its bun. The frazzled ends of stray hairs ringed her head like a halo.

'Well, we can't drive anywhere,' Ruby said. 'And the only place within walking distance is Billy Jack's, so . . .'

'I can't go into Billy Jack's!' Piper said. 'What if someone sees me in there?'

'Don't be such a snob,' Charlie said. He had the look on his face of a puppy who'd just placed the masticated remains of his owner's slippers at her feet. So proud, yet so very clueless. Just wait for the rolled-up newspaper, Ruby thought. Because it's coming.

Piper's mouth was a perfect round O. No one ever spoke to Piper that way, definitely not a man, and definitely not a man who had just bought her the most expensive meal in Beechfield. Ruby and Ethan's eyes darted back and forth between them nervously. What would happen next? Would she physically hit him, or just walk off in a huff? Not that she could get very far in those shoes . . .

Instead, much to everyone's surprise – including Piper's – she started to laugh. A full-throated, honest-to-God laugh. 'Come on,' she said, linking her arm through Charlie's. 'Let's go to your stupid bar. I'm warning you now, though, I'm not going anywhere near the bathrooms.'

'Suit yourself,' he said, leading her down the road. 'There's always the side alley, which I've used a few times in the past . . .'

Ruby and Ethan looked at each other with eyebrows raised. 'What the hell just happened?' Ethan said. 'Usually this is the point in the evening when his date slaps him.'

'This is usually the point in the evening when Piper slaps her date and flounces off in a huff,' she said. 'It's like watching some kind of ancient mating ritual from a previously undiscovered tribe.'

'Well, stranger things have happened,' he said, reaching out and taking her hand. 'Do you want to go with them?'

'Do you honestly think I'd pass up an opportunity to see my sister in Billy Jack's?' she said. 'Come on, let's go.'

Now

To: Bill Bailey
Sent: 17 July 2015 08:13
From: Ethan Bailey
Subject: re: Sox

I just said the twins seemed nice! Jesus!

Yeah, they've been on my case like crazy about the decision –
they want to make an announcement before Q3. Part of me
wants to sell up and get the hell out so I never have to attend
another board meeting ever again, but another part of me (the
one directly related to you, I'm guessing) has no clue what the
hell I'd do with myself without it. Other than drive you nuts,
obviously.

And of course I haven't brought it up with Ruby. Why would I? It
was years and years ago. A wise man once told me that there's a
reason dogs bury bones. I still don't really know what the hell
you were talking about, but I'm using it anyway.

Are you feeding Willy? Give him a scratch for me and an extra
can of Sheba.

E

Now

I woke up with a hangover. It was the second day running, and – after yesterday's pie-fest, my body was on the verge of revolt. There was a heaviness in my limbs and a dull ache between my eyes, and I knew immediately that the only thing that would make me feel human again was to lace up my sneakers and go for a run, even if it was the last thing I wanted to do. But sweating it all out was the only way, especially since I could already hear Mrs Willocks downstairs in the kitchen, baking something that smelled decidedly like blueberry muffins.

I forced myself onto my feet and stumbled to the wardrobe, pulling on a sports bra, shorts and a vest. I bounced lightly on the balls of my feet in the hope of getting the blood flowing, but it just made me feel light headed and I had to sit back down on the bed for a minute and take a couple of deep breaths before I was finally ready to hit the road.

It was a shockingly bright morning, with only a few lazy wisps of cloud lacing their way through the bright blue. I did a few cursory stretches and clicked my iPod until I found Kanye and set off. I hooked a left down a thin dirt trail marked by a small wooden sign: TO THE SEA. The path was rough and uneven, and brambles stretched in and caught at my legs as I passed. The path climbed up a steep hill fringed with long tufts of dried beach grass, which cracked and crunched satisfyingly underfoot. I took in a lungful of air and felt the fug in my head begin to clear.

Last night's game of charades had, predictably, ended in tears. Charlie had snapped at Piper for her inability to guess that the hand he'd placed on top of his head was meant to signify a shark fin – 'It's *JAWS*! How can you not get that?!' – and poor Candace had frozen, dumbstruck, after pulling *The Unbearable Lightness of Being* out of the bowl. Ethan managed to act out *Pulp Fiction* in two irritatingly clever actions, causing everyone to collapse into fits of rapture and me to turn sullen. Barbara fell asleep in a Regency reproduction chair, curled like a prawn and pinked with sleep, a well-thumbed Philippa Gregory open on her knee. A bottle of whisky had been emptied and another produced. At some point – I think it was around midnight – Mrs Willocks had poked her curler-wrapped head around the door and asked politely if we wouldn't mind being a bit quieter, but sadly for Mrs Willocks, we only got louder until the final crescendo, when Dad successfully re-enacted the Battle of Hastings using a fireplace poker ('Props aren't allowed,' Bob pointed out, but he'd been roundly shouted down). We all crawled off to bed shortly thereafter.

I reached the crest of the hill and stopped, bent over, lungs bursting, cursing myself for that last dram, but then I looked up and saw the wide arc of dun-colored sand stretching out to either side of me and the blue-gray of the ocean. I'd forgotten how much I loved the ocean: the smell of salt and seaweed and, ever so slightly, something sharp and slightly rotten, the rhythm of the waves as they washed in and out, the sound of the seagulls cawing as they flew in lazy, looping circles above. I pulled off my sneakers and tied them together around my neck: I wanted the feel of the damp sand packed beneath my feet when I ran.

To my left, a great hulking castle squatted at the edge of the bay, sitting atop a ragged bunch of rocks and scrubland and looking as though it had not so much been placed there as forced itself up through the earth. It was equal parts beautiful and terrifying: you could imagine people getting killed in it, or it at least being a persistent and convincing threat to anyone who saw it. I set off in the opposite direction, down a clear stretch of empty beach, my only company the occasional crab scuttling across my path.

For the second time in two days, I was alone. It was wonderful and also sort of disorientating, this sudden access to solitude. In New York, there were people. On the streets, in the windows of the glass skyscrapers that towered above, in the gym, in the elevator . . . everywhere, people. Even in the privacy of my apartment, I was still surrounded: the man downstairs yelling at the television, the couple in the next apartment bickering over whose turn it was to take the cat to the vet, the toddler rolling his scooter along the wood floor above. And always, always, the steady tick of emails streaming into my inbox. But here, now, there was nothing. I looked up and saw only an endless arc of ocean and sand. It was kind of amazing.

Just then, a tiny speck appeared on the horizon, followed by another, smaller, speck. I ran towards the two specks, gaining ground and perspective, and soon saw that it was a man and a dog – a scruffy, shaggy giant of a dog, nearly half the height of the man. The dog ran ahead in great loping gallops, charging towards me at alarming speed. I could hear the man shouting at the dog but the dog kept on charging. I couldn't think of anything else to do and was enjoying a rare surge of endorphins, so I kept running to meet it.

And then, in a great tangle of limbs and damp fur and muddy paws, we met.

'Archie, no!' the man shouted as he ran over to us. 'Archie! Get off her!'

I was pinned beneath the dog's weight (considerable) and fell into a fit of hysterical laughter as the dog lapped at my face. 'It's okay! It's okay!' I called up to the man. 'It's fine!' I managed to sit up and scratched the giant dog's head, at which point he collapsed in a heap onto my lap and nearly knocked the wind out of me.

'Christ, sorry about that!' the man said, reaching down to catch Archie's collar. 'He's a bloody nightmare, this one.'

'Don't worry,' I said, rubbing the dog's sandy belly. 'He's a good boy, aren't y—' I looked up and found myself face to face with the paperback man from the pub. 'Oh,' I said, not very enthusiastically. 'It's you.'

'Well, if it isn't my new American friend!' He held out his hand and pulled me onto my feet, the dog shifting and flopping heavily onto the sand next to us. 'I didn't recognize you from underneath six stone of dog. What the hell are you doing out here at this hour of the morning?'

I shrugged. 'Couldn't sleep, so I thought I'd get a run in. It's incredible here.'

He followed my gaze and nodded. 'It's magic, especially when you've got it to yourself. That's why I like to come out with him early, before I go to the surgery.'

'You're a surgeon?' With his wind-ruffled hair, faded board shorts and paint-splattered parka, I couldn't really picture him with a scalpel in hand, performing a delicate operation.

'No, nothing as glamorous as that. I'm just a regular old GP – old people's dodgy knees and the occasional bout of tonsillitis, that's my lot.'

'Oh. Well, it's still a . . . a very noble profession.' I don't know why I said that. I mean, I do think it's a noble profession, helping people and everything, but who says things like 'noble profession' other than a 1950s school marm? Me, that's who.

He let out a booming laugh. 'Yes, very noble – that's me! I'm Chris, by the way.' He stuck out an enormous hand and I shook it, feeling the rough callouses on his fingers as they touched mine. He couldn't have been much older than me, but his knuckles were thick and the tips of his fingers blunted and scuffed. He had the hands of a dockworker, not a doctor, and I felt momentarily sorry for anyone whose tricky knees needed fondling.

'Ruby,' I said, shaking his hand. I looked down at Archie, who was now rolling happily around in the sand, tongue lolling to one side. 'He's incredible. What a dog! What kind is he?'

'Irish wolfhound,' he said, leaning down to give him a scratch.

'He looks . . . primeval.'

'Excuse me! I'll have you know that he's a highly intelligent beast who only very occasionally eats his own sick. Aren't you, boy?' The dog looked up at him mournfully before scooting past to chase off a pair of seagulls. 'You see? A genius.'

'Obviously. So do you live near here?'

'Bit early to be inviting yourself round, isn't it?' he said, flashing a wicked grin.

'I'm not . . . I was just . . .' I stumbled and spluttered. It was too early for this sort of banter.

'Relax, I'm only joking. I live on the other side of those dunes there,' he said, pointing towards a few scrub-covered hills a half-mile away. 'Little cottagey thing. Nothing special, but it's quiet out there and there's no one around, so it suits me to the ground. You're at Bugle Hall, aren't you?'

I raised an eyebrow. 'How does everyone know that?'

'Come on, love. A group of strange Americans turn up, everyone knows where they are and what they're doing on a moment by moment basis. That's the village way.'

'We're not that strange.'

Now it was his turn to raise an eyebrow. 'I saw that tweedy couple haranguing the town drunk at the pub the other day, asking about his lineage,' he said. 'You can't fool me. A bunch of loonies.'

I held up my hands in admission. 'You're right, I can't defend it: we're all nuts. And yes, we're at Bugle Hall. It's . . . nice.'

'Come off it, it's like a bloody mausoleum there! I went there as a boy a few times: gave me the creeps. She still got all those animal figurines everywhere?'

'Like, thousands of them! And all of these commemorative plates with Princess Diana's face on them. It's kind of weird.'

'That's the English for you, love! Some of us, at least. Poor Mrs Willocks, still in mourning for our Diana. Never fully recovered from the loss.'

I remembered Mrs Willocks's kindly face and felt a crippling sense of guilt. 'God, I feel terrible. She's so nice!' I said hastily. 'And she's been such a good hostess!'

'I expect she's nice to you, making you pay through the nose to sleep with a bunch of creepy ceramic animals.' He caught the look on my face and looked sheepish. 'You're right, you're right – she's a lovely woman. I'm afraid that if you live in a small town long enough, you start to focus on people's . . . eccentricities.'

'No need to apologize,' I said. 'I live in New York – I silently wish at least three people dead on my commute every morning.'

'People, eh?' he said with a grin.

'Tell me about it,' I said. 'Anyway, I should get back. Mrs Willocks cooks a mean breakfast, and if I don't get there early, my dad will have polished the whole thing off.'

'Mrs Willocks a great cook?' he marveled. 'Well, you learn something new every day. Now, what are you planning to do with the rest of your day, once you've finished stuffing yourself full of Mrs Willocks's wares? I'm assuming you won't be wearing your shoes around your neck at the table, by the way. You don't need me to tell you that Mrs Willocks won't stand for sand in her doilies.'

I reached up and touched one of the sandy sneakers dangling by my shoulder and laughed. I was suddenly aware of what I must look like, and started tucking stray strands of salt-crusted hair behind my ears. 'I like the feel of the sand between my toes,' I said with an embarrassed shrug.

'Don't feel you need to explain on my behalf,' he said. 'I'd be out here naked as a jaybird if it wouldn't get me arrested.'

'And you think *I'm* the lunatic.'

'Tell you what: get on home and get yourself decent. I'll pick you up around noon and show you around this beautiful countryside of ours.'

The offer took me by surprise, and for a moment I was tempted to accept. I was desperate to see more of the place, and Chris seemed like a nice enough guy. Sure, I didn't know him at all, but what were the chances of this tiny village harboring a psychopath? A psychopath with a dog, no less? But then I thought about the look on Piper's face if I were to tell her that I'm abandoning my wedding duties to go joy-riding with a random northerner, and saw the folly of my thinking. 'I can't,' I said, 'I've got all this wedding stuff to sort out for my sister, and loads of the other guests are arriving today . . .'

'Tomorrow, then. I'll take you for a spin in the morning.'

I let out a laugh that was more like a bark. 'My sister would absolutely kill me if I left her side the day of the wedding, even for second. Sorry, it's not that I don't want to, it's just . . .'

'Say no more. You've left me a heartbroken shell of a man, of course, but I trust I'll recover in time.'

'You can always send me the therapist bill, if it comes to that.'

'This is England, pet! We don't have therapists, we have pubs.' He let out a whistle and Archie bounded towards us. 'First time he's ever responded to that,' he said. 'He must have taken a shine to you. Wants to impress.'

'I'm flattered,' I replied, giving Archie a goodbye scratch behind the ear.

'Right, good luck with the wedding, hope no one falls off a turret.'

'It's pretty much inevitable,' I said. 'Well, it was nice to meet you. Good luck with the tricky knees!' I started to jog away when I heard him call my name. I stopped and circled back to him.

'Here,' he said, thrusting a scrap of paper into my hand. 'Just in case you get a couple of minutes free before you go.' I looked down and saw that it was a slightly tattered business card. CHRIS DIXON: PHYSICIAN/MUSICIAN. 'Bit cheesy, I know,' he said, scuffing the sand with his foot. Archie the dog stared up at me expectantly.

'You're a musician?' I asked. I had always had a soft spot for musicians.

'Musician feels a bit strong,' he said. 'I play a bit of guitar in the Craster with my mates on a Saturday night, that sort of thing.'

'That's so cool!'

'I don't know if I'd describe us as cool,' he smiled. 'We specialize in Billy Joel's lesser-known work.'

I tucked the card into my sports bra. 'I'll give you a call if I get any free time,' I said. 'Or if I have any sudden Billy Joel cravings.'

'Careful,' he said with a grin. 'They can creep up on you. Give my regards to Mrs Willocks, by the way. And tell her my mam wants her Crock-Pot back!'

I could feel him watching me as I ran away, and heard Archie the dog give a mournful bark right before I slipped out of sight. There was a dull ache in my breastbone that felt something like regret.

Then

They were sitting in silence on the hood of Ethan's car, watching the stars wink above. Neither of them could think of anything to say that would be of comfort, either to themselves or each other, so the air was still between them apart from the sound of their breath and the occasional distant car passing by in the night.

It was Ruby's last night in Beechfield. Her bags were packed, her books were stacked in boxes, and her father had the route to New York plugged into his satnav. There was nothing left to do now except say goodbye, but right now that felt like an impossibility.

Ethan reached out and took her hand, his thumb gently rubbing her palm. She felt a thrill go through her at his touch, but it was quickly tamped down by the weight of her sadness. She knew that they should be tearing each other's clothes off right now, taking this opportunity to drink in every last drop, imprint themselves on each other's skin, but she also somehow sensed, now that she was out here beneath this black canopy of sky, that tonight would be a strangely chaste one. Both of them were crippled by the anxiety roiling in the pits of their stomachs.

'When do you start work?' Ethan asked finally, though he already knew the answer. She started on Monday. In two days' time, she would put on one of the business-smart outfits he'd gone with her to buy at the mall, get on the subway, walk down one of the wide, sweeping avenues he knew so well from the movies and would push through the door of some enormous glass skyscraper and be swept up in a world that he would never know and could never understand. Meanwhile he'd still be in Beechfield, serving shitty drinks to the same drunk loudmouths.

'Monday,' she said quietly. She felt a thrill of terror and excitement run through her, cutting through the sadness. New York, she thought to herself. For the past week, when the thought of leaving Ethan behind felt like a physical wound, she would conjure up an image of New York and marvel at it like a shiny new penny. New York will make all of this worth it, she told herself.

The silence descended again, each of them swallowed up by their thoughts. Ethan wondered how soon he'd be able to visit her. The thought of going to New York filled him with dread – he'd always hated the city because of its baseball rivalry with the Red Sox, and it wasn't doing itself any favors by stealing away the woman he loved – but he knew that, as soon as she got there, it would be the only place he'd want to be. He could go down for a weekend over Columbus Day, maybe, and then maybe she could come up a few weeks afterwards. Then, in the spring . . . well, he hadn't said anything to her yet, but he'd decided to go back to school. Ruby had been right: there were some interesting tech design courses around, some of them even in New York, so he'd sent out application forms to a couple. He knew that the only chance he had of keeping hold of Ruby was to try and make something out of himself. There was no way that she was going to stay with someone who was just a bartender, not when she'd soon have the whole of New York spread out at her feet. He had to try.

Ruby lay on her back and felt the residual warmth from the engine on her skin. There was a definite chill in the air, and the leaves on the trees overhead were starting to darken and droop. Soon the forests around here would be awash with brilliant color – reds and oranges and palest yellows – before the leaves finally gave up and dropped from their branches. She and her mother used to collect the prettiest leaves and press them between the pages of books to preserve them, though their color would always fade. After her mother died, she seemed to find them everywhere – each time she opened a book, brittle shards of dried leaves would flutter to the floor. Everything ends, she thought to herself, and felt a tear slide down her cheek and into the shell of her ear.

She looked over at Ethan lying next to her. His eyes were closed and the tips of his eyelashes cast a shadow in the moonlight. It would be so easy now to keep lying next to him and forget everything else: the job, the new apartment, Jessica, New York. She could stay in Beechfield with him. She could continue working in her father's office, maybe do some advertising work for him. She could spend her nights keeping Ethan company at Billy Jack's. They could move in together. It could all stay the same. It didn't have to change.

She sat up and wiped away the tracks of her tears. No, it didn't have to change, but it would. She'd worked too hard to give it all up for someone else, even if that someone else was the love of her life. She would move to New York tomorrow and start work on Monday – of course she would. How could she not? It was what she'd always wanted, and now it was stretched out in front of her. She hadn't meant to fall in love over the summer, but it had happened, and there was nothing she could do now to stop it. She couldn't give up Ethan, but she couldn't give up on what she'd wanted for herself, either.

Now

It was only noon, and already the house was overflowing with guests. Most of them were staying in B & Bs and Travelodges scattered across nearby towns, but Bugle Hall had quickly established itself as the central meeting point. Mrs Willocks was rushing around offering everyone cups of tea and an assortment of biscuits from a tin, a dazed expression on her face.

My hair was still damp from the shower when I came downstairs to find Ethan surrounded by a gaggle of young women. Taylor and Madison were perched at either side, their limbs somehow even more tawny and coltish than before. They threw their heads back and laughed every time he said something, and the rest of the room quickly followed. It was like stumbling across the court of Henry the Eighth, minus the threat of beheadings. Although at that particular moment, I have to say I wasn't completely opposed to the idea.

'Ruby!' Piper said, springing up from her seat. She grabbed me by the elbow and pulled me back into the hallway. I'd never seen her look so happy to see me. I was immediately suspicious. 'Thank *God* you're here. I'm having a total meltdown.'

'What's going on?' Please God don't let it be cold feet, I thought. I have traveled too far to have to negotiate a jilted groom.

'The wedding coordinator is *completely* incompetent. I told her that I wanted duck-egg blue trim for the place settings and it's *definitely* more like a sea green, and the florist has just called to say that she has a delivery of one hundred pink peonies waiting for me. Pink! I told her I wanted white!'

Organizational matters, however, were something I could deal with in my sleep. 'Piper, calm down. I'll handle it. Do you have the wedding coordinator's number?'

'No. Well, yes, but it doesn't matter, because I fired her.'

I stared at her for a minute, dumbfounded. 'You *fired* her? Piper, the wedding is tomorrow!'

Piper threw her hands up in disbelief. 'Ruby, how can I trust a woman who doesn't know the difference between duck-egg blue and sea green? And who orders the *wrong color* of peonies! She's obviously an idiot.'

I sighed. I should have seen this coming. If there was one thing Piper loved more than having staff, it was firing staff. 'We're in the middle of nowhere and anyway, even if we could magic up another wedding coordinator, there isn't time for her to start! Who's going to organize all the rest of it?' My heart began its rapid trajectory into my knees: I already knew the answer.

Piper beamed at me. 'You are, obviously!'

Jesus, take the wheel. I had calmed nervy clients about impending deadlines, I had soothed the ruffled feathers of sensitive creatives, I had even once redirected a plane for the MD of a Fortune 500 company. But I really, really wasn't sure that I could meet my sister's wedding expectations. 'I'm not a wedding coordinator! I don't know any of the people involved or the timings or anything!'

She looked up at me, green eyes wide and pleading. 'But you're so good at this kind of stuff – I mean, I know how much you love spreadsheets!'

'This is not helping to convince me.' It was true, though. I did love a spreadsheet.

'You know what I mean! You're, like, the queen of organization!' Piper took my hands in hers. 'Plus you're my big sister and my maid of honor and honestly if you don't agree to help me out with this I am going to flip out and then my face will break out from the stress and I'll look disgusting in the photos and oh my God I cannot handle this right now so please just say yes?'

I sighed and pulled her in for a hug. I was surprised once again by how brittle Piper felt in my arms, how delicate. Despite how absolutely nuts she drove me, I could never refuse to help my little sister. 'Of course,' I said, a familiar resignation settling in. 'Don't worry about a thing – I'll sort it all out.'

'You're the best,' Piper sniffled into my armpit, and I made a mental note to remind her of that fact later when she was throwing a fit over origami cranes. 'Okay,' she said, pulling me into the drawing room. The rest of the women barely looked up, all of them engrossed in whatever Ethan was saying. She handed me an enormous three-ring binder. 'This is the bible,' she said. 'It will tell you *exactly* what I want.' I rolled my eyes and she looked at me sternly. 'Do not deviate from the bible.'

I flicked through the binder, noting that each section was carefully tabbed and color-coded. I was impressed:

this was some high-level organizational voodoo. 'So you just need me to coordinate, right?'

'Basically, I need you to go around kicking ass and taking names. Just make sure that no one's slacking off or cheating me. Ruby,' she said, eyes shining, 'I'm trusting you with my *life* here. You can't let me down.'

I thought back to all of the times that Piper had said that to me: when I covered for her when she broke Dad's glasses, when she gave me her favorite Barbie doll to safeguard while she went to a sleepover, when I did her liquid eyeliner for her first high-school dance. There had been many, many life-entrusting moments between us. I smiled. 'I'll do my best.'

'Great. Ethan, can you ask Vic to come pick Ruby up and take her to the castle?'

Ethan looked surprised to see that I was in the room. 'Sure thing.' I was relieved to have a reason to leave – at least coordinating the wedding meant I wouldn't have to stand around here all day, feeling like a third nipple or a sixth toe.

Piper turned to me. 'Okay, so you need to be back here by four p.m. because that's when we're all going to get manicures, okay?' Group manicures. And so the nightmare begins.

I checked my phone. 'But that only gives me two hours!'

'That should be plenty of time!'

'Can't I just get a manicure on my own? I'm sure there's a place in town . . .'

Piper was appalled. 'Of course not! Everyone's nails have to be the same shape and color for tomorrow, which means we all have to do them together. Okay?'

'Okay.' I could feel a tension headache beginning to press at my temples.

'Don't forget to call the restaurant to confirm that they have a gluten-free option for the rehearsal dinner tonight. There is no *way* I'm going to be bloated tomorrow.'

'All right, all right! Jesus,' I muttered as I hefted the binder under my arm. I waved goodbye to the rest of the room as I headed out of the door, but no one seemed to notice.

Vic was already waiting in the driveway, which made me wonder if he was hiding in a thicket of trees at the end of the road, just waiting for Ethan to snap his fingers. He tipped his cap and opened the back door. 'I think I'll ride up front with you, if that's okay,' I said. I'd spent years being driven around New York by faceless taxi drivers, but I'd actually spoken to Vic now, so it felt weird to have him chauffeur me around. (Yes, I knew that was his job title, but still).

'Ruby! Wait!' I was about to climb in the passenger door when Ethan hurried up to the car, his jacket tucked under his arm. 'Do you need a hand with anything?'

I looked at him gormlessly. 'What, you mean the wedding?'

'Yeah,' he said, running a hand through his hair. I could feel my fortress crumbling and struggled to shore up the walls. 'I mean, I could come along with you to the castle, if you want. I'm the best man and everything, so I should help.'

'That's very gender-equality-minded of you,' I said, 'but I think I can manage to arrange a few peonies on my own. Besides, I wouldn't want to take you away from your adoring audience.' I am an ice queen, I thought to myself. I am some sort of lofty and elusive bird. Perhaps a swan.

He looked slightly stricken. 'I'm just trying to help.'

'You really don't have to,' I said. I am a lush tropical island, inhabited only by me. And with that, I slammed the door shut and waited for Vic to drive away. Which, embarrassingly, he didn't do until Ethan gave him the nod.

There was a tense silence in the car as we drove to the castle. I busied myself by thumbing through Piper's wedding bible, speculating on the exorbitant cost of the wedding favors (hand-engraved heart-shaped photo frames, each containing a black-and-white photograph of Piper and Charlie, and each encased in its own decorative pale-pink birdcage). All of this work – it must have taken her months. Where would all of Piper's energy go when the wedding was finally out of the way? Into making babies, I guessed. And then, after that, little pale-pink or pale-blue baby-shower favors, each encased in its own decorative birdcage.

I let out a sigh. Somehow, Ethan offering his help had been even more upsetting than him ignoring me, or watching him be fawned over by the bionic twins. That sort of solicitousness was so typical of him, or at least of the guy I used to know. He was so incredibly thoughtful when we were together, surprising me with little gifts and writing notes that he hid for me to find later, after he'd left. But now I knew it was just knee-jerk politeness, nothing more. I felt like someone's granny who needed help crossing the road, or an old mutt who'd got stuck down a well.

Vic glanced over at me. 'Rough day?' he asked.

'Sort of,' I admitted.

'Weddings can be very stressful,' he said with a sympathetic nod.

'Yeah, I guess.' You don't know the half of it.

'Anything else getting at you, love?' Or maybe he did. I looked over at him, surprised by the kindness in his voice. 'Go on, you can tell me. I'm like a bloody priest. I've been driving for twenty-odd years now, and the things people have told me would put hair on your chest. I can promise you'll not say anything that could shock us.'

'I'm fine, honestly,' I said, slightly more tersely than I'd intended, and immediately felt a stab of guilt. I knew that Vic was just trying to be nice, but that was exactly the problem. He was another man, looking at me pityingly and offering kindness. I didn't need kindness – I didn't need anything. I was a lone panther stalking through the jungle. I was an iron-clad torpedo shooting through the – I felt tears prick behind my eyes. 'Sorry,' I said quietly. 'I guess it has been a hard day.'

'Say no more, love. I'll leave you in peace.'

'I'm just a little on edge, that's all. It's not that I don't want to talk to you, it's just – well, I don't think I can bring myself to talk about it right now.' I knew that if I said another word on the subject, I'd burst into tears, which was an unacceptable and very un-fortress-like thing to do.

'No worries at all, we'll leave it at that. Now, have you seen Bamburgh yet?'

I saw that he was trying to change the subject, and swelled with gratitude. 'I saw it from the beach on my run this morning, but that's it. It looked . . . imposing.'

'You're not wrong there. Finest castle in the county, in my opinion, and gilded like the proverbial lily. Your sister will be over the moon when she sees it all done out for the wedding tomorrow.'

'You don't know my sister,' I muttered. Unless there was an actual coronation awaiting her, complete with coronet and sceptre, Piper would feel underwhelmed. And it was now my job to deliver it to her.

'Right,' Vic said. 'Where are we going first?'

I flipped through the binder. 'Looks like it's a florist called Bloomin' Gorgeous?'

'Christ, she's mad as a bat, that woman. Watch yourself, pet, she'll peck your eyes out if you're not careful!'

'Great,' I said. 'Just great.' But as I sat back in my seat, a little smile played at my lips. It was nice to feel useful. Besides, I was spoiling for a fight, even if it was with a crazy florist.

Then

Ruby arrived in New York with a face like a pie, eyes swollen to slits from crying. She was in her dream city, moving into her dream apartment with her best friend and about to start her dream job, and she was resolutely miserable.

Okay, maybe it wasn't exactly her dream apartment. It was a fifth-floor walk-up in Sunset Park, a neighborhood of auto-parts stores and bodegas (but not the nice bodegas they had in Park Slope or Cobble Hill). It was more off-brand dairy products and forty-ounces than organic kettle corn and choose-your-own craft six-pack. But it was cheap, and it was close to the subway and, on a hot summer's night, the smell of flautas and chicharrón wafting up from the kitchen of the little Mexican grandmother's apartment below was enough to make a grown woman weep. Well, an almost-grown woman at least.

Her father had driven her down from Beechfield, Ruby convulsing with sobs and him occasionally reaching across to give her an awkward pat on the back. She'd left Ethan standing in her driveway, staring after the car like a kicked puppy. He'd given her a mix CD when they kissed goodbye, and she had listened to it for the entire ride, eventually playing 'Yesterday' on repeat and keening all the way through the Battery Tunnel.

Jess opened the door and pulled her into a hug while Ruby's father silently unloaded the car. He didn't make a comment on the shitty neighborhood, or the fact the front door swung slightly off its hinges, or the endless flights of stairs he'd had to trudge up and down when bringing in mattress covers and shower caddies and favorite university hoodies, and box after heavy box of books she'd brought with her, most of which she'd already read and the rest of which she never would.

That evening, after her father had shoved the folded cardboard boxes into the back of his SUV – 'There's good money in them!' – and given her a hug so tight she could feel him holding his breath so he didn't cry, he climbed back into the car and drove off into the sunset, and Jess and Ruby got down to the business of getting incredibly, howlingly drunk.

Jess let her talk about Ethan for hours, listened as she told her that she'd never been so in love, that he was the one for ever, that being away from him would be unbearable, but that they'd make it work because they were made for each other, they were *destiny*, and silently poured more Ernest and Gallo rosé into the chipped Garfield mug Ruby had owned since fifth grade, and then finally, finally, right after she'd finished another crying jag, she sat her friend up, dusted her off, and told her to get a grip.

'I mean, I know you're heartbroken and I can totally see that you and Ethan love each other, and I'm sure you're going to do the whole long distance thing and it'll be fine, but this is *New York*! We are in fucking New York City! So tonight I'm allowing you to wallow in self-pity, but tomorrow, you and I are going to take this fucking town by *storm*, okay?'

'Tomorrow,' Ruby muttered, nodding weakly. And then, sitting bolt upright and wiping a dribble of rosé off her chin, 'Tomorrow! Shit, I start work tomorrow!'

'Fuck, yeah, you do,' Jess said, pouring more wine into the mug and swigging the rest from the bottle. 'And you are going to kill it.'

But the job, well . . . it wasn't exactly a dream, either.

Ruby emerged from the subway, blinking into the morning sunlight, and proceeded to head west, which was the exact opposite direction from the offices of Diamond Age Advertising. She realized her mistake half a block in, but was too embarrassed to turn around in case she was scoffed at by a crowd of seasoned New Yorkers who preyed on the weakness of newcomers, so she made a long, hasty loop down 59th, onto 5th Ave, and east on 58th before arriving, red-faced and sweating, in front of the wide, glass-fronted entranceway into her first ever adult job. She took a deep breath and pushed through the revolving doors into the marble foyer, ready to meet her future.

She took the elevator to the twenty-sixth floor and was greeted in reception by a stern-faced young woman, dwarfed by an enormous Plexiglas desk. Her tiny body was swathed in sample-saled Theory, and her face was slicked flawlessly in Mac. She did not smile. She barely acknowledged Ruby other than to roll her eyes slightly when she said her name and nod imperceptibly towards a lurid pink sofa shaped like a woman's pouting mouth. Ruby perched on the lower lip – hovered is a more accurate description considering her anxiety levels – and waited to be fetched.

Finally, after twenty excruciating minutes of sweating gently into the upholstery, a mop-haired man bounded into reception and shouted her name. It was Martin, the HR person – sorry, 'Head of People Movement' – who had interviewed her back in May. He was wearing a Stone Roses T-shirt, pulled too tight across his rounded stomach, and a pair of stonewashed black jeans that managed to be both too small and too large for him at the same time. There was a nervous, frenetic energy surrounding him, and when he smiled, revealing a row of smallish teeth capped by largish gums, he reminded Ruby of a jittery colt. She avoided making any sudden movements that might startle him as she followed him through the office.

'Here are our account managers, Tara and Melanie,' he said, pointing towards two interchangeably lacquered and bronzed blonde women. They both gave Ruby weak smiles before turning back to their laptops. He pointed across the room to an empty section of office bisected by a ping-pong table. 'That's the creative department, but it's still a little early for them – they were here until three a.m. last night, so they probably won't be in until ten.' She swallowed heavily at the thought of someone other than a bartender working until three o'clock in the morning. 'Here we've got our strategy guru, Simon' – a man wearing a cardigan and a knitted tie looked up from his Moleskine notebook and gave her a small wave – 'and down there we've got production.' She glanced over to see three people, two men and a woman, all albino-pale, huddled around a Mac Pro and whispering in harried tones.

There were two frosted-glass cubes settled in opposite corners of the otherwise open-plan space. She pointed to them and asked Martin if they were meeting rooms.

'No way,' he said, giving her a withering look. 'We don't believe in meeting rooms at Diamond Age Advertising. Transparency is one of our core beliefs. We're all about transparency here, right, guys?' No one bothered to look up. 'Anyway, those offices belong to the two big guys – the MD, Paul Gold, and –'

'Why didn't he just call it Golden Age Advertising?' she interrupted before she could stop herself.

Martin looked at her quizzically. 'I don't think we're connecting here – what do you mean?'

'You know,' she said, hating herself as the words left her mouth. 'Paul Gold, Golden Age . . .'

'Right, right!' Martin said, but she could tell it wasn't. 'It was a creative choice, actually. Because diamonds are worth more than gold, and we believe in clarity of thought . . .' he dwindled off.

'Of course! I get it! That makes total sense. Sorry, I was just being stupid.'

'Hey, there are no bad ideas here,' he said. He gave her an earnest, imploring look. 'But you should know that Paul is a true visionary.'

'I'm sure.' They blinked at each other for a few seconds. 'And the other office?' she asked. The subject of Paul seemed like a minefield and she was eager to move on.

'That belongs to our Head of Creative, Jefferson Peters.'

'Did somebody say my name?' Ruby turned to see a tall, tanned man with an easy smile striding towards her. He was wearing a light-blue button-down and worn-in jeans, the frayed hems of which crowned a pair of old Converse, and his hair was raked back from his forehead, revealing a pair of blue eyes lightly lined at the edges. 'What lies are you telling this poor, innocent young woman about me?' He was addressing Martin, but his eyes never left Ruby's.

'This is Ruby Atlas, our new office junior,' Martin said, presenting her like she was the prize pig at a county fair.

'Nice to meet you, Mr Peters,' she said, offering him a clammy hand. 'I read about your win at Cannes last year. Congratulations – it's an honor to work with you.'

'Flattery will get you everywhere,' he said, taking her hand in his and holding it for a fraction of a beat too long. 'And call me Jefferson – Mr Peters is my father, and he's dead.'

'I – I'm sorry,' she said, stuttering over her words.

'Don't be, he was an asshole. Which is why I don't want you calling me by his name. Now, I'm sure Martin here will take excellent care of you' – Martin beamed at this – 'but if you need anything, don't hesitate to ask, okay? This place can be a little rough at first, but my door is always open.'

'Thanks,' she mumbled, 'but I'm sure it'll be okay. I'm not afraid of hard work.'

'I bet you're not,' he said, in a slightly ambiguous tone. Something about him made her nervous on a deep, almost cellular level. 'Well, it's nice to meet you, Ruby, and I'm sure I'll be hearing great things about you. But right now, I'd better get to work.' And with that, he slid past them into his office, leaving her and Martin quaking with adoration in his wake. The door clicked shut behind him.

'Right!' Martin said, still pinked with pleasure. 'Let's get you indoctrinated!'

The rest of the day was a blur of meetings, Excel spreadsheets, diary bookings and taxi organization. Every time someone approached her desk with yet another task – usually Tara or Melanie, though she found it impossible to distinguish between the two – she would sit upright and alert, like a gopher peering up out of its hole. Every question seemed steeped in potential disaster and, she quickly realized, usually was. She booked a taxi for a client pick-up from the wrong airport. She served Earl Grey rather than mint tea to Paul. She accidentally deleted an important meeting from the internal calendar, sending the account team (Tara and Melanie again, who weren't even bothering with the pretence of politeness at this point) into a paroxysm of rage. After years of quietly shining at everything she did – class treasurer, captain of the soccer team, full-ride scholarship to a good university, universally praised and petted by various teachers and coaches and professors and guidance counsellors throughout her twenty-two years on the planet – Ruby was suddenly, decidedly, deemed lacking. And the more she screwed up, the more inclined she was to screw up again, until, by the end of the day, she was a giant, jangling ball of nerves.

She was still at her desk at 10 p.m. that night. She could see that she had eight – eight! – missed calls from Ethan, and she knew he was probably worried about her, but she was in too deep to think about calling him back, and was also convinced that she'd burst into tears at the sound of his voice. Her desk was covered in a light dusting of Post-it notes, each written to remind her of something she'd learned throughout the day or, more likely, something she had yet to learn but needed to urgently. The office was largely empty at this point, most of her co-workers having taken advantage of what was apparently a relatively quiet day to go to a late Pilates class (Tara and Melanie) or the Kurosawa film that was screening in the Bowery (the strategy team) or to do lines of coke off a mistress's taut abdomen (Paul, she would come to learn). Ruby lingered behind, playing a desperate game of Jenga with the internal office diary, and wondering if she needed to write a formal letter of resignation after only a day of work, or if she could just quietly evaporate.

'Rough day?' She looked up to see Jefferson perched neatly on the side of her desk. She hadn't heard him leave his office and she started slightly at the sight of him. 'Sorry to scare you,' he said. 'You looked pretty intense there. Everything okay?'

'Oh, yeah, fine!' she said brightly, swallowing the ping-pong ball of suppressed tears that had lodged itself in her throat.

'You sure about that? Because you don't look so fine.' He smiled in a concerned, paternal way that made the lines at the edges of his eyes crinkle, and she felt the ping-pong ball swell to a grapefruit.

'It's just a lot to get my head around,' she squeaked.

'I know, this place can be pretty nuts, and we don't exactly hand-hold around here, but I'm sure you're doing a great job. Hell, the fact that you're still here at the end of your first day is a pretty good sign. A lot of kids just disappear at lunch and never come back.'

She thought of the mournful taco she'd shoved down her throat while eyeing up the entrance to the nearest subway station a few hours earlier. 'Seriously? That's so irresponsible.'

'Well, not everyone's got what it takes. But it looks like you do.'

His eyes did that crinkly thing again, and even managed to twinkle, and she felt her heart soar a little. 'Thanks,' she said quietly, suppressing a grin.

'Any time.' He started to walk away, and then turned back towards her, as though a thought had just occurred to him. 'Hey, want to get a drink? I know a place that makes a killer Manhattan. Just the thing to take the edge off your first day.'

She wavered. Surely going for a drink with the boss was inappropriate, right? Or was it exactly the sort of thing that made someone a success? Ruby tried to imagine what Murphy Brown might do in her position, but her brain stalled. The image of the eight missed phone calls from Ethan bobbed into view and she shook her head. 'I'd better not,' she said, gesturing at her detritus-strewn desk.

'Nose to the grindstone,' he said, nodding approvingly. 'I like it. Don't stay too late – the guards lock the doors at midnight and you don't want to have to sleep over on your first night – people will talk.'

'Will do!' she said. 'Have a good night!' At this point, she just wanted him to leave her to her impending nervous breakdown in peace.

'See you tomorrow for more fun and games,' he said, giving her a salute as he walked out of the door. She heard it click quietly behind him, and pulled out her phone: 10:23 p.m. and another two missed calls from Ethan. She shoved it in her desk drawer: he'd have to wait.

Now

I got back to the house just in time for Mrs Willocks's afternoon tea. The smell of freshly baked scones greeted me as I walked through the door, and she immediately thrust a cup and saucer into my hands, overlooking the fact that my arms were already laden with shopping bags full of fresh flowers. 'They're just in the parlor, love,' she said, shooing me down the hallway. 'There's milk and sugar on the sideboard. I'll be in with the cakes and what-have-you in just a tick!' And with that, she scurried back into the kitchen. Poor Mrs Willocks still seemed deeply unsettled by the presence of guests.

I walked into the parlor to see everyone perched on various upholstered surfaces, saucers balanced on knees or placed on nearby tables. Ethan was, unsurprisingly, sitting between Taylor and Madison, the three of them deep in discussion about something (my guess was either sex or the Internet). My dad and Candace were playing cards with Bob and Barbara at a little table in the middle of the room, Dad's mouth pulled tight as he looked at his dwindling pile of chips. 'This game is rigged,' I heard him say.

'That's what they always say,' I said, swooping down to give him a kiss on the top of the head. 'Bob's got a full house,' I whispered in his ear, and my dad sighed and placed his cards face down on the table.

'Ruby!' Piper exclaimed, leaping to her feet and thrusting her cup and saucer into Charlie's free hand. 'You're back! Tell me everything. Is it a complete disaster? It's a disaster, isn't it?'

'Piper, let your sister take a breath,' Charlie said. 'She's only just come through the door.'

Piper shot him a dirty look. 'Do you not get that my wedding is tomorrow?'

'Hey, easy there now,' I said. 'Nothing is a disaster.' I placed the cup and saucer on a side table and dumped the bags on the floor before flopping into an empty armchair. The truth was, I was exhausted. The wedding, while not a disaster, had been on the cusp of becoming one. Piper had been right about the wedding coordinator – she had been completely incompetent. Now, after shouting, bribing and cajoling my way across the North East, I still wasn't entirely sure that it would all go off without a hitch tomorrow. I still had to arrange the bouquets – the florist had indeed been a madwoman, and had simply handed me several carrier bags filled with flowers, and shoved me out the door – and the photographer was claiming that he had shingles. Not that I was going to share any of that with Piper. 'Everything's fine,' I said, in the voice I used to soothe nervy clients. 'It's all under control.'

'Thank God,' Piper said, sitting back down on the sofa and grabbing her cup and saucer back from Charlie. 'I knew you could do it.'

'Yep! It's going to be great!' My phone bleeped in my bag and I was thankful for the distraction. It was a text from Jess.

What's happening? Are you still a fortress? Has he realized what a
total tool he's being?

'I've got to take this,' I said apologetically. 'It's work.' I
grabbed the bags and hurried out of the door.

'Clock never stops for you, does it, kiddo?' my dad
called after me as I ran up the stairs.

No, he's too busy being swathed in nubile twins. Am fine though.
Fortress strong.

I shut the door to my bedroom and sat down on the
floor. I pulled the flowers out of the bags and laid them
out in front of me – two hundred white peonies, huge
bushels of baby's breath, the occasional sprig of
greenery, and finally – bizarrely – a packet of rosemary.
I looked at it all in despair. Craftiness has never been my
particular forte – I once glued my thumb and forefinger
together when trying to fix a table leg – so I was pretty
stumped as to how I was going to make four bouquets
and a dozen table arrangements that would pass muster
with Piper.

I decided to channel the 'homespun and rustic' trend. I
grabbed a few peonies, stuck a wad of baby's breath next
to it and tied it together with a piece of twine. It looked
lopsided and sad. I sighed and leaned against the side of
my bed. Maybe if I had a little glass of wine, it might get
my creative juices flowing . . .

I was searching through one of the bags for the bottle
of red I'd stashed in there from the shop, when there was
a knock at my door. 'Yes?' I called.

'It's Maddie,' came the voice from the other side of the door. 'Can I come in?'

Shit. Just what I needed at this particular juncture in time. 'Just a second!' I started frantically shoving the flowers back into the bags – if she reported back to Piper that I had a small, unkempt greenhouse up here, I was toast.

I pushed the bags under the bed and opened the door. Madison was standing in front of me holding a pair of gardening sheers and a large spool of white ribbon. 'I thought you might need a hand,' she said in a conspiratorial whisper before pushing her way into the room.

'What do you mean?' I asked innocently, even though the jig was very obviously up.

'I saw the bags of flowers,' she said. 'I've been on enough sets to know a botanical nightmare when I see one. Don't worry,' she added when she saw the look on my face, 'I didn't say anything to Piper. Ignorance is bliss and everything.'

'Where did you get the gardening sheers?'

She shrugged. 'Mrs Willocks is the type of person who has an emergency flower-arranging kit on hand. I just asked.'

'Good thinking,' I said, quietly seething. As if it wasn't bad enough that I had to spend the rest of the afternoon frantically pulling together flowers, I now had to do it in the company of my ex's new love interest, who – and I was already certain of this without seeing her hold as much as a stem – was much, much better at this sort of thing than I was. Probably better than me at most things, I thought, being a multitasking hyphen-happy millennial.

'Should we get to work?' She folded her long legs under her like a particularly elegant piece of collapsible garden furniture and pulled the bags of flowers out from under the bed. 'Oh, this will be a piece of cake,' she said, inspecting the peonies. 'I'll arrange and you tie – deal?'

'Deal.'

We settled into a rhythm within minutes. As suspected, she was very, very good at flower arranging. Watching her work was like watching Blake Lively's Instagram account come to life, and each bouquet she handed me was beautiful, perfectly rounded and symmetrical.

'So,' she asked, after snipping the ends off another bunch of baby's breath, 'have you known Ethan a long time?'

Here we go, I thought. Nothing's free in this world, not even flower arranging. 'Yeah,' I said, trying to keep the guarded edge out of my voice. 'We used to know each other really well, but we lost touch over the years.' There, that was ambiguous enough.

'He's such a cool guy,' she said. 'Did you know he just set up a charity to provide Internet access in sub-Saharan Africa?'

'Yep, he's quite a guy,' I said quietly. 'Could you hand me the ribbon?'

'So were you guys just friends, or were you together together?'

I groaned inwardly. How was this turning into a very special episode of *Oprah*? 'We were together for a little while,' I said. 'But like I said, it was years and years ago. Before this wedding, we hadn't seen each other in a long time.'

'Do you mind if I ask why you guys broke up?' I do, I really, really do. 'Sorry,' she said, with a small apologetic smile. 'I know I'm being super nosy, but I'm just curious. It feels like you guys would be such a good fit, you know?'

I raised an eyebrow. 'You think?'

'Sure! You're both funny and cool, you both have these glamorous jobs –'

'His job is a little more glamorous than mine,' I pointed out. 'And yours isn't exactly unglamorous, either.'

She waved me away. 'I basically work in tech sales,' she said. 'People only think it's glamorous because it has something to do with fashion.'

'Well, yes,' I said, 'that and the fact that you're ridiculously gorgeous and are apparently running a small empire at the age of twelve.'

'I'm twenty-three!' she said. 'That's basically ancient in my industry. I'm like an old granny now.' We both let this idea sink in – if she was an old granny, I was literally Methuselah. 'So,' she said finally, 'you really don't think there's anything between you and Ethan anymore?' She busied herself with the next bouquet, but I clocked her watching me out of the corner of her eye, half coy, half shy.

'Definitely not,' I said, shaking my head. 'Like I said, it was a long, long time ago. Ancient history.'

I saw her smile and my heart felt like it had been sucker punched. 'Cool,' she said. 'Can you hand me that bunch of rosemary? I think I might stick a sprig in each of the bouquets. You know, "rosemary, for remembrance".'

She was the last person I expected to be quoting Shakespeare at me. She saw my expression and laughed. 'I minored in English Lit,' she explained. 'All of my friends made fun of me for it, but I just loved books too much to just go to school for business and coding, you know? I actually did my thesis on the significance of flowers in Elizabethan literature . . .'

I watched her face light up as she talked about the varied symbolic nature of the rose and realized that I actually liked her. She wasn't just some beautiful young girl with cotton candy for brains – she was smart, and funny, and thoughtful. All of which should have made the fact that Ethan had obviously fallen for her easier, but instead just filled me with a heavy, sluggish sadness.

We were nearly finished with the table centrepieces when there was another knock on the door. 'You guys alive in there?' Ethan opened the door without waiting for a response and grinned down at the two of us on the floor. 'Well, isn't this picturesque?' he said with a smile.

'Shut the door!' Madison and I chorused.

'Okay! Okay!' he said, stepping in and closing the door behind him. He produced a bottle of wine and a corkscrew from behind his back. 'I thought you guys might need a little liquid encouragement.'

'We really, really do,' I said gratefully. 'There are a couple of glasses by the sink.'

He retrieved them and poured each of us a glass of red. 'So how's it all coming?' he asked me. 'Have you glued your fingers together yet?'

He'd been on the phone with me during the table leg incident of 2005. In fact, he'd been the one to tell me to pour nail polish remover over my fingers to unstick them, getting the instructions out in little burst in between bouts of laughter. 'No glue involved, thankfully,' I said. 'Plus, Madison has basically been doing all the work. I've been demoted to string-tying, and I know that as soon as she's finished she's going to go back and retie all of the ugly bows I've made.'

Madison smiled at me sheepishly. 'Guilty as charged,' she said with a laugh. 'Hey,' she said, turning to Ethan. 'I was thinking we could go through that stuff we were talking about. Once we're finished, I mean,' she added, shooting me a glance. 'Stuff' was clearly a code word for sex. I sagged inwardly at the thought.

'Sure,' Ethan said with an easy grin. 'Happy to.' I'll bet you are, I thought to myself. Pervert. 'But I don't want to take you away from the flowers or anything. I can see important work is being done here.'

'I think I can take it from here,' I said quickly. 'There are only a couple of centrepieces left to do, and we can do the bows tomorrow. Or you can, I mean.'

'Are you sure?' Madison asked, but it was clearly rhetorical as she was already climbing to her feet and dusting herself down. 'I mean, I don't want to run out on you or anything.' She very clearly wanted to run out, but that was fine by me. As long as they left the wine, I was happy for them to clear out as soon as possible.

'Sorry, I didn't mean to break up the party,' Ethan said as they headed out. 'You sure you're okay up here?'

I tilted my glass towards him in salute. 'Never been better.'

'Well, if you glue yourself to anything, you know who to call.' He paused in the doorway for a minute. 'You still do that thing, huh?'

'What thing?'

'That thing where you tap your teeth with your fingernail when you're concentrating on something.'

'I don't do that!' I said, even though I knew that I did. It was one of my more annoying habits – I even annoyed myself with it. But I remembered now that Ethan used to think it was cute. Or at least he said he did.

'Don't try to deny it,' he said. 'You should knock it off, though. Bad for the enamel.'

'I didn't know that you were a dentist now, too. So many strings to your bow – watch out you don't hang yourself.'

'I'm a true Renaissance man,' he said. He slipped out of the room, shutting the door behind him.

I leaned back against the bed and took a long sip of wine. The floor around me was littered with the snipped ends of stems and little bits of twine, and I noticed a damp patch spreading on the carpet from where I'd placed a chill box full of greenery. I'd have to clean up before poor Mrs Willocks saw the mess and had a heart attack.

I closed my eyes, sank the rest of the glass, and tried not to picture the sort of stuff now inevitably being discussed in a room nearby.

I am a fortress, I thought to myself. An impenetrable fortress. In a couple of days, I'll be on a flight back to New York. Back to my apartment. Back to my job. Back to normal.

The thought didn't give me as much comfort as I'd hoped.

Then

'You heard from that girl of yours yet?' Charlie had made himself at home on his usual bar stool and was aimlessly chucking peanuts into his mouth.

'You know those peanuts have been touched by a thousand unwashed hands in this place, right?' Ethan said, moving the dish away.

Charlie lunged forward and took another handful. 'I'm not a pussy about germs like you.'

'Suit yourself, but answer me this: have you ever seen Mick Dewey wash his hands after he's taken a piss?'

Charlie dropped the nuts back into the bowl. 'Point taken. Have you heard from her or what?'

Ethan ignored him and kept polishing a spot on the mahogany bar until it gleamed with a deep shine. He hadn't heard from Ruby at all, not since she'd left him a drunken message late last night, her voice slurred and mumbling. Must have been wine, and lots of it. After a few years of bartending, Ethan was familiar with the intricacies of various drunks: the rageful gin drunk, the sleepy beer drunk, the happy-'til-you-puke tequila (or, in Ruby's case, bourbon) drunk. Wine drunk made people sound like they'd been hit with a tranquilizer dart, which in a way he supposed they had. Ruby had sounded specifically white wine drunk: too hyper to be red wine, plus he could hear her crazy friend Jess singing Destiny's Child in the background, which didn't really happen with red wine. Usually red wine drunk people passed out before they got to the Beyoncé portion of the evening.

He'd tried to call her back after he picked up the message, but it was at the end of his shift and she was asleep by then. He'd called again today, a couple of times – he knew she was at work, but surely she could take five minutes to take a phone call? – but her cell had gone straight to voicemail. It had been two weeks since Ruby had left, and he'd only managed to talk to her a handful of times thanks to their clashing schedules and the long hours she was pulling at the ad firm. Though why she was so dedicated to a job that treated her like such shit, he had no idea.

'I'm guessing that's a no, then,' Charlie said, a sly grin on his face. He'd already forgotten about Mick Dewey's unwashed hands and had resumed tossing peanuts into his mouth. 'I told you, man. You're fucking crazy to even try this long-distance shit. I mean, seriously, what's the point? You're going to get laid once every eight weeks – tops! – but she'll probably dump your ass for some rich banker asshole before you even get your first conjugal visit.'

Ethan dropped the cloth on the bar. 'You're a real asshole, you know that?'

'I'm not trying to bust your balls, I'm just trying to get you to see some sense. You could be having sex with a different woman every night,' he said, gesturing around the bar.

Ethan followed his gaze, taking in the table of divorcées who met at Billy Jack's every week to shriek about their low-life ex-husbands (Zinfandel drunk) and the few solitary women propping up the bar, the skin hanging loose on their sinewy arms as they raised their glasses to their lips (whisky – though it might as well have been motor oil for all they cared). 'Yeah, I'm clearly missing out.'

'Okay, tonight's a bad example. But there are plenty of hot chicks who come in here! Dude, Kelly Wallace was in here a couple of nights ago giving you the "come-fuck-me" eyes! I mean, Ruby's a nice girl and everything, but Kelly fucking Wallace! Come on!'

Ethan shrugged. 'I love her,' he said. He turned his back on Charlie and started polishing the bottles of liquor lined up on the back bar, hoping he would drop it. Which, of course, he didn't.

'I'm just trying to look out for you. I mean, I like Ruby, and obviously I love her sister, but –'

'Wait, you love Piper?'

'Yeah,' he said, staring down at the bar top. 'I do.' It was the first time Ethan had ever seen him look humble.

'Holy shit, man – are you serious? Have you told her?'

'Of course I've told her. I told her on our third date.'

'You told her you loved her on the third date? What are you, crazy?'

'Nah, I'm decisive.'

'What did she say?'

'That she loved me too, of course. What else would she say?' Ethan couldn't argue with his logic. 'Anyway,' Charlie continued, 'this isn't about my love life – which, as we can all see, is amazing – it's about yours. I just don't want to see you wasting your best years on someone who isn't in it to win it, you know?'

'My best years? You're working on your father's factory floor sweeping up scraps of toffee and I'm polishing bottles in a shithole. Would you seriously describe these as our best years?'

'Abso-fucking-lutely,' Charlie said, taking a long swig of his beer and tipping it towards Ethan in a silent toast.

'Then you've got a fucked-up sense of what's good.' He sighed and glanced at his watch. It was 11:30 p.m. – surely Ruby would be out of work by now. 'Look, will you watch the bar for me a second? I've got to take a piss.'

'Sure thing. Just don't blame me if there's a couple of beers missing at the end of your shift tonight.'

'Like you've ever paid for a beer in this place!' He walked into the stockroom and pulled the phone out of his pocket. He dialed Ruby's number, but the polite automated voice came on, asking him to please leave a message after the tone. He hung up. Maybe she'd gone for a drink with her colleagues after work, he thought, fresh-faced guys in button-down shirts called Ned and Teddy who would order 'Tanq Ten and Ts' and smoke roll-ups by choice and discuss the various merits of Bob Dylan B-sides. Guys who'd gone to college and had team track sweatshirts and the collected works of Pablo Neruda to prove it. Guys who were probably, right at this minute, placing a soft hand on the small of his girlfriend's back as they threw their heads back and laughed at the joy of being 'young professionals' in New York City, like they were the first and only people ever to grace God's earth with their special snowflake presence.

Fuck, he needed a cigarette. He leaned out of the stockroom and shouted to Charlie to give him another five.

'Have you got any more peanuts?' Charlie called back.

'Under the speedwell!' How a guy who came from that much money could have so little class, he'd never know, but he loved him all the more for it, in his own begrudging way.

Ethan went outside and leaned against the cool brick wall. It was dark in the side alley, with only the faint glimmer of a distant street lamp to help guide the cigarette to his lips, and then the red glow of the tip once it was lit. It had been hot earlier in the day, the muggy heat of August having pulled itself into September, but now the night air had a tinge of cold to it, and he could sense the oncoming crispness of autumn. Soon, it would be all pumpkin-spiced lattes and hay rides and apple-picking around Beechfield, and then the first few cotton-ball-bearded Santa Clauses would appear in the drugstore aisles, and they'd all pile into the sled for the long descent into winter.

He was pondering this, interspersed with images of a blond guy called Tad making out with Ruby, when his phone rang. It was her.

'Hey,' he said, trying to sound casual. 'How was your day?'

'Oh, you know,' she said, 'sort of shitty. Tara spilled her coffee in my lap – I'm pretty sure it was intentional – and I fucked up the lunch order. But other than that, it was okay.'

He didn't know, not even in the slightest, and the sound of her voice on the other end of the phone, tinny and slightly small, made him feel further away from her than he'd thought possible. 'Well, I hope she didn't burn you.'

'Nah, it wasn't that hot. Sorry I'm calling so late,' she added. 'The day kind of got away from me.'

'That's okay. I'm at the bar, Charlie's keeping me company. It's all good.' It's all good? Who was he now, Mark McGrath? 'Did you go for a drink after work or something? With your new work friends?' He could hear the wheedling anxiety in his voice now and kicked himself. Or, more accurately, he kicked the wall.

'No,' she said, sounding even smaller. 'Just working.'

'Still?'

'Yeah. There's a big pitch on next week, and everyone's freaking out about it . . . I think we'll all be here until at least midnight, but probably later.'

'So your colleagues are there with you?' He hated Teddy and Tad and Ned even more now, imagining them all gathered around Ruby as they ordered her to shovel more coal onto the coalface, their pink cheeks flushed with sadistic pleasure. 'I hope they'll at least get you a taxi home. It'll be way too late for you to be riding the subway.'

'I'm fine,' she said tersely, and he realized he'd got it wrong. There was a pause as the waves crackled between them. 'Only the partners get taxis home,' she said, her voice a little softer now, 'and anyway, the subway is totally safe. Little kids ride it on their own, so I'll be fine. Honest.'

'Well, give me a call when you get back to the apartment,' he said. 'Just for my own peace of mind.'

'I don't know what time that'll be,' she said. 'I'll probably just crash as soon as I get in. I'll have to be back in super early tomorrow.'

'Oh,' he said, hoping his disappointment wasn't too obvious. 'Of course, yeah. Just get some sleep if you can. And don't let them work you too hard.'

'Unlikely,' she said with a little laugh. 'I've got to get back inside. I'll give you a call tomorrow on my lunch break, okay?' He could hear her hurrying now, her breath slightly catching as she spoke, her heels clicking as she walked.

'Sure,' he said. 'Sounds good.'

'Sorry, I don't mean to blow you off or anything but . . . it's just been a weird day, that's all.'

'Don't worry about it.'

'God, I haven't even asked you about your day! I am a terrible girlfriend.'

'My day was fine.' He thought about the letter he'd received from the art college in Brooklyn, politely informing him that they didn't have space for him in the spring enrolment, but welcoming him to apply again next year. 'Totally uneventful. Now go back to work – go! I've got to get back before Charlie drinks himself under the table.'

'I love you, you know,' she said, and he could finally hear the Ruby he knew.

'I love you, too,' he said. 'Just do me one favor: if a guy called Teddy offers you a drink, don't take it.'

'Who the hell is Teddy?'

'Forget it.' They said their goodbyes and he headed back into the bar to find Charlie plugging nickels into the jukebox.

'A whole hour of the Stones coming up,' he said through a mouthful of peanuts.

Ethan leaned his elbows on the bar, helped himself to a beer, and let the opening strains of 'Goodbye, Ruby Tuesday' wash over him.

'Shit,' Charlie said, realizing the mistake. 'Sorry, dude.'

'It's cool,' Ethan said, and he nearly sounded convincing.

Now

'Ruby! Over here!'

I spotted Candace waving at me from across the room. I weaved my way through the crowd – which was full of people I'd either never met before or had met but whose names I couldn't remember – and slid into the seat next to her. 'Who are all these people?' I asked.

'Oh, who knows? Friends of the Armstrongs, I guess. Is that champagne?' Candace plucked a flute off a passing tray and raised it in salute. 'Good Lord, I've missed champagne.'

I shot her a sidelong look. 'Not a lot of champagne in Florida?'

'If there is, sweetheart, I haven't been drinking it. Your dad . . . well, he's tightened his belt so much that I wonder how he still has any circulation in his legs.'

'I thought he was getting back on his feet?'

'Well, sort of, but it's not exactly the lifestyle of the rich and famous around our house. He lost a lot of money when the bottom fell out back in 2008, and I don't think we're going to see it again, even though your father is dead set on working himself into the ground to get it all back.'

'I didn't realize it was that bad.' My dad and I hadn't had a conversation in a long time, not a real one. Our weekly phone calls consisted of a series of questions shot out by him like cannon fire, which I either deflected or absorbed.

'We're not in the poorhouse, if that's what you mean. But your father . . . well, it's been tough on him.' She paused. 'On us.'

I was worried now. My dad could be utterly absurd at times, and infuriating – but he had a big, soft marshmallow centre behind all that bravado, and I knew he loved Candace with all his heart. I turned to face her. 'You guys are okay, right?'

Candace necked the rest of her champagne and grabbed another glass from the nearby waiter, a far-off look on her face. 'Don't let anyone tell you that marriage isn't hard work,' she said. 'It should be unionized or something.'

Oh God, that didn't sound good. Not at all. I tried to rally. 'I know he can be hard to deal with, but he loves you.'

Candace patted my hand. 'I know he does, baby girl. I love him, too.' Her tone was more one of resignation than affection, like someone who'd been saddled with a kindly but meddlesome elderly relative, or a sickly cat. 'Anyway, here he comes, the man himself.'

I glanced up to see my dad weaving across the floor towards us. He was wearing a suit that I vaguely recognized from a funeral a few years ago, and his tie – too wide, too shiny – was slightly askew. I remembered when he had been voted Best Dressed Man in Beechfield – twice! – and the sight of him looking like something out of a Sears catalogue made me wince. 'How are my two favorite girls?' he asked as he sidled up next to us. He had a rocks glass full of whisky in one hand and an unlit cigar in the other. 'You two talking about me? My ears are burning!'

'They must be charred to hell by now,' Candace muttered under her breath. My jaw was clamped so tightly I worried I'd break it.

'We were just talking about the restaurant!' I said, as brightly as I could. 'How . . . modern it is!' The restaurant was a towering marble and glass slab perched on a headland with views overlooking the sea. Inside, it was all glossy surfaces and sharp edges, and from the look of the canapés emerging from the kitchen, the chef – a young gun with two Michelin stars under his belt – was very fond of foams. My heart sank at the sight of them – after a decade in New York, I'd seen enough foams and essences and emulsifications to last a lifetime. I had a sudden, deep desire to be back in the fuggy warmth of the Old Bell, the sound of darts hitting the board in the background and the barman glowering at me from his perch. And Chris, perched at the bar, sardonic smile on his face and Archie at his feet. I fingered the little scrap of paper in the pocket of my bag. Maybe I should have given him a chance. Or at least half a chance . . .

'Those Armstrongs know how to throw a party, huh?' Dad said, nodding approvingly. His cheeks were ruddy and I wondered how many whiskies he'd sampled so far. 'All class.'

'It's pretty fancy, all right,' I said.

'Lots of important people to rub elbows with, too. That's Dale Evans over there – he's a big cheese up at Intel now – and I think I saw Patty Drysdale earlier. Lot of money in this room,' he said, rubbing his hands together. 'Lot of money.'

I felt a flash of irritation. The man's marriage was on the brink of destruction and all he could think about was networking with a bunch of jerks who were probably all laughing at him behind his back. 'Jesus, Dad, you sound like Scrooge McDuck. Are you going to ask them to stick all their gold coins in a pile so you can swim around in them?'

He let out a hearty laugh. 'I wish, kiddo! I wish.' He narrowed his eyes and scanned the room again. 'I think I see old Jack Weathervale over there,' he said, gesturing towards an elderly man in golf slacks who was quietly dribbling one of the foams down the front of his polo shirt. 'Treasurer of the club now, apparently. He was always a man who liked to gamble, and I think he's got a condo down in Florida now . . . I think I'll go say hello, tell him about my idea. Give him a chance to get in on the ground floor, eh, honey?' He grabbed Candace's waist and squeezed, and she stumbled slightly in her heels.

'Go get 'em, baby,' she said, giving him a kiss on the cheek. I was amazed by her ability to still sound so upbeat, even when we all knew that Dad had more of a chance of getting money out of the foam emulsion than he did Jack Weathervale.

'Your father,' Candace said, shaking her head. But she didn't say anything more. I watched her watch him walk away and noticed the lines that had etched themselves into the corners of her eyes and mouth. I realized, all at once, how much Candace had aged. How much both of them had: behind Dad's bravado, it was pretty clear that he was strained and exhausted.

I looked over at Dad, hand already extended out towards a surprised and somewhat disheartened-looking Jack Weathervale, and realized, too, how hard it must be for him to be here in this room of people who had never quite accepted him when he'd had money, and who'd turned their backs on him as soon as he lost it. I looked around at all of the pleased white men in their starched Ralph Lauren, their bloated necks and their pink cheeks and felt suddenly, shakingly angry at the injustice of it all.

Candace must have sensed this change in mood, as she reached over and gave my hand a squeeze. 'How's it going with Ethan?' she asked, eyes kind.

This, despite Candace's best intentions, did not assuage my rage, particularly not when I could see him next to the bar, practically swaddled in lithe young women. 'Fine,' I said tersely. 'It was a long time ago, anyway.'

'Well, honey, that doesn't mean it's not awkward for you. I saw how you looked at him that night in the pub, so we both know that whole "I'm fine" thing is bullshit.'

'I didn't look at him in any way!' I could hear my voice turning high-pitched and squeaky. 'I swear!'

'Can't fool a fool,' she said. 'I know a girl in love when I see one. Are you worried about those girls over there?' she asked, following my gaze. 'Because you should not be worried about those girls over there. Piper's friends all have fluff between their ears and are just looking to score the biggest diamond they can get.' I looked at her quizzically. I'd never heard Candace talk this way. Usually she was so . . . nice. 'I know what you're thinking,' she said with a laugh, 'you're thinking that it takes one to know one!'

'I'm not!' I felt myself flush with mortification, because I did think that, just a little. At least I had when Candace had first appeared at breakfast one morning, swathed in a red satin dressing gown and bestowing kisses on my and Piper's unwilling cheeks. I shook my head firmly. 'I know you're not that.'

'Well, good. Anyway, those girls aren't going to keep his interest for more than a few minutes, so don't even think about them. Taylor and Madison are a little different – they're nice girls and they both have their heads on straight – but they're both way too young for him.' I raised an eyebrow at her: Candace was a good fifteen years younger than my dad. 'I know, I know, pot calling the kettle black again!' she laughed. 'But honestly, you're worth ten of those girls. Twenty.'

'I don't think Ethan thinks that's true,' I said. 'I'm pretty sure he'll be happy when he doesn't have to see me anymore.'

'Why? Because the two of you broke up a hundred years ago? So what? You were just kids! I bet he can't even remember why you broke up in the first place.'

'I doubt that's true,' I said, 'and anyway, I can.' And if he knew the real reason we broke up, I thought to myself, he wouldn't even want to be in the same country with me, let alone the same room.

'You always were a stubborn little thing,' Candace said, a fond smile playing at the edges of her lips. 'I remember the first time I stayed the night at your father's house – your house, I mean. Your face when I turned up at breakfast in the morning! Lord! I thought I was going to be turned to stone.'

'I was a brat,' I said, coloring at the memory. I had sat at the table and refused to speak, and when she had handed me a bowl of cornflakes I'd stood up and ceremoniously dumped them in the trash. In short, I'd been an asshole. But Candace had taken it in her stride – taken all of us in her stride – in a way I hadn't appreciated until I was much older.

'You were just protecting your dad,' she said now, 'and I respected that. But you were a tough little cookie, I'll give you that. What I'm trying to say is, I've always admired you for being so strong-willed and independent. I sure wasn't like it when I was your age. I'm not even like it now. But don't let your stubbornness hold you back from being happy, okay? Because you can bend a little, you know. You won't break.'

I smiled at her but didn't say anything. I had an image in my head of a slim branch, like the ones that hung from the silver birch that grew outside the window of my bedroom as a kid. I remembered stretching it into a makeshift bow and arrow, attaching thread to either end and pulling it tight, but when I'd tried to shoot an arrow with it, it had snapped in two on the first try. I tried not to read too much into the metaphor.

I glanced back over towards Ethan, who was now standing alone at the bar, watching the evening's proceedings with a faintly bemused look on his face. The young women had migrated south towards Piper, who was wearing – incredibly yet somehow inevitably – a tiny diamanté tiara and holding court at a large round table. I dreaded to think what she'd be like by tomorrow: I hadn't spotted any ermine in her suitcase, but that didn't mean she didn't have a stole or two stowed somewhere.

I took a deep breath and crossed the room. He looked up as I approached, and to my relief he smiled when he saw me coming. 'I'd buy you a drink,' he said, 'but I'm worried I'll get told off for being too helpful again. I mean, if flower arranging was such a contentious issue, I can only imagine your thoughts on bar etiquette.'

'Sorry I was kind of an asshole earlier,' I said. 'I'm just not used to . . .' I trailed off, unsure of what to say.

'People being nice?' The smile was getting wider now. 'Come on, I know you've lived in New York for a long time, but surely not everyone in that city is a callous bastard. Though I haven't personally come across one who isn't, I have to say.'

'Yeah, we're basically a zombie race there now,' I said. 'And yes, you can buy me a free drink. Vodka soda please.'

'What, no bourbon? I thought you were a bourbon girl to your core!'

The hairs on the back of my neck stood up at the mere mention of bourbon. 'No more bourbon for me,' I said. 'I'm a vodka girl now.'

'That's a shame. I liked you as a bourbon girl.' He took a sip of his drink. 'Well, to a point.'

We both paused for a beat before laughing. 'Thanks a lot,' I said. 'You sure know how to make a girl feel special.'

'I try. Vodka soda?' He signaled to the bartender and ordered a round of drinks while I tried to compose myself. The double mention of bourbon and the past had rattled me. 'So,' he said, handing me my drink, 'what do you think of the party?'

'It's nice,' I said with a shrug. 'I mean, I don't think I can remember being in a room with more Republicans before, but the canapés are decent and the drinks are cold, so I can't complain.'

'Yeah, there are an awful lot of red ties in this place.'

'I know, right? Piper and Charlie seem to be having fun though.' We glanced across the room to where Charlie was swooping Piper down in a low kiss. 'They're sweet,' I said quietly.

'They are. I don't know about you, but I'm still sort of amazed that it's worked out between them. Remember when they first got together?'

'Oh God. When we went on that double date to the Creamery and Piper wouldn't eat her ice cream because the man serving her wasn't wearing gloves and she became convinced he had Hepatitis C?'

'And Charlie would not stop telling us the blow-by-blow from last night's *Summer Slam*?'

'Disaster,' I said. 'But then the next thing I knew, they were curled up in the back seat with each other. I couldn't bring myself to look in the rear-view mirror in case I saw something a sister should never see.'

He nodded. 'That was one awkward car ride home.' We both fell quiet, remembering (at least on my part) what had happened between us after we'd dropped them off at Charlie's house. I was pretty sure that somewhere on my body I was still harboring the grass stains.

I was filled with a desperate urge to change the subject, kamikaze style. 'So,' I said, 'you're pretty popular at this wedding.'

He shot me a bemused look. 'What do you mean?'

I rolled my eyes. 'I mean that you might as well be wrapped in bacon the way those women have been looking at you. Actually, I guess it's probably more like wrapped in avocado toast for that bunch.'

'They're nice girls,' he said with a shrug. 'I don't know about anything more than that.'

'Please, I've seen the way Madison looks at you. And Taylor, for that matter.' I couldn't stop myself. It was like a scab that I knew hadn't healed underneath but I was nonetheless compelled to pick off.

He looked aggravated now, and I felt secretly pleased. He could do whatever he wanted, but I wanted him to at least admit it. 'Nah, I'm just helping them out with – oh shit.' Ethan pushed past me and started to run. I turned just in time to see my dad's legs give out from underneath him. He sagged to the floor like a bundle of rags, one arm clutching at his chest, his eyes wincing in pain. His head hit the floor, too hard, and then he was still.

'Dad!' I can't remember what happened next, but I must have run to him, because suddenly I was there kneeling beside him and cradling his head in my hands. A circle had formed around us, and a few of the suited men were hunched over us, whispering anxiously about what to do. I felt his breath coming in thin, shallow gasps. 'Dad? Can you hear me?' His eyelids fluttered briefly and then were still, and I felt my heart stop at that moment. I must have been crying at this point, because I saw a few tears splash onto his face as I leaned over him. They must have helped him to come round, because soon after his eyelids started fluttering again. But I knew we weren't out of the woods yet. 'Somebody call an ambulance!' I cried.

There was a murmur through the crowd as they debated the best number to call. 'Call 911!' someone shouted.

'That's for the US!' someone else yelled. 'We're in England!' '911!' '999!' and on it went, until I exploded. 'Ask a fucking English person!' I screamed.

'What do you need me to do?' I looked up and saw Ethan looming over me, voice calm but face etched with worry.

'Call the ambulance,' I said, 'and talk to them. Tell them I think he's having a heart attack. There's some aspirin in my bag – get it for me.' I suddenly felt preternaturally calm, like the still eye of a tornado.

'I've already called. They're on their way.' He crouched down and put an arm around me. 'It's going to be okay,' he said gently, and I let my head drop onto his shoulder, just for a second.

The ambulance arrived in a matter of minutes, but each of those minutes seemed to stretch into an hour. Piper was inconsolable, alternating between racking sobs and panicked hysteria, and Candace had slumped into a chair, looking on in shocked silence. When Ethan had been assured that the ambulance was on its way, he went and sat with her, wordlessly taking her hand in his and gently stroking it between his thumb and forefinger. I stayed with my dad until the moment that the EMTs wheeled him away. He had regained consciousness soon after Ethan placed the call to 999, and had accepted the aspirin that I had placed into his mouth as meekly as a child. He looked pale and shaken, but was able to sit up a little, and even muttered a few words of reassurance as he was being taken out on the gurney.

'Can I ride with you?' Ethan had asked as I followed the paramedics to the ambulance. We had Candace with us by then, holding up her weight between us.

'Only two in the ambulance!' one of the paramedics called back to us.

'Can you stay here and make sure that everyone leaves okay?' I asked. 'You can follow on with Piper and Charlie. Sorry, I know this isn't your responsibility, it's just –'

'Of course.' He reached over and gave my shoulder a squeeze. 'Whatever you need me to do.'

He stood in the parking lot and watched as the ambulance pulled away, holding up a hand just before we disappeared from sight.

'Looks like it might be a myocardial infarction,' one of the EMTs, the broad one with the tuft of ginger hair, said on the ride over to the hospital. Candace and I sat on either side of my dad, each holding one of his hands and staring intently at his grayed face, neither of us daring to look at the other. The paramedics must have sensed that we were both in shock, because blankets were tucked around our shoulders without us even noticing.

A thought struck me as we pulled up to the hospital, and I pulled out a worn scrap of paper and prayed that my phone would get a signal.

He answered on the fourth ring. 'Hello?' The voice on the other end of the line was thick with sleep and edged with suspicion.

'Chris? It's Ruby. My dad . . . something's happened. We think he's had a heart attack. Would you . . . I know it's a lot to ask, and I don't really know you, but . . .'

'Which hospital are you at?' he asked, voice suddenly sharp. 'I'm on my way.'

Then

'Is this yours?' Ruby asked, holding up a lacy black bra. It looked expensive, which was why it was even more surprising that she'd discovered it while cleaning the oven.

'I've been looking for that everywhere!' Jess said, plucking it out of her hand. 'Amazing. Now I can wear it tonight.'

'Do I even want to know why it was in the oven?'

'It's one of those stupid handwash-only things so I couldn't take it to the laundromat,' she said, rolling her eyes. 'Such a pain in the ass.'

'So . . . you thought you'd broil it instead?'

'It was soaking wet after I washed it in the sink – obviously – and it was taking for ever to dry and dripping all over the place, so I put it in the oven to dry out.'

'I'm not even going to go into all the reasons that was a terrible idea.'

'It was on a super low temperature! We're still alive, so I must have remembered to switch it off at some point – or maybe Kim did when she was making one of her weird dinners – but I guess I forgot to take it out. Seriously, though, this thing makes my boobs look incredible – Jay isn't going to know what hit him.'

'I'm very happy for you both. Just try not to burn the apartment down in future, okay?'

'I will promise no such thing. Now, what are you doing tonight? And please don't say you're staying in and watching television.'

'I thought I'd do a little cleaning, too . . .'

'Ruby, it's Saturday night. You're in New York – the city that never fucking sleeps, for God's sake! And you're going to spend it watching TV and cleaning our shithole of a flat, which, I can promise you, no amount of cleaning can make look good, so you might as well forget it and go out and get drunk.'

'I'm just super tired from work, that's all. And I haven't talked to Ethan all week, and he promised to call after his shift, and I want to make sure I'm around to talk when he does.'

'He doesn't finish work until, what, two a.m.? That gives you' – she glanced at her watch – 'seven hours to fill with fun and abandonment. Tell you what, I'll cancel my date with Jay and we'll go out, just the two of us.'

'You've got the magic bra now! No way are you canceling the date.'

'Please, this bra is probably too good to waste on that guy anyway. He always sticks his face in his plate of food and takes a big whiff before he eats it, and he's not exactly forthcoming when it comes to giving head. Let's use the bra's powers for good, like getting us to the front of the line at Wonder Bar.'

'Honestly, I'd be terrible company and the bags under my eyes would send us straight back to the back of the line. Go have fun with Jay and the magic bra. Tell him to get his head out of his plate and into your underwear.'

Jess gave Ruby a long, hard look. 'Okay,' she said finally, 'I'll let you off this time. But you can't be a hermit for ever, you know. I miss my partner in crime.'

'I'll be ready for active duty again soon, I promise.'

Ruby listened to the low hum of Jess's hairdryer as she scrubbed the bathtub. Little black specs, like iron filings, peppered the bottom, and as she wiped them up she realized they were tiny stubs of shaven leg hair. Her stomach curdled as she tossed the offending paper towel into the bin. Sharing an apartment with two other women was not the potpourri-strewn idyll that she'd seen in sit-coms and tampon commercials.

Ruby sighed and lay down on the newly cleaned bathroom floor, the tiles cool beneath her, the smell of bleach edging its way into her lungs. She could hear Jess misting herself with various hairsprays and perfumes now, humming to herself. Now there was the click of her heels on the living-room floor as she collected her bag, and a rummage in her vanity for the right lipstick. Ruby closed her eyes. Soon, she would be able to open the bottle of wine she'd bought for herself at the bodega and take her first, calming sip of solitary alcohol. She knew she could have opened it while Jess was still in the apartment – she was the last person who would ever judge her for drinking alone, or judge her for doing anything for that matter, but she'd come to savor the sound of the door closing, the hushed vacuum it left behind before the creak and pop of the cork.

Ruby was not adjusting to life in New York the way she'd hoped.

Work was terrifying in its intensity, but it was also a relief. It had clear rules and guidelines to follow, which

Ruby appreciated. She didn't mind the long hours, not really, and she didn't even mind the withering looks from Tara and Melanie, both of whom continued to regard her with the same unmitigated disgust they had for complex carbohydrates and generic brands of shoes. Hard work was something Ruby had been built and bred on, and when the CEO occasionally remembered her name or Jefferson thanked her for the coffee she'd made for him, she felt a little jolt of pleasure and pride.

No, work wasn't the problem. It was the city itself.

When Ruby had been a child, her mother would read to her every night before bed. Even when she was old enough to read to herself, after she acknowledged to herself that bedtime stories were babyish, and that her classmates would have teased her mercilessly if they ever found out, she would still ask her mother to read to her. Her favorite stories were about New York – Eloise, the little girl who lived at the top of the Plaza, and *From the Mixed-up Files of Mrs. Basil E. Frankweiler*, about a brother and sister who live in the Metropolitan Museum of Art. Sometimes, her mother would skip the books and tell her a story from her own childhood growing up in the city. The display windows at Macy's at Christmas. The taste of freshly churned butter spread on a hot roll at Le Pavillon. The dogs splashing in Bethesda Fountain on a hot August afternoon, ice cream dribbling down her arm and pooling stickily in the crook of her elbow while she watched. Ruby would close her eyes when she would tell these stories so she could better imagine her mother as a little girl surrounded by giant skyscrapers. She decided then and there that New York was her destiny.

But the New York Ruby found herself currently living in wasn't the pastel-colored dreamscape of ice cream cones and snowflake-strewn windowpanes she'd imagined as a child. This New York was all sharp edges and steel faces. Every time she emerged from a subway station, wide-eyed and blinking into the sunlight refracted off the buildings, she felt smaller, less sure. She got lost constantly and would wander down block after incorrect block, refusing to turn around or ask for directions or – God forbid – open a map in front of the teeming multitudes of more confident, better dressed and altogether more competent human beings who were her fellow New Yorkers. She felt, every time she walked down Madison Avenue or ordered a coffee from the cart parked near her office, that she was an imposter only inches from being found out.

It didn't help that Jess had taken to life in New York without so much as a backwards glance. Within six weeks at the *Examiner*, she'd gone from being a local beat reporter, covering *quinceañeras* in Queens, to being one of their 'On the Pulse' girls, which meant that she now spent her nights rubbing elbows with the city's bright young things in the hope of extracting some juicy gossip from them for the morning edition. Just last week, she'd caught a former reality TV star doing lines off a polished zinc bar top in NoHo. Her very self seemed to have swelled and expanded to embody this new, bigger life of hers. Meanwhile, Ruby was shrinking by the day.

Of course, she couldn't tell anyone how she felt. Jess would try to drag her to her terrifying club nights and gallery openings, where Ruby would inevitably be dwarfed by gleaming Amazons with unnaturally white teeth and enormous trust funds. Besides, she would never understand: they had spent four years at college tearing up campus, terrorizing frat boys and TAs alike, fearless and bold in their every move. For Jess to find out that Ruby had been a secret coward all along . . . it was too humiliating to contemplate.

Her father only cared about work. Their weekly telephone conversations consisted of him asking if she was still employed before offering up a few of his patented Alec Atlas 'pillars of success'. After she assured him that she would ask about the CEO's golf handicap (he played tennis) and his children (he had dogs), he'd pass her on to Candace, who would lecture her on whatever toxic foodstuff she'd heard about on *Oprah* and make her promise that she would treat herself to a pedicure, 'because a woman should never have to live with ugly feet'. Ruby didn't have the heart to tell her that her feet, like the rest of her, had swollen to a gentle plumpness over the past month, thanks to a steady diet of hydrogenated corn snacks, innumerable bottles of cheap white wine, and pure, unadulterated fear.

And then there was Ethan. Ruby knew that if she told him how she felt, he would be on the next bus down from Beechfield, ready to wrap her up in his arms and ferry her away from it all. He would reassure her that New York wasn't for everyone, that she had given it a fair shot, but that she didn't have to suffer for nothing, that there was no shame in coming back home, that she could come back and live with him, that he would look after her while she figured out her next move. She knew that he would be her knight in battered denim and that he would honestly love nothing more. But she couldn't let herself make that call. She didn't want to be a damsel in distress. She wanted to be a grown woman living in the greatest city in the world. It's just that it was harder than she'd thought it would be.

From the bathroom floor, she heard Jess call out her goodbyes before slamming the front door shut behind her. Ruby sat up, tucked the paper towels and the bottle of bleach back under the sink and picked herself up off the ground. She headed for the kitchen, trying not to break into a run, and opened the first bottle of red (two for twelve dollars at the bodega next door, it would have been wasteful to have only bought one). She poured out a large measure into one of their remaining balloon-shaped wine glasses, and drank while standing at the kitchen counter. She felt her stomach gently warm and then her fingertips begin to tingle, and she allowed herself a small smile before pouring another glass. It was Saturday night, after all. She might as well enjoy herself.

Now

All of my calm evaporated as soon as I set foot in the hospital. The smell of disinfectant mixed with something faintly sweet, the mournful bleeps coming from row after row of heart monitors, the sound of the nurses striding down the hallway in their soft-padded sneakers, all of it made my stomach clench in fear. The reality of the situation had finally set in: we were in a foreign country and Dad's health was in real danger.

Chris had arrived at the hospital shortly after Dad had been admitted, breathless and smelling faintly of toothpaste. 'Where is he?' he asked without so much as a hello, and I'd nodded towards the closed door of Dad's room.

'The A & E doctor is in there with him now,' I said. 'I tried to get them to let me stay, but he wanted to examine him on his own. He said something about tests . . .' I raised my hands in the air, helpless and lost.

'I'll be back in a second,' Chris said, already pushing open the door. Gone were the traces of the rumpled man I'd met on the beach the other day. In his button-down shirt, sleeves rolled to the elbows, and with a freshly shaven jaw, he looked every inch the professional doctor. I felt reassured just looking at him. He glanced back before he walked through the door. 'Don't worry,' he said and, for a minute, I felt the tension ease a little.

'Here you go.' I looked up to see Ethan holding up a paper cup full of coffee. 'Thought you might need it. I left Candace and Piper with Charlie and his folks – they're taking a breather. Piper's still pretty hysterical.'

I took the coffee from him and had a sip. It was too hot and my tongue went furred at the tip from the burn. 'Thanks,' I said.

'Was that the guy from the pub I just saw go in there?' he asked, gesturing towards the closed door.

'Yeah, I called him on the way over. He's a doctor.'

'Oh. Right. That's great.' His lips pulled into a tight line. 'Did he give you his number at the bar or something?'

'I saw him when I went for a run on the beach this morning,' I said. 'He gave me his card then, and I'd thrown it in my bag, and when all this happened I suddenly remembered he was a doctor and thought it would be helpful to have someone I know on the case.' I was rambling, but I couldn't seem to stop myself. 'Not that I know him, but . . . you know.'

Ethan nodded. 'Cool.'

We sat in silence, both taking tentative sips of terrible coffee and listening to the heart monitors bleep on. I felt the panic rise back inside me like a tidal wave. All I could think, over and over, was *What if he dies? What if he dies?* For the first time in a long time, I couldn't find a rational answer to the question. There was no reasoning when it came to these things – I should have remembered that from what happened with Mom. There was just chaos and hope and despair and sometimes just a glimmer of luck that meant that your world was spared, at least temporarily. But you never knew when the luck would fail to appear.

'I'm really scared,' I said finally. I felt myself deflate as the words came out of my mouth, and I slumped against the back of the hard plastic chair.

'I know you are.' Ethan reached over and took my hand. It felt odd to be touching him, both familiar and completely alien, but its warmth was comforting. 'But it'll be okay. Your dad's a tough cookie. Plus, he's got you fighting for him, and Christ knows you're a tough cookie, too.'

I stared blankly at a poster forbidding mobile phone usage on the ward. 'I could have done more,' I said quietly.

'What are you talking about? You were amazing back there. If he gets through this – and he will, I promise you – it will be because of how quickly you reacted, and how calm you were. You even remembered the aspirin, which could have saved his life.'

'No, I mean . . . I could have done more over the years. I knew that he and Candace had been struggling when the markets crashed. He lost everything, you know. Like, everything. And I didn't even help them.' I looked down at our hands entwined together and felt another pang of loss. 'I've been a bad daughter,' I said, but it was more than that. In that moment, I knew that I had failed at some fundamental part of being a person, that I'd allowed myself to become so closed up over the years, so singularly focused, that I'd lost the ability to connect with people. And, in turn, they had lost the desire to connect with me.

'Ruby, look at me. Come on.' I shifted reluctantly to face him. 'You can't blame yourself for this. You're a good daughter. You can't live someone else's life for them, and you can't protect them from every bad thing. Your dad knows that you love him, and that's the important thing. He wouldn't want you to put your life on hold for him.'

I shook my head. 'It's not just that,' I said. 'I've –' There was a moment, a single split second, where I was filled with an absolute certainty that I was going to tell him the truth. But when I opened my mouth, I couldn't find the words.

He took my other hand in his and smiled. 'Stop being so hard on yourself. Everyone could do more all of the time. That's the great catch-22 of life. Just when you think you're doing enough, that you're a good person, that you can feel a little pleased with yourself, something comes along to prove that what you're doing is jack shit. That goes double when it comes to family.'

His kindness just made me feel worse. 'Easy for you to say. You're taking care of your dad, and doing all sorts of charity work, and buying people random things everywhere you go. You're like Person of the Year.'

He let out a harsh little laugh. 'Hardly. Honestly, if I was a good son, I would have left him in Beechfield. Moving him here was selfish of me – he's miserable, and I'm not home enough to mitigate that. I thought I was protecting him, but really I was just clipping his wings.'

I shook my head. 'I'm sure that's not true.'

'Trust me, it is. That's what I mean, though: there's no right or wrong answer. Or, more accurately, there are only a series of ambiguous answers, all of which are designed to make you feel shitty. I think this is what they mean when they talk about parents getting their revenge on their kids in their old age.'

'I guess I didn't think it would happen so soon,' I said. 'I mean, I thought I'd front-loaded a lot of that misery when my mom died. I was banking on a few more years of carefree selfishness.'

'No offense, but it doesn't seem like you've been all that carefree. Kind of the opposite, really.'

'Fair point,' I said, embarrassed. The last thing I wanted was to let him think I was anything other than completely together, but at this point, after what had happened with my dad, I didn't have the strength to pretend anymore.

'It'll be okay,' he said softly. 'You'll do the best you can, because that's all you can do.'

I looked at him and felt something pass between us, like the moment I'd thought we'd had in the pub, only softer, kinder this time. 'Thanks,' I said, and I meant it.

The door opened and Chris strode out, followed by the A & E doctor. 'Thanks, Paul,' Chris said, shaking the other man's hand. 'I appreciate it.' It struck me again how composed he was in this environment, how . . . adult. I stood up and waited for him to face me. 'Your father is going to be fine,' he said. I nearly collapsed with relief, and he reached out to steady me. 'The ECG indicates that he's had a mild heart attack, but it seems to have stabilized and it doesn't look as though there's been any permanent damage. We're just awaiting the results of the blood tests to confirm – we should have them in an hour or so.'

I hugged him. It wasn't a conscious decision, but all of a sudden I found myself in his arms. I felt him tense with surprise at first, and then he pulled me towards him and held me there. 'Thank you so much,' I mumbled into his chest.

'It's okay,' he said, gently rubbing my back. 'It's going to be fine.'

'Sorry,' I said, pulling away. 'I got a little carried away.' I looked behind me at Ethan, who was now studiously reading a pamphlet on bowel cancer, face unreadable.

'You can go in and see him now,' Chris said. 'But go easy on him. He's had a bit of a shocker.'

I nodded. 'Would you mind telling Candace?' I asked. 'I know she'll want to see him, too. And my sister.'

'Of course,' Chris said, and he turned to head down the corridor.

Ethan stood up. 'I'll go,' he said. 'You stay here with Ruby.' He strode off without another word.

I walked into the room to find my dad marooned in the centre of a high-sided bed, the covers pulled tightly around his chest. Next to him, a heart monitor beeped steadily, the green line rising and falling on the screen. His arms lay limp by his side, and a thin white piece of tape secured an IV running from his right hand to a bag of clear liquid hanging on a metal frame above. His eyes were closed and his face, while not as worryingly gray as it had been earlier, was still pinched and sallow. Lost in the middle of the beige-walled room, the sickly-sweet antiseptic mixing with the smell of stale breath, he looked tiny and delicate, like a porcelain doll version of himself. I sat down on the hard plastic chair by the bedside and took his hand lightly in mine.

His eyelids flickered and stuttered open. 'Hey, kid,' he said in a quiet, rasped voice. 'How are you holding up?'

'I think it's me that should be asking you that,' I said with a small laugh.

He raised his free hand and waved away the thought. 'I'm fine, I'm fine. Doc said it was just a little blip with my heart, nothing serious. I'll be back on my feet and hustling in no time.'

I frowned at the word hustling. It wasn't the sort of thing you wanted to hear from your dad after he'd just had a heart attack. 'Just take it easy,' I said. 'You gave us a pretty bad scare back there.' That was the understatement of the century – I was pretty sure I'd aged at least a dozen years over the past few hours. I could feel the white hairs sprouting from my scalp already.

'I know, I'm sorry. Jeez, what a scene. Right in front of all those people, and on Piper's big night . . . how is she doing?'

'She was pretty upset, but she'll be much better once she sees you're okay.'

'Is she pissed at me?'

'Of course not! Dad, all anyone cares about is that you're okay.'

'But the wedding is tomorrow . . .'

'Don't even think about it,' I said sternly. 'Your job is to rest, that's it. I'll figure the rest of it out.'

'And Candace? Is she here?'

'Or course she is. She's been worried sick. Do you want me to tell her to come in?'

He nodded.

'Okay, I'll go get her.' I made a move to leave, but turned back to him. I knew I had to say something to him, and that I had to do it now, before I changed my mind. I also suspected I'd never have another chance to have my dad as a captive audience again. I sighed and sat back down. 'You know I love you, right?'

'Of course I do.'

'Well, keep that in mind when I say this. You have to take this whole thing as a giant wake-up call.'

'Now, Ruby –'

'Dad, just listen, okay? I feel like this is the universe telling you to stop, you know? Actually, I feel like it's the universe telling us all to stop. I know that I haven't exactly been the best daughter to you over the years, but I want you to know that that's going to change. I'm going to visit you guys more often in Florida, and if I can help you in any way . . . you know, I'm comfortable now. If you need money or anything like that –'

I saw his knuckles whiten as he grasped the edges of the sheet. 'I certainly don't need my daughter to bail me out.'

'I'm not saying you need me to bail you out. But let's just say I could make it so you didn't have to hustle all the time – why would that be such a bad thing? You've taken care of me all of my life. Just let me take care of you for once.'

'I don't want to talk about this now, Ruby. Besides, like I've been saying all along, my luck's about to change any day now. I've got the casino idea, and the market's already started to turn around . . .'

'If you keep going at the rate you're going, I honestly don't know what will happen,' I said. My eyes pricked with tears and my throat suddenly swelled. 'I want you to stick around for a while, Dad,' I said. 'Candace does, too. If you don't want my help, that's fine. But you've got to make a change for Candace's sake.'

He looked at me for a moment and then shut his eyes. I worried he was trying to shut me out completely, but when he opened them again I could see he had tears in his eyes now, too. 'I'm just sick of being a fuck-up,' he said.

I placed my hand on top of his. 'You're Alec Atlas. You're the best father a girl could ever ask for, and you're a good man. You could never be a screw-up. Fuck those country club guys – they're just a bunch of bloated white men. Who cares what they think?'

He smiled at me and gave me a wink, and I knew – like clouds parting in the sky to let the sun shine through – that it was all going to be okay. 'They do all have sticks up their asses,' he said. 'And that club has a damp problem they've never really fixed. Mark my words, in five years' time the whole place will be a swamp.'

'Perfect place for a casino!' I said, and to my relief he laughed. 'I love you,' I said, leaning down to kiss his cheek.

'I love you, too,' he said. 'You're a good kid.'

I opened the door to find the rest of them gathered in the waiting area, looking anxious. 'Dad wants to see you,' I said to Candace, who promptly dissolved into tears. 'You too, Pipes.'

They got to their feet unsteadily and walked into the room, shutting the door behind them. Charlie and his parents were huddled together, all of them struggling to keep their eyes open. Ethan stood up and walked over to me. 'How is he?' he asked gently.

'Okay, I think,' I said. 'He looks exhausted, but it seems like he's going to be fine. Better than fine, hopefully.'

'Glad to hear it,' he said. 'Ruby, I –' He paused, as if searching for something he'd lost and couldn't quite find. 'I –'

He was interrupted by Chris striding down the hall towards us. 'I've got your father's test results,' he called. 'It's all looking pretty good. He'll be in here for a day or two, just to keep him under observation, and he'll have to take it easy for a few weeks, but on the whole he's going to be right as rain.'

'Thank God,' I said, and I felt all of the tension drain out of me, like a plug had been pulled. 'I'll just go tell my dad,' I said, moving past him towards the door.

'I'm the doctor,' Chris said with a laugh, 'so I'll be the one delivering the medical prognosis. You just sit there for a minute. You've had a bit of a shock tonight.'

'Thank you,' I said, 'for everything.'

'Just doing my job,' he said, shooting me a grin before opening the door. 'Though I'm pretty sure you're now duty bound to go on that date with me.' The tips of my ears turned fiery hot and I was sure that I was blushing.

'He seems like a nice guy,' Ethan said when Chris was out of earshot.

'Yeah,' I said. 'I mean, I don't really know him, but he's been amazing tonight. I would have been much more of a wreck if he hadn't been here.'

'He's a real knight in shining armor.' There was more than a slight edge of sarcasm in his tone.

'What are you talking about?'

'I don't think he's here just out of the kindness of his heart,' he said. 'He's clearly got a thing for you.'

'I don't know about that,' I said, though I was being a little disingenuous. I could tell that Chris liked me, and I was secretly pleased that Ethan had noticed.

He turned towards me, eyes suddenly serious. 'Are you interested in him?'

'I – I don't know,' I said, flustered. 'He seems like a nice enough guy and everything, but I barely know him . . .'

'You should go for it,' he said abruptly. 'If you're interested, I mean.'

I looked at him for a long moment, but his face was like Switzerland – impassively neutral. A few minutes before, before Chris had interrupted us, I had thought that Ethan and I were on the cusp of . . . I wasn't sure what, but it felt like *something*. But looking at him now, his face open and earnest, I realized that I had got it wrong once again. The way he'd acted towards me all night was just another of those acts of kindness that came so easily to him. Just a guy helping an old friend in a difficult situation. I ignored the stabbing pain in my gut and forced a smile onto my face. I felt the walls inside me start to build again, stronger this time. I wasn't about to be made a fool of twice. 'Maybe you're right,' I said. 'So does that mean you're going to go for Madison? Have a little vacation fun, too?'

He blanched visibly, and I felt a perverse pleasure at making the mask slip a little. 'I hadn't really thought about it,' he said coolly.

'Don't give me that!' I gave his shoulder a shove that was intended as playful but came out a shade too aggressive. 'I know you're into it.'

He shifted uncomfortably in his chair and stared down at his hands. 'I mean, she's cute and everything, but . . . I don't know. I don't think your sister would take kindly to me hitting on one of her bridesmaids.'

'Oh, please, she would love it. She'd get to brag to all of her friends that she set her prettiest friend up with a millionaire.'

'I'm not really into the idea of anyone bragging about that.' He looked deeply unhappy, and I felt a brief flash of regret. But it was soon washed away by the memory of Ethan name-dropping Babington House to Madison a few days before. He couldn't have it both ways.

'Yeah, well, I can't say I feel all that sorry for you. Now, are you going to make a move on Madison or what?' I could see he was wavering. I felt the same inexplicable urge I sometimes felt on a crowded subway platform: to mete out a final, definitive shove over the edge. 'If the opportunity is there, you might as well take it.'

There was a long pause, the bleeping of a distant heart monitor and the occasional raspy cough of a nearby patient the only sounds. 'We'll see,' he said finally.

'Good!' I said brightly. I wasn't going to let him think for a second that I was anything other than totally, one hundred per cent cool with the idea, even as a small part of my heart withered and died.

Both of us fell back into silence. I plucked a pamphlet about heart disease out of one of the clear plastic holders mounted on the wall and pretended to study it, stealing occasional glances at Ethan, who looked lost in thought. After a few minutes, he caught my eye and opened his mouth as if to say something, but before he could, we were interrupted by Chris emerging from my dad's room, followed by Piper and Candace. Candace's face was slack with relief, but Piper's was tear-tracked and twisted. 'What are we going to do?' she wailed, throwing herself at Charlie. He woke up with a start and caught her in his arms at the last moment.

'What's going on?' he asked, eyes wide. 'Is your father okay?'

'He's going to be okay, thank God, but he has to stay in the hospital for the rest of the weekend.'

'Piper's a little upset that Alec won't be able to walk her down the aisle tomorrow,' Candace explained.

'That is a shame,' Bob said, nodding his head in sympathy. 'But as your father-in-law, I would be honored to walk with you on his behalf.'

'It's not just that!' Piper cried. 'How can I get married without my dad there to watch?' She collapsed in a fresh burst of tears.

'It's been an emotional day,' Candace said, lowering herself into a seat. 'You should all go home and get some rest. We can work all of this out in the morning.'

'There's nothing to work out!' Piper said between sobs. 'I'm not getting married without my dad, and that's that! We'll just have to call it off!'

'Isn't there any way around it, doc?' Charlie asked over Piper's bent head.

Chris shook his head. 'He's had a heart attack. Even if it's only a mild one, he still needs a couple of days of bedrest. It's too risky to let him out tomorrow, especially to go to a stressful event. Even though I'm sure it will be a lovely wedding,' he said quickly, with a respectful nod towards Piper.

Bob and Barbara were both sitting up very straight in their seats. 'I think you'll have to go through with it, sweetheart,' Bob said to Piper. 'Everyone's come all this way, and it's all paid for . . .'

'Yes, dear,' Barbara chimed in. 'And I think the people at Bamburgh would be very disappointed if we had to cancel at such late notice . . .'

'Guys, if Piper wants to cancel, then we'll cancel. It's only money we'd be losing,' Charlie said. Bob and Barbara swallowed in unison at this thought. 'She deserves the wedding she wants, and I'm not going to force her to do anything she doesn't want to do.'

Piper lifted her head off his chest and smiled at him, eyes shining. 'Do you mean that?'

'Of course I do!' he said, placing a protective arm around her. 'I love you, and I want you to be my wife, but I also want you to be happy on your wedding day.'

I crouched down beside them and took Piper's hand in mine. 'I know this is hard, but you know that Dad would want you to go through with the wedding tomorrow. He's already worried that he spoiled tonight for you . . . he would absolutely hate it if the wedding didn't happen because of him, too.'

Piper looked at me, eyes shining with tears. 'I can't get married without either of my parents,' she said. 'It's bad enough that Mom isn't here to see it, but I can't have a wedding without Dad, too.'

I stroked her hand. 'I know,' I said softly. 'I understand, but you have to be strong for Dad, okay? I know it won't be the same, but it's not like you won't have any family there with you. You'll have me.'

'And me,' Candace said, walking over and taking Piper's other hand. 'I know I'm not your mom, baby girl, but I do love you like a daughter.' Piper looked up at her and gave her a weak smile.

'Please, Piper. It's the best thing for everybody, okay? Including Dad.'

She looked at us for a minute and nodded. 'Okay,' she said. 'But this means I get to have a huge party for our first anniversary, and Dad's going to walk me down the aisle then. Deal?'

'Anything you want,' Charlie said, wrapping her in his arms.

Ethan stood up and gestured towards Chris. 'Have you got a second? There's something I want to discuss with you in private.'

'Sure thing, mate,' Chris said, and I watched the two men disappear down the corridor together.

'I wonder what that's all about,' Bob said.

'You guys should head back to the house,' I said, hoping to gloss over the awkwardness. In truth, I was just as curious to know what Ethan needed to talk to Chris about. Please God, don't let it be anything about me, I thought. 'Try to get a few hours of sleep before the big day. I'm going to stay here with Dad.'

'Me too,' Candace's mouth was pulled into a hard, determined line. 'I'm not going anywhere.'

Charlie hesitated. 'You guys must be exhausted. Are you sure you don't want to come back with us?'

Chris reappeared. 'There's an empty bed next to your father,' he said. 'I checked with the nurse and she said it was fine for you both to sleep there as long as you're prepared to move if anyone else needs the bed.'

'Of course,' I said, 'thanks for sorting it out. And for everything, really.'

'Don't mention it, pet,' he said.

Bob stood up and shook his hand. 'It would be our pleasure if you would come to the wedding tomorrow.'

'Oh, yes!' Barbara trilled, grasping his elbow. 'That would be just wonderful!'

Chris looked over at me expectantly. 'It might be fun,' I said. 'I mean, if you're not doing anything else . . .'

'You're coming,' Piper called from Charlie's arms, voice steely. 'And that's final.'

I glanced down the corridor and saw Ethan speaking in hushed tones down the phone, a pensive look on his face. He looked like he was miles away. Which, in a sense, he was. 'Yes,' I said, placing a hand on Chris's wrist. 'Come.'

Then

'Do me a favor and hand me the tongs, will you?'

Ethan's father was insisting on a final barbeque to see out the summer season, despite the fact that it was now well into October and there was frost on the ground most mornings. 'Never too late for a little fire,' he'd said earlier as he was rubbing a rack of ribs with a dry marinade. 'Good for the soul.'

It was his only night off that week. Charlie was taking Piper to the ballet in Boston – something that Ethan had delighted in harassing him about – and he couldn't face going down to Billy Jack's alone and sitting at the bar with the rest of the townies. When his dad had suggested a barbeque followed by a screening of *Rio Bravo*, he'd happily agreed, if for no other reason than it would take his mind off Ruby for a while.

'You got the hot sauce?' his father asked, poking at the coals. He didn't own one of the behemoth gas grills that hunched imposingly on decks throughout the rest of the neighborhood, replete with pizza stones and bun warmers. He was still using the same coal barbeque he'd bought when Ethan was a kid, despite the fact that the grid was caked with the charred remains of countless past kills. 'Adds flavor,' his father would say. He claimed he could taste the gasoline on the newer, fancier models, but really he just liked the primal thrill of piling up the round nuggets of coal and watching the whole thing go up in a massive whoosh of flame. Nothing better than cooking with fire, he'd say, a slightly maniacal glint in his eye.

'I made a salad,' Ethan said, placing a bowl of greens, cheese and thin slices of grocery store salami on the table.

'Candy ass,' he said, glancing over at it in disgust. 'Who needs salad when you've got meat?'

'Your colon, for one.'

'You sound like Cheryl.' His father had been dating Cheryl, a receptionist at a local swimming-pool installation company, for the past few months, during which she'd made it her personal mission to turn him into a vegetable-eating, hair-product using, bona-fide metrosexual modern man. Her efforts had been soundly rebuffed, and he would have ended things a long time ago if it hadn't been for the fact that she was a decade younger than him and held more than a passing resemblance to Christie Brinkley. 'She's the closest I'll ever come to being Billy Joel,' he'd said when he told Ethan about the vegan restaurant she'd dragged him to. 'Sometimes, a man has to make sacrifices to make his dreams a reality.'

Ethan sat down on the low brick wall that hugged the small, crabgrass-plagued backyard, and watched his father prod the ribs with the tongs until they flipped onto their side. It was cold out, colder than either would admit, and Ethan had pulled a moth-eaten sweater out of the hall closet on his way out. There were big tears along the seam of each cuff, one for each thumb. He suddenly remembered Ruby wearing it one chilly night back in August, her knees folded into her chest and the long hem pulled down over her legs, creating a woolly cocoon for herself in the middle of Memorial Park. She'd looked up at the night sky, hair curling under her ears, her eyes bright in the moonlight. She had looked so beautiful in that moment that it had taken his breath away. When she'd looked back towards him and asked if he wanted another beer, he hadn't been able to answer, just nod dumbly. He slipped his thumbs through the two holes now, hoping to hold onto the memory for a little longer.

'What are you looking so moon-eyed about?' his father asked, nudging him with a sneakered foot.

'Nothing. Just the stars.'

'First the salad, now you're gazing up at the stars? Jesus, give me strength – how the hell did I end up with such an arty-farty son?'

'The town water must have been contaminated.'

'Yeah, I should sue. Come on, Picasso, get up – dinner's ready.'

They ate at the white plastic picnic table, both of them shivering and trying not to show it. The dull hum of next door's television could be heard in the background, punctuated by the sharp sound of studio-audience laughter. Stella had lived beside them for over twenty years, but had never warmed into something that could accurately be described as 'neighborly'. Ethan had been terrified of her as a kid, mainly because once, when he and Charlie had been playing catch too close to her rose bushes, she'd come onto her front porch and wordlessly turned the hose on them. Most nights, they could hear the sound of her foghorn voice as she yelled at another goodfuhnuthin' son down the phone. Ethan occasionally wondered why they still bothered to call, knowing what was in store for them, but he knew enough about the thorny vines of familial entanglement not to question it for too long.

'So, you see the Sox game last night?' his father asked through a mesquite-smeared mouth.

'Yeah, I had it on at the bar. Sucked.'

'Tell me about it. Bunch of jack-offs.'

They nodded in commiseration and ate on in silence for a few minutes.

His father stripped the meat from a rib in a few sharp bites and dropped the gleaming bone onto the plate before reaching over and helping himself to another. 'You and Ruby still doing okay?'

Ethan picked a forkful of cheese and salami straight from the salad bowl and stabbed it into his mouth. He chewed until it was a fine mush, stalling for time. In truth, he had no idea how he and Ruby were doing. They talked most days, and she always said she missed him, but there was something in her voice, a slight catch of hesitance, that made him wonder if she really did. Sometimes, she sounded so remote, as if she were calling from a Russian space station silently gliding in orbit rather than a city a few hundred miles away. It made him feel deeply uneasy, but no matter how many times he asked her if she was okay, her response was always the same tinny 'I'm fine'.

Of course, he didn't admit any of this to his father. Instead, he shrugged and said, 'I guess,' before tearing a chunk of meat out of a rib with his teeth.

Next door, the studio audience roared with laughter.

'You need to go and see her.' His father didn't look at him when he said this. His entire concentration was still focused on stripping the last bit of meat from a bone, but it was clear from his tone that he felt what he was saying was important. In the resulting silence, he tossed another bone onto the pile on his plate and reached for another rib.

Ethan exhaled. 'I don't have the cash to spend a weekend in New York.'

'What the fuck are you gonna do, stay at the Four Seasons? You go to the bus station, you buy a ticket, you get on a bus. How hard is it?'

'Billy will never give me the time off. We're short-staffed as it is, and it's Columbus Day weekend coming up, which means the pissheads will be out in full force. He'll kill me if I ask for time off.'

Ethan's father set down his half-eaten rib and fixed his son with the kind of world-weary, disappointed look he usually reserved for Jetta drivers. 'Son, you say you love this girl. Right?'

'Right.'

'But you're telling me that you don't want to risk pissing off some dickhead owner of a shithole bar so that you can see her?' He reached into his back pocket and pulled out his wallet. The leather was scuffed and cracked from years of overstuffing, and when he opened it slips of paper and receipts spilled out before he shoved them back into captivity. He thumbed out a few bills and handed them to Ethan. 'Here's a couple of bucks. Go see your girl. If Billy gives you any crap, tell him he still owes me for the new carburettor and I'll be over with my baseball bat to collect.'

Ethan sighed. 'Dad, I can't accept this.'

'Of course you can.' He pushed back from the table and placed a gentle hand on his stomach. 'Jesus, I can feel the agita coming on already. I gotta get some Tums.' And with that, he got up and went inside, leaving Ethan with a pile of slightly congealed ribs and a mostly uneaten salad. He looked down at the bills, now crumpled and slightly sweaty in his hand, and smiled. Yes, he thought. I'll go to New York. I'll go get my girl.

Now

To: Mathius Sondergaard
Sent: 18 July 2015 03:34
From: Ethan Bailey
Subject: re: Buyout

I've made a decision. Let's talk in the morning.

E

Now

I woke up too early, the sun streaming through the latticed blinds and slicing me into thin, hot segments. I blinked at the ceiling, waiting for my brain slowly to crank into motion, when I felt a weight next to me shift, and what felt very much like a row of toes tickle my shin. I looked to my right and saw Candace lying in bed with me, wearing last night's dress and snoring fitfully in her sleep.

The cogs caught and whirred. Dad collapsing like an overbaked soufflé in the middle of the restaurant, the soulless hospital room with its bleeping machinery, Ethan's kind and unreadable eyes, Chris's steady arms around me. Piper's hysterics. Candace's blank terror. And now, here I was, tucked up in a spare hospital bed with my stepmother, a guard rail digging into my side. I sat up in bed and glanced at the clock ticking on the wall: 6:34 a.m. I had just woken up but my body already ached with exhaustion, and there was a wedding to coordinate and a bride to mollify and an ex-boyfriend to navigate and a doctor to – possibly – flirt with. I had miles to go before I could go back to sleep.

I leaned over and gently shook Candace's shoulder. 'I have to get back to the house,' I whispered as Candace's eyes squinted dimly at me. 'You get a little more rest if you can. I'll check on Dad before I go.'

'I'm up! I'm up!' she said, struggling onto her elbows. 'Jesus Christ, what do they make these mattresses out of – cement blocks?'

'Shh!' I said, 'you'll wake up Dad!'

'I've been awake for hours,' I heard a voice call from across the room. 'I thought you guys were never going to wake up. What do you think this place is, a Holiday Inn?' I looked over to see my dad sitting up in his bed and looking, frankly, pretty spritely. 'Morning!' he called to us. 'How are you guys doing today?' I watched in horror as he swung his legs over the side of the bed and hopped to his feet.

'Dad, what are you doing?' I yelled. He staggered slightly and I managed to jump out of bed and catch him just before he fell. 'Get back in bed, now.'

'I'm fine!' he said, waving me away. 'Just needed a good night's sleep, that's all. These beds, I tell you – like sleeping on a cloud or something! Candy, we've got to get one of these for the grotto.'

'I think it's probably the morphine rather than the mattress,' Candace pointed out. 'Now listen to your daughter and get back into bed. That nice doctor said you were supposed to take it easy!'

'I am taking it easy!' he insisted, sitting gingerly on the edge of the bed. 'Look at me, I couldn't be taking it more easy! But I'm telling you, I feel absolutely fine! There's no reason for me to take up a bed that could be used for a real sick person.'

'You had a heart attack last night,' I said. 'I think that counts as being sick.'

'I don't care what those doctors say – what do they know, anyway? I feel like a new man! And if you ladies wouldn't mind giving me a little privacy, I'm just going to get dressed and then we can be on our way. In case you've forgotten, we've got a wedding to go to.'

Candace sat next to him on the edge of the bed. 'Baby, you know you can't go to the wedding,' she said gently. 'You're not well enough.'

Dad struggled back onto his feet. 'If you think I'm going to miss my little girl's wedding, well . . . you have got another thing coming!'

'Dad,' I said, in my best teacher's voice, 'remember what we talked about?'

'What did you two talk about?' Candace asked.

'I know, I know,' he said, ignoring her. 'But this is different! This is Piper's wedding!'

'We've talked to Piper about it and it's all settled. Of course we would all love for you to be there, but it's too risky. The doctor said –'

'The doctor can kiss my lily-white American butt!' he yelled. In the corner, the heart monitor bleated urgently.

'You need to calm down,' Candace said, pulling him back down to the bed. 'Don't upset yourself!'

'You're telling me I can't go to my daughter's wedding and then you're telling me not to get upset? What is this, some kind of conspiracy?'

The monitor was beeping wildly now as it charted the erratic pulsing of his heart. A plump, harried nurse burst through the door, followed rapidly by an unfamiliar doctor. 'Clear the room,' the doctor said to me and Candace. We stared at him, stunned and frozen, as if we'd been caught beating my dad, or trying to smother him with a pillow. 'Please,' he said, more gently. 'Just for a moment.' We filed reluctantly out of the room.

From the other side of the door, we heard the sound of calm but firm words of caution being meted out by the doctor, followed by slightly more irritated, nagging words from the nurse. Dad tried to bluster, then cajole, then charm, then plead. The doctor walked out of the room shaking his head. His hair was still damp from the shower, and a clean, lemony scent followed him. 'Your father is a stubborn man,' he said to me.

'That he is,' I said, smiling proudly.

'Please try to keep your father calm. I can't have him shouting the place down – this is a hospital, not a football match.'

'I'm sorry,' Candace said, 'we will. We're just so happy to see him back to his old self.'

'If that's his old self,' he said with a sigh, 'it's no wonder the man had a heart attack.'

'We're working on it,' I said. We crept back into his room, cheerful smiles slapped on both of our faces.

'Are you going to be good?' Candace asked, perching on the side of the bed.

'This place is like a Gulag,' Dad muttered, but it was obvious that the fight had gone out of him.

'We'll take lots of pictures,' Candace said, patting his hand. 'And I'll come straight over after the ceremony to tell you all about it.'

'Oh no you won't,' he said. 'I want you to go to town at the reception! I want you to drink Bob Armstrong out of house and home! I want you to dance until dawn! I want to see photos of you swinging from the chandelier!'

'Alec!'

'I want you to enjoy yourself. I know you haven't had many opportunities over the past few years,' he added with a sad smile.

'Sweetie, don't you know by now that the only time I'm having fun is when you're by my side? It doesn't matter how much champagne is flowing – there's no point in drinking it if you're not around.'

She leaned down and placed a kiss on the centre of my dad's forehead, and I'm pretty sure I saw him wipe away a tear. 'I'll be outside,' I said, edging towards the door.

'No need for you to go, baby girl,' Candace said. She looked up at me and I saw tears in her eyes, which almost – very nearly, but not quite – set me off, too.

Dad rustled himself into a seated position on the bed. 'You two should get going anyways,' he said. 'I know you've got lots to do before the wedding, and Piper will be wanting you both to be around. You tell her that . . .' He broke off for a minute and took a deep, ragged breath. 'You just tell her I love her.'

'I'll bring you some cake,' Candace said. I nudged her and nodded towards the heart monitor. 'Oh, right. Maybe not cake.'

'Go on, get!' he said, and we kissed him goodbye before the heart monitor could start its frenzied ascent once more.

I glanced behind me as we left. All the bravado had left him, and he now looked slightly deflated, like a helium balloon long after the party had finished.

I dropped Candace off at the house and headed straight for the castle. I got a few curious looks when I walked in wearing last night's cocktail dress and a rat's nest of hair on top of my head, but I could tell that news of what had happened was spreading quickly as those looks soon turned to ones of sympathy. I chose to ignore them – if there was one thing I hated, it was sympathy from strangers.

'Okay,' I said to myself as I walked into the main hall, 'let's get this show on the road!'

The next hour and a half passed in a blur of baby's breath and tea lights and origami paper cranes. There were disasters small (a slightly lopsided wedding cake, nothing a few wooden skewers stolen from the kitchen couldn't fix) and large (a whole stack of place cards lost for an hour and then found, inexplicably, in the industrial refrigerator). The caterer was late, then realized she had forgotten the gluten-free blini bases. The registrar got lost. The gamekeeper's dog (can you believe they have a gamekeeper?) briefly rampaged through the marquee and ate one of Madison's artfully constructed centrepieces (thankfully there was one spare). One of the kids hired to hand out champagne before the ceremony decided to open a bottle and was found slumped by a toilet. In short, it was almost – but not quite – a disaster. Which was great, because I didn't have the chance to think about my dad lying in that hospital bed, looking so small and so lost.

Finally, order at least temporarily restored, I headed back over to the house to try to piece myself together into something vaguely resembling a maid of honor. I wasn't all that convinced of my chances.

The house was quiet when I walked through the door, the only sound that of a hairdryer moaning from somewhere upstairs. I sighed with relief and headed towards the kitchen in the hopes of begging a cup of coffee from Mrs Willocks.

'Ruby? Is that you?' Piper, resplendent in a hot-pink satin robe with the word BRIDE embroidered in delicate curlicues across the back, appeared at the top of the stairs. Her hair was piled on top of her head in enormous Velcro rollers, and her face had been perfectly made-up, but her eyes were tired and hollow. 'How's Dad?' she asked.

'He's doing fine,' I said. 'He sends his love and says he'll be thinking of you all day.' I decided not to mention his apoplectic reaction to being told he couldn't go to the wedding, and the subsequent heart monitor meltdown.

'I can't believe he won't see me become Mrs Armstrong,' Piper said. Her eyes began filling with tears.

I rushed up the stairs and placed an arm around her. 'I know,' I said, 'but it's your wedding day. He'd hate to see you crying. Not least because it'll spoil your make-up.'

She managed a small smile. 'I know,' she said, dabbing at the corners of her eyes with a tissue. 'Shit, the make-up woman is going to kill me. Come on, everyone's in my room.'

I followed her into the bedroom. Mrs Willocks's dolls and doilies were now covered in the detritus of wedding preparation. The bedspread was covered with make-up brushes and bottles of bronzer and still-damp towels. Someone had put Taylor Swift on an iPhone, and there was an air of false joviality in the room, as if everyone was just going through the motions of fun rather than actually experiencing it. Madison and Taylor were both wide-eyed and open-mouthed as they carefully applied mascara to their bottom lashes. They turned and smiled when I walked in, and I saw that they were both wearing T-shirts emblazoned with the motto #PipsGetsHitched. 'Madison had them made for the bachelorette in Miami,' Taylor explained. 'There's one for you, too.'

She had the good grace to look mildly sheepish when she handed me a shirt with HEAD BITCH in white lettering across the front. 'Because you're the maid of honor,' she explained. 'Sorry, it feels totally inappropriate now.'

'It's great,' I said, slipping it over my head. And it sort of was – when else was someone going to present me with a Head Bitch shirt?

'Is your dad okay?' she asked.

'He's a little tired, but he's going to be fine.' Relief flooded through me again as I said the words.

'Thank God,' Madison said. 'We've been so worried.' I'd never had a group of female friends – it had always just been me and Jess – but in this room, fuggy with hairspray and perfume and various fruit-scented bodywashes, and seeing the looks of genuine concern on their faces, I suddenly understood the value.

'Ruby,' Piper said, 'I don't mean to be rude, but it's three hours until my wedding and you literally look like a prostitute. And not even an expensive one. You need to get in the shower *immediately*. If you hurry, I'll see if the hair and make-up ladies can come back and work their magic on you.'

'I definitely need all the magic I can get,' I said. I ran to my room and closed the door behind me. My bed looked almost painfully inviting at that moment, despite the neat row of dolls surrounding it like tiny glass-eyed sentries, but I knew that I couldn't lie down, not even for a minute. In twelve hours, the wedding would be finished, and I could slide between the cool sheets and let myself slip into oblivion but, for now, sleep would have to wait. But there was one thing I knew couldn't.

I paced around the room as the phone rang.

'Hey, chicken, what's happening. Did you get rid of the twins yet?'

I burst into tears at the sound of her voice.

'Ruby?' Jess said. 'What's wrong?'

I took a deep, shuddery breath. 'My dad had a heart attack,' I said, before dissolving into a fresh wave of tears.

'Oh fuck. BEN!' she called, 'can you take Noah from me?' A pause, a muffled rustling, a door shutting. 'Ruby, are you there? Talk to me – what happened? Is he okay?'

'He's going to be okay,' I said, 'but oh, God, it was so scary. He just – collapsed. Just like that, in the middle of the room, with everyone around him. No one could help him. And then the ambulance came and they hooked him up to all of these things and – he looked so small, Jess! And so old! I thought he was going to die.'

'I know, sweetheart, I know. I'm so sorry. But they're saying he's going to be okay?'

I nodded.

'Ruby?'

'Yes,' I said, swallowing another sob. 'He's going to be okay.'

'Thank God.'

'I'm sorry I'm such a mess,' I said. I couldn't believe that I had lost control like that. I was supposed to be strong today, not crying like a crazy person. I couldn't be weak, not now. Not ever. 'I know you've got all this stuff on your plate, and you're pregnant, and here I am calling you up and crying down the phone at you! Just ignore me, I'm fine now,' I said, breath stuttering. I wasn't sure who I was trying to convince, her or me. I don't think it was working on either of us.

'Your dad had a heart attack. You're allowed to be not okay. And why the fuck are you apologizing? I'm your best friend – you're supposed to cry down the phone at me!'

'I'm sorry,' I said again, quieter this time.

'Ruby, listen to me. You are a human. You are allowed to feel sad, and scared, and whatever else you feel. You're allowed to feel things. Stop trying to out-tough life.'

'Sorry,' I whispered. Honestly, it was like I had a particularly apologetic form of Tourette's.

'Oh my God, stop!'

'I'm sorry! I'm sorry!' We both started to laugh, the wild, slightly manic sort of laugh that only happens at the most inappropriate times.

'I have to get ready for this fucking wedding,' I said finally.

'That's okay. I have to go get ready for this fucking baby. I'm in labor, by the way.'

I couldn't believe it. 'You are not. What the fuck are you doing on the phone to me?'

'It's fine! I'm only three centimetres dilated. I've got hours to go before she destroys my vagina. Did I tell you the doctor told me she had an unusually large head? Thanks for that, doc!'

'It'll be fine,' I said, though the thought made me queasy. 'You should lie down. Or are you supposed to walk around? You should go do whatever you're supposed to do when you're in labor.'

'Take drugs and shout at my husband?'

'Yes, that,' I said. 'I love you. You'll be amazing. Let me know as soon as she arrives.'

'I will. I love you too. Keep me posted about your dad. And please, give yourself a break, okay?'

'Never,' I said, but I was smiling now, and I felt lighter already. I hung up the phone and hurled myself into the shower, letting the hot water slough away the institutional smell of the hospital and stale adrenalin from the night before.

Clean, dry, and proudly wearing the HEAD BITCH T-shirt again, I headed back to Piper's room. I passed Madison in the hall and she gave me a quick smile before bounding down the stairs. I peered over the banister to see Ethan waiting for her at the bottom. He grinned when he saw her and said something that made her toss her head back and laugh. Her hair was out of the rollers now, and tumbled down her back in caramel curls. I could see now that her #PipsGetsHitched T-shirt was cropped, revealing a slice of hipbone and abdomen, and I silently said a prayer to the metabolism gods that their retribution would be swift and just. Sisterhood be damned. I watched the two of them head towards the door. They had the flushed, slightly guilty look of people who shared a secret and had no intention of giving it away.

I probably wouldn't have wanted to know even if they were telling.

Then

'Here you go, Atlas. You look like you need it.' Jefferson placed a cup of coffee on the desk and smiled down at Ruby like some sort of benevolent, golden-haired god. She blinked at the motto stretched across the blue paper cup and thought, At last! Something that's happy to serve me rather than the other way around.

'Thanks,' she said nervously. Jefferson always made her nervous. It didn't seem to matter that he was the only person in the company who acknowledged that she was an actual person rather than an enormous filing cabinet/coffee percolator. Or maybe that was precisely why he made her nervous: she had become so used to being viewed as another piece of beige office furniture that she found it genuinely unnerving to be addressed as a human. Well, that and the fact that he was very handsome and always called her by her last name, which felt sexually charged in some unknowable, amorphous way.

Ruby took a sip of the coffee. It was scalding hot and she felt her tongue go numb as it burned, but she refused to wince. That was the first thing she had learned on the job: never wince. Even if she was enduring a horribly humiliating and possibly painful experience in front of a group of peers and elders whom she was desperate to impress, she must never, ever show it. They were like vampires here, feeding off misery and guzzling down human tears, and the only way to survive was not to express weakness. Not even around Jefferson, with his wolfish grin and his free coffee and his calling-her-Atlas. In fact, especially not around Jefferson.

Ruby waited for him to leave – willing him to, in fact, so she could drink her coffee and concentrate on returning her blood pressure to a safe level – but he perched on the edge of her desk and said, 'Did you see what Martin is wearing today?'

'No,' she lied. Of course she had seen what Martin was wearing. It had been physically impossible not to see what Martin was wearing. Right now, from a space station orbiting Earth, they could see what Martin was wearing. He had stridden in earlier that morning wearing a deep purple suede trench coat and a pair of Chelsea boots, his hair combed flat to his forehead and pouffed alarmingly at the crown. He looked like a rooster in a Willy Wonka costume.

'Come on,' he said, leaning down conspiratorially, 'I know you saw him. Why do you think he's all dressed up? Mod convention? Swingers evening? Perverts anonymous meeting?' Ruby laughed in spite of herself, and he continued, encouraged. 'Seriously, though. Who wears that stuff? He looks like he fell out of an Echo and the Bunnymen video.' She didn't know who Echo and the Bunnymen were, but she knew enough to know that it was an extremely clever and funny thing to say.

'Date!' she blurted out. 'It's a date!' Ruby knew this because she had booked the restaurant – a pricey Italian place in Tribeca – and picked up his dry-cleaning the day before, including the offending purple trench coat.

'Son of a gun,' Jefferson said, 'I can't believe he actually persuaded someone to go out with him. I wonder how he managed it. What do you think? Blind date? One of those weird online chat room things? There's no way he could have just picked someone up in a bar, or on the street. Not even if she'd fallen down in front of him.'

Ruby shrugged, not wanting to get drawn in further in case it was an elaborate set-up that would lead to her immediate dismissal. Just last week, one of the copywriters had been fired for doodling a stick figure during a meeting. The MD had clocked it peeking out of his notebook and decided that the copywriter was making fun of him (there was some resemblance in the fleshiness of the chin). He was fired on the spot. Caution was the watchword around this place for everyone. Well, everyone except Jefferson, who was too talented for Paul to fire, and who, she had heard Tara/Melanie whisper in the corridor, was responsible for at least three-quarters of the business that came through the door. But Ruby had considerably less sway, and lived in constant fear of being chucked out the front door without so much as a reference.

'Well, good for old Martin,' he said, pressing on regardless, 'I hope he gets a little action. God knows he needs it.' Jefferson produced an apple from his jacket pocket and began polishing it on his trouser leg. 'So, what wonders await you this weekend?' he asked. 'What do kids get up to in the big city these days?' He took a bite out of the apple and gazed at her contemplatively as he crunched.

She still had no idea what people her age did in the city at the weekend – Adderall and horse tranquilizers, if Jessica's stories were to be believed – but for once she knew what she would be doing. 'My boyfriend is coming to visit,' she said, a touch of pride creeping into her voice. She hadn't mentioned Ethan at work before – mainly because no one had asked – so she felt of flutter of excitement in mentioning him. Sure, she might be a pathetic coffee-monkey here, but someone in the outside world actually wanted her, actually thought she was pretty damn great. The corners of her mouth winched up just thinking about it, as though pulled by two invisible bits of string.

'Is that right?' he said, in a tone she couldn't quite read. 'I didn't know you had a boyfriend, Atlas! I always knew you were a dark horse. What's the lucky guy's name?'

'Ethan,' she said, slightly too defensively. 'Ethan Bailey.'

He mulled this over as he chewed through another bite of apple. 'So what does this Ethan Bailey do?'

'He's a designer.'

'Oh yeah? Who does he work for? We've got most of them on the books.'

'He doesn't actually work for anyone.'

'So he's freelance? What sort of stuff does he work on?'

'He kind of just works on his own stuff,' Ruby mumbled. She pretended to study the to-do list that had been steadily stretching down the length of her notebook since earlier that morning, willing the tips of her ears to return to a normal temperature. 'He's a really amazing artist,' she said. 'He can draw almost anything. He bartends, too.'

'A real Renaissance man,' he said, and now she heard a new, unwelcome tone in his voice. 'Where does he bartend? Somewhere I'd know?'

'Just at the local bar back home in Massachusetts,' she said, now fully miserable.

There was a long pause as they both considered this. It was finally interrupted by Jefferson taking a last bite of apple and chucking it into the bin under her desk with a clang. 'Well, I hope you guys have fun,' he said. 'Make sure you show him all the sights our fair city has to offer: the vastly overpaid investment bankers, the displaced immigrants, the subway perverts, the hordes of gawking tourists. You know, the deluxe version.'

'The displaced immigrants are my landlords, actually, and I seem to have a knack for attracting subway perverts, so those two shouldn't be too hard.'

'That's the spirit,' he said, giving her an odd little salute before sauntering away. Ruby watched his retreating back with a sense of deep unrest. He hadn't said anything outright rude about Ethan, and she hadn't said anything untrue or mean about him, but it had still felt as though they were complicit in some kind of crime against him, a besmirching of his character. Jefferson had set Ethan a test in his questions, and it was clear that he'd failed. And now, in her eyes, Ethan seemed slightly diminished, and the excitement of his upcoming visit had been punctured.

She took another sip of coffee and tossed the still-full cup in the bin, splashing the mottled gray carpet in the process. She already felt wired, and any more caffeine would see her buzzing around the office like a hummingbird.

'I hope you're going to clean that up,' Tara/Melanie said on her way past. 'Martin goes mental if the carpets get stained.'

Ruby spent the rest of the day oscillating between frenzied work-based productivity and frenzied New York tourism-based research, consulting the Shecky's bar guide she had picked up on the way to work and making notes on possible cool bars that she could pretend to frequent. She was determined to show Ethan that she had mastered the bright lights of the big city. She would navigate the subway with ease, order a slice of pizza without feeling an undercurrent of paranoia, walk down the street without speculating on how she probably stuck out like a sore, poorly dressed thumb. She was determined that, for one weekend, she would somehow become one of those New York women: effortlessly cool, impossibly leggy, a look of hardcore badassery affixed to her face. For one weekend, she would not be Ruby Atlas, Terrified Rube. She would be Ruby Atlas, Urban Warrior.

In short, she would pretend to be Jessica.

At ten past seven, having narrowly survived being gassed by Martin's pungent aftershave as he wafted out the door, she made a break for it herself. Getting out of the office proved problematic: Tara/Melanie had caught her shakily applying eyeliner in the bathroom and snarked about it – 'Big night?' they had asked, giggling – and then proceeded to drop 175 envelopes on her desk just as she'd shut down her computer – 'They really need to be stuffed tonight, okay?' – but eventually, she made it out to reception, where she found Jefferson nursing a bottle of beer with one of the other creatives. 'Off to meet your boyfriend?' he'd asked in a slightly odd, strained voice. She nodded furiously, a manic grin plastered across her face, and charged out of the door. Freedom at last.

Of course, she got lost on her way to Chinatown, but for once she didn't dwell on it, because none of it mattered when the door whooshed open and Ethan stepped off the bus and onto the sidewalk and, in one graceful swoop, bundled her into his arms and kissed her. And then an ancient Chinese man hacked up an enormous gob of spit and launched it dangerously close to her left foot, but she didn't dwell on that, either. Instead, she dwelled on the exact green-gold shade of Ethan's eyes under the street lamp, and the smell of him – somehow undiminished after four hours on a discount bus – when she buried her face in his neck. She dwelled on the way he smiled when he saw her, like she was made of a million tiny stars, and the way all of the anxiety that had built up in her shoulders suddenly lifted. She dwelled on that, even as the ancient Chinese man took another shot, and this time made contact with the tip of her new shoe.

'Let's get the hell out of here,' Ethan said, throwing his ancient duffel bag over his shoulder and taking her hand. She led him up Canal Street and down to the R train, a route she had checked and double-checked before coming to pick him up. She handed him a pre-loaded MetroCard and swiped herself through, feeling quietly proud of the fact that it was a monthly card rather than cash. She was a local, after all, and locals had monthly MetroCards and could navigate Canal Street and didn't blink when an old man spat on their shoe. So far, she was doing so good.

She held onto the pole with one hand and him with the other as they rumbled past Rector, Whitehall, Court Street – places she only knew subterraneously, having never worked up the courage to venture above-ground and explore. 'This is where Junior's Cheesecake is,' she said as they screeched into DeKalb.

'Really?' he said, looking impressed. 'Have you been?'

'Yeah, a couple of times,' she lied.

At Prospect, they emerged, blinking, into a cacophony of noise filling the streets. It was cold out, the first night where there was a real chill in the air, and their breath emerged in pleasing puffs of fog.

'Hello, sweetheart!' the bodega owner called as they passed. 'What do you need? More wine? I'm just finishing my smoke but I can come back in now if you want to buy? One moment, one moment,' he said, fumbling to put out his cigarette.

'No, it's fine, it's fine,' she said, embarrassed. 'We're just heading home.'

'Who's this?' he asked, eyes lighting up. 'You have a friend? I didn't know you have a friend!'

'Yes!' Ruby cried, suddenly eager. 'This is my boyfriend, Ethan. Ethan, this is . . .'

'Roberto!' he said, taking Ethan's hand and pumping it up and down. 'Any friend of Ruby's is a friend of mine. She is my best customer, you know. Every night she comes in and asks for the same thing. Every night! She is a very reliable woman.'

'Thanks, Roberto,' Ruby muttered.

'Every night, huh?' Ethan smiled and raised an eyebrow.

'He's exaggerating.'

'Every night!' Roberto called from inside the shop, where he was frantically tidying the already tidy shelves.

Ruby pulled Ethan away from the doorway. 'Let's get back to the apartment,' she said. 'I have big plans for us tonight, and we need to get started.'

'Is that right?' Ethan said, waggling his eyebrows in mock-lasciviousness. 'Well, in that case, lead the way.'

They waved goodbye to Roberto, who reiterated his shock at her not buying 'the usual' two bottles of wine and pack of falafels from him once more, and then headed down Third Avenue to Ruby's apartment block.

'Is this where you live?' he asked, looking around warily. 'It seems a little . . . rough.'

'It's actually totally safe,' she said, and as she said it she felt herself believe it for the first time. She looked up at the red-brick building, took in the wisps of trash clinging to the branches of the leafless shrubbery in front of it, and was suddenly, immeasurably proud. 'This is us,' she said, opening the front door with a flourish.

Ethan took a cautious step into the communal hallway. 'It's kind of dark, isn't it?' The lightbulb had blown weeks ago, but no one from maintenance had come to replace it, and Kim had started to leave angry notes around the flat about it. Neither Ruby nor Jess were sure what she wanted them to do about it — they didn't own a ladder, and besides, wasn't it the landlord's responsibility? — but Kim was adamant that it be done. Thankfully, to them, Kim was just a ghost who paid a share of the rent and left passive aggressive Post-it notes all over the place, so they were able to ignore her easily.

'It's no big deal,' Ruby said, gesturing towards the broken light, even though she had been coming home every night from work paralyzed with terror at the thought of what might be waiting for her in that darkened hallway. She fitted the key into the door to the apartment and did the usual three shimmies and a shake needed to get it open. 'Home sweet home!' she trilled.

'So this is it, huh?' Ruby watched Ethan take in the tiny galley kitchen, the living room with its pockmarked floorboards and enormous, tattered orange sofa beached along the back wall. There was a pile of glossy magazines stacked on the heavy wooden coffee table, whose surface was dented and covered in ancient water stains. In the middle of the floor, there was a pile of clothing, state of cleanliness unknown, and an ashtray overflowing with cigarette butts and roaches. When she had left for work that morning, Jess hadn't yet got back home from her night out – it looked like she'd decided to take the party home with her.

'This is it! Do you want a drink?' She walked into the kitchen and pulled two beers out of the refrigerator without waiting for a response. She felt the soles of her shoes pull and stick on the linoleum floor. 'Sorry, it's not usually this messy,' she said, which wasn't quite a lie. She had cleaned the other weekend, or had at least started to before she had drunk a bottle and a half of wine and passed out in front of *The Hills*.

'Don't worry, I know girls are always dirty.' He took the beer from her hand and took a long, grateful sip before putting it down. 'Speaking of dirty,' he said, wrapping his hands around her waist, 'I've been going out of my mind thinking about you.'

'Me too,' she said, slipping away from him, 'but there's no time right now! I've made us a reservation at Hothouse, which according to Jess is the hottest restaurant in Park Slope. It's some kind of fusion thing – Thai and

Chilean? Italian and Indian? I can't remember. Anyway, it's meant to be amazing and we have to leave, like, now.'

'But I only just got here!' He made another grab for her, but she dodged it.

'I know, but there's a six-month waiting list at this place! Jess pulled in a favor to get us a table. I wanted to take you somewhere special on your first night. Somewhere *New York*.'

Ethan ran a hand through his hair and sighed. 'Rubes, I don't care about the hottest restaurant in Park Slope, wherever that is.'

'It's basically the new Williamsburg,' she said knowingly.

'Whatever. Look, I'm exhausted. I worked a late shift last night, and then I was on that disgusting bus surrounded by people who smelled like stale cabbage for hours.' He pulled her into him again and she resisted slightly at first, and then gave in. It felt good to let herself fall, even just for a second. 'Let's just veg out on the couch and watch TV and get take-out. Just a normal night, okay?'

'There are no normal nights in New York,' she said, feeling witty and urbane as the words came out of her mouth. 'Come on. It's going to be amazing, I promise.'

He sighed, then pulled off his T-shirt. 'Give me five minutes to shower, okay? But I expect to be repaid in sexual favors, just so we're clear.'

'Deal.'

Now

Piper, dazzling in Marchesa, smiled as everyone scurried around her. We took turns handing her flutes of champagne and retouching her lip gloss and gently pushing stray pins into the tower of blonde curls that crowned her head. All of us were itchy and slightly clammy after an hour in the chiffon monstrosities Piper had chosen for us (chartreuse was decidedly not my color) and our artfully made-up faces were starting to slide. Occasionally, a caterer or registrar or well-wisher would poke their head around the door, and Piper would hide herself in the bathroom. The rest of us would collectively beam at them while silently hoping that they had smuggled in food. None of us had eaten all day, and I was starting to worry one of us was going to end up on YouTube as one of those bridesmaids who faints at the altar and takes the bride out with her.

When we'd driven through the gates and entered the main hall of Bamburgh Castle, Taylor had frozen. 'It's just like Disney World,' she'd said, mouth slightly ajar. There was something unreal about the size and scope of the place: the towering stone walls, the vaulted ceilings, the endless acres of wood paneling. I knew that it had been built nearly a millennium ago, stone by stone laid by the hands of benighted peasants, but it was still hard to think of it as a real place and not something conjured up in a fairy tale.

Now we were all locked away in a spare turret some-where, away from prying eyes. I suspected we weren't the first women to be in confinement in the castle. Pregnancy, childbirth, contagion, madness – there had always been reasons to lock women away in remote places. This time, it was so the beauty of the bride wasn't diminished before she could be revealed to her new husband waiting for her at the top of the aisle. Until that moment, Piper had to be swaddled and protected and guarded like a secret. A secret who was currently a little bit tipsy.

'Do you want more champagne?' Madison asked, tilt-ing the bottle in Piper's direction.

'Ooh, yes please!' I was pleased to see that some of her sadness had been rubbed away and she looked like she was actually enjoying herself. I knew that the wedding wasn't turning out how she – or any of us – had planned, but I was happy that she was happy. It was her wedding day, after all, and Piper had been dreaming about it since she was little.

There was a knock on the door and Piper let out a little scream. 'Wait, I have to hide!' she cried. I wanted to point out that technically she wasn't required to hide from everyone – this wasn't a fancy game of hide-and-seek – but she had already locked herself in the bathroom again.

I opened the door to find Candace standing there, wearing a hot-pink bandage dress and teetering precari-ously on platform heels. Her make-up was immaculate and her hair had been curled into cascading blonde waves. From the top of her head sprouted a plumed fascinator, the feathers arcing over her face and tickling her shoulders.

She looked like an exotic, overblown orchid. I marveled at the strength it must have taken her to pull on that dress and stick those feathers in her hair. Here she was, at the wedding of her (not always easy) stepdaughter, in a castle, in a foreign country, with her husband laid up in a hospital bed across town, and yet she had still managed to paint her nails better than I could ever manage. I was filled with a sense of sudden, overwhelming admiration for this woman who had, sneakily and over the course of nearly twenty years, become my surrogate mother. I reached out and took her hand. 'You look amazing,' I said, and was glad to see her smile in return.

'So do you, baby girl,' she said, and I felt buoyed even though I was pretty sure she was lying. 'Can I speak with your sister alone?' she said, stepping into the room.

'Who is it?' Piper peered around the bathroom door. 'Oh, it's you.'

'Oh, Piper,' Candace said, 'you look so – so –' To everyone's horror, a tear fell from her eye, and then another.

'Your make-up!' we chorused, swooping around her with tissues. 'Don't cry! Don't cry!' we cried, but as much as Candace tried to get herself back under control, she had lost it. Her face crumbled like a snowbank during an avalanche, and all we could do was watch.

Piper walked across the room and placed an arm around her. 'Come on, I've got tons of make-up in here,' she said, leading her to the bathroom. 'I'll get you cleaned up in no time. Just don't get anything on my dress.'

We heard the door shut behind them and then the sound of murmured voices and the occasional stuttering post-sob breath. I didn't want to eavesdrop (well, I did, but knew I shouldn't) so I walked to the window and peered out to see if I could see the guests arriving. Instead, I saw a large white van pull up to the entrance, and Ethan get out of the front. Vic's car must have broken down, I thought, and I was having a little smile to myself at the idea of the great Ethan Bailey turning up to a wedding in a beat-up old van, when I felt a tap on my shoulder. I turned to find Madison in front of me, holding out a granola bar.

'I found it in the bottom of my bag,' she said. 'Do you want to split it? We'd better eat it quick before Piper gets back and starts yelling at us about crumbs.' She split it down the middle and handed me half. 'Are you okay?' she asked between chews. 'I know this must be rough on all of you guys, with your dad and everything . . .'

'I'm doing okay,' I said. 'Thanks though. And thanks for being so good to Piper. I know it means a lot to her to have you guys here.'

'Please,' she said, 'I wouldn't miss this for the world. Piper's actually my first friend to get married – isn't that crazy?'

'Totally crazy.' I couldn't even remember the first friend's wedding I'd been to – I felt like I'd spent the past decade trekking to various four-star hotels and country clubs and refurbished farmhouses and getaway resorts and wildflower fields and parental backyards around the country, toasting with mid-priced champagne, admiring letterpress placeholders and dancing barefoot to Van Morrison with a bunch of slightly-too-handsy uncles.

'Well, let me know if there's anything I can do,' she said.

'You got me a granola bar. That's basically life-saving at this point.'

'Don't forget to hide the evidence!'

The bathroom door opened and Candace emerged, fully restored, smiling a heartbreaker of a smile. Piper followed, dress still immaculate and now wearing a tiny silver tiara on top of her curls. 'Candace gave it to me,' she explained, and from the look on her face I could tell that something had shifted between them, or rather opened up.

'It's gorgeous,' I said, and we gathered around her and began cooing and clucking over it like a roost of hens.

She reached out and grabbed my hand. 'Candace is going to walk me down the aisle,' she said. 'Is that okay with you?'

I glanced past her towards Candace, who was now eyeing me nervously. 'Of course it's okay!' I said. 'Why wouldn't it be?'

'I don't know . . . you're my big sister, and you've sort of been like – weird, I can't believe I'm going to say this – sort of like a mother to me, but so has Candace, really, and with Dad not here . . . I just don't want to hurt your feelings.'

Candace stepped forward, hesitant. 'I would never want to cross any lines with you girls,' she said, 'and I know I can never replace your mother, but you're like daughters to me, and I would be honored.'

'I think it's perfect that you're going to walk her down the aisle,' I said decisively. 'And I love you both, but if you don't cut it out with this stuff, I'm going to completely lose my shit!' I wiped the tears that were threatening to destroy my liquid eyeliner, and pulled them in for a hug.

There was a knock on the door, and a nervous-looking waiter appeared. 'I'm sorry to interrupt, but the ceremony is supposed to start now, so . . .'

'Fuck!'

The room exploded in a frenzy of nervous energy. Feet were slipped neatly into heels, stray wisps of hair were tucked and sprayed, lipstick was retouched, last inches of champagne were swilled. We descended the precariously narrow stairs and gathered in the foyer, where the string quartet was awaiting its cue. I glanced into the great hall and saw necks craning anxiously in their seats. Charlie was standing at the front, sweating gently, face jaundiced, knees absurdly knobbly in the kilt he had insisted on wearing. Bob was standing next to him, face a bit less pale and knees even knobblier, and standing between them was Ethan, the knobbliness of whose knees were hidden in a pair of neatly pressed trousers. All three of them looked as if they were about to pass out from nerves.

'Are you ready?' I whispered.

Taylor and Madison's heads bobbed in unison, their bouquets clutched in front of them like tiny, fragrant shields. Candace was swaying slightly on her platforms, but was otherwise rigid, her expression a mixture of happiness and pure terror. Piper was flushed with the excitement of a born performer about to take her natural place on centre stage. She pulled her mouth into a perfect bridal smile – elated yet demure, it must have taken her weeks of practice in the mirror – and gave me a quick nod. 'Good luck!' I whispered. I took a deep breath and signaled the quartet to begin before taking my first measured step down the aisle.

It was odd, I thought as *Ave Maria* was teased out behind me, to be walking down an aisle towards Ethan without any possibility of becoming his wife. I suspected the irony wasn't lost on him, either. He caught my eye as I was halfway down and I could have sworn I saw the flicker of something – the ghost of a feeling long forgotten, like the phantom pains amputees are meant to feel in their lost leg – cross his face before disappearing. I was acutely aware of keeping my own face in check, and my jaw started to ache from the strain.

It was when I reached the altar that I saw him. There, sitting in a wheelchair in the front row, was my father. He had a blanket draped around him, but I could see that he was wearing his tuxedo underneath, and he grinned and gave me a wink. Chris was on one side of him, and on the other was a woman in nursing whites who was watching his vital signs on a small heart monitor. Dad gave me a small thumbs-up before turning to watch my sister walk down the aisle. I had no idea how he was here, but I was so, so thankful that he was.

The guests rustled to their feet as Pachelbel's 'Canon in D' began to swell. I watched the look of wonder on Charlie's face as he saw Piper enter the room. As soon as she saw him standing at the top of the aisle, the perfect bridal smile loosened its hold on her face and was quickly replaced with one that was broad, almost face-splitting. I could see the tops of her bottom teeth breaking above her lower lip – something Piper had always hated, as they were slightly crooked after years of refusing to wear her retainer. Seeing those little teeth poking out, and watching

Piper's eyes crinkle (also usually forbidden, as it causes wrinkles) made me realize how happy she was, and how much she loved this overgrown Labrador who was about to become her husband. My heart swelled – actually swelled, I swear it! – with joy.

Piper noticed him just before she reached the altar. 'Dad!' she cried, and immediately launched herself into his arms, which made everyone – including me – cry. 'You look beautiful,' I heard my dad whisper, which set off a fresh round of tears. Why does anyone bother to put on make-up for a wedding, I wondered, as I looked around the room through mascara-smudged eyes. I caught Ethan's eye and I saw that his eyes were shining, too – evidently no one was immune. He quickly looked away.

The ceremony was beautiful and blessedly brief. The couple exchanged promises and shakily placed rings on each other's fingers and kissed to great applause and yet more tears. They beamed at each other as they walked back down the aisle, stopping first to embrace my dad and Candace on one side of the aisle, and Bob and Barbara on the other.

Ethan walked with me as we followed them. 'Are you okay?' he asked.

I nodded. 'Seeing my dad tipped me over the edge.'

'I'm glad he could make it.'

'Me too. Thanks again for being so great at the hospital last night. I couldn't have got through it without you.'

'That's bullshit, but you're welcome.'

'It's not bullshit!'

'Ruby, you're the toughest woman I know. Strike that – you're the toughest person I know, and I once met The Rock.'

'Show-off!'

'I'm serious. You've never needed anyone's help, least of all mine.'

'That's not true,' I said, too quietly for him to hear. I was ashamed to admit that I'd needed him more than anyone, now just as much as I did back when we were together. But just as I was too proud to ask for his help then, I was too proud now to shatter this idea he had of me. I'd spent years building this fortress: I had no choice but to live in it.

We had reached the end of the aisle. Piper and Charlie strode through the doorway and onto the Battery Terrace, and behind us we could hear the surge of the guests as they discussed the ceremony, and how lovely the bride had looked, and how wonderful it was that her father could make it, and how grand the King's Hall was, and whether Charlie and Bob were chilly in their kilts. Ethan paused on the threshold. We stared at each other for a moment, the crowd swelling past us, eager to get their first taste of champagne.

Jess's words were still ringing in my ear. I knew this was my chance to say something, to set him straight on who I really was. 'Ethan –'

I felt a hand on the small of my back and looked up to see Chris's face grinning above us. 'Sorry, mate, do you mind if I steal her for a bit?'

Ethan looked at him blankly for a stunned minute before nodding his head. 'Go for it,' he said. I watched him disappear in the crowd.

'Nice guy, him, but he doesn't half look miserable all the time,' Chris said, steering me gently out of the room.

'How are you holding up? It must have been a shock to see your father sitting there.' He reached up and wiped a smudge of mascara from underneath my eye. 'You're gorgeous even when you're a mess,' he said with a smile.

'Chris, look –' I glanced past him to see Ethan already deep in conversation with Madison, his hand on the small of her back. 'Never mind,' I muttered.

'Here we are!' Chris grabbed two glasses of champagne from a passing tray and handed one to me. 'Now, what's the tradition at American weddings? Are there speeches? Is someone going to fire a gun at some point?'

'Yes to speeches, no to guns,' I said. 'At least I hope no to guns. The last thing this wedding needs is someone waving a firearm around the place.'

'That's a shame – I was hoping for a bit of pistols at dawn.'

I saw Candace steer my father into the room in his wheelchair. 'Do you mind if we go and say hi to them?' I asked.

'England is sadly still a patriarchal society, but I think forbidding you from speaking to your own father would be taking it a bit too far.'

We walked across the room to find the two of them giggling like a couple of schoolkids. 'I hope I'm not interrupting anything,' I said, leaning down to kiss his forehead.

Candace wrapped her arm around me and gave me a squeeze. I could smell her perfume – Poison, still, after all these years. 'Your father was just telling me a story about the nurse,' she said. 'He's being very naughty!' The two of them collapsed in giggles.

'Where is Nurse Clara?' Chris asked. 'Don't tell me you've given her the slip already, Alec.'

'Nurse Ratched is more like it!' Dad bellowed. 'That woman won't quit poking and prodding at me!'

'Dad, that's her job,' I pointed out.

'Well, I wish she'd at least warm up her hands first, is all I'm saying. Anyway, she just went to the bathroom to freshen up. I'm hoping she'll fall in.'

'Alec!' Candace admonished, but I could see she was secretly delighted to hear him back to his old self. Her face had lost some of its pinched look, and the color had come back to her cheeks. She looked happier than I'd seen her all week.

'Play nicely with Nurse Clara or we'll have to send you back to the hospital,' Chris said. 'And this time we won't be so generous with the pain relief.'

'You guys are a bunch of sticklers in this country,' Dad said. 'Must be all the socialism.'

'Not enough of it in my opinion,' Chris said with a laugh. 'If I had my way, we'd all be as red as the hair on my head!'

'I should have known you were one of them,' Dad said with a smile. 'Never trust a doctor who doesn't own a decent suit.'

'It'll be a dark day when I take sartorial advice from an American.'

'Boys, play nice,' Candace admonished. 'Chris, I think your suit is very handsome.'

'Why thank you, Candace,' he said, bowing with a flourish.

Dad reached up and shook Chris's hand. 'Look, I just want to thank you again for helping me out back there. I never would have seen my daughter get married if it wasn't for you and Ethan.'

I froze. 'What did Ethan have to do with it?'

'It was all his doing, really,' Chris said. 'He's the one who hired Nurse Clara and convinced the hospital administrators to discharge your father for the day.'

'Are you serious?' My heart was racing, but my blood felt like ice in my veins.

'Absolutely,' Chris said. 'Got it all organized last night, and he and Madison came around with a van this morning to pick us all up. I don't know how the hell he found an ambulance equipped for a wheelchair at such short notice.'

'He's rich, that's how,' Dad said.

'And kind,' I added. 'Really, really kind.' I felt the loss of him as keenly then as I had ten years ago. It wasn't about the money with him, or about success, or about how ridiculously handsome he looked in his suit – and he did. He was, and always had been, the most decent man I'd ever met. And I'd repaid him by running away from him and lying to his face, even now.

It all strung together now, like pearls on a necklace. I had to tell him how I felt. I had no idea how he'd react, or if he felt the same way, but I had to try. I also knew I had to tell him the truth, even if that meant ruining it all. I handed my glass to Chris. 'Will you excuse me for a minute?' I asked. 'I've just got to run to –'

'You're not running anywhere,' Dad said, grabbing hold of a corner of my dress. 'I'm about to give my speech!' And with that, he produced a spoon from his pocket – God knows where he'd got it from – and began tapping on the side of his glass. 'Excuse me! Can I have your attention please?'

The din of the room began to hush and the guests inched tentatively closer. 'Come on over!' he called, waving them towards him. 'Don't be shy!'

Silence descended. 'Now, I'm sorry I can't stand up, but you probably wouldn't want to see what I've got on under this blanket, anyway.' A ripple of nervous laughter went through the crowd.

'Something tells me your father is a born orator,' Chris whispered to me.

'I hope you're wearing comfortable shoes,' I replied.

'Ladies and gentlemen, I just want to welcome all of you to this wonderful occasion. I certainly didn't expect to watch my little girl get married from a wheelchair, but I'm just so happy I was able to be here at all. Thank you, Ethan, for making this possible for our family.' There was a round of applause, and I spotted Ethan at the back of the crowd, looking embarrassed and raising a glass in reluctant acknowledgement.

'You know, when my late wife was pregnant with Piper, I have to admit that I was hoping it would be a boy. You see, we were already blessed with a little girl, our Ruby, and of course every man wants a son who he can teach about baseball and cars and, eventually, women. But instead, we had another little girl, Piper. As soon as I saw those big blue eyes of hers, I was a lost man. Phew! I tell you, I cried like a baby when she wrapped her hand around my little finger – though I have to say that that was the first and last time she's ever been wrapped around my little finger, although I've certainly been wrapped around hers for the past twenty-odd years. Watching her grow up – watching both of my girls grow up – and become the beautiful women they are today has been the single biggest joy of my life. Bigger even than the time I beat Bernie Lipowitz on the golf course – you remember that, Bernie?' Another ripple of laughter, louder this time as everyone relaxed. 'I bet you do, you son of a gun. Anyway, I realize now that, if I'd had sons, I wouldn't have been able to teach them a damn thing about women. It's only through the pleasure of having daughters that I understand women now, though I suspect that my darling wife Candace would probably say that I still have quite a lot to learn on the subject.'

Candace smiled down at him indulgently and shook her head.

'So, here we are, at my little girl's wedding. Charlie, I have to say, when Piper first told me that she was seeing you, I had mixed feelings about it. I've known you a long time, and some of those memories aren't exactly golden. I think you still owe me some money from the time you got drunk at the club and threw up all over the hood of my BMW. But times change – Lord knows I know that better than most – and people grow up. I am very happy to give my little girl over to this man, because I know that he has a good heart. He also has a good deal of money, which certainly doesn't hurt!'

My stomach lurched at first, but then my face broke into a smile. Leave it to Dad to say the crassest thing possible at his daughter's wedding and get away with it. Glancing over at Piper and Charlie, I saw that they were laughing, too, and that even Bob and Barbara had stiff smiles on their faces.

'Well, I won't keep you much longer, and I've got a nurse standing here waiting for me – I think she wants to give me a sponge bath,' he said, eyebrows waggling, 'but I want to take a minute to acknowledge the woman who came into a house filled with sadness and anger and turned it into a home. Candace, I know these past few years haven't been easy – hell, I know that none of the years with me have probably been all that easy – but I want you to know that I love you, and that I am grateful' – he looked out and gestured towards Piper and me – 'that *we* are grateful to have you in our lives. I promise you that I will spend the rest of my life trying to make you as happy as you've made me all these years, and as happy as I hope Piper and Charlie will make each other in their future years as husband and wife.'

Candace leaned down and kissed him, and the room was filled with whistles and cheers. Piper made her way through the crowd to us and we all clutched at each other like the last survivors of a shipwreck. The room erupted in applause, and I saw my father – ever the ham – try to stand up to better soak it all in. 'Dad!' I admonished, and he sank back into his chair, a smile lighting up the whole of his face.

'He absolutely smashed it,' Chris said when I returned to his side. 'Brilliant speech. Your father's a class act.'

'He really is.'

The rest of the speeches went smoothly, with Charlie blubbing slightly when he talked about how much he adored Piper, and Ethan telling the standard embarrassing stories from Charlie's past, of which there were many. I kept hoping Ethan would catch my eye, give me a wink or some kind of sign, but he was a steadfast professional and addressed the crowd like a seasoned and somewhat world-weary pro. Finally, Piper took the microphone from him and proceeded to deliver a long, rambling speech about how much she loved everyone in the room, and how they'd all made her feel like a princess for a day. I didn't roll my eyes even once, which just goes to show the sort of emotional state I was in.

Once the speeches were over, we were herded down into the marquee, where tiny canapés were foisted upon us in a probably futile attempt to soak up some of the champagne before dinner. I kept trying to battle my way towards Ethan, only to be buffeted away by a caterer panicking about the vegetarian option or Piper asking me to hold the train of her dress as she went to the bathroom (yes, really) or Chris – lovely Chris, what a guy – handing me a glass of champagne, or a compliment.

The dinner bell (actually, rather theatrically, the dinner gong) was rung, and the guests crowded around the royalty-themed seating chart to find their places. Ethan and I were both sitting at the top table (the 'Crown Jewels', obviously), marooned at opposite ends. I leaned back during each course (smoked salmon on a bed of rocket, poached chicken and steamed vegetables, a slice of gluten-free wedding cake as hard as a box of thumbtacks) and saw him talking quietly with Charlie, or making Barbara smile and blush. I tried to make conversation with Candace and Dad, but found that I kept drifting off into stunned silence, trying to imagine the conversation I was hopefully about to have. None of the scenarios were particularly reassuring.

Plates were cleared and napkins discarded and the guests rose to their feet to watch the first dance, Charlie turning in slow circles like a bear at a circus as Piper flitted around him like a beautiful butterfly. Finally, the band struck up 'The Twist', and the dance floor filled. I saw Ethan leaning against a pillar, alone, watching Bob and Barbara mash potato with a bemused smile on his face. I knew it was my chance.

Then

Ethan's head juddered on the cold windowpane as the bus rumbled through the Holland Tunnel. He wiped a clear circle in the fogged glass and peered through, hoping to catch a final glimpse of Ruby, but she was already lost in the crowd. The man in the seat next to him, resplendent in a 'Yankees Suck' T-shirt tucked into elasticated sweatpants, pulled a jumbo-sized bag of Cool Ranch Doritos out of his rucksack and tore into them. The smell wafted over to Ethan, who sighed and closed his eyes. They felt gritty beneath their lids, and sore. The bus belched out exhaust fumes as the driver squawked into his cell phone and made a sharp turn onto the highway. Ethan's head hit the windowpane again, harder this time, and a dull headache bloomed between his eyebrows.

The weekend in New York was over.

If Ethan had been living in a 1950s Technicolor musical, he would have described it as a whirlwind. But he was not Gene Kelly, and New York was real rather than a studio sound set, so in truth the weekend had been more like a grueling endurance test. One he was pretty sure he had failed.

When Ruby had met him at the bus station, his heart had actually soared. The moment he locked eyes on her – windblown and harried and hair slipping into her eyes – he *had been* Gene Kelly and, if asked, he probably could have done that little skip-click with his heels. She had taken his breath away. All he'd wanted to do was bundle her into a taxi, lead her into bed, peel off her clothes and just steep himself in her. He had wanted to shut out everyone else – all of the huddled masses of New York – and just exist in a space outside of everyone. Just the two of them.

But, like so many dreams, it didn't quite work out as he'd envisioned.

First, there was the restaurant she had dragged them to on Friday – a Thai/Cuban place where they served drinks out of the husks of fruit and the dishes were created with the sole purpose of searing off your taste buds. They had been seated at a table next to the bathroom – the bitch's table, he knew from experience, so apparently whatever favor Jess had called in hadn't been all that valuable – and spent the next three hours shouting incoherently at each other over the too-loud samba music and trying not to cry as they speared chili after raw, explosive chili into their mouths. When they'd paid the bill – another opportunity for him to hold back tears – he'd wanted to head back to the apartment, but she insisted they take a taxi to a bar in Williamsburg. It looked like a fried chicken shop from the outside, but once inside Ruby had mumbled a password at the kid behind the counter and he had led them through the door of the deep freezer, down a narrow flight of stairs and into a damp, dimly lit basement bar filled with achingly hip people who looked like they were having a miserable time. 'Isn't this cool?' Ruby said, and Ethan had nodded wordlessly and proceeded to order the strongest drink on the menu. He'd slipped the bartender a twenty and asked him to be generous with the spirits, which, judging from the difficulty with which he'd ascended the narrow stairs a few hours later, he had been. When they finally got back to the apartment, they were both too drunk and too exhausted to do anything other than collapse wordlessly next to each other and let sleep pull them under.

When they woke the next morning, the rain pounding mercilessly on the barred window in Ruby's airless room, he'd hoped that they would finally be able to relax into each other.

'Morning!' Ruby said, bouncing out of bed and pulling on a pair of jeans and a sweatshirt. 'Did you sleep okay? I'm going to run out and get some coffee – do you want some coffee? You haven't lived until you've had New York coffee.'

'Come back to bed,' he'd croaked, but she was already out the door, keys jangling in her hand. He sat up gingerly and checked his head – it was sore, but he'd live. He pulled on his boxer shorts and padded into the bathroom, where he necked the three Advil he found in the medicine cabinet and took a long, meditative piss.

'Ruby, is that you?' He heard the sound of a somewhat throaty female voice cut through the silent flat as he walked back to the bedroom. 'Can you get me a glass of water? I'm fucking dying in here!'

'Uh, Ruby's just gone out to get some coffee!' he called back. 'She'll be back in a second!' He was suddenly aware of the sounds he'd been making in the bathroom and was deeply embarrassed.

'Ethan? Holy shit, I totally forgot you were coming! Hang on, I'm coming out there!'

He heard the sound of scrabbling, like a dog trying to get traction on a slippery floor, and then a crash. 'You okay?' he called.

'Yep!' A girl he presumed was Jess emerged in a whirl of limbs and teeth, peroxide-blonde hair poking up at strange angles from her head, and threw herself at Ethan. 'I can't believe I'm finally meeting you!' she cried. 'I've heard so much about you!'

'All good, I hope,' he said, delicately extracting himself from her embrace. It felt strange to be hugging Ruby's best friend – who appeared to be wearing an oversized football jersey and little else – particularly when Ruby wasn't there to sanction it.

'Totally,' Jess beamed. She walked into the kitchen and poured herself a mug of tap water, which she drank down in one breathless gulp before going for a refill. 'I am so completely fucked right now,' she said, and judging from her pink-rimmed, wide-pupiled eyes, she wasn't exaggerating.

'What'd you do last night?'

'The real question is, what didn't I do?' She star-fished on the sofa and blinked up at him. 'Did you guys go to Hothouse last night?'

'You mean the fusion place? Yeah, we did. Thanks for getting us the table – Ruby said you'd pulled some strings.'

Jess shrugged. 'No biggie. Did you love it?'

Ethan wondered how he could phrase his opinion democratically. 'It was . . . interesting, that's for sure.'

'Yeah, I know what you mean. It's kind of douche-y there, and the food is so spicy I was revisiting it for days. I was surprised when Ruby said she wanted to go. It's not really her thing.'

Relief flooded through him. 'I thought it was a weird choice.' He scratched the back of his neck, hesitating over what he was about to say. 'Hey, do you think . . . I mean, does Ruby seem okay to you?'

'What do you mean?'

'It's just – I know work's been really busy, and I know she's out with you every night, which is cool, you know, new city and all, of course she should be hitting up all the bars and going to parties and everything, but it's just –'

Jess sat up straight and folded her legs underneath her. 'She's definitely not out with me every night,' she said. 'I keep trying to get her to –'

They both froze at the sound of Ruby's keys in the door.

'Look,' Jess said in a hurried whisper. 'Don't worry, okay? I'm keeping an eye on her.'

'An eye on her for what?'

'Hey, guys!' Ruby burst through the door, balancing a cardboard tray of coffees in one hand and a paper bag full of still-warm bagels in the other. Her hair was wet and she was shivering slightly in her sweatshirt. Ethan was overcome with the urge to gather her up and swaddle her in blankets, but he could tell by her eyes – which were flashing slightly manically – that it would be like trying to bundle up a nervous cat. 'I caught Bagel World just as they came out of the oven – can you believe it? Ethan, wait until you have one of these – nothing in the world beats a New York bagel. Morning, Jess! What did you get up to? Thanks so much for getting us into Hothouse, by the way. It was so cool. Wasn't it cool?' She looked at Ethan expectantly and a little breathlessly.

'Yeah,' he said, 'it was cool.'

She beamed at him as she handed him a coffee and a bagel laden down with cream cheese. 'You are going to love this,' she said. 'You don't need to toast it because it's still hot.'

Ethan didn't have the heart to tell her that he hated cream cheese. 'Thanks,' he said, taking a cautious nibble at the edge.

'So, what are you two up to today?' Jess asked. She had helped herself to a coffee and was busy scraping the excess cream cheese from her bagel. 'They always put way too much on,' she said when she caught Ethan watching. He smiled and quickly followed her lead, sliding a slab of cream cheese off the bagel and onto the plate.

'I thought we'd just hang out around here,' he said, taking another, more enthusiastic bite. Ruby had been right: the bagel was delicious. 'Maybe watch a movie or something.'

'No way,' Ruby said, shaking her head. 'We have all of New York to see! I thought we'd start out at the Met and wander through Central Park down to Rockefeller Plaza.'

'Why do you want to go to Midtown on a Saturday?' Jess asked. 'Ethan's right, you're better off staying around here, especially in this weather.' She nodded towards the window, which looked out onto a gray, rainy morning. Ethan could tell that she was trying to be helpful, but

Ruby's eyes narrowed as she spoke and they both realized that she wasn't about to be dissuaded from her plan.

'He's only here for a day and a half,' she said pointedly. 'We can't just sit around here and watch movies all day. That would be lame.'

'I honestly wouldn't mind –'

'No!' Ruby cut him off. 'I want to show you the city.' She glanced up at the kitchen clock: 11:13. 'I can't believe how late it is! We need to hurry.' She took a single bite of her bagel before abandoning it on the kitchen counter and dashing towards the bathroom. 'I'm going to hop in the shower!' she called. 'And then we should get going!'

The bathroom door shut behind her and Jess and Ethan were left staring at each other. 'What the hell was that?' Ethan asked.

Jess shrugged. 'I don't know what's up with her today, but I hope you brought a pair of comfortable shoes, because it looks like you're going to be walking the length of Manhattan.' She glanced out of the window again. 'And maybe a parka.'

She wasn't wrong. Now, as the bus rattled through Connecticut, Ethan wondered if he and Ruby had managed to have a single meaningful conversation all weekend. He'd kept trying to talk to her about how she was doing: at the top of the Empire State Building, crowded next to groups of tourists snapping away at the gray, fog-obscured view of Manhattan below, in the dingy dim sum restaurant in Chinatown, their elbows knocking together as they hunched over the counter, as they waited in the endless line to be seated for brunch in SoHo the following day. But each time, Ruby would dodge and deflect his questions, slipping past them and into safer waters. He'd learned a lot of unnecessary facts about New York, but not a lot about his girlfriend's current state of mind.

Finally, he'd given up trying. They had spent the last few hours of the visit in relative silence, her nervously pulling him through the shops of SoHo, pointing out things he could buy if he'd had the money or inclination. He hadn't even told her about applying to schools: he'd been saving the news until he saw her in person, but the time had never seemed right, and eventually he decided to keep it from her entirely, maybe as retaliation for her own evasiveness, or maybe because, in the face of all the grandeur and excess of New York, the idea of junior college felt suddenly small.

And sex . . . well, that had been another thing that had been conspicuously lacking. Every time he tried to touch her she'd dart away from him like a startled goldfish. They'd had sex just once, in the early hours of Sunday morning, when they were both still gauzed with sleep and found each other in the half-darkness, a tangle of fumbling limbs and warm-breathed kisses. Afterwards, he'd pulled her towards him and run his fingers over the gentle slopes and dips of her body, but she had shifted away and wrapped the sheet tightly around her.

She was shy now, self-conscious in a way she hadn't been a few months before, when she would sit naked on top of his bed, peeling an orange and eating its segments slowly, the rind sticking to the sheets, the juice dribbling down her chin, laughing as he bent over to lick it clean. He could see that she'd gained a little weight, but he liked it: it had filled out her angles, made her pillowy and soft. He loved the new curve of her stomach, but she guarded it with a protective arm, and any move he made to touch it was rebuffed with a flick of the wrist and a quick, apologetic smile.

'The bus will be stopping for a short break,' the driver announced through the garbled intercom. 'If you want to eat food, you can get food. Bus leaves in fifteen minutes. Late people will be left behind!'

Ethan glanced out of the window and saw that they had pulled into a small service station with an Arby's attached. He wasn't hungry – the brunch, when it had finally arrived, had been huge, and besides, no one was ever hungry for Arby's – but he needed to stretch his legs, so he climbed down from the bus. He could hear the steady thrum of traffic from the nearby highway and the air was perfumed with exhaust fumes and frying meat. He lit a cigarette and inhaled. He tried to picture what Ruby was doing right now, but all he could imagine was her leading a group of Chinese tourists on a tour of Ellis Island, or spinning around in the middle of Times Square while tossing her hat in the air. He ground the cigarette out beneath his heel and headed back to the bus. Two more hours and he'd be home. And, he couldn't help but think, further away from Ruby than ever.

Now

To: Bill Bailey
Sent: 18 July 19:33
From: Ethan Bailey
Subject: re: For Christ's Sake

I know, I know, I will! I'm just waiting for the right moment,
that's all.
Go harass Jasmine or shout at the television or something.

E

Now

Ethan locked eyes with me as I walked across the dance floor. Time seemed to slacken, and the crowd I moved through seemed to be twisting in slow motion. And then he smiled at me, and the world cracked open again, and the music was suddenly too loud and the dancing too frenzied.

'Can we go somewhere and talk?' I said to him, and he nodded and took my hand.

We walked silently out of the marquee and down onto the beach below. It was dark now, and everything was colored a deep midnight blue, the stars bright in the sky. I took off my shoes and stretched my toes in the sand. I felt almost preternaturally calm. Whatever happened, I was finally ready to face it.

'Look,' I said, 'I'm just going to say a bunch of stuff now, and you can do whatever you want with it. You don't have to do anything with it if you don't want to.' He smiled at me, his eyes crinkling at the corners, and I felt a sudden flurry of nerves. 'Okay, here it is. I'm just going to come out and say it.' He nodded encouragingly. I took a deep breath, which only served to bunch my words up in my throat. 'It's – it's just that –'

'It's okay,' he said, placing a calming hand on my arm. 'Whatever you're going to say, it's okay.'

In that moment, I stupidly believed that could be true.

'I love you!' I said, too fast. 'I mean, I still love you. I never stopped loving you, I guess, even though I made myself think I did.'

'Ruby –' His face was lit up by the moon. The nub of his chin, the curl of his eyelashes, the soft, lopsided curve of his lips. I saw his eyes, black in the darkness, shine, and I knew then that he might love me, too, that those shadowy glimpses I'd seen over the past week hadn't been imagined. But I also knew that I couldn't let him say anything without hearing the truth. Even if I had never wanted anything more than to fall into his arms and keep lying for the rest of my life.

'No. Wait. I have to get all of this out at once, otherwise I never will,' I said. 'When we broke up, I –'

'That was the past,' he said, moving towards me.

'No, it's not. I've been living with it – living in it – every day for the past ten years, and I can't go another minute without telling you. If we're going to do this – do whatever this is – it has to be with clear eyes.'

'Okay,' he said softly. 'Tell me.'

'When I first moved to New York, I was miserable. I was lonely and work was awful and the whole city just completely terrified me. I'd made such a big deal about living in New York, about how it was my spiritual home and where I belonged and all of that shit, and then when I realized that it wasn't what I thought it would be, I decided that there was no way I could admit how I really felt about it. That's why I was so weird when you came to visit that time – I wanted to prove to you that I was a New Yorker now.'

'I remember. You made us go to that godawful speakeasy place. It was like you were on speed all weekend.'

'Yeah, well, that was why. And when you left, I just got more and more depressed and sort of . . . I don't know, helpless, which made me feel even worse. And Jess was having this amazing time going out all the time and meeting all of these fancy people, and I was either at work or at home missing you.'

'I thought you were tearing up the town,' Ethan said. 'Every time I talked to you, you told me about a new bar you'd been to. Why didn't you tell me? I wouldn't have thought less of you just because you were having a hard time in New York. Everyone has a hard time in New York.'

I shrugged. 'I don't know why I couldn't admit it to you, but I couldn't. I felt like I had to prove that I could make it on my own without you swooping in to help like some knight in shining armor.'

'I would have swooped, you know.'

'I know you would have. But I couldn't let you do that.'

He stepped towards me again and took my hand. 'You always were stubborn. I feel awful that you felt so alone, though. I wish I could have –'

'I'm not done.' I dropped his hand and turned away. 'There's more. One night, when I was at work late, this guy I worked with – Jefferson – asked if I wanted to go for a drink. He was the creative director there, so really senior –'

Hi brow knitted together. 'Yeah, I remember you mentioned him.'

'Well, he asked me to go for a drink, and I said yes. I don't really know why – he'd always been nice to me, but I also knew that there was something off about him, too, you know? But I went, and we drank so much – martinis and then bourbon, so much bourbon that I can't even smell it now without retching, and every time I tried to leave, he'd order another round and tell me he wanted to know more about me, and before I knew it, I was drunk and sobbing in this bar and he was helping me into a cab and then we were pulling up at his apartment and –'

'Don't.' I looked up and saw his eyes on me, steady and unwavering. 'Don't say it.'

'I have to,' I said quietly. 'Don't you see? I have no other choice.' What followed felt like an out-of-body experience, with me hovering above the two of us, watching the words come out of my mouth, watching him bow slightly as though he'd been punched, hard, in the stomach, watching me take a step towards him and try to take his hand, watching him push it away. Watching myself cry. Watching him walk away from me, up the sandy hill and back towards the party. I watched him go and I watched myself stay. I felt the howling vortex in the middle of my gut, and I thought, Well, it serves me right but at least it's done now. At least now, it's finally done.

Then

Ruby was late, again. In the weeks that had followed Ethan's visit, she'd found herself sleeping more than ever. If she wasn't at work, she was in bed, or lying on the couch, in a facsimile of bed, with the covers pulled up to her chin. Jess had tried to rouse her at first – at one point, mid-afternoon on a Sunday, she'd even poured a glass of water in her face to wake her from her seventeenth consecutive hour of sleep – but lately, she'd given up. 'You might as well grow a beard and move into a hollowed-out tree,' she'd say as she sailed out the door, leaving Ruby to wave half-heartedly from beneath her blanket.

At first, it had just been in the evenings when her eyes would begin to pull down like blinds, but now it was creeping into her mornings, too. The alarm would sound, but she wouldn't move. It was as if she were pinned beneath a ton of concrete as it slowly solidified around her. She started to press the snooze button. Once. Twice. Oh, fuck it, just turn it off. She'd called in sick twice in the past month, and Tara/Melanie had started giving her serious side-eye as she crept past their desks late every morning.

The drinking probably wasn't helping. Even she had to admit that her previous bottle a night had stretched to two, the warm fug of red wine calling to her constantly with its sweet, sleepy siren song. But it was more than that. The tiredness wasn't just red-wine-drunk, or the residue of a near-permanent hangover. It was bone-deep. She could sense the weather by it, like an arthritic knee. And, as it was December, it was pretty much always there.

She managed to stay on top of things at work, the fear-based adrenalin driving her through the daytime hours. In fact, the more uncertain she became about the rest of her life, the more competent she became at her job. Meetings were scheduled seamlessly, cabs ordered, flowers and anniversary gifts dispatched, coffees brewed and delivered without a drop spilled. Recently, the MD had correctly remembered her name and thanked her for picking up his dry-cleaning, which was a personal highlight. He'd even looked her in the eyes when he'd said it – or at least at the middle of her forehead, which was much better than her chest or ass. It was demonstrable progress.

As for the rest of her life, there wasn't much progress being made. The city still terrified her. Her world was still small, and getting smaller. Jess had lost patience with her. As for Ethan – well, it was hard to tell what was happening with him. They still spoke every night, dutifully exchanging scraps from their day (hers often plumped up with an injection of invented glamor) and, at the end of every conversation, reciting the same words of longing and love that had come so easily at the beginning. The phone calls were no longer acting as a blanket, wrapping her up and sending her off to sleep each night. Instead, she would lie in bed, the beginnings of a headache pressing against her temples, and quietly unpick the words until they were just a loose tangle of threads. How can he love me when he doesn't know me? she would wonder. And if he did know me, how could he possibly love me?

These questions trudged slowly through her head as she placed her bag beneath her desk and booted up her computer. She checked the clock on the monitor as it flashed into life: 9:47 a.m. They were meant to be at their desks by 9:30 a.m. sharp. Ruby found it vaguely offensive that the opening time was so rigid when the closing time was more pliable than a contortionist.

She sighed, popped an Advil and clicked open her emails, scrolling through and deleting as she went. Among the notices for sample sales she'd never shop at and bar openings she'd never attend was an email from her father and Candace's joint account entitled 'Christmas'. She groaned inwardly before opening it.

Hey Baby Girl,

Christmas is coming!!! Are you excited??? We are very excited!!!!
We put up the tree last week even though your father said it was too soon!! I got one of those tinsel ones that's all silver so it won't shed anywhere, so I told him we could put it up whenever!! I'm thinking hot-pink ornaments – what do you think???
I'm just planning Christmas dinner now (I know, I know – way too soon but like I said We're Excited!!). Would Ethan and his dad want to join us? I know that they're just the two of them and I always get way too much food so if they wanted to come they are More than Welcome. Your father said so, too!!!
Got to go, lots of love xoxoxoxo Candace
p.s. What do you want from Santa????

Xoxoxo

Ruby's cursor hovered over the Reply button before finally clicking Delete. Who asks about Christmas when it was still weeks away? Though it was early December, and the big tree had already gone up in Rockefeller Center (she'd seen it on the morning news), nothing about her life was feeling festive. The idea of having Ethan and his father around for Christmas dinner felt akin to inviting a pair of aliens who just happened to be passing through Earth. It was going to be hard enough finding things to say to Ethan when she was home for Christmas, never mind trying to negotiate the landmine field that would be a joint family dinner. As ever, Candace meant well, but had gone a step too far.

'Atlas, you look like you've just smelled something really terrible.' Ruby looked up to see Jefferson smiling down at her. He lifted an arm and took a tentative sniff. 'It's not me, is it?'

She broke into a fit of nervous giggles. 'Of course not! I mean, I can't smell anything bad, least of all you.'

'Phew! That's a relief. I just spent two hours with a client over breakfast, so I'd hate to learn now that she'd been holding her breath the whole time.'

Ruby felt a prickle of irritation at the thought of him having breakfast with an unknown, presumably glamorous, woman. She knew that this was irrational, but that didn't help to abate the feeling. 'Which client?' she asked, reasonably casually.

'Tracy Hornbridger from Ises – you know, the discount sportswear people? Sorry, the "active lifestyle brand". She's a total ballbuster, spent the whole time telling me that the entire campaign should be scrapped because she thought the print ads were the wrong shade of plum. They do a nice croissant down at Briar Street, though, so it wasn't all bad.'

'I'll keep that in mind,' Ruby said. 'About Tracy Hornbridger and the croissant.'

'Both are equally important,' he said. 'Actually, no. The croissant is definitely more important.'

'Duly noted. Do you need anything from me today?'

He smiled benignly at her. 'No, you're fine, kid. Thanks, though.'

'Okay, well, just let me know if you do!' Ruby could feel her cheeks beginning to flush and the rapid tap of her heartbeat in the base of her throat. Four months on and somehow she still wasn't able to interact with him without threatening cardiac arrest.

'Actually,' he said, turning back towards her, 'there is one thing you could do. I've got to go to this networking thing tonight – some new media bullshit drinks in SoHo.'

'What time do you want the cab?' she asked, hand already on the phone.

'No, it's not that, it's just – Tara was supposed to come with me, but she can't make it now, so I thought maybe you could come along and keep me company. It shouldn't be too long, and these things are always so boring on your own. Plus, it might be a good way for you to meet some people from the industry. A few fellow rising stars.'

Ruby's face was now almost unbearably hot. 'Sure!' she said, too enthusiastically. 'I mean, if you want me to, I'm happy to come along.' She looked down at her ancient H&M sweater and faded black pants slightly fraying at the seams. 'I'm not sure if I'm really dressed for it, though . . .'

'You look terrific. Besides, I promise you no one's going to be noticing your outfit.'

Ruby wasn't sure how to take this, so she just nodded. 'If you think so,' she said.

'Great. We'll just grab a cab outside at around eight. Sound okay to you?'

'Perfect.'

He gave her one of his crinkly-eyed grins before turning to leave. 'Looking forward to it,' he called as he walked into his office.

'Me too,' she said, though she wasn't sure that was exactly how she'd describe it.

The hours crawled by. Morning briefing. Burrito cart lunch. Several pensive trips to the ladies, where she stared into the mirror and wondered how she could possibly make it through a networking event. At four o'clock, a rush of emails flew into her inbox and she spent the next few hours chasing them back out again. And then, at a quarter to eight, she retreated back into the bathroom with her bag and proceeded to slick and blot several layers of too-bright lipstick onto her mouth. She remembered vaguely that Jess had once said that lipstick made every woman more confident, and she hoped – very dearly – that this was true now.

At five past eight, Jefferson opened the door of the taxi for her and ushered her in. She sat ramrod straight in the back seat next to him as the taxi careened downtown. She was desperately aware of every too-quick breath she took, every creak of the vinyl seat beneath her, every inch she slid towards him when the driver made a sharp right turn. For his part, Jefferson chatted blithely on, telling her about some recent humiliation of Martin's involving a drag queen and a pair of Jimmy Choos. She heard herself laugh, or at least make a sound approximating a laugh, but she felt as if she was floating above, pressed tightly against the duct-tape-striped roof of the car, and watching them below.

The car pulled to a screeching halt and she slid off the seat, reaching out a hand to stop herself from hitting the Plexiglas divider.

'Take it easy, man,' Jefferson said, hitting the glass with his fist, and the driver turned around and gave an ambivalent shrug.

'Nine fifty,' he said, gesturing towards the little hole in the partition.

Jefferson peeled a ten-dollar bill from his wallet and handed it through. He opened the door and slid out before turning back and offering Ruby a hand. 'You ready?' She took his hand nervously, registering the cool dryness of his palm and the clamminess of her own. Together, they faced an unmarked door, the thump of bass faintly audible from inside.

'Jefferson! Is that you? You sonofabitch, how've you been?' They turned to see a slick-looking man charging towards them in a too-shiny suit, hand already extended several paces away.

'Scott!' Jefferson said, taking the proffered hand and allowing his to be pumped enthusiastically. 'How the hell are you?'

'I'm good, man, I'm good. Making money, making money.' The man's face was unnaturally tight, and Ruby wondered briefly if he'd had work done.

'Good for you,' Jefferson replied, though he didn't sound entirely convinced.

'I hear you're at Diamond Age now! What the hell is that about, man?'

'Well, you know.' Jefferson looked suddenly uncomfortable, and Ruby screwed up all of her courage (or maybe it was the lipstick) and decided to intervene.

'Hi,' she said, holding out her hand. 'I'm Ruby.'

The tight-faced man looked her up and down and gave her a wolfish grin. 'I bet you are,' he said. 'Scott Tripper, at your service.' He did a low, swooping bow before raising her hand to his lips. They felt hot and too-soft against her skin, and she fought the urge to pull away. 'I see you're not once bitten, twice shy,' he said, reaching over and clapping Jefferson on the back. Both men's eyes were fixed on Ruby. 'You two heading in?' he asked, nodding towards the unmarked door.

'No, actually,' Jefferson said. 'We were just on our way out.' Ruby glanced up at him in surprise, but his face was calm and unreadable.

'Too bad. I guess that means there's more fish for the big shark to eat! Later!' The tight-faced man fist-bumped them both and disappeared into the bar, a blast of R & B welcoming him in. Ruby and Jefferson were left blinking and stunned on the sidewalk in his wake.

'What a fucking asshole,' Jefferson said, and then, with a sideways glance at Ruby, 'sorry.'

'Don't be. He seems like a total asshole.'

'He's a media buyer. I used to work with him before I made the shift to creative.' They stood in the middle of the sidewalk, two still points in a sea of office workers and partygoers flooding past in the icy evening air. 'Look, I'm sorry I made you bail on your very first networking event, but I promise you it's just filled with pricks like him.'

'In that case, you definitely don't need to apologize.'

'Let me at least buy you a drink.'

The relief that had been flooding through Ruby ever since Jefferson had said they weren't going into the bar suddenly made a hasty retreat. 'I don't know,' she said. 'It's a Tuesday night, so I should probably be getting back.'

'Come on, it's early! And you're young! I know this great little cocktail bar a couple of blocks over.'

Ruby pulled her coat tightly around her. 'I guess I could have one,' she said, plunging her hands in her pockets.

It had snowed the night before, and the streets were banked with blackened piles. Ruby's boots – cheap from TJ Maxx and decidedly not waterproof – skidded in the slush, and Jefferson held her elbow to steady her as they walked. It was a moonless night but SoHo was still bright from the shop-front windows and street lamps hanging above. Their breath formed little puffs in front of their mouths, like empty speech bubbles.

'Here we are,' he said, opening yet another unmarked door. This one led down a narrow set of stairs and into a small parquet foyer. A deep-red velvet curtain hung at the other end, waiting to be parted.

'Are we going to a bordello or something?' Ruby asked.

'Not quite,' he said. 'I think you'll like it.' He held the curtain open for her and she slipped through. Inside was the most beautiful room she had ever seen. The walls were painted a burnished gold, and the floors were laid with intricately patterned tiles that sparkled in the dim light. A long polished-brass bar hugged one wall, manned by supernaturally attractive bartenders, each locked in concentration on whatever potion they were mixing. Small wooden tables were scattered across the floor, candles flaring and guttering on each, and beautiful people held hands across them and spoke in low, intimate voices that came together as a collective satisfied sigh.

Ruby felt instantly ill at ease.

'It's cool, right?' Jefferson said, nodding hello to the maître d' (a dead ringer for Gwyneth Paltrow) and weaving his way to an empty table in the far corner. 'Is here okay?' he asked, taking her coat and pulling out her chair without waiting for a response. 'I come here pretty often, so they keep it free for me.'

'That's . . . awesome,' Ruby said, and she meant it in the literal sense. At that moment, she was filled with awe: for the place, for the people, and for this man – her boss – who was currently raising a finger and signaling a passing waiter.

'Hey, George, how you doing? This is my friend Ruby. She and I would both like two gin martinis – Old Raj, please, and with a twist.'

'Of course,' the waiter said with a wink. 'The usual.'

'You do like gin?' Jefferson asked after the waiter had floated away to the next table. He said it more like a statement than a question, so Ruby took it as one and smiled. 'Great, great. Even if you don't, you'll like it here. Best martinis in Manhattan.'

'Cool,' Ruby said lamely. She fiddled with the cuffs of her sweater and looked nervously around the room.

'You okay?' Jefferson asked, reaching across the table and touching her gently on the forearm. She reacted like she'd been stung by a particularly vicious wasp.

'Fine!' she said, too loudly. The couple next to them glanced over curiously. 'Sorry,' she said, more quietly. 'I'm fine.'

The waiter reappeared and placed two chilled martini glasses in front of them, both filled to the brim. Jefferson lifted his in a toast – not spilling a drop in the process – and took a sip. 'Perfection,' he said, and then gestured towards her glass. 'You've got to drink it while it's still ice-cold.'

Ruby lifted the glass to her lips and took a nervous gulp. The gin was cold and crisp and slightly pine-scented, and reminded her vaguely of New England winters spent sledding as a child. She felt the warmth as it slipped down her throat and the not-unpleasant burn as it hit her empty stomach. She looked up and saw him watching her intently. 'It's really good,' she said, and then took another sip as if to prove it.

'Good. I thought you'd like it. You've always seemed like a woman of discerning taste.'

Ruby wasn't used to being called either discerning or a woman by an attractive man who was (presumably) twice her age, so she smiled and took a third sip in response. The alcohol was working its way through her bloodstream now, and she felt a fizzing in her fingertips and a haziness settle in her brain. She placed the glass on the table carefully and surveyed the room again. 'So you really come here all the time?' she asked.

'Most nights,' he said. 'I like to come here after work, blow off a little steam. I've got a place up on Seventh Ave and 60th that I crash at some nights when I can't face the train back to Westchester. My wife hates it, but . . .' He gave a shrug as if his wife hating something he did was irritating but inevitable, like a winter cold, or a mosquito bite.

'You're married?' Ruby asked. She felt her shoulders loosen: somehow, in that moment, being in a dimly lit bar with a married boss seemed less threatening than an unmarried one. 'But you don't wear a ring.'

'Metal allergy,' he said. 'Makes me break out in hives. Anyway, enough about my dull life. I want to hear more about Ruby Atlas. How are you finding life in the big city?'

To Ruby's horror, she found her eyes filling with tears. 'Oh, you know,' she said. 'It's okay. The job is great.'

He sat back and let out a low whistle. 'Jesus, things must be bad if you think your job is great.'

She shook her head, but couldn't manage to squeeze out a single word.

'Hey,' he said, leaning across the table and placing a tentative hand on her forearm. 'You can talk to me, you know.'

'Do you know where the bathroom is?' she asked, leaping to her feet. 'It's fine, I'll find it!' She picked up her bag (the cheapness of which, like her boots, was starkly highlighted in contrast with the opulent room) and charged towards what she assumed was the bathroom, but which turned out to be a storage cupboard. 'The bathroom is through there,' one of the beautiful waiters said gently, and she managed to lock herself inside just before the tears spilled over. 'Shit,' she said to herself. 'Shit.' She sat on the toilet and took a few calming breaths.

The bathroom was completely covered in mirrors, floor to ceiling, like a fun house. Though at this particular moment, as she watched her eyes refill with tears, it was not fun in the least. What sort of sadist would design such a bathroom, she wondered? Even if she hadn't been having an emotional breakdown, she had never done anything in a bathroom that she'd wished she could watch herself do, and that included the time she pulled the Sigma Chi treasurer into the frat house bathroom and had sex with him in the mouldy shower cubicle. Especially that, in fact.

There was a soft knock on the bathroom door, and then, after a few minutes, another, more insistent one. She stared at herself in the mirror. She couldn't stay in there for ever – Jefferson might send someone in to find her, which would be mortifying. She took a deep breath and stood up, running a pinkie finger underneath each eye to wipe away her smudged mascara. She ran her hands under the tap and dried them with one of the little towels rolled up in a wicker basket next to the sink (a real towel! Made of cloth! She couldn't believe the profligacy of the place, the glamor) before rubbing in a few pumps of the expensive moisturizer for good measure. She pulled open the door, gave the woman waiting a haughty smile, and walked back into the bar.

Jefferson was where she had left him, gazing around the room like a man surveying his considerable kingdom. A pair of fresh martinis had been placed on the table. 'I thought you might need another drink,' he said as she approached.

She sat back down and immediately took a sip, then another. Her head felt pleasantly fuggy now, and all of the upset of the previous ten minutes began to evaporate. 'Thanks,' she said, gesturing towards the drink. 'I guess I did need that.'

He laughed and took a sip of his own. 'A wise man once said to me that martinis are like breasts. One is not enough, three is too many, but two is just right.'

'Sounds about right to me,' she said.

'Though sometimes there are extenuating circumstances.' He signaled the waiter as he sailed past. 'Two more, please.'

'Actually,' Ruby said, feeling suddenly bold. 'I'd like a bourbon, straight up.'

Jefferson raised an eyebrow. 'A bourbon drinker, eh? You're full of surprises.'

In that moment, gin-warmed and lifted by the unrelenting goldenness of the room, she felt sophisticated, even a little bit glamorous. She was a woman capable of surprising a man like Jefferson. She smiled at him across the table and he winked.

After that, there was another round, and then another. Ruby's vision tunneled and skipped. The waiter's smiling face appeared and disappeared, Jefferson's hand moved under the table onto her knee, and then there was the flickering rush of the street through the cab window. There was a doorman holding a door open, a bed with gray sheets, her sweater tossed over a chair, Jefferson's face looming above her.

She woke up on top of the sheets, wearing just her underwear. The room had the chilled air of a place not often lived in, and she clutched her arms across her chest and shivered. Jefferson was asleep next to her. He looked older somehow, the lines between his eyes deepening into a V, his skin chalky in the artificial lamplight. She sat up and looked around the room. The walls were painted a tasteful pale blue, and the carpet was thick under her bare feet as she padded unsteadily towards the bathroom. She stumbled through and was sick in the toilet, just once and as quietly as she could manage, careful not to wake him up. She pressed her forehead against the cool white basin as the scenes from the night flickered past.

Finally, once she was fairly sure she wouldn't be sick again, she gathered herself to her feet. She stared at herself in the mirror, taking in her slightly smudged eyeliner and the lipstick that had settled onto the chapped patches of her lips. She looked haunted, like a Victorian drawing of herself, all big hollowed-out eyes and pale skin. She carefully picked up her clothes from where they were scattered across the room, each item feeling like a piece of evidence at a crime scene. She dressed slowly. It was still night, but her hangover had already started to kick in, dovetailing seamlessly with her residual drunkenness. She checked the time on her phone: 4:34 a.m. She had thirteen missed calls, nine from Ethan, four from Jess. She placed the phone gently back in her bag and walked out of the apartment, shutting the door firmly behind her.

The night air was bitter, and the wind whipped down Seventh Avenue with merciless intent. The street was quiet now, all dimly lit doorways and shuttered windows, and she hurried into the subway. She would have taken a cab, but she only had six dollars on her, and besides, she didn't feel capable of communicating with a cab driver at that particular moment. In fact, she felt she might never be capable of speech again. Did they still take vows of silence in convents? she wondered. Was that avenue open to her?

She spent the ride home with her eyes half closed, head tilted back against the window. The stations rushed past: 34th Street, Union Square, Canal Street. She knew now that everything had changed. She would get a new job. She would never again accept a drink request from an older, married man. She would meet the city head on and fight her way through it. She would no longer be afraid. She would be smarter, harder, tougher. She would be an adult.

She would also end things with Ethan. She'd send him a letter, and she'd say goodbye. She knew that she couldn't live with herself if she told him what she'd done and he hated her for it, but she also knew that she couldn't live with herself if he forgave her. She had to let him go, cleanly and without explanation, so she could keep on living.

She closed her eyes and let the rhythm of the train soothe her. Court Street, DeKalb, Atlantic. She would live with herself, alone. It would be some sort of penance, or maybe some sort of salvation. Prospect Avenue. Her eyes shot open and she darted off the train and into the late-night morning.

Now

It was early again when I woke up the next morning – it seemed my body had made an executive decision to resist the new time zone and would hold out until the end. I didn't feel hungover this time, or tired. Instead I was almost too-awake, my heart was racing in my chest from the moment I opened my eyes.

It came back to me in pieces, snatches of memory dropping into my mind like slides in a projector, and then the reel began and I saw it play out in full. How did that song go again? Didn't we almost have it all?

I sat up and looked out of the window: the sky was a muted gray and it was misting gently. The fluke sunshine had disappeared and I was finally going to get the English weather I'd been promised in so many picture books and bad romances.

I pulled on a pair of leggings and a sweatshirt and unspooled the waterproof cagoule from its little protective travel pouch. I laced up my sneakers and headed down the stairs. No one was up yet, not even Mrs Willocks, and a hush had fallen on the house, as though a spell had been cast. I pulled open the door and hurried down the driveway, worried that someone might hear me. I wanted to escape unseen.

I'd eventually returned to the party, brushing the sand off my feet and slipping them back into the heels that had started to hurt. I'd put a smile on my face and drunk champagne and laughed at Dad's jokes and cheered when Charlie's thirteen-year-old cousin did the worm in the middle of the dance floor. I'd danced with Chris and tossed my head back and laughed when he said something funny, and I hugged my sister at the end of the night and told her she was the most beautiful bride I'd ever seen. At one point, I saw Ethan typing furiously on his phone, but I didn't speak to him. I'd gone to bed without seeing him. His flight home was scheduled for early this morning – around eight – so I figured I'd stay out of the way until I could be sure he was gone.

I let myself through the kissing gate and walked through the field and past the sheep and up the steep hill. The mist turned heavy and the thin fabric of the cagoule stuck to my body. My sneakers squelched. Across the fields, the fog that had been rolling in gentle waves rose and joined up with the rain, turning the hills a hazy blue-green.

I found it without much trouble. The seat of the bench was beaded with rain and I used my hand to brush it off, wiping my wet hand on the edge of my sweatshirt. The plaque had fogged up in the cold, and I wiped that clean, too.

I hadn't realized where I'd been headed until I'd arrived, but I was glad I'd come. The bench was still wet and the backs of my legs were soon damp as I sat. The cagoule, I was discovering, wasn't all it was cracked up to be. I shivered and hugged my arms to my chest and looked out across the hills to the sliver of dark-gray sea.

I pulled out my phone and sent a text.

Little specks of rain appeared on the screen and I shoved it back into my pocket. I thought about Jess, pushing a new life out somewhere across an ocean, and smiled.

I knew I should be upset, and of course I was – the dull ache in my chest was making me feel slightly nauseated – but I could feel something else behind it. Something that felt a little bit like relief, or excitement, or a combination of the two.

In a weird, slightly masochistic way, I was glad about what had happened the night before. It hurt, sure, and that sucked. But it had also made me free. I realized that I'd been wearing my guilt like a hair shirt for years, taking it off only to admire the hardened, shiny scars beneath. I was the girl who did something terrible to the boy she loved, and I turned myself into the woman who had done something to the man she'd loved and could therefore never be loved again. After a while, it had stopped being about Ethan and had become about me trying to prove to myself that I didn't need love from anyone. I decided that, instead of opening myself up to the possibility of being hurt (or, worse, inflicting hurt), I would turn myself into a single, solitary, Teflon-covered bullet. Sad about something? Tough it out. Feeling lonely, or overwhelmed or scared? Tough it out. There was no room for sympathy. How could there be, after what I'd done?

When I was a teenager, I'd drive around Beechfield on my own at night, aimlessly heading down back roads and singing along with Joni Mitchell, thinking someday I'd get out of this place and I'd never, ever look back. I was going to follow my mom to New York. I was going to slough off my small-town skin, and the bright lights of the big city would embrace me as one of its own.

But when I moved to New York, I realized that it wasn't all that keen to open its arms to me, that I'd have to work and work and work in order to pry them open even an inch. So I did. I worked and worked and worked, and one day, I looked around and realized that I'd made it. I'd spent ten years trying to prove a point to myself, and I'd finally proved it.

But here's the thing that I'd realized: I sort of hated my life. Not entirely – pieces of it were great – but I'd been living on autopilot for too long, wearing grooves in the sidewalk between work and home and the gym. It was as if I'd been eating the same meal over and over again and had suddenly remembered that the world was full of other dishes waiting for me to taste them. Pasta covered in tomato sauce and parmesan, freshly baked bagels slathered in cream cheese, a slice of the triple-layer chocolate cake with vanilla frosting that Jess had made for Noah's second birthday: all the things I'd passed up over the years, shaking my head and begging abstention. From now on, I was going to eat the damn cake. I was going to sleep in on Saturday mornings. I would forget about the laundry and the dusty skirting boards and instead I would take a book – one I actually wanted to read, not one I felt I should out of some compounded cultural obligation – and sit in the park with a coffee and a croissant and fall asleep in the sunshine. I would cut myself a little slack.

I was going to quit my job. The thought came to me fully formed and iron-clad. I was going to travel, but not in a 'run off to Italy and take a pasta-making course' kind of way. I'd go down to Florida and spend some time with my dad and Candace. Maybe I'd go back to Beechfield and stay with Piper and Charlie, though not for so long that we'd end up killing each other. I'd visit Jess in New Jersey, and get to know Noah better, and the new little one, whoever she might be.

Maybe I'd go back to New York at the end of it, maybe I wouldn't. The thought of not having to fight so hard every day made me feel almost giddy. I had forced myself to love that place for so long. The idea that I didn't belong there – that I couldn't belong – had been so crippling that I'd moulded myself into someone who did belong, sharpening my elbows and edges every morning before I left the house. I had no more axes to grind now. I could finally let myself soften a little.

My phone buzzed with a text message.

It's a girl. Eliza Jane. 8 lbs, 9 ounces. It hurt like a bitch, my vagina will never recover, but she's perfect. Love you. J xx

I closed my eyes and let the rain fall, and felt, for the first time in a long time, grateful.

Then

Dear Ethan Bailey,

On behalf of the Admissions Committee, it is my pleasure to offer you admission to the Massachusetts Institute of Design. Upon assessment of your portfolio, you stood out as one of the most talented and promising students in a hugely competitive applicant pool.

We would like to take the unorthodox step of inviting you to begin your academic studies immediately rather than commencing the course next academic year. Please find enclosed all the necessary paperwork to enable this.

We firmly believe you are the ideal fit for the course and will thrive within our academic environment, and are delighted to welcome you to the Massachusetts Institute of Design.

Many congratulations, and we look forward to hearing from you in due course.

Yours sincerely,
Mr B. Harris
Admissions Committee
Massachusetts Institute of Design

After

It happened on the walk back to Bugle Hall. I was soaked by then, the pretense of the cagoule having entirely collapsed, and my hair was plastered to my face, yesterday's hairspray stinging my eyes. I was bent down retying my shoelaces – caked in mud now, and tangled – when I heard footsteps. I looked up just as he reached me. He held out his hand.

'What are you doing here?' I asked. 'I thought you had an early flight.' A very small part of me thought that I might now be starring in a romantic comedy, one in which the hero decides not to catch the plane home and come get the heroine instead.

Ethan shrugged and pulled me to my feet. 'Delayed,' he said. 'The fog.'

'Of course. The fog.'

We blinked at each other.

'Is everyone up now?' I asked.

'No, it was quiet when I left. I'm pretty sure everyone's still sleeping off their hangovers. What time did you leave last night? I didn't see you go.'

'I left around eleven.' I'd invented an excuse about a headache, and slipped out the back. I'd walked the mile back to Bugle Hall in the dark, my fingertips brushing the hedgerows so I wouldn't get lost. 'What about you?' I asked.

'About one, I think. I rode back with Chris and Madison,' he said.

My eyebrows shot up. 'Chris went home with Madison last night?'

He laughed at my shocked expression. 'Yep. He spun her around the dance floor a couple of times, and the next thing I knew they were making out in the corner like a couple of teenagers.'

'I thought she only had eyes for you,' I said.

'Nah, she just wanted some professional advice,' he said with a wry smile. 'I spent an hour and a half talking to her about three-dimensional imaging.'

'Huh,' I said, unable to keep the grin off my face. I thought back to the night before when I'd spotted the two of them deep in conversation and assumed they were declaring their deep mutual lust for each other. Turns out they were just declaring their deep mutual nerdiness.

We blinked at each other again.

'I sold the company,' he said finally. 'The deal will go through in the next couple of weeks.'

'Oh!' I couldn't hide my surprise. 'What made you decide?'

'Your dad,' he said. 'Seeing him in that hospital room made me realize how little time we've got – all of us. We can't afford to waste it on things that don't make us happy, you know?'

I nodded. 'I know exactly what you mean. So what will you do now?'

'That depends, I guess.'

'On what?' I asked.

'On you.' He paused and my breath caught in my throat like a tiny, trapped bird. 'Look, I'm not going to sugar-coat this. When I read that letter, it blew a hole in my heart that I've spent years trying to patch up, and what you told me last night was the emotional equivalent of pouring iodine into the wound.'

'Fuck,' I muttered quietly.

'I was fucking pissed off when you left, and I was pissed off last night when I found out why – what you did with that douchebag you used to work with.'

'I know,' I said, 'and I'm so –'

'I'm not finished!'

I raised my hands. 'Sorry, sorry!'

'The thing is, I never really forgave you for leaving me like that. You just sent some mysterious letter and then disappeared without a trace. Do you know how that felt?' I was silent. I suspected I knew how it had made him feel, but that didn't mean I wanted to hear it, however much I deserved it. 'I spent years making myself into someone who would never feel that sort of hurt again. I got successful. I got rich. I got all the things I thought I could ever want. And you know what happened?' He stopped and looked at me. His breath was coming out in foggy little puffs and I could see his ribcage quickly rising and falling from underneath his thin, damp T-shirt. I wondered if he was cold, and the thought made me sad.

'You got laid a lot?'

'Well, yeah,' he said with a little shrug, 'but it didn't make me happy. Nothing seemed to make me happy – the money or the fancy apartment or the awards or the women – none of it. The work made me forget about it for a little while, but over the past couple of years, when all I've been doing is worrying about stock valuations, I've just felt . . . empty. The point is, I'd been chucking all this – all this *stuff* into this massive hole and the only time I felt like it could be filled was when I saw you sitting there in the airport. There you were, jet-lagged and fidgety and frankly not smelling all that great after the plane ride, but suddenly I didn't feel so fucking empty anymore. I tried to deny it at first, but I did a pretty shitty job – Charlie called me on it when were at that castle and I had to come up with some bullshit lie because I wasn't ready to admit it to anyone, not even myself. How do you tell the world that the only person you can possibly seem to love is the person who hurt you the worst?'

'All I can say is I'm sorry,' I said quietly. 'I'm so, so sorry.'

He shook his head. 'No more apologies. Like I said, there isn't enough time. Because here's the thing: the more time I spent with you, the more I realized I wasn't angry anymore. Even after what you told me last night, I tried to feel angry about it – I spent all fucking night trying to be angry with you, trying to make myself hate you. But I couldn't do it.'

I could feel a smile nudging at the corners of my mouth. 'You couldn't?'

'No,' he said, stepping towards me. 'What happened between us, it was a lifetime ago. I've spent ten years try-ing to forget about you, and here you are in front of me again. I'd be a fool if I let you go again. In a way, I'm glad what happened between us happened. It was horrible, obviously, but it sort of shaped me, you know?'

'I do,' I said.

He lifted a hand and cupped my chin, and my heart stalled and swelled. 'The thing is, the only thing that can fill the giant hole you blew in my heart is you. And I don't want to waste another second of our life together. If you'll have me, that is,' he added with a nervous laugh.

I'm pretty sure I was crying at this point, though it was hard to tell with the rain. In any case, he reached up and brushed my cheeks. 'Are you sure?' I asked. 'Even after everything?'

'Especially after everything,' he said. 'I should have fought for you back then. I knew you were unhappy in New York, I could tell something wasn't right. As soon as I got your letter, I should have got on the first bus down there.'

'I did something horrible,' I said. 'I definitely wasn't worth fighting for.'

He slipped his hands around my waist with the ease of a pair of favorite jeans. 'You've always been worth fighting for,' he said. 'Take it from someone who's been trying to fight against you for ten years. It's much easier to fight on your side.' And with that, he leaned down and kissed me, and this time I knew I was crying because I could taste the salt in our mouths.

We walked back hand in hand, stopping only to kiss and giggle like the kids we used to be. The rain kept on falling, heavier now, and our shoes slid in the mud, but neither of us took any notice. It was just him and me now, like it had been before. Only different. Better.

'So what next?' he asked as we neared the house. 'I've got nothing but time on my hands now. I could head back to New York with you, or . . .'

'Actually,' I said with a smile, 'I've got something else planned. You up for a little adventure?'

He swooped down and lifted me off the ground. 'More than I can say.'

To: Bill Bailey
Sent: 19 July 2015 12:28
From: Ethan Bailey
Subject: Home

Dad,

There's a flight out of Heathrow to Edinburgh tomorrow – a car will pick you up tomorrow morning at around 10 a.m. Pack a bag and your passport – whatever you'll need for a couple of weeks. (Actually, maybe ask Jasmine to do it, to be on the safe side. Knowing you, you'd only pack a box of crackers and a spare pair of underwear.) We can get the rest of the stuff sent over later (including the cat).

We're going home. All of us. I sold up, and Ruby and I . . . well, you'll see for yourself tomorrow. It's good. I'm happy.

Go pack. Don't think about it, just do it. There's no time to waste – too much has been wasted already, not least by your jackass son. So come on, let's go.

E

Acknowledgements

Thank you to my wonderful editors Kimberley Atkins and Maxine Hitchcock at Michael Joseph, and to the whole Penguin team, particularly Sarah Scarlett, Sophie Elletson, Hattie Adam-Smith and Jenny Platt.

Thanks to my super-agent Felicity Blunt at Curtis Brown for the pep talks and the tough love, both necessary and appreciated. Thanks, too, to Jess Whitlum-Cooper. Thanks to Helen Manders for always turning around in her chair and listening when I began a sentence with, 'Can I ask you a book-related question?'

Thank you to my parents for all you have given, and continue to give, me. And thank you to my parents-in-law John and Christine for being generally excellent. I am very lucky to have two amazing families in the Pimentels and the Robertsons: thank you for being so much fun.

Thank you to Katie Cunningham for her steadying words, constant hand-holding, and overall perfect best friend-ness. Not a day goes by that I am not grateful to have you in my life. Finally, thank you to my husband Simon for his encouragement, kindness, and willingness to watch Gilmore Girls. I love you.